Acknowledgements

Steve and Chuck would like to gratefully acknowledge the support and encouragement we received from numerous friends when they became aware of this project. And we would like to offer special thanks to Doug Streuber, Leslie M. Carringer, Dorothy Lance, and Kathleen Nowak for reading drafts of this novel and providing feedback on everything from plot integrity and character development to grammar and spelling. Their support and input were extremely valuable as we worked our way through the writing and editing process.

We would also like to thank Dorothy Lance and Cathie Bishop for their patience and tolerance during the multi-staged development of this novel. Cathie's and Dorothy's support and encouragement was essential, and greatly appreciated!

Thank you!

The Authors

Steve Lance and Chuck Markussen have over 75 combined years of aerospace engineering experience in the areas of tactical missile development, defense electronics, and modeling and simulation. Both moved to Tucson, AZ during the mass exodus of Hughes Missile Systems Group employees from Los Angeles in 1994, and retired from Raytheon Company in February, 2011. This is their first collaborative effort in writing fiction.

Disclaimer

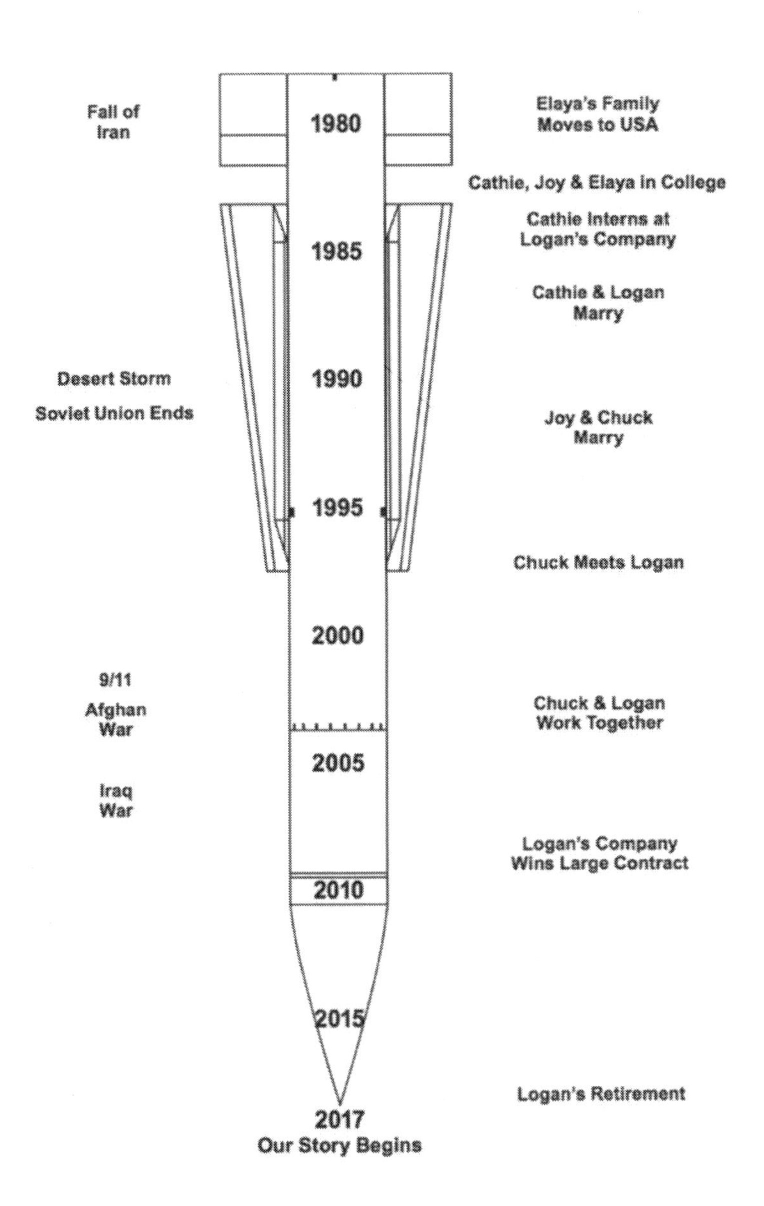
Fall of
Iran
1980
Elaya's Family
Moves to USA
Cathie, Joy & Elaya in College
Cathie Interns at
Logan's Company
1985
Cathie & Logan
Marry
Desert Storm
1990
Soviet Union Ends
Joy & Chuck
Marry
1995
Chuck Meets Logan
2000
9/11
Afghan
War
Chuck & Logan
Work Together
2005
Iraq
War
Logan's Company
Wins Large Contract
2010
2015
Logan's Retirement
2017
Our Story Begins

Prologue

April 1989

The alarm klaxon continued to sound in a distracting manner as General Alexi Groebnick made the final preparations to evacuate the base. For two days he had hastily organized transportation for the small stockpile of nuclear weapons under his command, housed in dreary concrete bunkers burrowed under the Caucasus Mountains northeast of Tbilisi, Georgia. The fall of the Soviet Union, which his superiors had assured him was quite impossible, had come with astonishing swiftness, as had the orders to immediately remove all weapons and fissionable material from the far-flung outposts such as General Groebnick's. The general silently cursed the stupidity of the bureaucracy that had failed to foresee what now seemed an obvious political shift, and had then failed to provide the means—transport, communications, and soldiers—to complete this hasty pullout. A wide-eyed lieutenant ran up to the general, and saluted perfunctorily. The young man, a fresh graduate from the military academy, and not particularly well-placed in his class, had been given his assignment at this dusty old base with the presumption that he could neither cause nor come to harm in a remote outpost guarding old-technology weapons of little value. As with most on the base, he was ill-trained to deal with an emergency.

"What is it, lieutenant?" the general asked. "Is all prepared?"

"Sir, the last truck is loaded but for one weapon, the small one, which requires your key. But sir, there are armed men approaching from the south—not Russian."

"Yes, yes, well, let us go …" A sudden rattle of automatic weapons fire, echoing down the dimly lit corridor in which the two men stood, halted the general's words. Indistinct shouts were heard along with more gunfire. "Never mind," the general spoke. "Tell the men in the trucks to leave immediately with the remaining escort. They are not to stop, do you understand? Then bring two men from your squad and meet me at the vault. We will retrieve the weapon and leave in the personnel carrier."

The lieutenant, in a state of near panic now, stood motionless, his head cocked in the direction of the gunfire.

"Lieutentant," the general spoke loudly, "the last truck is to leave and you are to bring two men of your squad to the small vault—NOW!" The terrified soldier took a few tentative steps, turned back to the general and saluted (the general returning the salute with growing irritation), and then sprinted down the corridor.

The general did not run, but walked briskly down the corridors and stairways that led to the small vault, where the only "suitcase" nuke in his care was kept. The general waited impatiently for the young man and the two other soldiers that were all he could now spare to take up this last device. He cursed again the stupidity and incompetence that had led to this, and fingered the key on the chain around his neck. The weapons fire had ceased, and he waited in silence until at last, steps were heard descending the last flight of stairs to his location.

As he entered the light, the lieutenant's face glistened white, covered with perspiration, for the men behind him were not Russian. The general guessed Chechen, but it hardly mattered. The man immediately behind the frightened lieutenant spoke in accented but perfectly understandable Russian.

"Thank you, lieutenant," he said, politely, and fired a burst into the young man's back, the sound echoing loudly in the bare, concrete corridor. With no hesitation, the man turned to the general. "The key, sir, if you please," he said, extending his hand.

The general dropped the key and reached for his sidearm. With a smile of pure satisfaction, the man raised his weapon in what seemed a slow and lazy fashion. A single shot rang out, the bullet entering the general's forehead and exiting his head with a spray of blood, bone, and brain matter. The door of the vault ran with reddish ooze.

"Allahu akbar!" the man cried.

"Allahu akbar!" echoed his men.

The leader turned to a very young man at his side. "Hasim, kindly relieve the general of his key and open the vault. We have little time."

***

January 2017

Nearly thirty years later and five thousand miles distant, Derrick Michelson, skipper of the Bering Sea crab boat *Emma B*, lit another cigarette with the last drag of the one he was smoking, which was simply one in an uninterrupted sequence whose chewed and snuffed remains had long since spilled out of the ashtray at his elbow.

"This is bullshit," he snarled, looking at the display on his navigation equipment. He grabbed the microphone and said, "Jerry, get your butt up to the bridge." He added, "The fucking GPS has gone batshit," but had released the button on the mike just before this last vent. His crew was exhausted and they had been fighting through some of the ugliest weather the Bering Sea could dish out. No need to worry them over some messed up equipment they could live without, or to let them see how close he was to popping a gasket. He himself had been in the wheelhouse for sixteen hours with barely a piss break and his eyes were as red as a ferret's. And now, after steaming south-southeast for the last five and a half hours, this piece of crap navigation system was telling him he was within spitting distance of Ostrov Mednyy, a Russian island nearly five hundred miles west of where he knew he was! Jerry, Derrick's cousin and a permanent member of the crew, was the best man on the electronics and knew quite a bit about this particular GPS navigation system, new to the *Emma B*. If he couldn't get it sorted out, well, they still had a compass and the navigation beacons and were at least well out of the monster storm.

"Yeah skipper, what's up?"

"You know, all's I want is to get a decent fix on our location. I mean, we've been steaming along this path," he motioned to the monitor, "and now it says we're fuckin' here." He jabbed at a location near the Russian island, hundreds of miles off. "What the hell is wrong with this thing?"

"Give me a minute, boss," said Jerry. After a few diagnostic commands had been tried and indicated that the equipment was functioning normally, with a good signal from six satellites, Jerry shook his head.

"I don't get it. There's nothing here that looks like trouble. The only other thing I can think to try out here is a total reboot and satellite reacquisition. Want me to try?"

"Might as well. The useless thing does me no good telling me we're about to ram Russia. But I swear to God, I'll be using this hunk of crap as a boat anchor if it's gonna act like this. It's a damn good thing I don't have to rely on it entirely. It's also a damn good thing the error was big enough to be obvious instead of just small enough to be believable but to screw us royal. I'm going to get on the horn to a couple of other boats; see if anybody else is having nav problems. Piece of shit," he added, for emphasis.

Chapter One

Retirement, A New Phase

Logan Fletcher leaned back in his chair and took another long, slow, voluptuous pull on his Monte Cristo, and let a thin stream of fragrant, blue-grey cigar smoke trickle past his lips. After a productive and challenging thirty-two year career in aerospace, his first week of retirement had not gone poorly at all, and he was finishing it off in the gorgeous outdoor courtyard of Santa Monica's St. Mark's plaza, his spicy penne pasta with artichoke hearts and Napa Valley Cab settling nicely under the tiramisu and cognac that was now sharing his palate with the fine Churchill cigar. The sunset still burned a smoldering campfire red behind the silhouette of the Santa Monica Mountains, the tall palms at the edge of the plaza reduced to two-dimensional dark cutouts, waving in the gentle breeze that was fading with the sun.

Thirty-two years! At times, every day had seemed an eternity, with the pressure, the frustrations, the intransigent customers and the unsympathetic supervisors. But then, years seemed to speed past in an instant, and Logan had gone from a wide-eyed college grad, with reverence and admiration for his colleagues, mentors, and bosses, to a jaded program manager, grown impatient and intolerant of the Byzantine structure of his company and the U.S. government agencies with whom he'd contracted. He had felt pride, disappointment, exhilaration, and exhaustion. He had met and worked with many customers and staff that he had openly admired for their intelligence, skill, courage, and dedication, and he had met his fair share of butt-kissing sycophants, fakes, backstabbers and cowards. There had been no more than two or three programs over all the years that had brought him an intense satisfaction which combined an esoteric victory—the knowledge of having truly advanced technology—with a certainty that his product had saved lives in gritty, perilous, combat situations.

This visit to Los Angeles, where he had done considerable business over the years, was a first move towards uniting him with a true friend and grateful customer, Chuck Johnson. Logan smiled at the thought. The fact that Chuck and he had become close friends, combined with the irony that Joy, Chuck's wife, and Cathie, his, had shared a dorm in college and were also extremely close, was an unexpected bonus. The real triumph had been that Logan's team had delivered an incredible set of prototype communications electronics to a team of CIA operators (Chuck among them), and it had saved their lives. Yes, that one topped Logan's list. But the smile slowly melted from Logan's face. In the end, he had found it more and more difficult to go to work, where stress and politics seemed to be replacing technology and teamwork as his steady diet. He hadn't been bitter (at least, far from wholly so), but he had woken one day with the certainty that it was time to call it quits. Other wide-eyed techies would take his place—easily. He had come to the end of his career with some regrets, a strong feeling of accomplishment, a group of true friends, and an overwhelming desire to wake up each day ... relaxed! And so, the beginning of the second part of Logan Fletcher's life was well begun. A vacation, with no need to check his available Paid-Time-Off balance, and then back to Tucson where he had lived as an employee for so many years, and where now he would live as Logan Fletcher, happily retired man.

The last set by the five-piece jazz ensemble that had played throughout his most enjoyable dinner was drifting on the breeze while the fragrant mesquite smoke from a large stone-rimmed fire pit complemented the smell of wild rose and oleander planted throughout the courtyard. The fountain at the far end of the plaza played music of its own for him and thirty or so equally relaxed and sated patrons seated in groups of twos and fours at tables covered with alabaster linen, scattered on the pavers of the main courtyard like so many lilies on a dark pond. Logan absently fingered chords to match those of the pianist, whose easy fingering delivered an almost poetic progression that blended with the horn, drum, guitar, and bass. With his newfound luxury of time, it was his earnest desire to take lessons and improve upon his moderate but still quite amateurish musical skills; and since he was devoted to jazz both as a patron and a hopeful participant, this evening provided a jumping off point for his musical venture.

The only wisp of cloud to darken the sky in this fabulous evening had been that his wife Cathie seemed extraordinarily ill at ease. Logan knew that she was not as passionate about music, particularly jazz, as he was, but a fabulous dinner and a spectacular Southern California sunset would usually be very much to her liking. He had to remind himself that she was anxiously waiting to hear from her publisher on the status of her fourth novel, a continuation of a chain of spy thrillers (she absolutely hated when he referred to them as such). Liz, her serial heroine, was a young, beautiful, and extremely capable woman with a PhD in engineering and expertise in networks, communication systems, and encryption. She was employed as a technical director at a large, fictitious aerospace company that might be mistaken for Boeing or Lockheed. While bringing a degree of dull satisfaction to Liz's life, this rather mundane job had never completely sated her spirit of adventure. But by exploiting connections she had made through her business dealings, she had ultimately secured a contract as a freelance consultant to the CIA, specializing in protecting or cracking secure networks. It was this work, and Liz's inevitable interaction with interesting members of three-letter agencies, that had been the basis for all of Cathie Clarke Fisher's novels.

Cathie's most recent installment introduced a serious romantic interest for Liz: a lean, steely-eyed former F-14 Radar Intercept Officer; highly trained in fighter weapons and tactics and an instructor to the young pilots of Iran's growing air force before the fall of the Shah. After retiring from the Navy, Cathie's new character had worked in the defense industry, primarily in weapon-systems modeling and advanced tactics development for networked systems. Slightly older than her heroine, he was still the epitome of masculine self-confidence, and his military experience and his involvement with advanced communications networks were both natural connections to her main character. The love interest had seemed to develop on its own as this intriguing character had been woven into Cathie's imagined world.

Her publisher had warned her to avoid the romance angle in pretty clear language. "Look, you've gotten this franchise really rolling, but the demographics of your readers indicate a surprising number of young males, attracted no doubt to the action, the adventure, the world stage, and your faithfulness to technical detail and believability. They also seem to enjoy the female version of James Bond that you've created and how she's been evolving. So go ahead and let her screw as many enraptured guys as you want, but please don't turn this into a Hallmark 'made for TV' special." Cathie had fumed for weeks over this one, but had written in a love story all the same. Hell, she could always kill the character off if it wasn't working.

During dinner and the ensemble's performance, she had dutifully turned off her Blackberry, her iPhone, and her pager. But it was clear that as soon as both the dinner and tonight's musical entertainment were at an end she would re-wire herself to her own little universe and get back to business. The voice of the pianist broke in on Logan's abstraction. "Hey, thanks for being here and showing us some love. Enjoy the rest of your evening now." Logan joined in the enthusiastic applause and glanced sidelong at his wife who was joining in, but had a noticeable look of relief on her face. He sighed inwardly. Why spoil a beautiful night?

"Listen, honey," she said as the applause died and a general murmur of conversation had begun, "I just need to check messages. Do you mind? Why don't you grab another drink at the bar? I'll be there in, oh, ten minutes."

Logan smiled and leaned over to kiss her cheek. "Take your time, babe, you know where to find me."

On warm summer evenings, La Florentine would open an outdoor bar bordering on the plaza, which was in fact a horseshoe shaped extension to the large semi-circular bar on the interior of the restaurant. Tonight it was quite busy, with additional ones and twos migrating in that direction with the conclusion of the jazz concert. However, the sound system had filled the void and thankfully, the restaurant's manager had directed that the evening's musical theme not be broken. Logan approached the bar just as Diana Krall finished a series of provocative A minor seventh and

B flat thirteenth chords and began to croon the Frishberg classic "Peel Me a Grape."

This restaurant was extremely popular with the local aerospace execs who ran Northrop-Grumman, Alpha Defense, Raytheon, Boeing, and others from nearby El Segundo, and who would often bring important customers, business partners, or military officers to wine and dine after a dull day of business. And so it was with no great surprise that Logan recognized a few of the "wheels" from Boeing that he had briefed, not long before his retirement, on a potential joint venture to develop a secure tactical communication system. They gave him a courteous nod as he passed, but didn't invite him over, and Logan turned to look ahead just in time to avoid a collision with one of the most stunning women he had ever seen. She was Asian, but with an unmistakable Hawaiian or Tahitian influence, layers of wavy dark hair and brilliant, intelligent eyes that were well at home in a gorgeous, high-cheekboned face and beautifully shaped lips beneath a smoldering lipstick that might have been painted from the same palette as the sunset sky. Her skin was a flawless bronze, and her dark blue silk dress, which flowed from well below her neck to the middle of her shapely calves, made her look as though she were standing naked in a luxuriant jungle waterfall in moonlight. A quick glance had also revealed that her small feet were clad in dagger-like heels of cobalt that should have been registered as weapons.

"Excuse me, I'm so sorry," he exclaimed when he could finally draw enough breath to speak.

"Oh no, not at all," she replied with a brilliant smile. "My fault entirely. I am very grateful that our meeting wasn't even more abrupt. A collision would have been most unfortunate." *Yeah, that would have been a real bummer*, thought Logan ironically. Though her speech was flawless, with a melodious voice that added additional grace to her appearance, it might have had a slight "English" ring to it. Logan contemplated this while rather tactlessly admiring her more obvious features. "Well, I'd best get back to my hosts," she added, smiling once again, and showing no apparent resentment for his stupefied behavior. She seemed to be quite accustomed to her impact on men.

At the moment, Logan felt very much like a man. At fifty-five, he had prided himself on staying in good physical condition. And though he continually fought a tendency towards an expanding waistline, a tendency he would have scoffed at even ten years ago, he was still fighting successfully, and as a result, his relative thinness made him look taller than his actual six foot one. And while his dark brown hair had been yielding at last to grey, he retained a sufficient quantity of the original color, so that the grey still tended to make him look "dignified" rather than old. Perhaps even this incredibly lovely woman would still find him attractive, he thought.

The subject of Logan's fantasy moved away and he gazed at her with a lack of self-control that he thought he had overcome in college, thinking of the immortal words of a long-vanished grad school buddy with a philosophical bent, "I hate to see you go, but I love watching you leave." The heels, of course, made her taller, but he guessed her to be a slender but athletic five foot six, without them, and they certainly did not inhibit her movement in the slightest. She glided through the tables and people with the calm, smooth and unerring certainty of a jungle cat in search of prey, and reseated herself with the Boeing execs. *Must be tough*, Logan thought, jealously. *Wow! I seriously need that drink now.*

As if reading his mind, the bartender smiled. "It is probably unwise to bring alcohol this close to an open flame," motioning in the young woman's direction, "but would you like to risk it?"

"Hell yes I would like to risk it!" Logan replied enthusiastically. "Oh, you mean the drink. Sure. Ahhh, how about a Glenfiddich, straight up and 'stat' please, I feel faint." The bartender turned chuckling and came back quickly with a double. "On me, sir. Please enjoy. Sometimes I could love this job!"

"You know," said Logan to the smiling bartender, "I've just retired from a truly dreary job that kept me mostly in drab buildings with no windows and minimal female interaction, and though I probably don't have your skills, I could stand another job like this. Not a bad office, especially the view!"

"Got that right! I'll check up on you in a bit and make sure you're recovering from the shock."

Logan gave up on attempting a civilized lack of interest and settled for staring in what he hoped was not an overly boorish manner in the direction of the stunning woman he had internally dubbed Miss Blue Hawaii. No one seemed to notice. All of the men and most of the women in the immediate vicinity seemed as drawn to stare as he. *Wow,* Logan thought again, *moths to flame!* But it appeared that the group was preparing to leave, the lady simply returning from powdering her nose, no doubt, and it was amusing to see the three middle-aged Boeing VPs who could terrorize the greater part of a huge corporation, behaving like high school suitors of the same cheerleader, trying to outdo each other in gallantry. The lady wisely remained neutral, and the group moved amiably off and was soon out of sight.

Logan looked back in the direction of the bar and took a sip of his single-malt scotch and was astonished to find that the brilliant and colorful bottles, the multi-hued back-lit glass behind, the scintillating light refracted by the lines of suspended wine, martini, and champagne glasses all seemed to have suddenly lost their sparkle. Even the Glenfiddich seemed, well, a little flat. *Really?* thought Logan. *Unbelievable!*

But he settled back into his comfortable bar stool, and by the third or fourth sip, the world had regained its balance, its unfortunate normalcy. Logan now had an opportunity to glance around him and he noticed a news story running on the silent fifty-five inch LED screen hung above the rows of bottles. A news story that was being related by an anxious and serious-looking reporter wearing a hooded parka to protect him from a slanting, driving sleet, and standing on what looked to be a very shabby dock in a small port. Mountains rearing up in the distance were snow covered and forbidding and the reporter droned silently on as he pointed towards an empty dock area. In the banner running below this picture were the words: "Second crab boat, *Glacier Challenger,* now missing and feared lost in strong Bering Sea storm. The *Annabel* was reported overdue 16 hours earlier, and efforts by the Coast Guard to locate either ship or crew have been, so far, unsuccessful, and have now been suspended due to the ferocious weather ... Their disappearance is a mystery since both had acknowledged several warnings ... Navigational failure had been suspected but seems unlikely for both vessels."

Logan's attention drifted for a moment as another group nearby rose to their feet and said their goodbyes, and for a few moments he just surveyed the quiet evening and the deepening darkness of the night sky. But a feeling of "something missed" had snagged in his mind. It was the feeling that you get when, despite the calm of your surroundings, and a sense of security and comfort, there is an interloping feeling on the edge of anxiety that has no rational basis but will no longer allow you to fully relax. It was a bit like the onset of a dull toothache, or being halfway through a relaxing weekend in the mountains and realizing you forgot to lock the door on the way out of your house.

And as we all do, Logan began to rerun the last few minutes in his mind and so isolate the source of this unexplained feeling. He cycled back to Miss Blue Hawaii. No problem there! True, her departure had somewhat sapped the energy from the evening. But that wasn't it, as he remembered being pretty well recovered halfway through his "Glen". Then, what? And it suddenly occurred to him that somehow the news story of the disappearance of the two crab boats had, for an instant, sounded familiar. Had he heard it earlier in the day? No, he was certain that this was the first he had seen or heard of it. Then how was this familiar? He thrashed it in his mind repeatedly and scanned the television for any other news that might give him a clue, but no luck; just an ad for a new book-reading tablet, with the gorgeous young woman cheerfully explaining the features and benefits of this wonderful device to the young stud that just happened to be sitting next to her and appeared to be fascinated. But Logan no longer cared whether the two would live happily ever after, twin tablets at their side, for the notion of "books" had come just that immeasurable amount close enough to the story of the ship disaster, and a spark of association had leaped the gap. That was it! His wife's first novel had contained a similar theme. What exactly had it been? Something about terrorists hacking into the guidance systems of U.S. weapons. But before they actually carried out the attack, they had tried a dry run on commercial fishing boats and they had used the cover of a storm to hide their trial. Interesting, but not that practical, had been Logan's thought at the time. It had been a minor aspect of his wife's book which neither defined its success nor could have prevented it. And having identified the mental hangnail that had been eluding him, Logan let it go with just the afterthought that he'd mention it to Cathie. It was an interesting coincidence, after all.

A few moments later, Logan was joined by his wife who had the look of a pressure cooker with its safety valve disabled, just about three seconds from exploding. She went right to the bartender and ordered a shot of tequila, which she downed swiftly, sending the bartender back for a second, before ever acknowledging her husband's presence. Logan watched as the cowed bartender nearly ran for the bottle, refilled the shot glass, delivered it to Cathie with a sorry attempt at a bright smile. She turned her back on him, and he glanced at Logan, rolled his eyes, and made haste to the opposite end of the bar, where he made himself extremely busy.

"Bastard!" she snapped.

"Whoa. I'm gonna guess that call did not go well."

"Bastard!" she repeated. "Where's that bartender gone? I think I need a drink."

"Easy there, babe. Just tell Don Loganioni all about it, and I'll have some of my boys give him a little, you know, friendly advice. Or would you prefer that he find a horse's head beside him in his bed tonight? You know, I've met a few guys in special ops over the years that might just do that for fun."

Cathie teetered for an instant on the edge of detonation and suddenly relaxed just a tiny bit, the shadow of a smile just touching the corners of her mouth. She reached a hand up to touch his face and said "And this is why I love you. Thank God you can make me laugh you tall, handsome, retired old guy. And thank God you know how to pull my fuse when I need it. That was close to being a scene. But do me a favor, love, see if you can coax the nice young man back. I promise I won't castrate him. I think I will have one more."

Logan made a slight motion with his hand, which "the nice young man" acknowledged with a nod.

"So, are you in any frame of mind to tell me about it? Or is it best to let the wound heal a bit?"

"Oh, I should've known. Geoffrey has decided to play hardball with the love interest in my latest book. Says he will absolutely not go to publication unless I tone it down, preferably remove the character entirely. And to rub salt in the wound, he says it's for my own good. Did I mention he's a bastard? Oh, and I might have called him one, that is, right before I hung up on him. Oh hell. Take me back to the hotel and make passionate love to your darling wife. Between that and the tequila, I'll get a good night's sleep. I suppose room service can deliver a large helping of "crow" tomorrow morning before I call him back."

Logan grinned and put his arm around his wife's shoulder. "You know," he said smiling, "I'm quite young to be retired. Really. I've been mistaken for fifty-four and been ID'd in the grocery store when I bought booze … once or twice … well, a few years ago. But still …"

Cathie just smiled and took his hand. "Just shut up before your luck runs out and you lose the chance of a lifetime."

***

And as Cathie and Logan drove off to their hotel, Ms. Luana Chu kicked off her heels and buried her toes in the lush carpet in the backseat of a platinum Bentley driving down Wilshire Boulevard towards the coast. She spoke quick, perfect Mandarin to her driver, instructing him to take her back to her condo in Marina Del Rey. It had been an extremely productive day, but a much more productive evening, and the executives she had dined with had not only picked up the tab for her passable dinner, but they had fallen over themselves to demonstrate their importance and connectivity by divulging information about many of the projects in their advanced programs portfolio. Nothing classified, per se, but information that did a gross disservice to the concept of op sec, operations security. Her father would be pleased

Ms. Chu was the president and CEO of a small but rapidly growing company specializing in the efficient backup of critical software and data, primarily of a sensitive, or in many cases, a highly classified nature. The need had grown with the times: rapidly expanding networks; massive data storage; extremely sensitive personal, competitive, or military information. And with that growth had come the vultures: the hackers, the competitors, the unfriendly foreign governments employing all types of malware, worms, Trojan horses and carnivorous bugs of all descriptions. She had started as a consultant to industry and several government agencies but had been encouraged, and sponsored by her father, to establish her own corporation, employing only the brightest graduates from MIT, Cal Tech, Stanford, etc., to leap-frog the existing technology of the day, and to build a firm foundation to support the future needs of data security.

Headquartered in Honolulu, Infinity Services Group, or ISG to the rapidly growing family of subscribers, still had a relatively small staff, and because of this, and because of her natural inclination and ability to dazzle, she had continued to be the chief interface with business and military leaders and the key speaker for many seminars. Ms. Chu's credentials were sterling. Born in Honolulu to a Chinese father and native Hawaiian mother she had several distinct advantages besides her striking looks. And though her father was Chinese, she was an American citizen by birth, which had smoothed her path in schooling and in acquiring access to sensitive and classified information. Her mother had been an elegant daughter of a wealthy Hawaiian businessman, whose lineage was traceable to Hawaiian royalty. And though extremely successful in business, there was a barely veiled resentment of the haoles who had stripped his family of their royal status and honor, a resentment that ran very deeply, and was transmitted from birth to Luana's mother and so to Luana. What had also been transmitted was a grace and aristocratic air, carefully veneered to avoid offending her clients, but which exuded confidence, capability, and leadership.

Luana's father had been born in Mao's China but had lived most of his life in Hong Kong, beginning as a menial worker in a small, shabby plastics factory, using resourcefulness, callousness and brutality to his co-workers to earn himself a supervisory position. Through a highly political and loveless marriage to the daughter of a businessman, followed by her untimely death, he ultimately became a managing director of a company with interests in chemistry, plastics, and more recently, semiconductors. A careful examination of Mr. Chu's past would have revealed very little. And that was exactly as it was intended to be. As a boy of no more than fifteen—poor, homeless, and rejected by his parents—he had entered the Chinese military, which had become his family, his source of food, education, and direction. Recognized quickly for his intelligence, his responsiveness to command, and his hard, even brutal approach to getting a task accomplished, he was chosen to become part of a not-inconsiderable group of similar youngsters that were taught to both covet and hate the decadent capitalistic swine of Hong Kong. But they were also taught to mimic the men they despised so as to blend in within their corrupt business structure. The goal of this unique cadre of pliable Chinese youths was to ultimately help smooth the anticipated transition of Hong Kong to Chinese control and to apply the appropriate leverage at the appropriate time to ensure the proper alignment of this rotten but massive economic giant with its new masters. A few simple skills were taught to these young trainees, including blackmail, extortion, bribery, and assassination. Graduates of this training were injected quietly into the seedier ghettos of the metropolis, given a small stipend and left to their own resources. Those who failed simply ceased to exist. Those who succeeded saw a slight increase in their stipend along with much higher expectations.

It was the farsighted plan of a massive, patient, and evolving superpower, with no guarantees of success, no very specific goals, but with extraordinary potential payoff. In fact, some of the participants had done well, some had done very well, but few had succeeded to the degree of Luana's father, delighting his superiors and earning praise and a successively more difficult portfolio of tasks. Wan Chu took to traveling frequently to San Francisco and the Hawaiian Islands, expanding his commercial contacts and seeking relationships that could be exploited in the future.

Throughout, Wan Chu (his name for public consumption) remained fiercely loyal to his military family, hating the corruption that he had been forced to bathe in and longing for the word that would allow him a share in the glory of bringing it down, bringing about its total annihilation and cleansing.

Marriage to Luana's mother opened new vistas for his handlers, as did the birth of his daughter, an American citizen with a remarkable pedigree of disgust, envy, and loathing for the West, through both bloodlines. The inherited traits from her father and mother including high intelligence, charm, brutal efficiency, determination, self-confidence, and callousness could be molded to suit a philosophy that was hardly divergent from her parents' natural feelings. And so, Wan

Chu received his greatest challenge: to help his daughter to become a powerful, influential force within the American industrial complex and then, to wait for the word.

Luana's education proceeded through exclusive private schools where she excelled in academics and social graces. At home, she was daily reminded of the disgusting quality of her classmates and their parents, mere money-grubbing usurpers with no honor, no philosophy of societal fairness, no claim to personal achievement of any kind, simply lining their pockets by the sweat and labor of others. Her father's frequent absences did not diminish this indoctrination, as her mother felt it with equal vigor, and by the time she graduated from high school, she was already convinced that these people were meant to be manipulated by her as she saw fit, always with a charming smile, in order to bring about a better good. And she had already learned the skills that would allow her to manipulate them in such a way that they would thank her for it.

Her own academic, extracurricular and social skills, along with the influence of two powerful and savvy parents who knew the value of a timely donation to higher learning, brought her a scholarship to Stanford. There, she dazzled her advisers, professors, and classmates with a triple major in English communications, computer science, and math, completed with honors. While working on her undergraduate degree, she had interned with several dotcom companies in the Bay Area, establishing invaluable contacts, and not a few unconditional job offers awaiting her graduation. Her subsequent MBA had put the finishing touches on a woman who could now write her own ticket.

She had had several lovers over the years, but none that she had cared the least about, considering them decadent, unpolished, and not worthy of her and her higher goals, and they had been discreetly discarded when she grew tired of their foolishness. Her friendships had the appearance of sincerity, which she considered much more important than sincerity itself, and seemed quite to satisfy her "friends," since an acquaintanceship with Ms. Luana Chu was becoming a valuable property. In fact, she had developed an unbelievably complex and almost wholly disingenuous façade, every facet of her personality and behavior designed to manipulate, control, and dominate, with her resentment of the western world, skillfully camouflaged by her total immersion in it, her only honest emotion. Wan Chu could hardly accept the praise of his superiors. This prodigy had created herself.

***

It was after midnight when Luana, lounging on the balcony of her Marina Del Rey condo, decided to call her father. And in truth, it was her condo, or at least would be at the death of her father, who had quietly bought the spectacular oceanfront residence through an obscure holding company which he owned. No very great amount of information would ever be transmitted by the highly un-secure means of the telephone, but then, few words would be needed to communicate what she needed him to know.

"Luana, my bright angel, how are you my dear?"

"I'm doing very well, father. Today's was a most successful business engagement, and I am sure that the executives at Boeing were very interested in my product. They do some very interesting work there, you know, and we agreed that I should conduct several lectures on advanced products and capabilities for their leadership, in the hopes that they will engage my company to continue to provide for their data security needs."

"That is excellent news, and when will you be meeting with them next?"

"They are very busy men, but they managed to find time for me next week. At that meeting, we will agree on the days for the seminars. It is quite settled already. And by the way, I will use my time here to even greater profit, as they introduced me to some of their fellow executives at two other firms. I shouldn't be surprised if they too decide to take advantage of me, that is, my company's fine services."

Wan Chu laughed appreciatively. Since Luana had turned eight, it was always she that had taken advantage of her companions, dazzling the boys and men, and overwhelming the women.

"Good, good, very good! But you know, I do miss you. I plan to be back in Honolulu the sixteenth of next month. It would be lovely if you could join me and your mother for a few days. It seems that business always keeps us apart. But speaking of business, I have a fascinating business acquaintance that I'd like you to meet."

"Father ..." Luana began, for the one weakness of Wan Chu outside his passion for his own version of world justice, was to see his daughter matched to another superior intellect, with similar beliefs.

"No, no, my dear, truly, a business associate, no more. Much your elder as well, but still a very energetic and knowledgeable individual who should be able to stimulate your thoughts, perhaps to a remarkable degree. And you certainly know him by reputation. He was the individual that brought us the most interesting idea that ultimately led to the birth of your now thriving corporation. Such an amusing concept, and so childish in its way. An idea he captured from a novel!"

And though Wan Chu was extraordinarily perceptive he neither knew, nor would have thought it significant, that his business associate had not been the originator of this theft.

"Ah, that gentleman! Yes, an amusing concept. Well, then I am sure I will enjoy his company. I will be certain to keep the sixteenth, plus several days following, clear. It would be a shame if my new clients wanted to meet then, but if so, perhaps I can convince them to change their minds."

"Quite simple. Just mention that you are otherwise engaged, but that your director of operations, the august Mr. Peyton, can easily come in your stead. I would think they would cheerfully reschedule."

"Yes, quite likely. You are always so kind to my ego."

"And you never fail to live up to all my praise."

"Love to you then, father, and mother if you should speak to her before I do."

"And love to you as well."

All that had been necessary to communicate had been accomplished, without any doubt, but this acquaintance her father mentioned had already piqued Luana's interest. To earn her father's respect was no small achievement. This man must be one of extraordinary capabilities and decisive action.

Chapter Two

Friends & Wine

Logan eased the rented Mustang convertible through another series of curves along the picturesque California Highway 1 near Pismo Beach, the fresh ocean scent whistling past Cathie and him, making an untidy mess of Cathie's hair. But what the hell, the contented smile on her face spoke nothing but relaxation and enjoyment. They had agreed to take this ride with the top down as a treat and as somewhat of an homage to the California coast scene and neither regretted it for an instant. In fact, they had decided to stay on the Coast Highway past the point where it would be logical to turn off for Paso Robles, today's destination, in order to enjoy the sights as the road wound its romantic way past Morro Bay.

"I've gotta say, dear," began Logan, "this doesn't suck."

"No it doesn't," Cathie replied.

Part two of Logan's post-retirement celebration had begun, and both Logan and Cathie looked forward to their upcoming time in the wine country with their best friends Chuck Johnson and his wife Joy. Cathie had known Joy since their first years in college, and their friendship had grown and flourished despite some long periods when they had rarely seen each other. Frequent phone conversations as well as some old-fashioned letter writing, for which both had an odd, throwback passion, had gotten them past these intervals easily. And when Joy had first introduced her then fiancé Chuck to Logan, the two men had hit it off immediately, both having a passion for golfing, jazz, and good wine. Of course, their relationship had developed through another extremely powerful connection, almost, but not quite, by accident.

This connection had begun in 2002 and solidified substantially in 2005. On both occasions, Chuck had been a very active field operator for the CIA. Long before the passage of UN resolution 1441 requiring Iraq to fully cooperate with UN weapons inspectors, the CIA had decided to make their own assessment. Chuck's team covertly monitored communications, hacked into networks, planted sleeper bugs, monitored the deployment and operational status of air defense units, and generally helped to prepare the battlefield should a military strike be deemed necessary. Politics was not Chuck's business, cyber warfare and intel were, and Chuck aggressively went after the equipment that would give his team the winning edge.

During that effort, several rather unique experimental pieces of hardware and software had been delivered to the field. These tools had been produced through an extremely confidential, very well-funded, and extraordinarily rapid development activity. To meet the deployment deadline, an equally extraordinary contractor team was formed. Composed of "A" players only (electronics, communications, and software engineers taken, regardless, from other company projects), the team was given free rein to tailor standard company practices and procedures and to shortcut time-consuming system engineering processes. Both the customer and the contractor realized that these shortcuts reduced the likelihood of a successful development to something like 20 percent. The team had ultimately succeeded beyond all expectations due to superior capability, extreme dedication (ten hour days, no vacations, holidays or weekends for five months), and outstanding leadership. Chuck knew the company involved in the development, but only later found out that it was his friend Logan Fletcher who had led the team. During the same period of time, Cathie and Logan had been told by Joy that Chuck was involved in some dreary, tangled paperwork at a U.S. military base in Saudi Arabia. Neither, of course, had believed that for a moment.

By 2005, Chuck's mission had evolved. He was still responsible for a team whose primary mission was cyber warfare and intelligence, but his base of operations had changed to Afghanistan, and the stakes had become, if possible, even higher. So had his personal level of exposure, and he had requested support specifically from Logan and his team.

Deployed along the Afghan/Pakistan border, Chuck and his team had caused a fair bit of chaos and confusion, and had helped end the careers of several mid-level Taliban leaders. Chuck knew his team was being hunted, and moved his outpost often, but he had not discerned the level of force and resources that had been deployed against him. On a cold night in a crumbling, abandoned shepherd's hovel on a dusty mountainside, Chuck's new gear had allowed him to crack a secure enemy communication link and determine that a large, well-armed group was approaching their position. A bare minimum of time was available, but Chuck and his team had made an orderly withdrawal, leaving nothing of value and only one sheet of paper with a hastily scrawled and cartooned "Kilroy was here."

Of course, during the time this deployment had occurred Joy had explained Chuck's absence as merely, "Chuck has been assigned out of state for a while," and no more was asked. Only Logan and one other contractor team member had ever been out-briefed, some months later, on their product's successful field test. It had been Chuck himself who conducted the out-brief, and specifics were still kept to a bare minimum except as regarded the performance and potential upgrades of the unit, but it had been clear that Chuck believed he owed his life to Logan and his team.

And so the bond between the couple, begun with the women's relationship at school, had been cemented with clay from a hillside in Afghanistan.

***

"You know, I'm looking forward to seeing that old cowboy. Do you think he still gets assigned out of state much?" Logan asked.

"Oh no. Joy said he's getting too old, like you, and the climate wouldn't suit his delicate health."

"Hey, watch that! I'm not that old. Well, I am old enough to retire, which in my opinion is a perfect age. Besides, Chuck is at least, what, five years younger than me?"

"Eight, dear, but who's counting? In fact we're all about eight years younger than you. How did my parents allow you to rob the cradle all those years ago?"

"Hmm," he replied a bit sourly. "Yeah, well, they must have recognized that I was the perfect companion for a young and reckless starving authoress, and that if your career didn't work out, the stodgy old engineer would at least keep you off their payroll."

"Oh, c'mon, don't be an old grump. I mean don't be a young, virile grump. We're having fun, right?"

Logan smiled and jabbed the gas petal for emphasis. "Yeah, we're having fun. But my fun meter says it's almost lunchtime. Let's stop in Morro Bay and grab a bite before we press on to Paso Robles."

***

From the terrace of Benny's Seafood, Logan and Cathie stared out across Morro Bay towards the massive Morro Rock. A sea breeze kept the air fresh and cool, despite a cloudless sky and dazzling sun.

"You know," said Logan between bites of his grilled grouper sandwich, "I'm gonna have to hit the gym some time on this trip. Food like what we've been enjoying plus a few days in the wine country will turn me into a blimp, a large, soft, round blimp."

"Hmmm, well, I guess it's OK to splurge. After all, how many times do you expect to retire?"

"Just the one, babe, just the one. This is pretty awesome," he added looking out over the sparkling bay and the absurdly steep, green-clad rock. "Just check out all the birds flying on and off that rock. You know, I wouldn't mind taking a class or two, now that I have all this free time," he added with a grin. "You know, get a better education on birds, trees, native plants. I mean, there must be a dozen species out there, and the only one I know for sure is the California gull."

"Did you know the California seagull is the state bird of Utah? Seriously. They flew in during some kind of biblical locust invasion, ate the bugs, and saved the Mormons. Pretty cool, actually."

"Yeah, I guess I heard that one about seagulls in Utah. Kind of a long flight. Good thing they got a meal of biblical proportions out of it."

Logan yawned. "Good thing Paso Robles isn't as far as Utah. What do you hear from Chuck and Joy?"

"I got a text a while ago. Chuck was delayed getting out of the office. They'll be a little late getting in, but wanted to be sure we made reservations at the Artisan for dinner at 7:00. They promise to be there. More or less. Actually, they said if they were late, have another drink."

"Like Chuck needed to tell us that! Duh."

***

Highway 41 rapidly left the coast behind, climbing and cutting through the rolling, golden hills of central California and directly towards some of the finest wine country in the contiguous forty-eight. With the sun beginning to roll towards the Pacific, shadows were starting to form in the clefts between the successive hills, casting early shadows on the California live oaks that nestled between the tawny, grass-covered slopes. There was a scent in the air, too, hard to define, but Logan was sure that if he had been dropped here blindfolded he could, with one whiff, exclaim "California" without fear of contradiction.

Check in at the La Bellasera Hotel and Suites had been smooth, and the couple was now enjoying a happy hour drink at the hotel bar. At least, Logan was enjoying his drink and letting his eyes drift lazily across the pool where a few children were busily splashing their father, and beyond the hotel to the sunlit hills, now alive with the orange gold of the rapidly setting sun. Logan glanced at his wife, but she still seemed extremely engaged with her Blackberry; texting, he guessed, with her publisher, and Logan silently prayed that the mood wouldn't be spoiled by another long-distance argument. He glanced at his watch. They'd have to leave soon anyway to get to the Artisan restaurant by seven. He hoped Joy and Chuck wouldn't be late, and he hoped that Cathie would put away her electronics for her old schoolmate and best friend. If she didn't, Joy was just as likely to ask to borrow the Blackberry, for just a second, and then blatantly remove its battery and hand the disabled machine back to Cathie with a shrug. Logan smiled at the thought. The one time he had tried that little gambit he had slept on the couch for a week. A news ticker on the television announced that wreckage of the crab-boat *Annabel*, including a few empty survival suits, had been found, far off course. "Poor bastards," Logan thought. But the news quickly rolled on to a happier tale of a modern day Lassie saving her 7-year-old master who had fallen into a racing river. Logan yawned.

"Time to go, babe," he said, tapping his watch face. No response. "Cathie, time to go. Hello, earth to Cathie, do you copy?"

A distracted, "What? Oh, yeah, sure, five-by-five. Just let me finish this one little point."

Logan had deliberately added a ten-minute buffer to his call to leave, and he was quite pleased when precisely nine minutes and twenty-two seconds later, Cathie surfaced for air. "Ready?" she asked. "Well, let's go then, don't want to lose our reservations."

***

Logan and Cathie had just begun sipping their second before-dinner drinks and Cathie had regrettably resurrected the Blackberry from her purse when Chuck and Joy thankfully arrived. Hugs, handshakes and greetings were passed enthusiastically all around, and as the waiter quickly arrived to take drink orders, Logan heard Joy say, "Hey, is that the new Blackberry? I believe it is! Could I just take a peek at that for a second?"

"Actually, no," replied Cathie with a giggle. "I'll just turn it off and put it away, shall I?"

"Oh yes, dear, that will be just fine," Joy laughingly replied. "So I want to hear all about your new book, but first tell me about your princess. Still in school and not married to some Greek billionaire?"

"Still in school, and more or less enjoying it. God, for the price you'd think we were billionaires. Still, she's doing well, with some potential prospects after graduation. I get a blow-by-blow description every weekend."

"I'll vouch for that," said Logan. "My God, when that call comes in I can count on at least one uninterrupted hour of free time. Of course, I get a hell of a lot of free time these days."

The two conversations split at that point, with Cathie and Joy still catching up, and Chuck turning an envious eye to Logan. "So you really did it, you old bastard you."

"Please, I'm getting enough of the 'old' harassment to last me to the very short end of my days. I can only say that I highly recommend it, and besides, I think I bloody well earned it. I've got a few things to be proud of and to reminisce on in my declining years."

"You can say that again, brudda, including my still being around to harass you."

"Yeah, well not all of my decisions were faultless, nor all of my programs successful," he joked dryly.

Chuck laughed appreciatively. "Yeah, guess I deserved that one. But I tell you what, spending all that time out of state has kind of worn my bony ass out. It's desk work for me from now on, and a freakin' early retirement too, if I can swing it. You know our son, Marcus, just got into the agency. Damn, I'm proud of that kid, well, proud of both of them, but Marcus is gonna do well in the agency. I mean, brilliant, young, energetic, studly. Reminds me of me, a few years back."

"A few! You mean like twenty-five or so? My, my, they say the memory is the second thing to go."

"What's the first?" Chuck asked with a grin.

"Well, I guess I forgot. Oh hell, better look at these dinner menus before the waiter gets back."

"No, c'mon man, check this out instead," and Chuck pulled a battered piece of paper out of his pants pocket and unfolded it to reveal a slightly better than Google Earth image of the nearby area. "Look, I've got all of the wineries we talked about marked on the map and the appropriate sequence of visiting consistent with A, hitting every one we talked about; B, mixing the appropriate vineyards to provide the optimal assortment of tasty wines daily; and, most importantly, C, sequencing each day's visits in such a way that the outbound leg is the longest, while the final stop is still within striking distance of the hotel even if we are totally shitfaced," he laughed loudly. "Logistics, man. UPS doesn't have jack on me!"

Eventually dinner was ordered along with a bottle of Turley Vineyards Zinfandel, a well-known and well-loved varietal.

"So, not to get all serious here, but have you been watching the news?" asked Chuck.

"Yeah, of course, with all the time I have now I've become a regular junkie. My 'cable favorites' are MSNBC, CNN, Fox News; you know, left, middle, and right." But Logan's half-formed smile faded as he saw cold, deadly seriousness in Chuck's eyes.

"Sure, but, have you noticed anything a little odd, maybe a little like something that maybe someone might write into a novel, you know?"

The seriousness of Chuck's tone along with the look in his eyes surprised Logan a bit. He took a sip of his wine. "Yeah, well, yeah at least one instance. Couple of crab boats presumably lost. Speculation about nav failures. I just saw today that wreckage of one was found."

"Not wreckage. At least not the kind that would leave forensic information. Sure, survival suits, bits and pieces, but no sign of the boat. Gone to Davy Jones. Which is pissing a few people off, I can tell you. The other one, *Glacier Explorer, Glacier Something, Big Freakin' Glacier …*"

"*Glacier Challenger*," interjected Logan.

"Yeah, that's it. Well, so far, not so much as a life preserver or a bait box from that boat. What's worse, there may never be anything."

"Why's that?"

"Well c'mon brudda, think. If it was a nav error, then looking in the area where it was supposed to be fishing before that killer storm blew in is just about likely to get you squat. On the other hand, the Bering Sea is pretty damn huge, and the resources just aren't there to open up the aperture. Besides, the crew is long dead and everyone knows it." Chuck paused and took a sip of his wine. "Say, Cathie hasn't talked to you about this, has she?"

"No. I've been meaning to mention it to her, actually."

"Don't," said Chuck with surprising vehemence. "I mean, no need to bug her about it when we know next to nothing."

"Next to nothing ain't nothing, brudda," Logan responded, mimicking his friend's expression. "You must have a whiff of something."

"Folks, your dinner will be right out. Care for another bottle of wine?"

As dinner arrived, conversation drifted back towards family and friends and, of course, to the planned agenda for the next several days. "Honestly, he's been like a little kid with his satellite photos and itinerary," said Joy to Cathie. "Got to admit, though, it sounds like a rather good plan. Creds to you, Mr. Logistics Man," she said, smiling at Chuck.

"So, Mr. Logistics Man are we going to do the dinner cruise in Morro Bay or hit Anthony's in Cambria tomorrow night?" asked Cathie.

"So many decisions, so little time, so much food, so much wine. Say, I believe that was poetry. I just might have a competing career in literature, albeit not prose," Logan grinned at his wife.

"Trust me darling, stick to being retired. But I believe I asked a question of Mr. Logistics, so would he, and no one else," with a significant look at Logan, "please let me know what's for dinner tomorrow."

"Now this is serious business," said Chuck leaning over the table in a conspiratorial manner. "You know that if you don't have reservations, in advance, the cruise is damn near impossible to get. Same goes for Anthony's. However, I know a few people, and I called in a few favors, wasn't easy, and it's gonna cost me in the future, and maybe a few people are going to get hurt, but for a good cause ..."

"Oh pipe it, Charlie," Joy interrupted. "We made reservations last month for both. Thursday at Morro Bay, Friday at Anthony's. Tomorrow we freewheel it."

"My cover blown, my carefully crafted story ruined. But yeah, that's more or less the truth, if you're into that sort of thing."

"Truth I can live without, dinner, however, is mandatory," Cathie concluded.

"Gotta admit," whispered Logan to Chuck, as the waiter dropped off dessert menus and there was a moment of confused questioning and perusing of the choices, "I could handle a little more truth, if there's any more to have."

Chuck considered, and then cautiously said, "You put it well, there is a whiff of something, and to me it smells of skunk. So far, just a few coincidences, some like the boats making a splash, pardon the pun, and some others are well below the radar horizon, at this point it's no more than a white Zinny, if you get my drift. But there is either a literature-admiring copycat out there with some resources at his disposal, or these are some damned freakish coincidences."

"Others?" asked Logan.

"Brudda, I think I've said enough, for now. Like I said, it may be nothing more than a white Zinny."

Logan smiled at Chuck's second usage of "white Zinny." In the years when the two were communicating regularly, they had developed a slang method of stating a judgment on situations based upon their mutual love and understanding of wines. It was designed to be used, quite unofficially, over open com lines that were possibly, or perhaps likely, to be compromised. It was never intended to give specific information, but more of a gut feel, an overall impression of a situation. But the two men had come to rely on it and were often able to glean a very keen understanding with a wine name applied to a specific situation of which they both had knowledge. In this context, Logan could safely conclude that there was uncertainty in Chuck's office as to the nature of the events and their connection with his wife's novels, white Zinny indicating something of an amorphous nature; confused, uncertain, possibly nothing at all, but having at least "a whiff."

Logan sat quietly during dessert, answering somewhat at random and not really participating in the conversation. He knew that he was getting a few sharp glances from Chuck, but he either ignored them or met them with a rather insipid "gee I'm enjoying my dessert" smile. Logan realized that he had pushed Chuck for information, maybe pushed a bit too hard. But unlike other strictly professional interactions with this very capable and determined man, there was an apparent level of personal involvement through his wife and her novels. Logan hadn't needed a trained CIA agent to make the connection, however tenuous, between the navigation failures of the missing crab boats and the subplot of his wife's first novel. Coincidence was a much more likely solution at this point, and Logan had nearly dismissed the connection from his mind. He recalled a philosophy class, taken many years back, and the professor that had patiently explained the concept of Occam's razor to a largely bored and disengaged group of college students in a half-filled lecture hall. Logan had retained the essence of this principle which was that if there existed multiple explanations for an event, then the simplest of them was most likely true, and certainly terrorists taking ideas from a novel to carry out attacks was far from the simplest explanation available. Logan also recalled the interesting theory of one Sherlock Holmes that when all possible alternative explanations have been eliminated, then that which remains, however unlikely, must be true. Certainly, it was far, far too soon to remove all other explanations, and based on Chuck's comment regarding lack of forensic evidence, there might never be a satisfactory resolution.

This thought brought Logan back to the frustrating realization that it was Chuck who had reopened the topic that he, Logan, had very nearly forgotten. This set off warning bells in Logan's head that had not triggered with his initial casual notice of the news story and its similarity to the novel. Why would Chuck even bring this up? And the answer was obvious: There was a whiff all right. Chuck was no less human for being a very highly trained CIA agent with a rather impressive resumé of "out-of-state" assignments. But the need to occasionally share theories or concerns with someone outside the agency had been made possible through his unique professional and personal relationship with Logan. Chuck and Logan were both professional when it came to handling sensitive information, but a certain degree of judgment and discretion could and had been used, and this symbiotic relationship had been beneficial to both. But that wasn't it, not in this case, Logan felt certain. He thought back to the conversation, struggling to find the true objective for Chuck initiating it, and realized that the entire point might have been to determine whether Logan had spoken to his wife about the matter, and more importantly, to discourage him from doing so. Logan's first reaction and natural instinct had been to assume that this was to prevent Cathie from any possible feeling of responsibility for the tragedies of the lost boats, to spare her from any possible feeling of guilt. It wasn't until much, much later that Logan realized that Chuck's actions had an alternative explanation. This left Logan, whose extremely analytical mind had not retired when he had left work, with three possible explanations for the nav failures and the loss of the boats. The first, coincidence, still seemed the most likely by far. Copycat use by people who were opportunistic and less creative than his wife was the second.

And the third, a nasty one that Logan could barely acknowledge and that he quickly banished from conscious thought, was that his wife was somehow intentionally providing concepts or constructs of plans to some very bad people.

A sharp glance from Logan to his friend Chuck caught the studying look on Chuck's face as he watched his friend, and Logan wondered how much of what he had been thinking had been apparent to Chuck. Logan returned the look, no insipid smile this time, but a hard and serious gaze that told his friend that all joking had gone out of this subject.

***

"Honestly, dear," Cathie began as Logan and she got ready for bed, "you just seemed to clam up. Is something wrong? I would have thought you'd have been really glad to see Chuck and Joy. I mean, we've been planning this for so long and it's, well, I just don't know."

"Dear, you are imagining things. I'm as happy as a bushel full of clams to see Chuck and Joy. Hell, Joy got you to banish the BB, at least for a few minutes."

This last bit of highly affected banter changed the current in Cathie's mind quickly and she scowled. "You know this is a critical time for my publication. I need to stay in contact with that toad Geoffrey whether I want to or not."

"OK, OK, just joking, babe. But look, I'm fine. I guess I just lost the thread of the conversation and got off into my own little universe. You know how I do that. But I'm really happy to see Chuck and to have this little trip to kick back, and well, to prepare me for my continuous life of sloth."

Cathie relaxed a bit, accepting Logan's explanation not so much because it was believable, but because it coincided with her desire to make this a memorable and most enjoyable trip.

In Chuck and Joy's room, a not dissimilar conversation was playing out. "Sugar, you must've said something to Logan to piss him off. I mean, he went into silent mode right around dessert. Did you call him old or something?"

"You know I didn't. But even if I did, it was all in fun. I guess I'm just a little jealous," Chuck replied evasively. "I think maybe it was just a long day of driving, drinking, eating, drinking, and, oh yeah, drinking."

"You are so full of crap, lover. Just in the DNA I suppose. But maybe, just maybe you're right. How about we just 'lax it tomorrow? Whatever it is that set things to mute, can we please avoid it? Your life and manhood may depend on it."

"Ooooh baby, I love it when you threaten my manhood," laughed Chuck. "Deal! All smiles, rainbows, and unicorns tomorrow. Besides, we've got some serious tasting to do!"

***

The next morning, the couples met for brunch, and the events of yesterday that had led to two evening discussions seemed as though they had never happened. Chuck had pulled his satellite photos out again and he and Logan were deep into their planning before omelets had even arrived, while Cathie and Joy continued to catch up on family and friends. The scent of fresh coffee drifting up from their four cups was nearly as satisfying as the flavor, and a basket of fresh, hot biscuits was keeping them quite satisfied for the time being. They were seated at an outdoor table of the Pony Cafe, and the early day was gorgeous: a near cloudless sky and a brilliant sun, with a steady breeze gently playing through the fresh flowers at their table to take the edge off the heat.

"Hey, can we finish up at Turley? After having that zin last night I want to buy a case. That can be say, three o'clock, then we can get back here and kick back for a bit before we get to more eating and drinking," Chuck concluded.

"You know, we have seriously got to work in some sort of physical activities here, or we could be leaving in a wheelbarrow," Logan said.

Chuck smiled a conspirator's smile. "Look," he began, "I know you must've brought your clubs, right? So leave it to Mr. Logistics. Tomorrow, bright and early, you and I hit the links at the Morro Bay Country Club, I've got a tee time for six-forty. They've got a great layout that gets you up into the hills overlooking the coast. Lots of fresh air, some upper body exercise, particularly for those among us, and by that I mean you, who have a slightly elevated handicap. We play eighteen, which I win handily, meet the gals for a light lunch, they having enjoyed a lovely spa morning courtesy of two charming men who need about five hours of free time; we take in the two wineries that are closest to Morro Bay marked in blue on the photo, and are back at the pier by 4:30 to catch the evening cruise. So, that only adds up to two meals and one round of golf. Not too bad, eh?"

"A good plan but for the prognostication. I intend to wipe your bony ass ... net, that is. But give me a few months of blissful leisure and I believe I can take a run at your gross score as well."

"Dream on, brudda, dream on. Still, I know you've heard the one that says 'a bad day of golf beats a good day at work.' I think I can enjoy this even if I don't end up on the happy side of eighty."

"Boy, you've got that right. Ah, food has arrived," he added as the waiter appeared with a packed tray.

***

The golden day continued as they wound their way through rolling hills from one winery to the next, toasting with amber glasses of liquid sun. Evening found them on the *Morro Dreamer,* still sipping wine and watching the swollen disk of the evening sun set the western sky and sea ablaze; a dazzling light which evolved from pure, otherworldly radiance, to a tawny lion's mane, a spectacular orange, and finally into a decidedly mellow and gentle green.

"Well," Logan began, "that was a more than satisfying day." He and Chuck were seated in the open air on the *Morro Dreamer's* upper deck, their wives doing a little shopping in the small boutique area on the deck below that boasted handmade jewelry, paintings, and ceramics from local Morro Bay artisans.

"No, not so bad," Chuck agreed, pulling two cigars from the pocket of his light jacket, trimming the ends of both, and tossing one in Logan's direction. He ignited each with a lighter, guaranteed wind resistant, that produced a powerful blue flame like a propane torch. A cloud of fragrant blue-grey smoke drifted out over the *Morro Dreamer's* wake. Both men were silent, watching the golden sunset, and then resumed a game that they had played since first becoming friends, a variant of their much more serious code for communicating sensitive information, that involved wine and women. Logan gestured with his cigar towards a petite blond woman leaning out over the rail, her floral-patterned skirt waving about her knees, and a smile of enjoyment on her sun-bathed face. "Have you noticed the Riesling?" Logan asked, admiring the lovely amber tan on her bare arms and slender legs, and smiling appreciatively.

Chuck lifted his sunglasses to facilitate a better view, and indicated his approval. "Yep, light and sweet. But you know, for my taste, I think I prefer an excellent GSM," he replied, motioning in turn towards a young couple, the female of the pair being tall, dark-haired, and olive-skinned, a tight-fitting sweater and jeans clearly highlighting her more prominent features.

"Ah," said Logan, "well-balanced, full-bodied. An excellent choice as well, my friend." And so the game went until every female within eyeshot had been associated with an appropriate wine variety to which both men could agree. This installment of their game was complete, a tie by mutual agreement. A few minutes later, the ship was nudging the side of the dock and the dinner crowd, dined and sated, began to gather their things and prepare to disembark. Chuck and Logan gently hauled their spouses away from their shopping and towards the gangway.

The drive from Morro Bay back to their hotel in Paso Robles passed by in companionable silence. Upon their arrival, Chuck and Joy excused themselves with a hopeful wink from Chuck to Logan as they headed towards their suite. "Well babe, it looks like just us two for the evening," said Logan. "We happen to have this odd bottle of Late Harvest Sauvignon Blanc that I just know isn't going to fit in the car and it just so happens that the Jacuzzi is currently unoccupied. What do you say?"

"You read my mind, lover. So should we get our suits on or just skinny dip?"

***

A very few minutes later, the dull thud of plastic cups toasting added a punctuation to the pleasant bubbling chatter of the Jacuzzi. "Eight wineries, forty wines, a nap, an outrageously excellent meal, a Cuban cigar, and my lovely wife, tantalizingly close and seductive. As my wise father, God rest his soul, would have said, 'This really doesn't suck!'" Logan exclaimed, exhaling a fragrant cloud of smoke that hung gently in air.

"That can't really be a Cuban, can it, darling?" Cathie asked. "Won't Chuck arrest you or something?"

"Got it from Chuck," Logan grinned.

"Well then, just pass that over here, would you." Cathie drew in deeply, leaned her head back and blew out a delicious cloud towards the darkening sky. "Oh my God, that is awesome. Did you bring one for you?" she asked, teasingly. "Actually, my dear … ," Logan replied with a grin, pulling another Cuban from a leather pouch.

"I knew I married you for a reason! You are very nearly perfect. Well, you're pretty damn good, that is, not too bad. Shit, you brought two cigars! You're my hero!"

"Gawd, we had some good vino today, didn't we? The varietals were pretty awesome, but I've got to say, I loved the red blends from Paso Robles."

"Me too. Oh, and before I forget, don't you forget to split the Tobin James Club half and half," she added, meaning a combination of white and red wine. "Gotta have those whites for summertime."

"Your wish, my command, et cetera, et cetera." Logan took another sip of the Sauvignon Blanc as Cathie wrapped her lips around the Cuban. "How did I get so lucky to get a female Bacchus for my wife?"

Cathie blew another fragrant cloud. "You know, Logan," she began in a more serious tone, "I think I'm the lucky one. I love the fact that we share this hobby, I love the fact that we can get away on trips like this. Hell," she laughed, "I even love the fact that you put the entire inventory of our not inconsequential wine cellar into EXCEL."

"EXCELLL!" Logan drawled, sounding exactly like Homer Simpson saying "Beer!"

"But sweetie," Cathie continued seriously, "I just love the fact that you love me."

Logan responded with equal seriousness, "That's not too hard, actually."

Cathie continued, following her own thoughts, "I know it can't be easy, sometimes, with me. Hell, I never thought I'd be, well I guess I'm lucky to be writing and to have people that want to read my work, but I know that the pressure and the nonstop availability and interruptions can be a drag. Sometimes, I think I should just kill off all the characters and hang it up."

"Don't, babe! You're good, really good. Besides," he added with a grin, "we need the income!"

"Bullshit! You know, babe," she added after a brief pause, "I can't think of the last time I felt so relaxed. Thanks so much for this little getaway."

As Cathie spoke these last words, Logan had the wonderful sensation of several toes tickling his calf, camouflaged by the bubbling jets.

"When you're done with that cigar," he said with what he hoped was a loving and passionate look, "I think I know where another bottle of the Sauvignon Blanc might be hiding."

"Might it be hiding near our bed?"

"It just might!"

As the two walked hand in hand towards their suite, Cathie asked, with some seriousness, "What were you and Chuck going on about last night? I caught a few words, and it almost sounded like the plot line from my first novel, which would be odd," she said, punching his shoulder in a very gentle way, "since you NEVER read my novels!"

"Not true!" Logan replied with sincerity and complete honesty. "You know I love your books. Hell, I could probably recite them from beginning to end. Let me see, how did that first one begin? Was it 'It was the best of times, it was the worst of times,' no, that was from a very dull story involving guillotines. 'Call me Ishmael,' no, not it either. Bit of a tall fish story, that one. 'Chapter One, I am born.' Hmm, not that one either!" Logan was blabbing on, and he knew it, as he searched for a way to deflect this question in a way that wouldn't offend his wife or, worse yet, ring false in her ears and cause her to cling like an irate Gila monster to an intrusive hand until he finally fessed up. Through years of marriage and a long working career full of Machiavellian politics, Logan had discovered that, quite oddly, a simple (partial) dose of the truth actually worked best. "We were just hacking over some of the depressing news of the day. A bit dull, actually."

Cathie gave him a sharp look that seemed to say she wasn't buying that, at least, not in full, but by then they had reached their room. Her face relaxed as she pulled the room key from her purse and let them in. "OK, sweetheart, you can keep your boring news and super-secret conversations to yourself … for now. In truth, the Sauvignon Blanc is sending out its siren call. You fetch the vino and I'll locate a couple of very elegant plastic cups. It was a glorious day!"

Chapter Three

Introductions

Luana sat relaxed on the terrace of the penthouse atop the Hilton's Tapia Tower in Honolulu. From where she sat she had an unobstructed view up the shoreline of Waikiki, a view of the hotels and restaurants, tourists walking along the pathway, and a number of evening surfers still trying to catch one last wave. The stately bulk of Diamond Head provided a backdrop, its upper heights catching the last rays of daylight as the sun settled into the vast Pacific. The steady trade winds rustled the leaves of the small palms and liana vines that bordered the terrace.

She sipped her mai tai and felt not the slightest feelings of contradiction that she, who was so much a champion of equality, fairness, and social justice, should enjoy such luxuries. There would always be superior individuals whose station was above the general populace as she was physically above them from this towering eminence. No contradiction whatsoever. She and her father were true believers in bringing about this equality and their version of justice that would naturally place them in a different stratum as was due their energy, zealousness, fervent belief, capability, and above all, their success. Those that needed taking down would be taken down, those that needed raising up would be raised up, and those who had been granted the wisdom to see this need, to adjudicate the distribution, and to bring it about were entitled to the best of what life had to offer. And those few would graciously accept, from the masses, the gratitude that they had so righteously earned.

Since her childhood, Luana had been taught the difference between crass capitalism and its lust for wealth and power and the rise of the true aristocracy with their benign enlightenment. She had grown more than accustomed to the notion. But beyond that, she had learned to manipulate greed, desire, even lust. Her own venture into the corporate world had been as a means to an end, and she had grown adept in turning the weaknesses of others into her own strength. Childish boyfriends, young lovers, college professors, business associates, and now the leaders of corporate America had all fallen to her aggressive charms and—she flattered herself—had enjoyed their fall. Her own ultimate destination was still evolving, but in the fantasy world of her imagining, the aristocracy, herself a prominent member, ruled with calm benevolence, savoring the decadence of their station.

And as Luana watched the shoreline come alive with the twinkle of torches, lanterns, strings of colored lights, and the dazzling brilliance of the dozens of hotels—watched the masses of tourist, vacationers, businessmen, and locals moving about—she relaxed even further, allowing her mind to wonder about this friend of her father. She would know soon. He was expected for dinner at seven-thirty. And they would not be fighting the masses for a seat at a noisy and overcrowded restaurant. Luana's mother had sent her own cook from Maui to prepare tonight's meal, and they would be dining on some of the finest Hawaiian fare, a mixture of traditional cuisine and Manu's own creations, that the islands had to offer including taro in a coconut sauce, roast pork and chopped Maui onion, and steamed seaweed-wrapped grouper, fresh pineapple skewers with lobster and scallops marinated in seawater and grilled with a butter sauce. Of course, the islands didn't really have this to offer. But she and her father did, and she assumed her guest would be both pleased and impressed, which was the main point of this meal.

Luana glanced at her watch. Nearly seven. Her father would return shortly, and she would take a moment to freshen up, though she was already dressed in a tight silk dress printed with dark green tropical vegetation twining around and blending into a deep sapphire sky, as though she were wearing a bit of the living jungle tangle torn from a romantic night. Her eyes would pass for stars. And this too was calculated, by her father's design, to both impress and distract their guest, putting her father at a tactical advantage. Once Luana was thoroughly convinced that this wasn't one of her father's ill-advised attempts to find her a companion, she had enthusiastically agreed to the strategy. It was, after all, her own approach in so many meetings with the corporate executives that were her potential customers and sources of information.

***

At seven-thirty precisely, the elevator buzzed, announcing the arrival of their guest. "Ah, punctuality. That is what I mean, my dear, a most extraordinary visitor. Manu, please see our guest out to the terrace and be sure to ask him his drink preference as he enters."

"Ivor, my friend," Wan Chu greeted. "Please come and meet my daughter while Manu prepares your aperitif. Ivor, allow me to introduce Luana, my daughter, my only child, and the pride of my family. Luana, this is Mr. Ivor Vachenko, a business associate."

"Mr. Vachenko, it is a distinct pleasure. My father has said the most flattering words about you, and although you may not know him sufficiently as yet, his praise is most difficult to obtain."

"Please, no," said Ivor in a surprisingly deep and resonant voice. "This will not do. You must call me Ivor, as your gracious father has honored me. And as for pleasure, I assure you, Luana, it is completely and thoroughly mine."

"Come and sit, Ivor," Wan Chu invited.

During this early banter, Luana's practiced eye had not been idle. She had quickly taken in Ivor Vachenko's physical appearance. He was approximately six feet tall, well-built and still in exceptional physical condition for his age, which Luana judged to be about fifty-five. His weather-worn face was of a light mahogany, and his short grey hair and beard were trimmed meticulously. His English was perfect with only a slight accent that might be Middle Eastern to a highly perceptive ear, but by appearance and demeanor he could easily pass for a successful Spanish or Italian businessman. He wore a simple, though obviously quite expensive tan sport coat over a three hundred dollar Hawaiian shirt and tan pants. He very much gave the impression of being wealthy, intelligent, well bred, and openly friendly. But Luana had been around many powerful, aggressive, and successful men, and she immediately sensed quite a bit more about Mr. Vachenko. The name itself did not readily fit the image, being eastern European, possibly Czech or Russian. That would make an interesting story, she was sure. But she had learned much from looking into his eyes. They were dark brown, with a lively intelligence to them that seemed to fit his cheerful and open nature. But behind the outward sparkle that, along with the beard, weathered face, and grey hair made you think of a friendly uncle, there was an unmistakable and un-concealable hardness and strength. She sensed that this man had seen and done things of an extraordinary nature and despite her and her father's plan to dazzle and disarm him, he remained cautious and on guard, and those eyes were evaluating them just as Luana's were assessing him.

Dinner was served to the continuation of pleasant dialogue, Ivor expressing disappointment that Mrs. Chu had been unable to join them and speaking with open admiration of the success of Luana's company and the numerous well-placed connections she was cultivating. He said very little about himself, however, and following her father's lead, Luana accepted this and spoke only of his travel to the islands and whether he was enjoying the sights and the lovely weather.

"Ah, Luana, one would be called blessed indeed to call the Hawaiian Islands their home. I find that I love the relaxation and casual luxury of Maui the most, however, and I hope to visit there once again before I must depart for my own home of heat, scorpions, and sand," he said, smiling.

"I believe Mr. Vachenko must be referring to Arizona, my dear," Luana's father joked, "and yet somehow I feel that perhaps I am mistaken." Wan Chu had thrown this calculated dart and was inwardly pleased to see that he had hit his target. Vachenko's expression perceptibly tightened for a moment, immediately followed by a charming smile and laugh as he regained control.

"Yes, parts of the Arizona desert do in some ways resemble my home, though they are generally greener and much more hospitable. But perhaps we might sit for a while out on the terrace and talk briefly of business. I find the steady breeze exhilarating. And Miss Luana?" Ivor paused with a significant look at Chu.

"My daughter will, of course, join us. She is my daughter in every way, and I believe no more need be said."

"Of course, of course," Ivor replied smiling graciously, "I was only concerned for her possible boredom during the discussions of two old men."

"Manu," Chu called, "You may bring out the fruit, cheese, and of course the cognac, then you may go." Manu silently laid out the after-dinner fare, poured three glasses of the amber liquid and retired as silently as a ghost.

"Yes," began Wan Chu, "I too adore the steady, warm trades. And an outdoor setting is so much more appropriate for discussions such as ours," he smiled reaching for a slice of guava.

"We have much to discuss," began Ivor.

"Yes, yes," Chu interjected pleasantly. "Let me clear the way for you and perhaps our discussion will go quickly and we can enjoy the pleasure of the evening for a bit longer."

Vachenko sat silently and nodded. Still smiling, Chu began. "You and your companions wish to bring about, how shall I say it, a more equitable arrangement of world order. Happily, we, that is, I and my esteemed Eastern business associates, agree. We are in a position to help you in many ways. These should be obvious to you, for I am a conduit to very substantial resources. Not to belabor the obvious, but these include, most importantly, intelligence and finances. Now, our paths, while not leading to the same destination, follow the same course for a considerable way. My associates and I are willing to negotiate for the resources you need, but of course, there are things we need in return."

Vachenko sipped his cognac and remained silent, which Luana much admired both for its formidable self-control and for its wisdom. It was unfortunate folly to interrupt her father, who also took a sip of the cognac, and continued. "So Ivor, my friend, to not be too wordy, we have only one small request to make in return for our support. To be crude, you wish to fuck the Americans as they have fucked your people, taking their holy land, killing the men, raping the women, and corrupting your country. Your methods involve killing, terror, and punishment to make both a physical and a political statement. Simple and effective, in its way, but it can be more. It can be strategically significant as well."

Here was the punch line. Vachenko straightened himself in his chair. Her father's use of crude language was, like everything Wan Chu did, calculated to have an effect and in this case it made a point of the hardness and authority behind his civilized manner. The message was clear and unambiguous, and his masterly use a delight to his daughter. Her eyes sparkled with the primordial fierce joy of the wolf closing on its prey. Luana was a twenty-first century wolf, and like the wolf she was committed to hunting with the pack, surrounding and ultimately overcoming even much larger, much stronger prey. But like the wolf, she realized that there could be no effective pack without a single alpha leader, and this was her father. She quietly put aside the thought that one day she might become the leader, and if that occurred, it would be the result of a bloody conflict for power, the strongest prevailing. The alpha wolf did not cede power to a subordinate, nor did a subordinate inherit by virtue of calm, methodical succession. A brief moment passed and the palms rustled lazily in the steady, sea-tinged breeze.

"My daughter and I will provide targets for you and your associates. These will not be your only objectives, and the others I leave to you to best meet your own desires to discommode the Americans. But you will attack the objectives that we provide. My daughter and I will provide these targets as they are developed and refined, and these will contain those appropriate to achieve our strategic ends, which, I do assure you, are in line with your own of destroying American hegemony. There will be others which are more in the nature of obscuration. It is unimportant to you as to which of these is which. They must all be destroyed. We leave it to you to make a political statement with blood and violence as you see fit. Our resources of intelligence and finances we will provide for both our objectives and yours." Wan Chu paused briefly, momentarily letting Ivor believe he was finished, and then a fraction of time before Ivor began to respond, continued, "We only ask, my friend, that your independent objectives be made known to us in advance. After all, it wouldn't do to have a resource conflict develop due to poor communication."

Ivor struggled to control his emotions and his reaction. His thoughts ran rapidly to the members of his own organization and to their highly variable dedication and reliability. Still, they were drones and subject to command. It was to another that his thoughts now flew; she whom he knew so intimately, body and soul; she who had manipulated her Western acquaintances, extracted critical vulnerabilities, and authored many of his most successful, and bloody, operations. What would she think of such an arrangement? She would, of course, be kept anonymous, but this demand smacked of control, of domination. Ivor's long-standing relationship with this woman, passionate both physically and philosophically, gave him insight into her potential reaction. It was doubtful she'd be pleased. But how far did he dare push back with Wan Chu? Still struggling with these questions, he spoke at last with an affectation of nonchalance, "My dear friend. I am afraid this is not acceptable. As you know, our operations are of the most sensitive nature and the fewer people who are aware the more likely the success."

"You distrust me?" Wan Chu asked in a voice of brass. "Then perhaps we may not do business after all."

"No, no, you misunderstand, my friend. It is just that with many people involved, there is always a risk of, let us say, an incautious subordinate making an error."

"This will not happen," replied Wan Chu. "Incautious subordinates have a very short life expectancy in my organization. Your information will be handled most discreetly. To save much time I will say that this is not negotiable. Deviation from this policy will, sadly, result in the termination of our cooperation."

"And yet, I and my people will be the ones at risk: risk of betrayal, capture, injury, death. Surely we are the most committed to this endeavor and surely we deserve some consideration for this willingness to accept the most difficult and dangerous aspects of our partnership?"

Luana sensed that her father's patience was nearly exhausted, and felt that the outcome of this dialogue was seriously in question at this time, but Wan Chu held up a hand palm outwards towards Ivor and said with icy calm, "My friend, your dedication and that of your associates is well known to me. Who among my compatriots has not remarked on your zealotry and commitment? It is said that you would fight on, with your bare hands alone, to free your country and your people. What are resources or intelligence to people with so much zeal, so much passion, so much fervor for justice? Hardly needed at all. So, if it must be so it will be so. And yet, we stand to gain so much from this partnership. But, I grow tired, my friend. My patience is at an end. I have stated that this point is not negotiable and I know you understand me well, yet you attempt to negotiate. It simply will not do. Do we not know each other well? My poor monologue is now complete."

A long pause ensued, and Luana gazed at her father with open admiration.

The tension was broken as Ivor took the last sip of cognac in his glass and casually refilled it from the decanter. "I believe we can do business, my good friend, and on behalf of my associates, I accept your generous proposal."

He's lying, thought Luana. *Good, very good. He is afraid and will be all the easier to manipulate.* "Another slice of mango, Ivor?" she asked, smiling her dazzling smile.

"Please," he replied, matching her smile. But the broken-glass edge of that hardness she had sensed during their first moments together was dulled. He had lost. A more sympathetic observer would have said that he had been forced to compromise, but Luana knew only a simple truth. She knew it in her heart. He had lost.

"Well, since that aspect of our negotiations is complete," began Ivor, eager to salve his stinging pride, and hoping that Wan Chu, having won his point, would be flexible in terms of an immediate grant of money, "there is some need of the, ah, resources, that you just mentioned."

"To be sure. But first, have you the personnel to carry out near-term operations? I am sure you must have some ideas, and I await them with great expectation."

Ivor smiled. Here he believed he had something to impress even the man of stone that sat across from him. "My friend, we have made the most extraordinary acquisition: a man of strength and intelligence; a man of absolutely amazing skills; trained in combat, stealth, observation, communications, explosives; an expert with many weapons and a skilled tactician."

Wan Chu sat politely with his hands resting on the table in front of him, the fingertips lightly touching, an inquisitive look on his face. "Such men are rare, and all too difficult to hide … and control," he added after a significant pause.

Ivor laughed a hearty laugh. For the first time this evening he had the advantage of Wan Chu. "Yes, yes, normally quite true, but he is an American, trained by them, ingrained in their culture and their military, understanding both their tactics and their weaknesses, a gift from God. I will not lie to you, he killed many believers until he too faced Allah, or his own God, I do not quibble. But having recognized the error of his ways at last, he now accepts the true faith and the true cause that we so justly pursue with that same zealotry that you have so rightly acknowledged."

Ivor laughed even more heartily at the look of skepticism on Wan Chu's face. "No, no, but I embellish slightly. And yet, he is ours to command. He has proven his faith in blood on several occasions. Of course, we do not completely trust him, but he has a lieutenant, a believer, a man of good faith, in fact my nephew, who swears that he is ours, and is positioned to guarantee his good faith in the future."

Though the look of skepticism did not entirely fade from Wan Chu's face, Ivor proceeded. "But one man does not make a cadre. Others are needed and this man has been given the responsibility to bring others, eight others to be precise, across the border through a most disagreeable though often-used corridor for immigration and the transport of other commodities. As I said, a most disagreeable area, and the weather and landscape are quite hostile as well," he added with bland sarcasm.

"Does your trusted man involve the cartels?" asked Luana, with a nod of approval from her father.

Ivor shrugged and opened his hands in front of him to show the inevitability of this connection. "They are involved, of course, to some extent, but are not knowledgeable of the nature or the nationalities of the immigrants that Mister …" and Ivor hesitated. "But why trouble you with names," he said, smiling. "He will be there personally to ensure the success of the mission. The involvement of the cartel personnel, those infamous coyotes, will be minimal."

"Very good," Wan Chu responded, nodding.

"And yet," added Luana, "they are not without their own forceful inquisitiveness should they feel in any way threatened. Your man must move very cautiously."

And Ivor smiled a very hard and thoroughly non-jovial smile. "Though 'discretion' is his middle name, I assure you, my man need not fear the coyotes, and he has been instructed to leave no loose ends once his charges are safely across the border, no loose ends whatsoever."

"Very good," repeated Wan Chu, as he handed Ivor a sheet of hotel note paper. "You will be so kind as to memorize this sequence and return this paper to my daughter before you go. It is the number of an account in which you will find a current balance of one hundred thousand dollars, which should be sufficient for your immediate needs. Luana will discuss with you the means by which we may easily communicate in the future. She has a rather elaborate Facebook page where many friends stay in touch, though she may desire you to use several others in preference. I will leave you in her capable hands and withdraw, by your leave."

It was clear that with or without Ivor's leave, Wan Chu would be departing. But having received twice what he had planned to ask for in immediate funding, Ivor rose graciously and bid his host a good evening. By Wan Chu's departure it was also clear to Ivor that Luana enjoyed her father's complete trust to not only be aware of operations or to carry out specific assignments, but to develop tactics and plans and authorize them independently. With Wan Chu departed, Ivor returned to his seat, swirled his glass of cognac and stared with renewed interest and respect at this beautiful and capable woman.

Luana caught his gaze and smiled a charming smile. "Well, Ivor, shall we begin?"

"Of course!" he answered.

Chapter Four

Circling Buzzards

Jason Stone snapped upright in his sleeping bag, his .45 in his hand in less time than it took him to open his eyes, the pain throbbing raspily in his head. He did a quick check, and the campsite was quiet. Miguel, who was technically on guard, but had been leaning lazily against a mesquite, shot him a rapid look and quickly turned away, seeing the fire in Stone's eyes. Stone put his left hand to his pounding forehead and rubbed for a few moments; safety'd his weapon, and lay back down. He tried to close his eyes, but when he did, all he saw was the doorway and window of a shabby, rundown stone and mud building and the look of astonished terror on the face of Sam Cochran, his teammate, who had turned back to the building just as the IED had gone off behind Jason with a blinding flash; leaving an image Jason's doctors had told him had been imprinted on his retinas.

The blast had sent a jagged piece of steel through Sam's jugular, nearly removing his head as it whistled past. Jason had been hit in the back by multiple shrapnel fragments, miraculously missing his spine and major arteries, and the concussion had knocked him forward, though not quickly enough to avoid a large stone fragment that had hit him in the back of the head, causing a much more serious injury than the spectacular wounds to his back and legs that had nearly bled him white. Working in the pitch black with night vision goggles, the brilliant flash from behind had illuminated the scene in a painful way, and Jason still suffered, as the doctors said he would, from the afterimages.

Jason opened his eyes and looked up at the dark night sky. They were all still in Mexico, perhaps a half-day's travel from the Arizona border.

He and his eight Middle Eastern companions were being guided at the moment by four disreputable coyotes, expendable pawns of the cartel. Jason didn't trust them, and in fact despised them from their first meeting where one of the group had sauntered up to him with a leer on his face and had insolently asked who Stone worked for and why he wanted the glum and silent group of men that Jason was escorting. Jason had eyed the man carefully and gently eased his hand to the butt of his semiautomatic and replied quietly, "You don't have a fucking need to know. Got a problem with that?" His relationship with the coyotes thus established, they had each done their respective jobs with as little interaction as possible, but that little bit had only succeeded in lowering Jason's already subterranean opinion of them.

He was only a trifle less critical of the eight that he was looking after, the eight he was bringing into the states to work for Ivor. They seemed nervous, clumsy, and ill-trained for any challenging assignment, but Jason still retained a certain qualified trust in Ivor. Not everyone could do every assignment. He assumed Ivor had something appropriate for this lot.

***

Jason was an enigma. A powerfully built six-foot-two, he had followed his father's example and had entered the army when he was barely eighteen, where he had shown immediate promise. He had successfully completed both sniper and explosives training, had made the cut for the Rangers, graduating at the top of his class, and had volunteered for duty in Afghanistan. His father had been proud of his son, more so for his service to his country than his individual military accomplishments. But a strong part of Jason's personality had come from his mother, who had instilled in him his feeling of self-worth and the belief that to serve an inferior commander or, for that matter, an inferior cause, was beneath him, worthy of scorn. His pride of individual accomplishment grew, therefore, rather than the pride of being a part of a team, even a winning team. And though his father tried to suppress it, there was a feeling of disappointment in Jason's inability to be wholly engaged, to be a part of something bigger, and this shadowy, poorly veiled disappointment had communicated itself to Jason. Misunderstanding the cause of his father's disappointment entirely, Jason interpreted it as being due to his own lack of achievement. And so, Jason continued to challenge himself, pushing to do more, to achieve more individual recognition, and to be a better son for a father who seemingly could not be satisfied. And in fact, his father felt sorry for Jason as well as dissatisfied. What he wanted to see in his son was simply the ability to play on the team and to honor the team's goals, to share their success, to be a brother to his fellow soldiers. To feel the satisfaction of being a member of a truly supportive, extended family had been his father's most precious reward when he had served. Jason was wired differently.

Several disciplinary actions against Jason for arguing with superior officers over tactics and missions had apparently been dealt with when Jason was assigned to some of the toughest and most successful commanders. Jason acknowledged and admired the fighting records of these men, and he served without reservation … at first. Still, Jason kept his respect for them individually well in reserve, and judged his superiors with a cold, hard, analytical adjudication that he applied equally to himself. And as he continued to succeed personally, he became more and more alienated from his father, from his fellow Rangers, from his commanders, and from the cause for which he was fighting. His mother would have completely agreed with his callous assessment of those around him, and in fact continually encouraged him to think independently, to seek personal recognition, and never, never to be subservient to those who were less capable than himself. His own extraordinary abilities had caused him to arrogate to himself judgments regarding both tactical and strategic objectives, to believe that he was capable and in fact deserving of the right to direct his own missions, to choose his own destiny. Ultimately, he began to challenge even the most fundamental elements of his deployment, and the nation's goals and commitment in the Middle East.

In the span of time between when he was struck by shrapnel and rock and the moment his face impacted the packed earth floor, Jason saw, as sharply and blindingly as the image of his partner's face and the filthy interior of the building, that his mission here was wrong, completely wrong, and not worthy of his participation. The revelation, or rather the culmination of his growing conviction, had occurred instantly. In the months of rehab that had followed his evacuation by rescue choppers that night, he had never doubted his resolve to take a new course, one that he would feel was worthy of himself. He kept his own counsel on the matter. There were no peers for him in the U.S. military hospital in Ramstein, Germany, in any case, and when offered a medical discharge from the service, he had disappointed his father for the last time by eagerly accepting. His mother applauded his independence and discerning judgment. Jason accepted a job with Tactical Associates Incorporated, a private security company which operated in Afghanistan, and he later led an operational group in Iraq.

Jason didn't give a rat's fart for his role within TAI, but played the part as a talented actor will sometimes be forced to play a part in a movie with a poor plot line and childish script in order to satisfy the politics of the studio. He had received what he really wanted, which was access within Iraq to those that he felt might be worthy of his talents, an access that he had patiently and skillfully exploited. For the second part of the revelation that had sprung into his traumatized mind was that the people he had been fighting, those even who had planted the IED that had nearly killed him, were in fact fighting for the more worthy cause, fighting within their own country against a powerful outside invader to keep their freedom and their way of life. What that way of life might entail no longer held any interest for Jason. What did interest him was what he perceived as the simplicity, purity, and righteousness of their cause. He had witnessed the brutal, efficient commitment to that cause, carried out with bare hands, courage, and a zealous "win or die", or if necessary, "win and die" philosophy. In his mind, this philosophy contrasted quite favorably versus a sterile, bureaucratic, hierarchical, totally uncommitted endeavor whose primary objective seemed to be to return home to beer and babes as quickly as possible.

Many months of discreet inquiries had finally brought him into contact with Ivor Vachenko, to whom Jason openly offered his explanation as to his extraordinary change in allegiance. Vachenko's lieutenants had been inclined to hold Jason indefinitely, extract what information they could, and then return his body to Tactical Associates Inc. one piece at a time. And Vachenko, who saw a potential, fantastic opportunity here if all was as Jason suggested, was nevertheless inclined in that direction. He had put it to Jason plainly, why should they take a chance and trust him? Jason's candid reply that, in their position, he certainly would not trust him, but that he believed he might be able to demonstrate his good faith and skill, if given the chance, and could, in fact, make a few recommendations that Ivor might find useful. The balance had been delicate enough, but with extraordinary caution and skepticism, Vachenko had allowed him to suggest what might be done.

Without hesitation, Jason had described two options; one involving a lonely ranger outpost of which he was aware. Jason had argued bitterly with his team commander at the time the outpost was established regarding both its placement and the level of firepower to be stationed there. The fool had overruled him and had disciplined him for insubordination as well. To Ivor Vachenko, Jason said he could easily recommend an approach and an attack strategy that would succeed with minimal risk.

Stone's second suggestion involved attacking a chow tent at a larger army outpost, situated much too close to the armed perimeter, as though eating was considered a non-hostile, and therefore safe business. What was more, the tent was crowded at chow time with at least thirty men, lightly armed at best. Jason had, of course, noticed this poor operational situation and recommended to the commanding officer extending the armed perimeter and limiting the number of men in the tent at any given time, rotating men through over a longer period of time. Once again, Jason had been faced with ignorant stubbornness and arrogant hostility (the CO had told Jason to do his own fucking job and let him run the base). Jason could easily point out two small hills with easy egress that would allow for a crossfire of RPGs and automatic weapons.

Ivor had been astonished with Jason's recommendations, but after days of careful surveillance and dry runs, Jason being held the entire time, they had successfully carried out both attacks. Stone had been released to the care of Ivor's nephew, where his short leash was gradually lengthened as his hands became so covered in the blood of his own countrymen that there could be little doubt that the conversion that he had spoken of, the result of his revelation, was in fact true. Any lingering mistrust shifted to a certain wariness that if the allegiance of this man could so radically change once, it might do so again, and they would do well to be prepared for that awkward moment. A badly burned and mutilated headless corpse was deposited and discovered where an anonymous tip had told Tactical Associates to look. A few damaged but identifiable personal items were left with the body. And so, Jason Stone ceased to exist. Jason's greatest regret was that he would miss his mother's encouraging, supportive letters.

***

Jason lay staring at the night sky for a while longer until an unmistakable smell touched his nostrils. Someone was smoking a joint. He rose slightly and looked over at Miguel who tipped his head back and took a drag as the joint glowed brightly. He released a cloud of smoke and gave Jason a foolish look.

"Hey gringo, you want one? Ees free!" he chuckled.

Stone said nothing, but lay back again. *Fucking incompetent morons*, he thought. *It'll be good to be rid of these bastards*. His anger died quickly. It would be light in a few hours. By this time tomorrow, he'd be in Arizona with his group and this cartel scum would be just a bad memory.

That evening, Jason performed a very careful assessment of their campsite. Though he was always disciplined in this regard, an accurate knowledge of his surroundings having saved his life before, he wanted to be particularly certain of cover points, his location relative to the campfire, and the location of his eight men relative to the coyotes when everyone was settled down for the night. The location of the fire was obvious, this filthy site obviously much used by the cartels. He selected a favorable location for himself and his group and relaxed as the evening deepened.

***

"Hey, Eddie, pull it over for a second, will you?" Eddie did as he was asked and the border patrol vehicle ground to a stop on the shoulder of a rugged, parched dirt road in southeastern Arizona. Zach Kreski rolled down his window and sneezed from the self-generated cloud of dust still surrounding their truck. Zach waited for most of the cloud to disperse and then raised a pair of battered binoculars to his eyes, focusing quickly at what looked like a sparse cloud hovering over a ravine about three miles away. The cloud sharpened and disappeared under the powerful magnification of the binoculars and evolved into a large, slowly revolving group of buzzards. "Yeah, looks like buzzards," Zach announced, "a hell of a lot of them." Both Zach and his partner, Eddie Munoz, got out of the truck and Eddie copied his partner's movements with his own set of binoculars.

It was somewhat amusing to see the two side by side. Eddie Munoz was a short, stocky, barrel-shaped man with the dark skin that spoke loudly of his Mexican ancestry, though he was a third-generation American who had grown up in Tubac. His round face held a pair of expressive dark brown eyes, and was capable of containing an enormous smile that was often followed by loud, energetic laughter that surfaced often, though not nearly as much on this assignment as in the past. His short dark hair contained no grey as yet, making him look somewhat younger than his forty-three years. Zach Kreski, on the other hand, was tall and lean in a lanky, somewhat out-of-proportion way: arms and legs seeming just a shade too long for his torso. His light brown hair invariably came out from under his cap pointing in all directions and refused to yield to a comb. Light-skinned and blue-eyed, Kreski was never far from a tube of SPF 50, which accounted for his looking as pale as though he had stepped from a gloomy winter scene in a Polish peasant village into the blazing Arizona desert not five minutes ago. Ironically, he was a first generation American, his parents having emigrated from Poland in the eighties just before he was born, a fact regarding which Eddie never failed to tease him. "Damn Polack illegals," he'd spout off at random times. "We need to tighten up the border on the east coast." More taciturn than Munoz, they had still hit it off and had become the Mutt and Jeff partners of the local Border Patrol office, but no one at any time would have impugned their capability and dedication. They had done some amazing work together, and so had gotten this plum assignment.

"You've got that right," Eddie added a few minutes later. "That's more birds than I've seen in a long time. Can't see what they're after from here, too much mesquite and scrub. That's Tilaquia Ravine, isn't it?" he added a moment later.

Eddie pulled out a well-used map of the San Bernardino National Wildlife Refuge and the surrounding area, noisily shaking out several folds. After a few moments of study, he replied, "Yeah, yeah, pretty sure it is. There's Diablo Butte and The Teeth to the northeast and San Pedro rock just the other side of the border. That's Tilaquia for sure. About two and a half, three miles into the Refuge."

"Not much breeze. Do you smell anything, Zach?" A sensitive nose was nearly as valuable as a good pair of binocs to a border patrol agent, especially an agent assigned to monitor the perimeter of one of the most notorious human and drug smuggling corridors along the Arizona-Mexico border. For one thing, it was as valuable at night as it was during the day, and even the night vision goggles that both Eddie and Zach frequently used could not penetrate extensive foliage. In the nature of their business, both agents had located camps of illegals, drug runners, and coyotes by smell, and had often located the remains of those who had fallen behind or had gotten the worst of a quarrel along the way, sometimes interrupting packs of actual coyotes, buzzards, and once an irate mountain lion enjoying an unexpected banquet. Zach's nose, acknowledged by both as the most highly tuned to detect the smell of decay, tested the air for several minutes.

"Nada, but that doesn't prove anything. Still, it's more likely that whatever is down there is relatively fresh, maybe not even completely dead. But I'll tell you, you've heard the joke, 'Eat shit, ten million flies can't be wrong'?"

"Yeah, I might have run across that one."

"Well, a couple hundred buzzards are never wrong." Zach paused, not really wanting to ask the next question, but knowing that he and Eddie both were thinking the same thing. He sniffed the air once more and finally said, "So, I suppose we need to go and check that out?"

"Yeah," replied Eddie, a humorless smile quickly crossing a serious face beneath his focused brown eyes. "Yeah, a couple hundred buzzards and two underpaid BP agents can't be wrong. I'll tell you what, though,

I say we take the truck and to hell with squashing a few endangered bugs. It's our call, and I say we may need the gear, especially if someone is alive."

Zach Kreski unconsciously checked the firearm at his side and glanced back to the vehicle, the shotgun barrel protruding conspicuously above the level of the dash. "You mean the med kit and stretcher, right, partner?"

"Absolutely. I'll call in and let them know we're investigating and that we'll be on wheels. Man, I can already see the stack of shittin' paperwork we're gonna have to fill out on this one." He shook his head and walked back to the truck.

"You'd think after five years of this BS Homeland Security and the Interior could come up with a solution to this crap?" Zach directed at his partner's back.

"It's at least ten. And let me see, I'm not exactly shocked."

For years, Homeland Security and the Interior Department had been feuding over access to this land. Though Border Patrol agents had been allowed to enter on foot or horseback, motorized vehicles had been prohibited for years because of potential damage to the environment, as had road construction, or the construction of surveillance structures. Homeland Security had even been obliged to pay millions to Interior to mitigate "environmental damage" caused by incursions, held to be necessary, by the Border Patrol. The murder of rancher Robert Krentz in 2009 had caused angry lawmakers to draft legislation that would allow Border Patrol more access, but subsequent litigation and counter-litigation had failed to yield a satisfactory solution, and it was often at the agent's discretion, and legal risk, that exceptions were made. And so the Refuge had become a refuge indeed to some of the worst scum of the feuding cartels trafficking in people and in drugs, using illegals as mules, and very often fighting amongst themselves or murdering reluctant participants in their operations. Ironically, for at least ten years, the only humans having seeming unrestricted access to the wildlife refuge pounded rough paths through the dense brush and made campfires with whatever wood came to hand: mesquite, palo verde, or live oak. These groups killed and ate whatever animal life offered, pissed in the streams, and left trash of all descriptions, sometimes human corpses, littering their camp sites.

Eddie returned a few minutes later, exasperation written on his face in the form of an unhealthy red flush that sat very poorly on his nut-brown skin. "You'd think all we wanted to do was go four-wheeling in the virgin wilderness, dine on snail darters and spotted owls and sleep on fresh jaguar fur!"

"Did they OK us? You know, just this once I might take no for an answer."

"Yeah, reluctantly, with many a reminder of our environmental obligations. I told them that if there were still a few surly cartel snakes with AK's and they got us, we'd try not to stink too much. So keep that in mind, all right?"

Zach leaned his head towards his right shoulder and sniffed in the area of his armpit. "Too late. I stink already."

"Oh c'mon, let's do this."

A careful approach brought them within a quarter of a mile of the epicenter of circling buzzards. "I guess this'll do," said Eddie softly. "Check side-arms, I've got the heavy artillery."

As they prepped near the truck, Zach said, "You know, Arizona is famous for raptors."

"What?" asked Eddie as he checked the load on the shotgun.

"Raptors, you know, birds of prey, hawks, eagles, owls, vultures, buzzards." Zach was clearly nervous as they moved slowly towards the ravine, and Eddie thought it best to let him talk a bit. "Yeah, they're pure hell on small pets. My neighbor lost a cat. Just got plucked out of his yard one day by a hawk."

"No foolin'! Well, I had a Chihuahua that disappeared right from my backyard one evening. Got out there just in time to see a bird that had the wingspan of a C5 just easing away towards the hills behind my place carrying Pepe as though he were a feather."

"Probably a great horned owl. They can pick up things the size of my wife's Prius. A little dog wouldn't give one much of a fight. Sorry about your dog, by the way."

"That little pecker? I never liked him. All he ever did was eat, shit, and bark. He probably gave that owl indigestion."

"Yeah, raptors," said Zach distractedly, "I really need to spend time learning more about them. Most of them are really beautiful, but not these guys so much," he said, jerking his chin at the circling cloud. "Man I hope they're not already at it. I've seen 'em pop out of a carcass before, heads covered in goo, looking like they just loved it in there. Fucking disgusting."

"OK," said Eddie more softly, "just take my right wing, about twenty feet, and let's go in easy. Eyes and ears, eyes and ears."

Zach nodded and drifted off to Eddie's right and both worked their way through the sparse and widely spaced creosote bushes towards a line of heavier vegetation; grasses, mesquites, a few palo verdes growing in bushy profusion near the line of the infrequent watercourse. Fortunately, the trees were not too thickly spaced, and they both began to relax somewhat as they became more confident that there was no one and nothing alive at ground level. But this anxiety was rapidly replaced with another type of fear and disgust, for there were clearly bodies present: two, three, maybe more, at various distances from the remains of a still smoldering campfire. There was near silence now, as they approached, an almost peaceful quiet that one might expect in a wildlife refuge far from any roads or towns, but the evidence that met their eyes as they entered the clearing with the campfire spoke of noise and extreme violence that had taken place here less than six hours earlier.

***

The man near the campfire lay on his back, a very small trickle of blood, dried black, from the entry point of the bullet on his forehead tracking across a dirty cheek to his left ear. Very neat, clean entry about a half inch across. Likely a .45 caliber. Eddie gently turned the man's head with a rubber-gloved hand, disturbing it in a still gooey pool of brain matter, blood, hair, and bone fragments. Not so neat, but confirming Eddie's suspicion that a hollow point bullet had been used, simply disintegrating the back of the man's skull. The remainder of what had been in his skull, that which hadn't been ejected at high velocity, spraying the campsite, had run out after he hit the ground. There was still a look of surprise on the man's face, and his thin mustache was drawn up on one side of his mouth, as though in the beginning of a snarl.

***

Miguel was the first to go. Having confirmed the location of his eight charges (safely to the side of any counter fire) and located the coyotes (Miguel here by the fire, Benito and Jose near the backpacks, and Emilio pissing near the edge of the flickering light), Jason had simply risen quietly and casually pulled the H&K .45 from its holster. Though cautious regarding his own people, Jason really didn't expect any counter fire; not from this scraggly, undisciplined crowd. They might terrorize each other and wave machetes and AKs at the usual wetback mules that they prepped for a border crossing, and they might spray bullets promiscuously at their counterparts in other cartels, possibly even hitting something other than dirt, trees, and bystanders, but Stone had nothing but contempt for them. His conclusion, arrived at early in their association, was that there was not a man among them, and his instructions to leave no loose ends seemed a trivial request, and one that he was happy to oblige. Miguel had turned at the movement, and in less time, much less time than it would take for him to form a thought, his ability to form a thought was permanently terminated. A simple, short-range head shot.

***

"Two more over here," Zach called. Eddie moved off to the shade of several larger mesquites about twenty feet from the fire. Two men, also on their backs, neat head shots again, and Eddie thought briefly "execution style," but it really didn't make sense. Neither man was bound, and it appeared they had been facing the fire when shot. Neither had drawn a weapon, but that didn't signify. Their attackers had just moved quickly and accurately. This had less the look of a battle than an ambush. He once again checked to confirm the same type of weapon load, but hadn't even begun to consider that, in fact, these shots had been fired from the same weapon. Zach was quietly losing his breakfast about ten feet away, and Eddie didn't grudge it of him. Zach could vomit and then be back moving decayed bodies in the blink of an eye. Unlike Zach, Eddie's stomach never gave that involuntary rejection, though he felt the gut-churning disgust no less than Zach. It was just that way. If Eddie ate it, it stayed eaten.

***

Of the four coyotes, Benito was perhaps the most agile, the most capable, and so he was next. Benito and his compadre had risen from fumbling in the backpacks and turned at the sound of the gunshot, and Jason waited calmly until both were upright, facing him, the firelight reflected from their faces. A deep-throated crack, an instantaneous flash, and the solid thud transmitted from Jason's hands to his shoulders, and Benito was kicked backwards off his feet, following the spray that had been his brains. Before the body landed, there had been a rapid, machinelike adjustment in azimuth and elevation, and Jose's forehead rested at the top of the H&K's sights. Jose was a slug in Jason's opinion, and true to form, he had barely moved, the stupid look of astonishment spread across his filthy face. Another crack and Jose lay on the ground five feet from Benito, the stupid look preserved.

***

"Is this it?" Eddie asked, surveying the campsite.

"Seems to be," replied Zach, spitting some bile-tasting phlegm to one side. "Let me just check the perimeter." Zach paced the irregular edge of the clearing, and was about to announce that there was nothing else, when he spotted another body at the north edge, slightly on its side, in a tangle of broken cholla cactus. Though partially covered in cholla pickles, if was clear that this man's head had also been demolished, and while looking for an entry hole, Zach had been puzzled until he realized that one of the man's dark eyes was simply an empty socket, the bullet passing through and blooming to create the carnage behind. Zach's dry retching caught Eddie's attention, and he made his way to where Zach was standing and spitting once again.

***

The fourth shot was the only one that Jason had considered anything like a challenge. At least sixty-five feet from his firing location, barely at the edge of the inconstant firelight, deep shadows jumping, retracting, creating figments of plants, rocks, fallen tree limbs, his target had turned, struggling with his zipper as the echoes of the first three shots died. Jason, of course, knew Emilio's exact height, an advantage that he enjoyed, having spent several days with these men. It was not like an ambush against an unknown force, though under those conditions, he might be working with night vision gear, difficult here with the fire so close by, and not really necessary. Stone waited for what he believed was sufficient time for Emilio to react, and here was his night's only minor, trivial miscalculation, for Emilio was even slower than Jason had estimated, and though nearly upright, he was still turning slightly when the forty-five round reached him, entering slightly to the left of Jason's ideal aim point; in fact, entering through Emilio's right eye. The result was somewhat of a disappointment to Stone, who always strove for perfection, but he consoled himself with the thought that it was a long, poorly lit shot, and if Emilio had shown the energy and quickness of, say, Benito, he would have been standing as expected, and it would have still been a perfect headshot. Having convinced himself that the fault lay therefore with Emilio and not with himself, he de-cocked the gun, set the safety, re-holstered and walked to the other side of the camp to the eight men who sat or stood in stunned silence. "We really don't need those guys at this point," said Stone, with a gritty lack of emotion, "so just get your shit together and be ready to move in five minutes."

***

"Hey Eddie," Zach began when he was once again able to speak, "I think I know this guy." Zach motioned to the fourth body, the one with the blood-clotted hole where his right eye should have been.

"No shit?" Eddie moved closer to the face and gently turned the head towards him. After a moment of careful consideration, Eddie agreed. "I know him too, partner. He was a regular on the border. Sneakin' in to try for the California farm country. We must've picked him up what, two, three times? What the hell was his name, anyway?"

"Emilio. I remember some of his fake papers weren't too bad. Poor fucker. When they started cracking down on the farmers, he got handed over to ICE, sent back, and then just crossed the border again. Persistent SOB. He must've gotten tired of the routine, just for the chance at breaking his back picking tomatoes. Poor fucker," he repeated. "I'll bet the little shit wishes he'd stuck to farming and not thrown in with the cartels."

"And I'll bet you're right. Still, it was getting so hard to even get in to the interior; and then hard to find a farm that wouldn't just toss you to ICE if they felt the heat, always with an understanding that if you made it back, there'd be a job for you. Temporarily."

"Poor fucker," Zach said for the third time. "So what do you think? Rival cartel hit? Pretty neat if you ask me."

"Maybe," replied Eddie with a side-to-side shake of his head uncertainly. "Maybe, but something just doesn't seem right. Do me a favor, check those backpacks over there by the other two.

Eddie continued to examine the dead man, Emilio, noting that his handgun, a Glock 22, was still in its holster. None of the four men had drawn, confirming to Eddie a surprise attack. There were a lot of footprints all around, making it impossible to tell how many assailants had struck. But a night attack with this kind of precision just didn't jive with the usual cartel ambush where automatic weapons were the firearms of choice, not .45 semiautomatics. And the precision of the shots! None of the bodies had any other bullet wounds, just the one shot to the head: neat, clean, and very unusual.

"Jesus Christ!" exclaimed Zach. Eddie quickly spun around to face his partner, his heartbeat madly accelerated.

"Whoa, sorry Eddie, didn't mean to startle you, it's just that these packs are both still full of shit. Buddy, I may be wrong, but this looks like horse to me."

"Bullshit," snapped Eddie, both irritated at Zach's outburst and annoyed with this obvious misjudgment. Cartel members didn't leave two backpacks of heroin lying on the field of battle after snuffing their rivals.

"Well this is just pot," Eddie said, looking briefly in the first pack.

"Yeah, got that. I am a highly trained BP agent you know. Got a passing grade in drug identification 101. Look underneath it, the small sausage at the bottom." Eddie dug around, still unconvinced, but his hand brought up a cylinder of dirty white powder, tightly wrapped in layers of plastic.

"No fuckin' way! And I mean no fuckin' way!" And as Zach watched, Eddie hefted the bag and stared in disbelief. "I suppose we could test it—if I'd brought the kit, which I didn't. But I guess we both know the answer."

Zach nodded and replaced the contents of the backpack. Both rose to their feet, and Eddie said, now in a choked whisper. "None of this makes any sense. Why leave the drugs? Was it just a revenge hit?"

Zach shot Eddie a skeptical look. "A revenge hit? Not a chance. These guys would have been tied up and carved like last year's turkey as a message to their compadres 'Fuck with us and you die screaming.' Besides, they still wouldn't just leave this shit lying. No fuckin' way."

Both men looked cautiously around them with grave uncertainty. There was an awful lot of cover here and they were vulnerable. The clearing was quiet except for the buzzing and churring of insects. A nearby cicada began its rhythmic chatter, answered quickly by another further off. The sun, well up now, was turning serious, and its heat was penetrating the thin mesquite canopy. Sweat glistened on both of their faces.

Eddie considered briefly. "Look, whatever happened here, somebody might want to come back and claim their booty. Eyes and ears, eyes and ears! And let's move fast. Pictures of everything pronto, including close-ups of the entry wounds. Then we take the two backpacks and get the hell out of here, and I mean fast!"

"What about the bodies?"

"It'd take us at least an hour, maybe two, to get them back to the vehicle, and my intention is to be out of this clearing in under five minutes and back to the truck in ten more, with enough time to smoke a Lucky on the way. Then we roll."

"And so?" asked Zach, poking a stiff thumb in the direction of the camp.

"Looks like the buzzards will get a meal after all."

Chapter Five

Engineers Playing Golf

Logan paced through his house restlessly. Since returning from his wine-tasting tour he had been unable to shake the feeling that something was, well what? Not wrong exactly, but ... He shook his head in frustration and looked at the clock in his bar area. Shit, seven forty-five. He still had at least an hour before leaving for the golf course to meet up with some of his work friends. Of course, they were now just "friends." But a long association with the three of them meant that they would give him an update on all the news and company politics that didn't involve direct disclosure of classified information. Still, with the history they had shared, he could certainly get an update on the progress of even very sensitive programs by seemingly innocuous comments like "So has Dave fucked up the 'Third Gen' program yet?" or "Did Jay ever get the algorithms to give him an ID probability anywhere near 70 percent?" It was more than enough to keep him satisfied and in touch, and he enjoyed feeling the total absence of pressure when, to a depressing story of frustrations and failure, he would shake his head sadly as he walked back to the cart to select his next club.

Still restless, he went outside onto his patio. It was a clear, dry, Tucson day with temps heading towards the nineties. He had hoped for an earlier tee time, but no luck. He wandered back into the house and checked the bar clock: 7:48. This just wasn't going to do. With a determined stride, Logan walked back into the family room, pulled back the bench, and sat down to the keyboard of a gorgeous Steinway baby grand, a gift from his wife on his retirement. Logan cracked his fingers and began by playing a series of chords.

A piano had been a part of Logan's life since childhood, and many an anxious, frustrating, confusing, exhausting day at work had given way to the joy and peace of even a half hour of jazz, inexpertly but passionately played. Sitting at this magnificent piece of musical architecture had been somewhat intimidating at first, but there was no doubt that this machine produced a beautiful, powerful, resonant sound that put a smile on his face. Logan ran through several changes and then smoothly transitioned into "Satin Dolls," a piece that he had been working on, arranged by Steve Bulla: a few mistakes, a few false starts, but still quite good, quite sufficient to take the nervous edge from his mind. Logan relaxed. A quick glance at the clock showed that it was now almost time to leave. As he rose, Logan spared a conscious thought at the marvel and magic that was music. He played a few last chords and headed towards the garage.

As he drove towards the Esperero Country Club, his radio tuned to a local talk station, his mind half registered a story of violence along the Arizona-Mexico border. Living in Tucson, these stories were sadly much too common. The most noteworthy part of this story seemed to revolve around rival cartel violence resulting in four dead, presumably coyotes, found a day or two after their deaths, badly decomposed, which Logan interpreted as "eaten." There had been some unusual aspects to these deaths, not the least of which was that no cartel had claimed responsibility. The story ended and an ad for an ambulance-chasing law firm began. Logan quickly switched the radio to a jazz station. Maybe one of the guys would know more about this.

Logan was the last to arrive, a point not missed by his companions.

"Jesus, Fletcher, all you do all week is sit on your ass. You'd think you could be on time to a Saturday golf game," began Bart Wiley with a grin. Bart was a short, sandy-haired engineer who had worked on several of Logan's programs. He had a dry sense of humor, very little patience for incompetence, and was generally recognized as the most brilliant signal processing expert currently working at Alpha. "I say Fletch buys the first round!" A growl of unanimous approval.

"You know, I'm actually on time, people. Besides, you just can't imagine the pressure and stress of retirement. Honestly, there are times when it takes me almost 'til noon to figure out what to do that day!

Besides, since I've been here playing every day this week, I figured I really didn't need to get here early to warm up this morning."

"Oh bite me!" broke in Kevin Flahrety. Kevin was a tall, bulky man with a smile never far from his face. A retired Air Force fighter pilot, he had flown primarily in F-4s and F-15s. Logan was always amazed that someone Kevin's size could be jacked into the cockpit of an F-15. Kevin may have been thinner then; he certainly hadn't been shorter, but somehow all of his six feet five inches had been squeezed in. His call sign, "Too Tall," had been an easy one to come up with. Kevin had worked at Alpha for nearly five years now in the Operations Analysis organization, a perfect fit for his combat fighter experience. His most common, witty repartee when challenged on his assessments—the same he had just tossed in Logan's direction—was "Oh bite me."

"Hey Logan, how's retired life treating you?" asked Gary Walkin. Gary was the closest to the public caricature of an engineer in this odd, tightly knit group. He was average height, with dark, rather messy hair, a bit too thin, with clothes that looked like his mother had helped to pick them out, usually a bit short at the wrists and ankles. He was extremely shy, usually serious, and fell into the category of the introverted engineer, the one that, in the worn joke, looked at his own shoes while talking to you, as contrasted to the extrovert engineer who looked at your shoes while talking to you. However, his capability as a computer systems engineer spoke eloquently enough on his behalf, and he had earned the respect of some extremely capable customers over his twenty-plus-year career. Also, if you were designing a computer network for your office, or a virtual ether-linked cyber network, this was the guy you wanted on your team.

"Retired life is not bad, good in fact." Gary had asked him in a serious tone, and so Logan decided to reply seriously, avoiding any of his cache of witty rejoinders, often used with other jealous individuals. "Yeah, actually I've been working on my golf game, playing a lot more jazz. Cathie says she almost likes it when I play now, plus I had a great time with Chuck and Joy up in the wine country. You remember Chuck, don't you?"

"Oh yeah, absolutely," replied Gary, using a grimy towel to wipe the grass and dirt from his pitching wedge. "That man had an interesting resumé. I believe he benefited from that last project we worked on, you know, the HAWK project."

Logan laughed. "HAWK! Man, that brings back some memories, all of them unpleasant. I remember that you guys kept referring to it as HAWK and I could never figure out what you were talking about. I finally cornered Bart one day and with that dry deadpan delivery of his he said it stood for Holiday And Weekend Killer! Man was that the truth. Still, I think Chuck appreciated it."

"Are you guys gonna play golf or just make out all day?" yelled Bart. "Let's move, old retired guy."

"Oh bite me!" Kevin added for emphasis.

Gary and Logan hopped into the golf cart and headed off in pursuit of the rest of their foursome. As they drove, Gary leaned over and said in a serious tone, "I actually came up with that, you know, HAWK. Kevin actually preferred POFS, which stands for Piece of …"

"Yeah, got it," interjected Logan.

***

By the fourth hole, it was apparent that Logan's alleged practice had not been of much value. After a slice off the tee box that sent his ball into some very nasty desert rough, Bart commented, "Nice shot, Fletch. You probably killed some wetback hiding in that scrub. In fact, if we put you and your driver on the border with an infinite supply of balls we could probably stop the influx of illegals cold!" Bart took a drag on his pipe and let out a long blue curl of smoke, a clear sign that he appreciated his own humor.

Logan pulled another ball from his golf bag and prepared to tee off again. "Speaking of wetbacks and border crossers, you guys keeping up on the killings in the San Bernardino Preserve? What was it, four guys shot execution style?"

Bart waited until Logan had hit his second tee shot, a hook this time that ended in a bunker to the left of the fairway, barely avoiding the thick desert just beyond the sand trap. "Damn," said Logan with real vexation, "I'd be better off throwing the frickin' ball!"

Bart took another pull on his pipe, and the fragrant smoke floated on the wind past Logan's nose. "Profound lack of concentration. You see, your mind is thinking 'illegal border crossers hiding in the scrub,' and the only thing that gets translated to your swing is 'scrub,' and so that's where you hit the ball."

"Don't tell me you're a psychologist as well as an aerospace engineer?"

"Minored in it at USC. It was the only way to meet women when your major is engineering. Ended up with my first wife that way," he concluded somewhat sourly, taking a much more somber pull and emitting a weak little trickle of smoke.

"Oh yeah," said Logan, glad to return the sarcasm, "you're working on, what was it again, number three?"

Bart teed his ball and gazed straight down the fairway. "Nope, I've sworn off marriage permanently." He took two practice swings, and then sent the ball rocketing out to land neatly in the center of the fairway at least two hundred fifty yards downrange. "Straight and long, straight and long, if you know what I mean. And speaking of that, I've taken up cougar hunting with the rest of this motley crew. That's about as far as my commitment will take me for now. Kind of odd," he added as Kevin teed his ball, "the three of us have all been divorced, some more than others, but you have remained steadfast to your one and only. Still, you ought to join us for a drink on Wednesday at Gulliver's, that's 'half-off martini night,' making that prime cougar territory for Wednesdays. It's probably not as much fun as a spectator sport, but what the hell, you might still get a laugh at Kevin using his 1970s pick-up lines."

"Oh, bite me!" The swish and strike of the ball, a solid connection. "I believe I'll claim long ball on this hole. Pay up gents!"

A few hours later, the four were enjoying the pleasures of the nineteenth hole, cold beers and quesadillas, when Logan reiterated his previous question. "So what about those guys on the border? More cartel rivalry I suppose."

"Bit of an odd story actually, if you mean the killings in San Bernardino," said Kevin, downing the remainder of his beer and making a circular motion in the air to the waiter, indicating the need for another round. "What got reported, and it wasn't much, didn't quite fit the usual cartel MO. One of the first reports even said that drugs were left at the site of the killings. Haven't heard 'boo' about that since then. It's all a little odd."

"Anyway, it's yesterday's news," put in Gary. "Today's news is about a half a dozen Mexican cops dead in Ciudad Juarez. Actually, it's more like five point five cops, since none of them had a head."

"Gee thanks for the graphic, Gary," grumbled Bart. "Can we get another quesadilla here," he directed at the passing waiter. "Just cheese, no meat," he added, with a gloomy look at Gary.

"So on a cheerier note," Logan began, "what kind of cool stuff do you guys have in the pipe?"

"Well," began Kevin, "lots of the usual beeps and squeaks. Say Gary, aren't you working on some stuff for the new drone project?"

Gary nodded and took a bite of his quesadilla and appeared to be somewhat hesitant to reply, but finally commented, "It's a network, of course. The trick is to keep it flexible, able to add or delete new systems incorporating evolving protocols, including semi-autonomous weapons, but be virtually impossible to crack. It's a little tricky, but the processing horsepower is finally coming along in a reasonable size, weight, and cost to do all the algorithmic work."

"How much processing horsepower," asked Logan.

"Well, more than you have in that prehistoric machine you've got at home," said Bart. "What's your operating system again? DOS?" Bart chuckled and automatically moved to light his pipe, then abruptly halted, with a frown.

"You'd think he'd remember after, oh, twenty years," said Gary. "No smoking indoors. By the way," he added, "it's like multiple teraflops."

"A big multiple?" asked Logan, somewhat surprised.

Gary shrugged in a noncommittal way and continued working on the quesadilla.

"Problem is," Kevin ventured, "most of the systems out there depend on GPS for either midcourse or terminal guidance or both. Someday, someone with a big satellite swatter is going to just smack the network out of the sky, and we'll be left with a bunch of very expensive paperweights."

"Sour grapes," said Bart. "Kevin is just pissed that not everything that flies these days comes with a guy in a bag and a white scarf. It's about the video games now, old man. My kid could fly an F-15 drone from his home computer and kick your ass."

"Oh bite me."

"Speaking of GPS, though, have you guys heard any news on those crab boats that wrecked?" asked Logan. "They were thinking GPS failures were a possibility."

"Jesus Christ, Fletcher," replied Bart. "Is that all you do all day, watch the news?"

"Damn right," said Logan, smiling, and taking his turn in making the circular motion with his hand to the nearby waiter. "Let's see, my cable favorites are CNN, MSNBC, and Fox News."

"Yeah, and mine are the Playboy Channel, ESPN, and the NFL network."

"I think you need to bite me," put in Kevin.

"Right, but c'mon, any internal poop on that story?"

"I ran into Hal the other day," began Gary, "you know, Hal Kaminski in security, former CIA. He still talks to some of his old buds, and they gave him the old brick wall response, which makes him think that something is still unresolved and a little weird there. Wouldn't say if anyone in the agency was investigating or just monitoring. Sounds kind of like BS to me."

"So are we splitting the tab, or … ?" asked the waiter who had strolled up and was now looking around the table hopefully.

"Just give it to the old retired guy," said Bart, abstractly rubbing the bowl of his empty, unlit pipe. "The one with the pension plan that's still worth a shit."

***

Chuck sat in his dingy Oakland office abstractly rubbing the bristles on his face. The day was growing old, and the smoggy sunlight filtered in through the rather grimy windows facing west towards the commercial docks nearby and the bay entrance further off. During certain times of year, the sun seemed to be heading out towards the western sea, directly through the bay entrance past the Golden Gate Bridge. Today was one of those days, and Chuck stared at the ghostly remains of the orange ball painting a soft-focused sky that shaded from dazzling orange to gold to pale green and then through a spectrum of blues often hidden by an impenetrable marine layer that would settle over the bay like a sodden grey blanket. Today was unusual, and despite the old and rundown interior of the building and the less-than-charming view of nearby offices and commercial buildings, it was as lovely as could be hoped for from where Chuck sat looking out his fourth floor window.

But the view was wasted. Chuck rubbed his hand over the bristles once again, vaguely registering the scratchy, sandpapery sound, but his mind ninety-five percent occupied with several mysteries. He had been trying for the better part of the day to gain ground on at least one of them, but as the clock pushed towards six, he felt as though he might as well have stayed home, or played a round of golf. The affair of the lost and misdirected crab boats was growing old. Everything that could hope to be recovered from the sinkings, a painfully slim collection, had been recovered, examined, catalogued, and sent to storage. Chuck was convinced that there was no additional informational juice that could be extracted there. This included the last transmissions from the two boats before they vanished. Interviews with three other captains that had experienced GPS failures but through superior seamanship, better initial circumstances, or pure dumb luck had lived to tell the tale had, in fact, told their tale. Chuck had interviewed Captain Michelson of the *Emma B* personally, and his account, liberally laced with strong invective towards the GPS manufacturer, had provided what seemed like a few glimmers, the most significant being that Michelson's cousin Jerry had downloaded a software update less than a month before the incident. One of the other surviving boats had done so as well, but the third had not. Chuck's intern, an eager, young, recent SFU graduate, was attempting to track down the GPS unit manufacturer and software version being used for the two lost vessels, so far with limited success. Still, it seemed, based on the data from the survivors, this lead had fizzled. Unknown to Chuck, it would be months before he would be able to finally get the owner of the third boat to admit that he had acquired and loaded an illegal copy of the same software version used by the other boats, and had simply lied,

stating that his boat still used the previous revision, the last one he had actually purchased.

"Chuck. Hey, Chuck. A couple of us are going down to Murphy's for a quick one. Want to join us?" This was Cesar Nunez, a long-time resident of this office, somewhat of a plodder when it came to drawing a conclusion, but sure and steady, exactly the kind of agent Chuck would not want pursuing him if he were a bad guy.

"Yeah, hey Cesar, that sounds, yeah that sounds great. Are you boys leaving now?"

"Hey, check the chronometer, my workaholic friend. After 6:00. C'mon man, that shit will still be there to confuse you in the a.m."

"OK, Cesar. Tell you what, I'll just tidy up a couple loose ends and meet you guys there, OK?"

"OK, buddy. But if I'm not home by eight, the spousal unit will have my nuts, so no bullshit, shut it down and come on."

"You got it. Out in a flash," he added abstractly, his glance drawn back to a stack of reports on his other mystery, and waving his hand at Cesar's departing back.

His second mystery involved a border shooting he had been asked to investigate. Why, he wasn't sure to begin with, but this thing had gotten weirder and weirder. He had spoken to the two border patrol agents who had reported it, what were their names again? Oh, yeah, Kreski and Munoz. He had read their reports and begun to understand why the agency had taken an interest. The news stories about cartel hits were bullshit, of course, and he had quickly decided that he needed to talk to both men. They had both more than exceeded Chuck's expectations as observers and communicators. These were men who knew their business and were pros. Both had known almost immediately that something was out of the ordinary there, long before the discovery of 20 kilos of heroin and 100 kilos of pot left at the scene of the killing. Their descriptions of the scene, the bodies, and the evidence were so nearly identical, that Chuck was as nearly 100 percent convinced of its accuracy as if he had been there himself. Even the photos, taken under serious threat of the return of cartel personnel, were clear, logical, and with no shot wasted. And in a backward way, Chuck hated them for it.

"So what do you think now?" his branch chief had asked after Chuck had been investigating the killings for a week. "Still think I put you on a bullshit, run-of-the-mill, border-war killing?"

And despite the coherent descriptions, the accurate statements, and the outstanding photos, Chuck was forced to grumpily admit he couldn't make shit out of it. It simply made no sense at all, every bit of verbal or visual evidence seeming to contradict the others and destroy any theory he could conceive. His branch chief, an older, former field agent, and now a long time office monkey, had smiled in that way that made Chuck wish he could bitch slap him into the next county. "Keep at it, Einstein," he'd said.

Chuck had kept at it for over two more weeks. He had had several follow-on conversations with Kreski and Munoz that, while enjoyable as one professional to another, had not yet shed any light in the gloom.

There were, in fact, three primary things that Chuck couldn't fathom from this hit. The first and most obvious was leaving behind a quarter-million in drugs after successfully killing off the previous owners. Chuck's intern, Randy O'Neil, had coined the phrase "Like clubbing baby seals" to describe this evidence, which was glaringly and painfully obvious. The second less obvious fact was that there had apparently been many men at this campsite during or after the killings. Kreski's photos had captured the apparent tracks and movements of, well, Kreski had estimated a dozen, Munoz ten to twelve. Having this small army arrive after the killings was inexplicable considering the booty left behind. But then, why were these guys here to begin with and why leave the drugs in any case? More questions, more contradictions. The third, and to Chuck, most puzzling aspect of all, and definitely too subtle to be described by Randy as "clubbing baby seals" was the precision of the killing. Munoz, that incredibly able BP agent, had actually snatched up the only casings he could find at the site: four, located within a two foot radius near the fire. Just four. Forty-five ACP, confirming the caliber of the rounds that went through all four coyotes. But c'mon! Just four. No sign of fire, at least no casings recovered, near any of the victims near the backpacks or the one at the extreme end of the camp. It had taken Chuck over a week to consider the possibility that there had been only one shooter, the man near the campfire, and that with four shots, he had made four perfect head kills. Chuck was more than a reasonable shot, but if the distances that Kreski and Munoz reported were accurate, and Chuck was convinced they were, he himself could not have made these shots, not in the time before someone could have drawn, fired, and maybe ruined his day. So if this were a single shooter, he was damn good: special ops good. But that left one tiny little mystery, perhaps the most provokingly puzzling of all. How the hell did this killing robot happen to be standing in the middle of the camp with the men he intended to kill?

"Chief, aren't you leaving?" It was the voice of Randy.

"Hey, you stud worker you, what're you still doing here, it's after six?"

"Uh, actually boss, it's 7:25."

"What? Aw fuck! And I needed that drink, too!"

"Hey, I'll buy if Cesar and the gang have left. C'mon, let's roll. By the way," Randy added as they locked the office and set the alarm, "I'm nearly done with that white paper you asked me to write on the novels of one Cathie Clarke Fletcher. Interesting stuff. Not my style for light reading, of course. I prefer Dickens or Twain."

"Light reading? Dickens? You are one warped mother. But thanks, maybe that'll shed a little sunshine on the crab boats."

***

By the time Chuck and Randy arrived, Cesar was at the register settling his tab.

"You blew it, Johnson. I bought tonight! See you people tomorrow. Hey Randy," he shot back as he walked towards the door, "isn't it past your bedtime? What's your mommy gonna say?"

"What's that? Sorry, I seem to have something in my eye!" Randy shot back, rubbing his eye with the outstretched middle finger of his right hand in an exaggerated manner.

"That's right, I'm number one!" Cesar responded laughing. "See you guys manãna."

"What'll you have?" asked the bartender, as Randy and Chuck seated themselves at the end of the long wooden bar near to a large bay window looking out on a gloomy night.

"Jeez, what happened out there? That fog came in on a freight train," Chuck said absently, then turning to the bartender, "Umm, yeah, how about a 'Town Drunk,' it's been a hard day."

Murphy's "Town Drunk" was a dark but surprisingly smooth microbrew with an 8.2 percent alcohol content. The "surprisingly smooth" usually meant that the first went down quickly and was followed by a second. After two, the drinker's judgment departed the premises, with the usual sad consequences. On one occasion, with contractors invited to join them, Cesar and Jerry, one of the most unusual characters Chuck had ever met, had each managed four "Drunks," and Jerry had insisted, for reasons that still seemed unclear, on giving Cesar a hug out in the parking lot. In truth, none of the group present that evening saw anything out of the ordinary in this behavior. Of course, they had all been hammered. "And how about a brat and fries too. This is gonna be dinner."

"You got it. And you, sir?" he nodded towards Randy.

"Hell, I work for this guy. If he's having a 'Drunk,' I'll have one too. And how about a Bay Burger, medium, and some fries. It'll be the best meal I've had this week."

"Could I see some ID please?" asked the bartender.

Chuck was still giggling as Randy returned his wallet to his pocket. "Oh to be young again," he chuckled, feeling the stubble on his chin, much of it a shade of dirty grey.

"Yeah, well, it's a failing we all have once in our lives," replied Randy. "I'm sure I'll outgrow it. I guess I never told you, but they actually wanted to see my ID on my last airline flight back to visit relatives, you know, to sit in the emergency exit seat?"

"No shit! What've you got to be to sit there, twelve?"

"Fifteen, boss, but I've aged a hell of a lot since then." After a pause, he added, "So, Joy not expecting you home for dinner tonight? I figured you'd need to drink and run, boss."

"Oh, she's out of town. Some girly sorority reunion, oddly enough with your Ms. Cathie Clarke Fletcher. They've know each other for many long years. In fact, she and her husband Logan joined us for an outstanding wine-tasting trip. That was my big vacation. But I get to meet up with all of them in LA for a fine night of drinks and debauchery."

"So you know her, I mean them. So boss, I don't get it. Why not just ask her for a thumbnail on her books?"

"Now let me explain something to you, young apprentice," Chuck said, turning to Randy and placing a fatherly hand on his shoulder, "because what you just said has caused a great disturbance in the force on multiple levels. Firstly, this is a company business matter. Now, do we mix business and pleasure?" Randy shook his head in the negative. "Correct," Chuck continued, "we do not. And in all seriousness, what I want, what I need, is the view from outside looking in, right?" An affirmative gesture. "Secondly, and most seriously important, I have the complete works of Cathie Clarke Fletcher, and I just haven't read the sumbitches! There, what do you think of that? So, am I going to ask my wife's best friend and my best friend's wife for a Cliffs Notes summary of her Christmas present to me? WTF, Over!"

"Forgive me, master," said Randy with a grin. "I guess that's why you're the boss, boss."

"Yes, yes I am and …" A sudden buzzing at his hip brought Chuck up short. "Spoiled my damn punch line!" he said irritably, as he pulled the Blackberry from his hip.

"Now what the fuck!" he commented coarsely, after a quick glance at the Blackberry display. "The branch chief," said Chuck sourly, as Randy gave him a querulous look, "has just dumped another load of shitty goodness onto my plate, that is," he added, with a raised eyebrow and a significant stare, "onto OUR plate. Now let me see, let me do the math on this, that's gonna make three insoluble problems that'll make me look even more like a washed-up agency operator trying to drive a desk, and make you look like the 'Dumber' part of 'Dumb and Dumber.' Yeah, that'll be cool."

"Uh, I can always transfer out, you know, go work for someone smart."

"That's funny, oh yeah, real funny. You did say you were buying tonight?" A rapid gesture brought the return of the bartender. "Two more 'Drunks' por favor. And what'll you be having, Randy?"

Halfway through the second "Drunk," Chuck's equanimity was on its way to being restored, and he began, after swallowing a large bite of his sandwich, "I guess I could tell you about this e-mail," pointing at the Blackberry. "It's pretty vague, and we'll need to chase some details in a hurry, 'cause this shit will hit the news rooms pretty quick, and there's liable to be a splash. Basically, there are two trucks and four dead guys parked near a lake northeast of here about 90 miles. That lake happens to be the water supply for a couple of resort towns up there, uh, what were the names? Oh yeah, Audubon and Sierra Crest, population about forty-five thousand total. And in the trucks are some dozen 55 gallon drums of what the e-mail describes as real bad shit. Helpful! And oh yeah, there's a dead zone around the vehicles for about a hundred yards. The first people that came near the spot—a couple of day hikers—got dizzy and puked their guts out before they managed to get far enough back. Law enforcement arrived and brilliantly approached the vehicles. There are now three officers in the hospital puking their guts out and one unconscious. So I figure, we'll just sort this one out by nine tomorrow, get a breakthrough on the crab boats by eleven-fifteen, and solve the mystery of the cartel hit by noon. That'll give us time for a quick bite of lunch and a leisurely round of eighteen, leaving me with enough time to write my resignation letter!"

"You know, boss, when I think of you, I think 'organized and practical,' yep, that's just what I think! My boss Chuck is organized and practical. I love this job!" After a brief pause, the grin on Randy's face melted away like a wax sculpture under a blowtorch. "Holy shit!" he began, sitting up straight and staring directly ahead, but with his entire focus turned internally as if fiercely concentrating on recalling a thought or lost memory. "Jesus tap-dancing Christ!" His blank stare vanished and he turned wide eyes to Chuck, who held his drink halfway between the bar and his mouth, waiting for Randy's next words.

"Boss, I've read about this before! If this isn't just some industrial fuck-up trying to unload toxic waste, I mean, if this is what it looks like—someone deliberately trying to poison a water supply—then I've read it before. It's from book two of C-squared Fletcher's novels, *A Tangled Web*."

Chuck's beer hung in limbo for a long moment before he drained the glass and set it on the bar with a thump. "What the fuck is going on?" he asked. After another long pause in which Chuck seemed to be making some internal calculations he turned to Randy, a hard look in his eyes. "Are you game?" Randy gave a tight nod and called for the check. A few minutes later Randy was brewing a pot of double black coffee in a semi-dark office, while Chuck was downloading additional details of the poisoning from the classified system and trying to shake the remaining cobwebs of "Town Drunk" out of his head.

Chapter Six

Lost Faith

Wan Chu sat on the patio of his Maui villa staring out towards Lanai and fumed. That he, Wan Chu, should be forced to fume at this point in his lifetime was perhaps more insulting, more irritating, than the actual breach of faith by Ivor; Ivor and his ignorant minions who had made fools of themselves by this ridiculous attempt at poisoning a water supply for two insignificant towns in California. Such complete ineptness, such unbelievable incompetence would have been enough to upset Wan Chu extremely. But it would not, in fact had not, caused him to fume. It was Ivor's failure to inform him in advance that his band of Keystone Kops had planned and would be carrying out an attack. Wan Chu had left no ambiguity regarding the requirement to inform him or his daughter in advance if Ivor hoped to build a cooperative partnership with Wan Chu. And then the message on Luana's Facebook page had come, encrypted in such a way as to communicate Ivor's desire to present himself in person to explain, to apologize, to be forgiven. Wan Chu fumed, and continued to resent that he should need to fume.

When Ivor arrived, he was shown out onto the patio, the beautiful scene of green hills sloping away to a spectacular, sparkling ocean, and the distant island charm of Lanai entirely spoiled by the expression on Wan Chu's face.

"My dear, dear friend," Ivor began, but Wan Chu waved him to silence as he would have shooed an annoying fly.

"There has been a serious breach of faith, perhaps a fatal one, and I do not speak figuratively. I will now ask questions and you will answer. Think carefully before responding. No," he added in a sharp commanding voice as Ivor had made his way towards a rattan patio chair, "do not sit. We will not be so very long."

Ivor straightened and tried to calm his internal anxiety. He had never seen Wan Chu this furious, nor had he ever seen such an overt show of force; he had passed at least five well-dressed Asian-looking men with large bodies and grim expressions on the way through the outer courtyard and into the villa. At the end of the patio where he and Wan Chu now stood, staring placidly out towards the ocean, was a huge Hawaiian man who gave every impression of simply not being there with his stoic silence and rigid, mahogany chiseled face.

Wan Chu began quickly. "You have broken your commitment to inform me in advance of your independent operations. Why?"

Ivor's first tentative attempt at a response, the words already forming on his lips along with an ingratiating smile, would have immediately implicated his lieutenant, the man in charge of the operation. The same man had also been given the assignment of informing Wan Chu through his daughter's Facebook page, utilizing a fictional "friend" name and an innocuous message regarding a vacation in the country. His lieutenant had disregarded this direct order from Ivor, and had proceeded with the action. The dismal failure of the operation, Ivor suddenly realized, was not nearly of the same importance to Wan Chu as the failure to keep him informed. Ivor wisely bit off his words before they escaped his lips. His blossoming smile died on the vine.

"My friend," Ivor began, with deadpan seriousness, "it is I who have failed you. I alone am responsible. While it is true that I delegated the important task of informing you to a trusted subordinate, it was that decision and my failure to confirm his action that have caused you this distress. Please forgive me."

Ivor's answer, was in fact, the only one that would have kept him alive, as Wan Chu had already decided.

"Good," replied Wan Chu. "You are a man. I can deal with a man. How will we ensure that this error is not repeated?"

"I will personally see to the communication with your daughter. The message will be sent by me, and I will wait for a confirmation from Luana before proceeding."

"Very good. And this subordinate who has disobeyed you, you have disciplined him?"

"He was among those who died in the trucks. I understand their deaths were quite gruesome."

"And the cause of this pathetic failure? I speak now of the mechanical cause which brought about these deaths rather than the incompetence of leadership which was so apparent."

"My friend," Ivor began with embarrassment, "I am sorry to say that we were unable to make a direct assessment. By the time we were aware that something had failed, the police, as well as several other agencies, had cordoned off the area. By posing as a small local news agency, we were able to interview the two who first reported toxic odors before law enforcement completely clamped down on all information, and as I'm sure you know, the two hikers never came near enough to the vehicles to provide detailed information. Based upon what we know, it would appear that the drums were improperly sealed, and that the fumes, which are extremely toxic and fast-acting, overcame the men."

"In both vehicles? So not a simple foolish error, but a systemic lack of understanding of the methods for safely handling this material. More incompetence!"

Ivor flushed, but was forced to admit to himself that the words of Wan Chu were true.

"I believe that this material was a derivative of carbon tetrachloride," Wan Chu stated. "Six large drums per vehicle, if I am not mistaken."

Ivor failed to hide the look of surprise on his face. "A mixture of carbon tetrachloride, insecticide, and … other chemicals. Very potent. And, yes, there were a dozen drums in all, but how …" he began in amazement.

"Please, we all have our sources of information. Mine may even have access to some of these details, though sadly, not all. Men with expertise have informed me that a hermetic Teflon seal would be desirable to contain such materials for even a short period of time, and of course, the mechanical sealing requirements for transportation over bumpy fire access roads would far exceed those for standard storage of, say, crude oil. Only an incompetent fool would simply mix your devil's brew, pour it into used, unprepared drums, and then jostle it for eight miles or so, and expect to return with a happy tale of jihad and success. And yet," Wan Chu added with emphasis, "even if they had succeeded, they would have failed."

Ivor stared at Wan Chu in amazement, but said nothing, and Wan Chu continued with a satisfied smile on his face. "You are not familiar with Adams Lake, I take it? It was formed with the damming of the west fork of the White River. The valley which once was has become the lake that now is. It is surprisingly long and deep."

***

Chuck and Randy pulled off the head-covering of the hazmat suits they were wearing and stared at each other, Chuck grim, and Randy a delicate shade of green.

"You OK?" asked Chuck. "You look like you drank five 'Town Drunks' when your limit was three."

Randy spit some phlegm from his mouth and wiped it with the sleeve of his shirt. "Jesus Christ, Chuck, I never expected to see bodies like that in my life. It was like the flesh was rotting off the bones. And did you see their eyes? It was like someone poured acid into their sockets. And everything, and I mean everything, in that van except bare metal was fucked up. The vinyl was turned to putty, the cloth seats and the clothes on the guys discolored; falling apart. Shit, even the rubber bits and seals looked like hell. I knew carbon tet was bad, plus what did the lab guys say, large quantities of commercial insecticide, and some other shit they haven't identified yet, possibly a hallucinogen and anesthetic cocktail, but Holy Christ, it's unbelievable what that stuff did!"

"No wonder those poor cops got sick when they approached those trucks. And did you notice that there were dead birds scattered all around? I swear, even the nearby plants looked yellow to me. Damn."

"Well, I've seen enough, including the IDs they pulled from the four dead perps. You notice anything odd?"

"Young Grasshopper, you are learning!"

"Grasshopper? What's up with 'Grasshopper'?"

"Right, sorry, you'd be too young for that. Young Jedi apprentice, your observation skills and memory are well above normal. Yeah I noticed. The first thing I noticed was that three out of four of those fake IDs were pure shit, Mexican garbage. The fourth was a lot cleaner, looked newer and a lot better quality, a bit of local work. We may be able to chase that down."

"And?" asked Randy, with a smile of expectation.

"Yeah, and, and then I noticed the guy's name, Humberto Joaquin Ramirez. Nice name, really. In fact, sounds like right out of *Treasure of the Sierra Madre*."

"Badges? We ain't got no badges. We don't need no badges! I don't have to show you any stinkin' badges!" Randy mimicked.

"Hmmm, not bad, but I'd keep my day job if I were you. Yeah, the name struck me, and then I remembered looking through the box of treasure that those two BP guys, Kreski and Munoz, had collected before high-tailing it. Did I mention that those guys were solid gold?"

"Not more than a hundred times, boss."

"Yeah, well, they're damned good men. What was it Kreski said, 'I picked this up near where the larger group seemed to be congregated. Just a flash out of the corner of my eye. Maybe it'll be helpful, even though it's just a crappy old Mexican fake ID.' Solid gold. And the name on the crappy old Mexican fake ID?"

"Humberto Joaquin Ramirez!" answered Randy with a grin.

"Could be, just could be that our four rotting corpses over there witnessed a hell of a gunfight down there on the border. And I'm guessing that maybe those fellows weren't exactly day laborers, either. Be sure we check the photos on the bad guy database. Wouldn't surprise me if Humberto wasn't really Ahmed."

"Already on it, boss."

"Well, I think we've picked the ground clean here. Thank God these fuckers didn't dump this stuff in the lake!"

"You know, boss, that's the really odd part. It looks like they were approaching the lake from the end closest to the dam. The water supply for the towns is towards the other end, where the White River enters the lake."

"So? This shit'll mix, you know," said Chuck, feeling that Randy was now off in deep weeds.

"Yeah, yeah, I understand, boss, sorry, but what I mean is, since I figured that because of the physical separation, I could assume a uniform mix as a worst case basis for an effects analysis, you know. If they had dumped right at the intakes, the concentration would have been higher, and that would throw off the kind of simple calculation I wanted to try."

"They couldn't have gotten that close. The park ranger station is right there, along with a few businesses, some cabins, hell, even a critical care center for the local towns."

"Ok, so assuming a uniform mix, and assuming the primary component was carbon-tet, it just doesn't make sense!"

"Randy, I'm tired, I have the taste of that shit in my mouth, I need a bath real bad, and I have to pee. What the fuck are you trying to say?"

"What I'm saying is, regardless of how nasty that shit is, 660 gallons in a lake of roughly 20 billion gallons gives you a concentration of .03 parts per million. It might have tasted or smelled a little off, but it wouldn't have killed anybody! It wasn't enough; even though I wouldn't want my beagle drinking it out of the toilet."

"Are you serious? Are those numbers right?"

"I ran 'em four times, boss, and I checked with Benny at the downtown lab on the concentration needed to be lethal. Still, there were some assumptions."

Chuck stared in amazement and with a certain fatherly pride at his protégé. "Nice!" After a short pause, he turned back to Randy. "I'm still checkin' those numbers, man! Twenty billion gallons! Don't ever be doin' math in public with me," he added with a lopsided smile. "There were parts of Philly where I grew up where you'd get your ass kicked for public math!" Randy just grinned. "And why do you let your beagle drink out of the toilet? That's just disgusting!"

As the two walked back to their car, Randy turned to Chuck with a slightly guilty but amused look on his face. "I don't actually have a beagle, boss."

***

"Not a lethal concentration?" asked Ivor incredulously.

"Not nearly," answered Wan Chu with a humorless smile. "Incompetence! You did say that the architect of this comedy died in the trucks?"

"Yes," replied Ivor blankly.

"Excellent," said Wan Chu, coldly. "I believe you would agree that this incident is best put behind us?"

"Yes, of course, Wan Chu."

"Good. Very good. Because I now have need of the services we previously discussed. This must be a discreet mission, and my daughter Luana will be directing."

"Certainly, Wan Chu. Would a meeting be suitable? The man I mentioned, the soul of discretion, would handle the actual execution, and it would be best if Ms. Luana could speak directly with him."

"He had no part in this debacle with the poison?"

"None whatsoever, my friend. He had been looking after business ..." He paused. "... elsewhere. In fact," he added shamefacedly, "he was furious when he discovered what had occurred. We have discussed the situation, and he will be involved with the design of all tactical missions in future, with full authority over execution."

"Good. My daughter will contact you. Now our conversation is at an end." He motioned to the huge Hawaiian bodyguard. "Please see my guest out."

As Ivor left the villa, his fear and anxiety in anticipation of this meeting drained away like dirty bath water from a tub, to be replaced with first embarrassment, then resentment, and then finally anger at the patronizing way in which Wan Chu had treated him. He was angry that what he had hoped would be a partnership had devolved into a master/servant relationship. As he considered, he wondered whether this relationship could be salvaged, returned to something of the equal balance that he had hoped for, or whether it was doomed to deteriorate to the point where he, Ivor Vachenko, would need to find other allies, other more reasonable allies. It was always risky, however, and not just in the development of relationships with new friends, for Ivor knew that one didn't just walk away from an agreement with Wan Chu and expect there to be no consequences. He would have to bide his time, cultivate relationships very carefully, and present Wan Chu with a fait accompli:

a powerful new ally that even Wan Chu would hesitate to threaten. Who that might be and how the change might be brought about were still in the fetal stages within Ivor's mind. Perhaps through her. She was in an extraordinarily influential position.

In the meantime, however, Ivor felt he still held one powerful trump card in the person of Jason Stone. He felt that even the huge Hawaiian would hardly have been much of a challenge for Stone. Ivor considered this and smiled. He would explain the situation to Stone and then see what Ms. Luana had in mind. Ivor's ego grated at having to relinquish even tactical control of a large mission to a woman. There were certain definite advantages within his own country, but here it would be one more irritation to bear from the arrogant Wan Chu. He would be sure Stone was well briefed in advance.

Chapter Seven

A Class Reunion

Joy and Cathie sat sipping Cosmos at a beautifully decorated, linen-covered table in the Crystal Room of the LA Bonaventure. They had arrived early to their college sorority's reunion dinner and had been seated at a table near the podium, from where they anticipated several dull speeches from the sorority president of their year, as well as from other dignitaries. Chief among these was the university chancellor, a divorce′, who still fancied himself a ladies' man, and could not resist the opportunity to be in the same room with nearly sixty lovely, and potentially available, ladies. The Cosmos were designed to take the edge off the boredom of the speeches and to add sparkle to the conversations with former friends and classmates.

"You know, Jenny Griffith seems to have aged a bit," Joy said somewhat jealously, inclining her head in the direction of a tall blonde in a gleaming silver dress and heels, currently being accosted by the chancellor and two liveried male staff of the hotel, offering drinks.

"Oh yes," replied Cathie smiling. "She's definitely lost her edge. You can see it at a glance. Not at all like us!"

"Yes, well, what we may have lost in pure gorgeousness, we've made up for in refinement, charm, character, and excellent manners."

"Yes? You mean like never criticizing someone who could steal our dates at a party with one flash of those perfect teeth?" asked Cathie with a smile.

"Absolutely," Joy replied with aplomb. "That would be boorish. And I believe she is trolling for her third husband, by the way." Joy and

Cathie clicked glasses together, sipped their Cosmos, and scanned the room for another historical rival to savage.

In the course of making his rounds, the chancellor stopped by the table where Joy and Cathie were seated and engaged them in an amiable conversation about their old school days, wagging a finger at the reputation for trouble that these two had apparently acquired; a somewhat truthful account provided by the helpful Jenny Griffith. In fact, the chancellor was a tall, attractive, charming man who wore middle age extremely well. He was obviously in good physical condition (he had been a former college basketball all-star, and still had a lean, athletic look) and his tanned face, neatly trimmed brown hair, silver sideburns, and strong jaw made him look like a presidential candidate.

At his departure, with a promise to re-engage the two troublemakers later in the evening, Joy leaned towards her friend with a smirk. "I believe you were flirting with that man, Cathie Clarke Fisher! You shameless hussy!"

"Nonsense," she replied in mock seriousness. "After all, he's old enough to be, well, I guess he's old enough to be my husband!" And both laughed. "Besides, he kept leaning in your direction, and I'm sure he wasn't admiring that pendant you're wearing."

"Well that's just naughty! Your mind is just in the gutter. That my best friend would have such rude notions is just appalling!" They clinked glasses once again.

When Cathie looked up from her drink, she said, "Hey, isn't that Elaya? No, over there by the podium. Wow, pretty fancy western rig for the wife of a Saudi sheik!"

"Yeah, well, she wasn't always the wife of a sheik. I vaguely remember her as the quiet, kind of mousy, foreign-exchange student who seemed a little awkward, a little out of place with the rest of the girls, though truth be told, I never really got to know her that well."

"I did, and don't let looks deceive you. She could be quite, let's just say 'lively,' under the right circumstances. I mean, take a look." Joy did, and what she saw was a beautiful, dark-haired, olive-skinned woman in a rather low-cut silky brown dress that rippled to just below her knees as she moved about talking to other sorority members, easily managing the three-inch heels she was wearing like someone with considerable practice.

"Well," said Joy somewhat sourly, "another sister who's managed to hold up better than us. It hardly seems fair. But I'll bet she doesn't get to wear that outfit much in Riyadh."

"I believe she travels a lot. Europe, Asia, Australia. Would you mind holding down my seat? I'd like to go and chat with her for a minute."

"No, go ahead. The rest of our table should be here shortly, and I can always flag down the chancellor and throw myself at him."

"You're a dear. Back in a minute."

But in fact, many minutes passed, and though Joy talked enthusiastically with the other sisters who had arrived, she kept glancing to one side of the room near the tall doors that opened onto a patio with a spectacular view of Los Angeles. Cathie and Elaya were standing near a table of appetizers, heads close together, in what seemed at this distance to be a very animated and serious conversation. They had avoided any attempts by others to engage them, and were still standing alone, deep in dialogue, when the lights were dimmed and their sorority president stepped to the podium to make a few opening remarks before dinner was served.

"I was beginning to think you fell off the balcony," whispered Joy in a somewhat accusatory tone.

"Sorry, sorry. It's just that I haven't spoken to Elaya in person for so long. We were just catching up. Plus she always gives me a few bits of local color from her perspective on the world that I can morph into one of my stories."

Joy said nothing, but settled back in her chair and tried to look interested in the opening remarks. Her focus soon drifted, however, and as the monologue droned on she found herself thinking that Cathie and Elaya hadn't had the look of people who were "just catching up."

The opening remarks droned on, but at last came to a grateful close. Waiters began serving salads and refilling drinks. In the extreme mild and fuzzy mood brought on by their second (or was it third?) Cosmos, Joy and Cathie began reminiscing about the "good old days." "Oh Gawd," Cathie began, do you remember that night at the Hollywood

Bowl? I thought Chuck was going to die of boredom. 'Mozart Night' wasn't really his thing, I guess."

"Not so much. The Earth, Wind and Fire concert we saw later that year was much more his speed. Mine too, if you must know. Hell, dear, Mozart was a bit, well, dull."

"Oh, I don't think Logan thought so. For one thing, it took the edge off the Lakers beating Philly the night before, kind of hard to take for a man of the 'brotherly love' persuasion. He misses the days of the ever-eloquent Moses Malone and his famous playoff prediction. What was it, again? Oh yes: 'foh, foh, foh.' The man had such a command of the English language."

"Brotherly love maybe, sweetheart. But Logan was staring at you all that evening like a drowning man stares at a life jacket."

"And that would be the other thing. I believe Mozart was responsible for one of the most, let's just say 'fulfilling,' nights of my life. God bless the man!"

***

Logan stared around the empty room, reached for the phone, but then, looking at the clock, realized that Cathie and Joy would still be enjoying their sorority dinner. Frustrated and restless for reasons he couldn't fathom, Logan sat down at the piano and randomly played a few chords. Then he began to play with more concentration, a little something of his own devising, something of an undeniably jazzy persuasion, to be played against Mozart's Minuet in F Minor, a concept he'd borrowed from the Moody Blues, combining classical orchestral music with, not rock, but jazz, a musical style that he felt might blend even more effectively. Logan stopped for a moment, pressed play on his iPod, and Mozart's Piano Sonata no. 11 in A Major, K. 331 gently began. Logan joined in, soon lost in the beautiful harmony and delicate phrasing.

***

A cultural world away, Wan Chu was having a serious discussion with Luana.

"You understand, I am sure, my daughter? The attack has gone extremely well; through the Pentagon firewall and that of the major platform houses, Boeing, Lockheed, Northrop. Your admiring corporate leaders will have red faces and apologetic lies to tell their government counterparts, who will also be attempting to preserve their dignity with great fictions of their wisdom in preserving software backups in carefully isolated locations, locations which we have penetrated through long, long years of effort. And yet, one remains that prevents, as the Americans love to say, a 'clean sweep.' Unfortunately, the producer of many rather effective tactical weapons has managed to block our intrusion. We therefore need a more direct approach to force them to their so called 'hardened' backups."

"Of course, father. I have a very simple, yet, I believe, very effective method for forcing this move."

"Yes?" Wan Chu asked.

"A fire, caused by poor electrical installation and equally poor warning systems should suffice. Astonishingly, only two buildings need be targeted to wipe out the servers for all of the fielded tactical systems. They are adjacent and share the same 'defective' electrical installation by the Brumos Corporation. I do not envy the Chief Executive Officer of Brumos."

"Casualties?"

"Some, of course, and I will be relying upon Ivor, his trusted man, and his associates, whom I will meet tomorrow. The fire, a rather terrible blaze, will eradicate any traces."

"Good," said Wan Chu. "Daughter, may success shine upon you!"

***

"Where did you say Elaya was from?" Joy asked, as their sorority reunion dinner drew to a close. She sat, quite relaxed now, toying with her medjool date gelato and an elegant snifter of cognac. Her mood was now sufficiently benevolent to, if not enjoy, then at least pleasantly tolerate the after dinner speeches. The grinning chancellor now approached the podium.

"Tehran," answered Cathie. "Got her BA in Liberal Arts with us at USC, then graciously took daddy's money and headed to Oxford for her master's."

"Good evening, ladies," began the chancellor, "it is my distinct privilege and pleasure to be with you all tonight, both the naughty," turning a beaming countenance towards the table where Joy and Cathie sat, "and the nice," turning towards Jenny Griffith's table. "Your sorority has been an important and integral part of the USC campus life for many years …"

"And so?" Joy continued in a whisper.

"And so, she met Hasim bin Wazari, cousin to the Sauds. A family of high regard, if corruption, belligerence, political intrigue, oppression and rape don't bother you too much. Notwithstanding that, the money is good."

"Sounds like complete scumbags to me!" said Joy with surprising force.

"And I might just agree with you," Cathie responded.

"So I don't get it," responded Joy with a disapproving tone, "why would this woman, any woman accept that? And you're her friend?" she added with a surprisingly sour, incredulous expression.

"Easy there, sweetness. When I knew her, she was young, impressionable, kind of wild, but with a strong sense of self-esteem. Where the fuck that went, I couldn't tell you, but I've been told that money talks and bullshit walks. And I didn't say I admired her for her outstanding matrimonial decision, so just back the hell off, okay?"

Joy nodded silently. "Sorry. I guess I just don't understand why any woman with a head on her shoulders would jump in the sack or join a harem for any amount of cash. I didn't mean anything by it."

"Hmm," Cathie replied, somewhat mollified. "Well, it ain't just 'any amount of cash.' This guy is not only connected big time to the royal family, but he has oil shipping contracts that enabled him to buy a yacht with a swimming pool on board big enough for most other yachts to sail in. Serious money. Deadly serious. I stay in touch to get that local color I talked about. Frankly, I don't relate to her much anymore. And tonight, she just kept pumping me for plot lines for my newest stories.

Hell, not just plot lines but details. I mean, I guess turnabout is fair play and all that, but she was becoming obnoxious about it. Satisfied?"

"Said I was sorry. I'll say it once more if it'll make you feel better. Meantime, I believe the chancellor has been throwing you the 'love to get to know you better' look. Best pay a little attention, dear."

Cathie and Joy focused on the brief remainder of the chancellor's speech, and watched as, with a smile, he stepped down from the podium and headed in their direction.

But before he could make his way to their table, the chancellor was intercepted by the effervescent Jenny Griffith who simply took his arm and guided him away, flashing a brilliant smile back in the direction of Joy and Cathie as she passed.

Joy and Cathie both smiled a poison-filled smile back at her. "Bitch," Joy whispered through clenched, still-smiling teeth.

"Just as well. I'm getting too old to have strange men chasing me, and me a happily married woman, too."

"Just so you know, you're never too old and never that happy, and if you ever mention that to Chuck I will strangle you," Joy laughed.

"Funny thing is," Cathie said a moment later, resuming their previous topic, "I thought I could get Elaya to release her moray eel grip on me if I just loaded her up with details of my ill-fated love story, you know, the one where the F-14 RIO connects with my main character, Ellen, but she latched on to that like a leech! 'Oh how interesting!' she says. 'When I was a little girl in Tehran, the American pilots from the base were so handsome and so revered. What model F-14 was it? How far could that big missile, the Phoenix, really fly? Did they use them to attack ground targets or airplanes? Could they use it to attack, say, a building? How terrifying it must be to fly in combat! Surely they would never send one airplane up alone. How awful! Why did America stop using F-14s? They seemed like a wonderful airplane to me when I was a girl. And so fast! The Iranian military still had a few that worked, that they kept just in case.' On, and on, and on."

"Apparently she's a bit hyper in addition to being a rich, well-dressed …"

"Ladies," the chancellor said, "I haven't interrupted some scheming for another of your well-known bursts of indiscretion?"

"Chancellor, join us," Joy said, with a sly look towards Cathie.

"Actually, ladies, I was wondering if you'd like to come over and join my table. You seem a bit lonely over here."

"With pleasure," said Joy. "I believe we may just need to powder our noses first."

As Cathie and Joy walked towards the ladies' room, consciously aware of eyes upon them as they went, Cathie leaned towards her friend and said, "You know that ex F-14 RIO who's won the heart of the fair lady in my story?"

"You mentioned him," Joy responded with anticipation.

"Well, in my mind he looks just like the chancellor!" she said, and both continued on, laughing.

***

Elaya had made her final trip around the room and paid her respects to both the chapter president and the chancellor before Cathie and Joy returned. She had spoken to those she knew and had stayed at the reunion for a fashionably sufficient amount of time, behaving with a dignity fitting her current station in life. She had, perhaps, been overly aggressive with Cathie, but that had been necessary. If it puzzled her one-time friend, it would soon be forgotten.

It would have surprised Cathie tremendously to realize how little she really knew about Elaya, and not simply about her history since leaving USC, but in regard to her deeper nature. Within Elaya there were two primal forces that drove her behavior. Passion was one. Elaya felt things in the extreme. Her relationship with the man she loved was the most profound example of this. The fact that he was not her husband might have surprised anyone but herself and her lover, for she was discreet to the point of frustration, her discretion being the progeny of the other force, a cold, machinelike, disciplined determination to have what she desired. The coldness enabled her patience, and moderated her desire to act rashly. In Cathie's exposure to the young Elaya, she had seen only a glimpse of the passion, undisciplined at the time, that had led Elaya to some of her more rash and wild behavior. Age and maturity had dulled neither the passion nor the determination, but had encased Elaya's actions in a diamond-hard veneer of civilized behavior. To the public eye, she was neither passionate nor determined, but polite, not overly intelligent, and conforming. In London, she was gracious and deferential, in Paris, sparkling and cheerful, in Riyadh, humble and subservient. An individual whose life intersected hers at only formal occasions, as at her reunion, might describe her as a global chameleon, adapting her behavior perfectly to her current environment. But that assessment would be pathetically shallow. In fact, she was a passionate spider: patient, relentless, and deadly.

Only one man truly understood her nature. They had met at Oxford, at a time when Elaya's soul was inflamed by the overthrow of the Shah and the usurpation of the Iran she had known as a child, and she burned for the day when she could set things right. She had gone to secret, forbidden meetings to plot the days of the ayatollah's downfall and the return of modern ways to a country that was being torn from the world stage and driven back to the Stone Age by the tyrannical theocracy of bearded, old men. This man had been the leader of those meetings. Eight or ten years older than herself, but mature, weathered, and strong, his brilliant eyes sparkling in a face of carved granite, he had won her heart and soul with his zealous words and bold schemes, as well as his strong hands and eager body. And her passion was ignited by the dual flame of physical love and the politics of righteousness.

Years had passed. Radical plans and grand actions were tempered by reality, but maturity brought patience without ever dimming the fire of their common desires. By mutual agreement, he went into near exile; plotting and scheming, often against the western world that had turned its back on Iran, a world content—indeed, acting—to see that Iran remained weak and isolated. She re-emerged within London, to seek a relationship of convenience and power that could be used, at some point in the future, to fulfill their mutual dreams. Her marriage (that is, her nominal marriage to bin Wazari), was reluctantly accepted by both as a means to this end, and the passionate spider spun her web.

And now, Elaya was the wealthy, dignified beauty who was accepted anywhere in the world, her charming façade obscuring her true nature, her true goals, and her true passion. She and her love would one day succeed. They would be masters in a new Iran, a free Iran, a powerful force in the Middle East and the world.

Chapter Eight

Target Practice

The sun was beginning to clear the mists from the secluded foothills valley near the Rose Hill Cemetery, thirty miles outside Oakland. Randy yawned but kept walking, carrying a life-size human target into position at the outdoor range, shared by the Oakland PD, the local military, and the regional CIA and FBI offices. False fronts of buildings, old burned-out automobiles, and other structures littered most of the site. Randy and Chuck were off near the perimeter, away from all of the structures, in a clearing among a small cluster of California live oaks. Chuck had been looking over the ground since before dawn and was now directing Randy as to where he should place the four targets, looking at a series of notes that he held in his hands. The range was empty on this early Sunday morning, and when the final target was placed, Randy returned to where Chuck was standing, stifled another yawn and commented, "Don't get me wrong, boss, nothing I like better than the smell of gunpowder and the ringing din of small caliber firearms on a quiet Sunday a.m., but exactly why are we out here? Don't you have a flight to LA this afternoon to meet up with C-squared and your wife? If it was me, I think I'd be packing."

"I am packing," Chuck replied flatly, patting the H & K .45 semiautomatic at his hip. "And actually, I'd have preferred to do this at night. It would have been even more realistic. Yes?" he asked, a look of amusement now lighting up his eyes as Randy tried to process this last comment, quickly surveyed the site again, opened his mouth to speak, and then clamped it back shut. "Does the light begin to dawn?" Chuck asked.

"This setup has a certain familiarity to it. You and I here, one target close by, two next to each other, off a ways, and another at least sixty feet off standing solo. This wouldn't happen to be the scenario that your two bubba Border Patrol agents described from down San Bernardino way, would it?"

"Full marks, young apprentice, though a bit slow, and you did need the hint about a night exercise being preferred. We'll call it an A minus."

"So I get the setup, but you may have to dock me a few points, since I'm still wondering what we're trying to discover here."

"Well, I guess you might just say it's one of the sub-mysteries within this entire border shooting mystery that I just can't shake. Look," Chuck began, "We now know that one of the guys in the larger party was Salim al Rabat and not Humberto Joaquin Ramirez. We also know that none of Salim's buddies took gunfire. And we know that some very efficient mothers came down on the four coyotes. This would lead one to believe that these same mothers were shepherding Salim, et al, and could afford to dispose of the coyotes once they no longer needed them."

"There's still the possibility, boss, that these were two separate events. Kreski and Munoz had no way to confirm that both the larger group and the coyotes and their killers were really all there at the same time."

"True, no proof," replied Chuck as he dropped the magazine on the forty-five and checked his load. He snapped the mag back into place and deftly fingered the slide release. The first round pulled smoothly into the barrel as the slide snapped forward with a solid "klatch." "But in my mind," Chuck continued, "it might explain why none of the drugs were snatched by the killers."

Randy narrowed his eyes, but still had an uncertain look. "It's simple," Chuck continued, "If the group of guys was the cargo, and the drugs were only camouflage, then it would make sense to a determined group, and one that needed to move fast, to take the cargo and leave the rest."

"Wow, kind of a stretch, boss. I mean, who couldn't use a little extra cash. Baby needs a new pair of shoes!"

"A stretch," said Chuck sourly. "Like trying to put a girdle on a whale. But you've got to admit, it's actually less of a stretch than postulating a couple of hard-ass killers who take out four coyotes and just leave the booty, for no damn reason."

"Yeah, yeah, I guess you're right. But I sure wish we had more of a solid motive. So," Randy continued, looking around the site, "I take it we're the assassination squad." He pulled his own .45, a Glock, checked the load and re-holstered it. "So where do you want me?"

"Yeah, well, back over there by the dumpster where I can't accidentally shoot you."

Randy looked back to the dumpster, another fifty feet away, clearly out of range for any logical scenario.

"And here, take this with you," Chuck added, handing Randy a stopwatch.

"OK, master, I'm completely lost. WTFO?"

"Well," began Chuck, "that's actually kind of good this time, 'cause what I have in mind is kind of crazy. The little sub-mystery I'm trying to solve is whether this could have been done by a single shooter, right from this spot."

"No fuckin' way!" Randy exclaimed.

"Language," Chuck chided. "That's 'no fuckin' way, sir!'"

"Right," Randy drawled back at his boss. "So, what exactly?"

"So, you get back over there by the dumpster, then when I fire the first shot, you hit the stopwatch. I'll try for four head shots, you time it, and we'll see what I actually hit. Then, it'll be your turn."

"Me? But boss ..."

"Don't give me no bullshit, Randy. I've seen your scores. You try next. Then I'll try again, and so on and so on. Look, what kind of reaction time do you figure for that guy at max range, I mean, from the first shot to when he could either draw or take cover?"

Randy considered. "Maybe five seconds?"

"You shittin' me? I could write my memoirs in five seconds."

"Four, no less than four. I mean, c'mon, boss. It's night, he's off on the perimeter doing what? Jerkin' off or takin' a whiz? Four, no less."

"Even with subsequent shots?"

"Four," replied Randy sullenly.

"Fine. I'm gonna go slow first time around. Make sure I get hits. Well, go on, get your lazy ass back to the dumpster."

"Right, boss," Randy responded crisply. "No fuckin' way," he muttered as he stalked off.

"I heard that! Now be ready."

CRACK. Randy started the watch. CRACK, a pause, CRACK, a much longer pause, CRACK.

"So?" asked Chuck.

"Nine seconds flat."

"Check the body count."

Randy made the rounds of the target dummies. "Sorry boss. You only killed three. One guy of the pair lived to snuff your ass."

"Fuck!" snarled Chuck. "OK, Mr. Sharp Shooter, take your place."

A repeat of the firing sequence followed. "Shit," said Chuck, after tallying the score. "Eleven point five seconds, but they're all dead. Nice shootin', Tex, but, sadly, you died too. My turn."

Chuck and Randy repeated the experiment until both their times and accuracies began to drop off.

"Thass it. We're done," said Chuck. "What was our best score?"

"Well, I killed them all, but my best time was 10.8. You got three in seven seconds, but missed number four, and right now my arms are so tired, I'd be better off throwing the gun at the bad guys. So, what do you figure, boss."

Chuck considered for a long time. "Look," he finally said, "If it was one guy, he did it at night with poor lighting, he had no prior knowledge of his target locations, and he had no practice. I am deeply inclined to say 'no fuckin' way.'"

"Except?" Randy prompted.

"Except, I still think it could be done by someone with exceptional, no, check that, with extraordinary skills." He paused while he let Randy absorb this. "And if it was one guy, one guy with skills like that, then we could be in deep fuckin' do-do."

Chapter Nine

She's a Lady

Luana arrived at a nondescript house in a nondescript upper-middle-class neighborhood in Thousand Oaks, California, at around three that afternoon. She had shared communication with Stone by his adopted name, "Shirley," on the designated friends of LGBT group on her company's Facebook page. No photos had been exchanged, but Shirley had described an "acquaintance" and loyal LGBT supporter to Luana (buried in long, dull, descriptions of trips to exciting locales such as Fresno and Milwaukee), with sufficient detail that when Luana saw a tall man apparently repairing a lighting fixture on the house's front porch, he actually seemed familiar. Stone had simply surfed Luana's company website from a computer in the local library, and there had been more than a few photos of the company's lovely, young president and CEO.

She had parked the modestly small BMW, appropriate to the point of invisibility in this neighborhood, and strolled up to the door. Stone stopped his pointless adjustments, casually held the fixture in place and fastened the decorative cap screws before turning to Luana.

"Ms. Chu, a pleasure," he said, holding out his hand, which Luana accepted and shook with a firm grip. "I'm Jason Stone. I advise Mr. Vachenko on special projects."

Luana mentally recorded that Stone had clearly avoided stating that he "worked" for Vachenko. Stubborn independence. She respected that.

"So not 'Shirley' after all?" she asked. She inspected the man from head to toe. Tall, lean, and hard had been expected, but it was the face—strong jawed with a smooth forehead, short-cropped, no-nonsense dark brown hair, but with a very expressive mouth that might have been almost feminine—that was remarkable. But above all, the grey-green eyes (unusual and very attractive in his well-tanned, rectangular face), contained a sparkle of both humor and intelligence that Luana hadn't expected.

"And so why 'Shirley,' may I ask?"

Stone offered a hint of a smile, a slight shrug and replied, "Shirley you jest? No, I don't, and stop calling me Shirley."

Luana enjoyed a good laugh. "One of the funniest movies of all time, and an excellent choice. At the risk of offending, I'd say it suits you."

"No offense taken."

For his own part, Jason Stone had made his own assessment of Ms. Luana Chu. There was a beauty about her that could be distracting if a weak-minded individual allowed it. He was not weak-minded. But, he could still distinctly enjoy it. Luana had been advised to dress modestly, and she had, according to her own lights, in a dark brown fitted business suit with pants rather than a skirt, and modest shoes with reasonable heels that tried to be inconspicuous, but probably cost several hundred dollars. She would need to change into something much less modest before her dinner tonight with the corporate executives who would fall over each other to entertain her while she sold her company's wares. Still, she was unmistakably female, and he hoped it wouldn't be a distraction to the small group of Vachenko flunkies within.

"Please, come in, Ms. Chu," Jason said, opening the door.

"Thank you, but perhaps you could call me Luana?" she said, as she brushed past him, leaving a tantalizing scent of orchids lingering in the air. Stone followed with a smile and a mental note to be very careful around this woman. He escorted Luana into the living room where a group of four men wearing Dockers and Eddie Bauer shirts and looking completely uncomfortable and false in them, were waiting. This was actually worse than Luana had expected, and the thought, "You can put lipstick on a pig …" flashed through her mind. These men looked as out of place as a two-headed ogre to her. But, she reminded herself, she had been trained to observe, and most Americans, especially Angelenos, wouldn't take a second look at a two-headed ogre.

As Stone introduced them, the men stared at Luana like a piece of raw meat in an insolent and lascivious way. Luana immediately adopted the look of haughty disdain acquired from her mother who had perfected it when forced to tolerate unwelcome haole visitors in her home. These men were beneath her, and she would treat them as mere servants of Ivor Vachenko.

Jason noticed the look on the men's faces, and interposed himself between them and Luana. "Listen up," he said in a voice of command. "After the complete fuck-up your compadres made with the poison, Mr. Vachenko's sponsor has insisted that the next operation be directed by Ms. Luana. Does she have your attention, your full attention?" he asked with a hard edge to his voice.

The four men randomly nodded, and Stone stepped back. "Please carry on, ma'am."

Luana acknowledged Stone's courtesy and was impressed that he hadn't been squeamish or apologetic about his use of language. It was a message not lost on the men in the room, whom Stone clearly dominated.

She began without hesitation, "We have an assignment of extreme importance that has been agreed upon by your employer. It will require *discretion*" (she emphasized the word), "and precise action. Please listen carefully as I provide an overall outline, and do not interrupt. There will be the time for questions when we discuss details." She paused and waited for an affirmative response. There was none. She continued, "The target will be two buildings at a guarded aerospace company in Tucson, Arizona. You will be provided with all maps and logistical information. It is imperative that this action be carried out and appear as an accidental fire. There will be no evidence of foul play whatsoever."

As Stone listened, his opinion of Luana rose rapidly. She was well prepared, not intimidated by the men in the room, and spoke clearly and succinctly. But above all, he was impressed by the plan itself, a creation of her own it was clear. The objectives were well defined, the details well thought out, problems anticipated, fallback positions and lines of retreat simple and easy to understand. It had the feel of success about it, the feeling that it could only fail if bumbled by one of the fools in the room. At that moment, one of the "bumbling fools" broke in gratingly, interrupting Luana as she once again stressed the need for complete secrecy and anonymity.

"Why should we do this and then not claim credit? This does not advance the cause of jihad. We will burn these buildings and then cry out in the name of Allah!"

Luana fixed the man with an icy stare. "I believe you might not have understood me. Perhaps I should have said no questions or foolish comments until I am finished."

"You ridicule us! We are not fools, and we are not dogs to be treated so!"

"Sir," said Luana, "be silent or leave now."

The man leaped from his seat and began to shout. "You cannot talk to me so! I am nephew to Ivor Vachenko, respected leader in Mazani Province, faithful servant of Allah. You are an insolent, disrespectful, shameless woman. It is you who will be silent, unfit to be in my harem, infidel and whore!" The other men in the group had stiffened, and through gestures and mumbled words showed their support for the man whose face was distorted in anger, white spittle dribbling from the corners of his mouth.

During his tirade, Luana had stood perfectly still and, it seemed, with complete composure. Only Stone had noticed her right hand ease gently into her tan leather Coach handbag. As it opened, slightly, he caught the dull look of angular metal. "Compact .45! Nice!" he thought.

But gunshots and bloodshed were not really how Stone wanted this meeting to end. *Well*, he thought with some amusement, *at least not with gunshots*. During the time Ivor's nephew had been ranting, Stone had moved imperceptibly within arm's-reach, and as the tension increased, the invective growing hotter, Ivor's nephew had drawn his hand back to slap Luana, and the gun was halfway out of her purse. In a movement that was a blur, Stone's fist had come up, backhanded, into the man's mouth with a dull thud, and before the blood even began to run from the man's shattered teeth, Stone had taken the cocked arm, twisted it behind his back, and snapped it near the wrist like a child would snap a dry branch. The man was now on his knees, grimacing in pain, bleeding profusely from his mouth, one oddly-twisted arm cradled in his other.

"I believe that the lady asked for silence. If you can manage to sit there and bleed quietly, you can stay, otherwise, get the fuck out of this room."

The man struggled to his feet and looked with intense hatred at Stone. "My uncle will hear of this, I swear it."

"Yes he will," Stone replied quietly, unperturbed. "From me. Now, you have just exactly 15 seconds to stay not dead if you keep standing there. Or you can withdraw now and live a while longer."

Though furious, the man was thoroughly terrified, and he stumbled from the room, wincing in pain.

"Now, I'm not going to ask nicely again," Stone said to the other three. "Keep silent, listen, and learn."

"Thank you," Luana directed to Stone as she eased the .45 back into her purse. She turned to the others and said, with some irritation. "We will begin again."

***

Luana lingered for a private word with Jason after the conclusion of the gathering. Ivor's toadies had hustled the still furious and bristling nephew into their Chevy Tahoe and had driven off to Stone's comment, "There go some unhappy campers. They were poor risks to begin with, and now they'll require the most careful observation. I know that your father has an arrangement with Ivor, but I wish he could have found more capable subordinates."

Though still very wary of this exceptional man, Luana had been impressed with his commitment, dedication, commanding presence, and obvious capability, and was tempted to trust him in as much as he had trusted her with this candid expression of concern. "At times," Luana began, phrasing her words with extreme caution, "I wish that it was unnecessary to involve Ivor and his band, present company excluded, of course. I appreciate the, hmm, gallant behavior that prevented me from having to kill that fool. It's always so messy when unexpected accidents of this sort occur. I doubt the man himself is quite as grateful, however."

Stone turned and his face caught the westing sun, turning his bronze features to gold. He smiled a thoughtful smile. "He doesn't need to love me, and I certainly don't love him, but after today, his behavior is simply too undisciplined to be tolerated. Ivor can find another watchdog for me, if he wants to."

Luana gave Stone a questioning look, which he shrugged off. "I've been more or less on probation with Ivor since I was recruited. It's illogical, given my dedication, but there you are. I suspect he will never fully trust me, and as for him, well I guess I'll judge him on his behavior and his decision making."

"I see that neither of us is overwhelmed with admiration for Mr. Vachenko, and after the last botched operation, where not the tiniest bit of blame has fallen to you, I believe even my father became somewhat out of sorts."

"I don't think I'd enjoy having your father be 'out of sorts' with me. But I will guarantee the success of this next mission, provided I can convince Ivor to let me use several of the least incompetent of his minions. Actually, the three remaining today should suffice if I provide a little on-site supervision. By the way, I very much admired your plan: neat, clean, efficient. It was yours, wasn't it, and not your father's?"

"Yes. He leaves many of these details to me. But you mean to say that you will actually be present on this mission?"

Stone ran a hand thoughtfully through his short hair. "Seems best. The risks are low, and the chances of success much higher if I'm there. You don't mind, do you?"

"Not at all, at least, not from the perspective of getting the job done. But it would be a shame, Mr. Stone, should anything happen to you. I have seldom been so impressed with someone at a first meeting, and it would be a shame to have our relationship end here."

Jason actually laughed a very amused laugh at this point.

"Do I entertain you, Mr. Stone?"

"Well, yes, actually. Mostly because you took the words out of my mouth. I've rarely been so impressed with someone at a first meeting, and I'm what you might call a very skeptical man. And secondly, that you'd think there is much risk in this mission. Of course, I'll get a good look at everything first and make a final risk assessment before we proceed. That shouldn't be too difficult. There are a lot of ways to get access, and I already have a badge. I'm Jerry Nelson, and I have a top secret clearance."

"So you won't be going in as 'Shirley'?"

"I'm afraid my skills at disguise don't quite extend that far. And by the way, if you're going to insist on calling me Mr. Stone, then I'll be obliged to return to Ms. Chu."

"Jason it is," she smiled.

"Also," Jason added, as he walked with Luana to her car, "I would very much like to continue this discussion over dinner some time. There is a truly exceptional seafood restaurant with an outstanding terrace overlooking Malibu. They have great food, excellent wine, and amazing sunsets. Would you be interested?"

Again, Luana admired this man's direct approach and confidence. She smiled a more sincere smile than she would normally employ with potential customers or business associates. "That would be delightful, Jason. We can make arrangements through our mutual friend, Shirley."

Jason laughed again. "I guess I'll never live that one down. I'll look forward to it!" he said, as he handed her into her car.

Chapter Ten

Seeing Blue Hawaii

Chuck was still somewhat flustered from his early morning target practice, a hurried trip home to shower and pack, and then a frustrating and nearly fatally late drive to the airport to catch the only Southwest flight that would still get him to dinner on time. His second margarita was beginning to take the edge off, and as Joy and Cathie compared notes from their late night sorority gathering, Chuck turned once again to Logan.

"Man, that Randy is one in a million. A really good kid with all the raw material to be a great agent."

"Yeah," laughed Logan, "He's probably brilliant, handsome, and modest, just like you!"

"Yeah, right," Chuck replied with a half-smile. "Actually, he's smarter than me, much more handsome, but don't tell Joy I said that, and one hell of a shot. He was fast and accurate. I tried to convince him that if it wasn't for my extreme age, I could have matched his skills, but the truth is, I never had those skills. He's damn good, and will probably get better." A shadow passed over Chuck's face, and he rubbed the stubble on his chin in a motion that always indicated extreme thoughtfulness or doubt.

"But?" Logan prompted.

"Yeah, it's the 'but' that's killing me. But the guy at the border, if it was just one guy, is way, way better than both of us."

"Look, you've been around the block. Have you ever actually known a guy with skills like that, or is this some fictional character brought to life by incipient senility?"

"I'm not that senile, you old retired fart. I've known two, maybe three guys in 25 years that might, and I emphasize might, be able to do that trick. Shit!"

"Hey, relax a little, buddy. C'mon, here we are at St. Mark's, acknowledged by the collective Fletchers and Johnsons as the finest dining experience to be had in the greater El Segundo area …"

A flash of silver like a barracuda turning beneath crystal-clear water caught Chuck's eye, and he interrupted with a, "Holy shit, did you see that? Check your three o'clock, buddy, pronto."

Logan turned slightly in his seat and gazed across the plaza and then gaped in amazement. "Miss Blue Hawaii," he said, stunned.

"Miss Blue … what the hell you talking about?"

Logan managed to regain some of his composure. Joy and Cathie had caught the thread of the discussion and had turned a practiced eye to the woman across the way, returning to their respective spouses with a look that said, "Grow up!"

"Yes, well, she was here the last time Cathie and I were here, you know, celebrating my retirement, only dressed in blue. I almost collided with her, more's the pity." Cathie struck his shoulder with her small purse for that comment. "And hence, the Miss Blue Hawaii." Three older men, somewhat tuna-shaped, followed the young barracuda to a table and fussed with trying to help her take her seat, a noncommittal smile adorning the lovely woman's face.

"Chuck, do I need to come over there and wipe the slobber off your face? 'Cause if I do, I'll be takin' some flesh with it."

"No, my lovely, darling, precious wife. You know my heart will always be true to you."

"It ain't exactly your heart I'm worried about, lover."

All four laughed and (the barracuda thankfully hidden from view) settled back to their drinks.

During dinner the conversation was general, trivial, and amorphous. The girls related events from their college reunion when they could get Chuck and Logan to pay attention. The men preferred discussing the merits of the latest Scotty Cameron putter and the finer aspects of their respective golf games, whenever they could politely redirect the topic.

“I was saying, Logan,” Cathie repeated with emphasis, as his concentration had once again drifted, “that I wondered whether you were ever surprised by how your college buddies turned out when you got together after ten or twenty years.”

Logan shrugged noncommittally and Cathie continued. “Well, I don’t really think I missed all that much by skipping our tenth. From what I could tell, the people that were jerks twenty years ago were still jerks, the ones that seemed to have something on the ball did well, and the ones that were sent off to school to get them out of mummy and daddy’s house were neither here nor there, but they still had mummy and daddy’s money to fall back on.”

“Maybe one exception, wouldn’t you say?” Joy asked. “I mean, your friend Elaya. How do you figure her, marrying that Saudi princeling or whatever?”

“Well, like I told you, even though she seemed kind of shy and withdrawn, she could be a little wild thing in the right environment. How that fits in with marrying a Saudi—I think he was only a sheik, second class, dear—I really couldn’t say.”

You know, Charles,” began Joy, with an emphasis designed to secure his undivided attention, “this Elaya person had Cathie by the ear right up until dinner started.”

“Really?” said Chuck, directing his gaze towards Cathie and trying to appear more interested than he really was. “Telling you about her sugar daddy’s latest oil field or his second yacht?”

Cathie smiled a tolerant smile. “He’s on his third, actually … yacht, that is. She didn’t mention whether or not there were other wives. But like I told Joy, it was a bit annoying. I was trying to get a little Middle Eastern vibe, you know, something for a character I’ve been developing, and instead, she was grilling me on the plot for my latest book, and I mean grilling me. It got to be quite annoying, but she was a veritable limpet, and it wasn’t until they dimmed the lights that I was able to get away.”

As she had spoken, Chuck had straightened slightly and was trying his best to not appear to be as focused as he had suddenly become. A lightning, covert glance over to Logan had communicated this interest to Logan along with a silent plea to not encourage this discussion.

"So babe, isn't that weird how she kept bugging Cathie?" Joy asked in the direction of Chuck. Chuck hadn't responded when a cataleptic movement by Logan knocked his half-full water glass over, and a flurry of napkins, mopping, recrimination, and abuse covered the dangling query. A near state of calm had been restored when the dinner fortuitously arrived.

***

Back at the Hilton, Chuck was pouring himself and his wife a nightcap of Courvoisier from the well-stocked mini-bar when he asked, with as much affected nonchalance as his professional career had developed, "Say, babe, what did you say that Elaya person's hubby's name was?"

***

Cathie's opening salvo was somewhat less subtle. "Logan, you are a clumsy bastard!"

Though startled by his wife's angry tone and apparent serious remark, he just shrugged resignedly. "Look, I just moved wrong and knocked the damn glass over. It wasn't like it was full of sulfuric acid. Hell, nobody even got wet."

"Oh, sweetie, I couldn't give a short damn about the water glass, and don't try to cover up clumsy with even clumsier. What the hell is it that you keep dodging and refusing to talk about. You and Chuck both!"

At first, Logan was genuinely confused. He had honestly felt that his wife had been referring to the episode with the water glass. And of course she was. But a very little thought brought him to the realization that she had been referring to that as "clumsy" only in how he had used it to bury Joy's question about Elaya and squelch any further discussion on the matter. Logan sighed. He knew she was smart when he married her. Sharp as a damn tack, one that he had just sat on.

"So I suppose my creative lying skills have no chance here, huh?"

"None. You may have to resort to the truth. And I've got a pretty good notion, so I'd suggest you just stick to the straight and narrow. And by the way, this little incident is jingling a tiny bell that goes all the way back to a Jacuzzi discussion in Paso Robles."

Shit, thought Logan, *smart AND a memory like a hard drive*. "Well, look," he began, licking his dry lips.

"Oh, this is going to be good," said Cathie sitting down on the corner of the bed and crossing her legs, with an expression like a professor listening to a student's lame excuse for a grossly late delivery of a report. "Please, carry on."

"Well," he began again, "Chuck had recommended, strongly, that I not bring this up with you."

"Whoa right there, buckaroo," Cathie interrupted, holding up her left hand and pointing with her right to a gold ring on her finger. "Unless I'm badly confused, I believe you and I are the married couple, and I'm not sure, but I do have this odd notion that there is a trust basis in that relationship. Yes, I'm pretty sure. Now I've lived with you and your super-double-secret career long enough to realize that there are things you can't and won't tell. I got that. But I'm also pretty sure you signed away all those clearances when you left the whole military-industrial scene. But even if you hadn't, you can't tell me that this is something you can blab about with Chuck in some restaurant but can't share with me."

Logan had waited patiently for Cathie to vent. He realized he wasn't exactly standing on the high moral ground, but he continued with a firmness and seriousness. "Chuck recommended it and I completely agreed. Look, it seemed pointless to bother you with something that seemed, well, so unlikely."

Logan paused, but Cathie said nothing and seemed content for him to continue.

"So, let's have this discussion. I'll tell you everything that I know. Just please promise me you'll sit down with me and Chuck and clear the air. It isn't exactly super-double-secret: no paperwork, no program name, no classification guide, but Chuck is playing this one very, very close to the vest. So we have a three-way discussion, OK?"

"A ménage à trois. How delightful," Cathie replied, sweeping the harsh edge of tension from the room.

And Logan related his "white Zinny" discussion with Chuck, and his concern that some very bad people were using ideas from Cathie's books; at least two potential cases now. "The lake poisoning was an obvious terror attack, but the whole GPS thing is much more iffy and a hell of a lot more obscure. Obviously, when you mentioned your old college buddy pumping you hard for plot lines, and she married to some wealthy mystery man with unknown allegiances, well, I could see Chuck was about to have an aneurism, so I knocked over that damn glass."

"Oh, darlin'," Cathie said gently, putting a cool hand to his face. "It was actually not a bad effort. About a B+, and I'm sure Joy didn't catch on, it's just that it's hard to pull off between two old married folks like us. As for the secrecy, I get it, and I'm happy to have that little chat with Chuck. And I think it's sweet of you to assume he was just trying to spare me anxiety. But you know Chuck: professional to the core. Come on now, he has to retain at least a tiny, healthy suspicion of me in all this. So let's just have that chat."

***

Four hundred miles to the east, an equally uncomfortable conversation was taking place in a small suburban house just west of the Tucson mountains.

"And so you have received your instructions and made your preparations for the Alpha operation?" Ivor had deliberately thrown the comment about receiving instructions into Jason's teeth, as a reminder that he, as well, was merely a tool in this exercise. He was disappointed to see no visible reaction.

"The meeting with Ms. Chu went very well. It's a well thought-out plan with minimal risks. I've added a few minor adjustments, approved by her, and assuming a competent level of support, I believe I can pull it off." The fling about competent support was also a calculated jab, and Stone had considerably more satisfaction in drawing out a reaction from Vachenko at this point.

"I am reluctant to bring this up, Jason, but my nephew, Hamid, has informed me that this woman, Ms. Chu, was rude and offensive, and that you took her side in front of the men, resulting in a scuffle."

"And I'm sorry to say, Ivor, that your nephew has lied to you on several scores. By the way, that was his pickup truck I saw around the corner, right? Well hidden! I'm sure the little rat is lurking somewhere in this house right now. He's welcome to join us, for my part." Ivor had stiffened with thinly controlled anger, but said nothing. "As I said," Stone continued, "lying on multiple scores. It was he that was rude to the young woman, treating her as I'm sure he treats his own wife, or is it wives, like a piece of property with no rights, like an ignorant inferior, like a foolish, subservient woman. Since we were gathered to hear her plan, and since he was not contributing to the discussion in any meaningful way, I felt he should remain silent. He disagreed. Also, there was no scuffle of any kind. I simply dropped him like a sack of rotten potatoes, and he slunk off to lick his wounds. The meeting then proceeded in a much more productive manner."

"And did you truly find it necessary to break his arm?" Vachenko inquired with barely controlled fury.

"Well, it seemed better than to have him pull that ridiculous pig sticker he keeps in his sock or that cheap-ass gang-banger piece tucked in his belt behind his back. And incidentally, the young lady was about to put him down permanently. She seems to be quite capable. So all in all, I believe he should be thanking me. A card would be nice."

Vachenko steamed furiously in silence, and a long pause ensued, Stone sitting quite relaxed while Ivor slowly reeled in his rampant emotions.

Finally, Ivor swallowed painfully and, putting the best face he could upon it, asked gruffly, "The plan. You mentioned support. The three at the meeting, will they be sufficient?"

Behaving as though the previous discussion had never occurred or had receded to the distant past, Stone answered with professional calm, "They seemed to grasp the plan completely, understand their roles and responsibilities and be capable of carrying them out. Those three should be more than sufficient."

"When?" Ivor asked curtly.

"Two weeks and two days. A Friday evening, late. That'll minimize the likelihood of random employees about and should minimize the possibility of casualties."

Ivor scowled and roughly rubbed his nose. "I don't give a damn about casualties. If I had my way ..." He stopped abruptly. This constant reminder that he was not in charge—that he was merely supplying manpower—was becoming an unbearable irritation. His focus drifted as his mind returned to a topic of growing importance: finding a new sponsor for his activities. Though his ego had been badly bruised, he still recognized his own abilities as well as the value of his organization, already well-manned and in place on American soil. There was one name that kept surfacing in his mind, a potential ally with a decidedly more similar philosophy than Wan Chu, though equally as dangerous when disappointed. His mind was jarred back to the present as he thought he heard Jason say, "Besides, I need a few more days to fully lay things out, prepare and test the accelerants, and catch a family of raccoons."

***

Stone had left shortly after with little more than a dissatisfied grunt from Ivor. Within moments of his departure, Vachenko's nephew, his arm in a short cast, and his face with a yellow and black bruising around his lips, entered the room.

"Pig!" he snarled.

"Sit, Hamid," said Ivor, shortly. "You heard all, I presume?"

"Yes. Let me kill him for the insult to our house. I myself will carry out this mission! And uncle, there will be many casualties!"

"Listen, nephew, and be patient." Hamid waved his good arm impatiently through the air in a gesture of negation.

"Come," Ivor continued, his hand on his nephew's shoulder. "We must be practical. You do not have access to the Alpha facility for one, nor are you yet recovered enough to participate. Listen, please!" Ivor interjected as his nephew made as though to protest. "Also, we have made an arrangement with Wan Chu. Stop, I beg!" Hamid finally seemed cowed, at least for the moment, and Ivor continued. "It is not necessary for you to tell me that this arrangement with Wan Chu has become less than desirable. But as you grow in years and wisdom, you will understand, you MUST understand, that with people of this kind, one must move with extreme caution. This mission carries little risk and less reward for us, but if successful, it will remove the microscopic scrutiny by Wan Chu under which we must now operate. With a relaxation of this scrutiny, we may evaluate other courses of action. Do you understand?"

A silent scowl and a grudging nod from Hamid.

"Good. And we have another complication. It would appear that our valued Mr. Stone has become enamored of the talented Ms. Chu. Whether he shares her bed is of no importance to me, but it would appear that his allegiance has begun to drift once again."

"Let me kill them both, the arrogant American and his whore!"

"An honorable sentiment, nephew, but we must be extremely cautious. Do not think that you can simply walk up to Mr. Stone and easily send him to hell. He is wise, cautious, and extremely skilled. For now, we must live with this scorpion in our tent. But we will watch him, most carefully." Ivor thought for a moment, and added, "When the scorpion is otherwise engaged, when his mind and body are focused elsewhere, then it is a simple matter to ..." and Ivor lowered his foot with a decided thud, and made a grinding motion with his heel, while his nephew grinned a broken-toothed smile.

Chapter Eleven

Beer Conversations

It was late at the Oakland CIA office where Randy sipped badly burned coffee from a mug with a broken handle. More accurately, it was very, very early on a hypothetical non-working Saturday. Randy rubbed his exhausted eyes and tried to concentrate. He sat alone in the larger of the two conference rooms within the secure area of their facility. It wasn't much, just two institutional metal and plastic tables shoved end to end surrounded by about a dozen mismatched chairs, another eight or ten shoved up hard against the walls. Randy had actually counted the different chair styles at around eleven-thirty the previous night when he had temporarily lost focus. There were five, including one mysterious single that the knowledgeable office members avoided since it had a nasty tendency to eject its occupants at random times. Between the chairs at the table, drawn up tightly, and those against the walls, an aisle existed, presumably large enough for a slim person to pass through. He had been in many meetings in this room when it was packed with no fewer than thirty people, many standing near the sign that announced "Maximum Safe Occupancy—18."

For his purposes tonight, however, the room was sufficient. He had pushed back all of the chairs on one side of the table so that he could readily move between the piles of material that he had stacked from left to right by subject, and vertically by chronology. There were five distinct piles: one with intel on the crab boat sinkings, one regarding the shooting at the Wildlife Refuge, one for the failed lake poisoning, one stack containing synopses of the Cathie Clarke Fletcher novels, and a relatively new one with the names Hasim bin Wazari and Elaya Andoori hand-scrawled across the top of a thinly populated folder. This last hastily prepared folder was the result of of a secure phone call from Chuck, who had spent a few days at the Santa Monica office. During that conversation, Chuck had told Randy simply to check the "bad guy" lists for one Hasim bin Wazari. Randy had checked, and was planning to fly out to Tucson on Monday to meet with Chuck at Rickman Air Force Base, attend an all-day briefing by Southern Command, and then give Chuck a data dump on bin Wazari, who in Randy's opinion was dirty as hell. Of course, the data didn't support that. Bin Wazari was scrupulously unconnected with any known terrorist organizations or with known mid- or high-level operatives. He was filthy rich, and enjoyed the favor of the Saud family, including being a pet industrialist when lucrative contracts were being handed out. But none of this meant shit as far as Randy was concerned, and Homeland Security agreed, not restricting bin Wazari's travel, but putting him on a watch list and surveilling his movements when he visited the US. The connection with Elaya, whom Randy affectionately thought of as, "the nosy, nasty, towel-head tramp," a nice bit of alliteration, made him more than a little suspicious.

For a young man, Randy was surprisingly old school. While his contemporaries might have entered all of the relevant data into the computer and performed a dozen correlative searches, Randy preferred this approach, with all his material laid out and within reach, color-coded based on the assortment of Post-it notes available: purple, blue, yellow, pink, and green. Where he discovered a potential correlation between piles, he would apply a Post-it of the source pile's color, including a date and document reference, and stick it to the page of the pile where the would-be correlation occurred. Now, with about seven hours behind him and his vision blurring, it had begun to look like a group art project made by psychotic third graders. He took another sip of the stale, cool coffee and nearly gagged. "Enough!" he said aloud. "Shit, am I ever fried. Time to lock up and start again tomorrow … well, later today. Shit!" He tried to recite in his head the key points that he felt he had discovered, but the tiny colored Post-its seemed to be re-arranging themselves as he stared. He would have sworn that he could actually hear them laughing at him, and he peevishly flipped the bird to the entire table. "F-you, Post-it Notes," he grumbled.

Still, he knew that something was connecting here. Luckily, today being Saturday, he could just spin the lock on the room and leave everything in place. This room wouldn't be needed for any actual meetings until at least Monday, and by then, he'd be off to Tucson. As he secured the office and set the alarms, he allowed himself to smile inwardly, if just a bit, for he knew that he had done well in digging up the intel on bin Wazari. Good enough to warrant the trip to see Chuck ASAP. But that wasn't all. Oh no. Randy had two other nuggets with which he planned to dazzle Chuck. He also planned to accept the copious praise that his tired mind felt he was due.

The first nugget was a resolution of the mystery of the crab boat GPS software. Randy had tracked down the software versions used on the two lost boats, and found that it was the same as that used on the *Emma B* and one other of the three survivors. But that wasn't the best part. Randy had also managed to bluff and bully the third surviving captain, the one who had claimed that he had been using an older version of the software, into admitting that he had, in fact, installed an illegal, bootlegged copy of the newer software. It was now a clean sweep. With all of the affected boats having used identical GPS algorithms, it was time to engage some GPS gurus to sift through the code and try to reverse engineer its functionality and try to locate any gremlins.

Randy's second little gem, still in the embryonic stages, involved the possibility of poisoning C-squared F's next novel in such a way that, perhaps, it might lead to the puppet master pulling the strings on these capers, for Randy was becoming more and more certain the actual terror events had their origin in the books. A sting operation of the type he had in mind would be complicated, possibly dangerous, and in the end maybe fruitless. Still, a tiny part of Randy's conscious mind had the hint of a hopeful smile.

***

Later the same day, Randy returned to the office. Upon opening the facility, a shocking smell—a nasty blend of carbonized coffee and melting plastic—triggered the unwelcome thought that he had forgotten to turn the coffee pot off. Only a thin trickle of smoke, not enough to set off the alarm, was wafting from what looked like a Salvador-Daliesque mutant coffee maker, the glass pot still upright, its plastic handle and lid melted and sagging, the handle having oozed near enough to the hotplate to begin gently bubbling and emitting a sickening stench. The plastic structure of the water tank behind the pot had also deformed lopsidedly, with the overall impression being that of an appliance that might be found at the Mad Hatter's tea party.

Randy spared a brief moment to give thanks that his forgetfulness hadn't destroyed the office, or in fact, even set off the fire alarm. He pulled the plug to the coffee maker, propped the door open, and set the ventilation system to work before seating himself in the conference room and catching his breath. He was in a state of confused thankfulness—after all, the building was still standing—and peevish frustration. He had come here to work, but now would also have to find the time to remove this odd sculpture and go out and buy a replacement unit (with an automatic shut-off function!) before Monday. *Shit! Thank God I have no life*, he muttered inwardly.

However, even halfway across the room he fancied he could feel the waves of heat coming from the still-smoldering machine. He didn't dare touch it until it was well and truly cool, and that time could be spent on his real mission. In the light of day, with a few hours of sleep behind him, it still seemed feasible to poison the new Fisher novel, assuming his boss would OK it. It would also require some serious cooperation from Ms. C-squared, and Randy was certain that Chuck would need to call in a few markers on his friendship with Cathie and Logan. Thinking of Cathie Clarke Fletcher had reminded Randy that he also wanted to refresh his memory as to how the sabotage of GPS systems had played into her story's terrorist plot. Randy remembered the basic plot line: at a pre-planned time, already programmed in the infected software, GPS systems of commercial aircraft would simultaneously malfunction. In the book, the plan resulted in mass confusion as well as the destruction of a few aircraft; the hypothesis being that a little human error or carelessness coupled with faulty navigational data during a trans-ocean flight, particularly at night or in severe weather, would cause a number of flights to end badly. Randy flipped through the book and noted how many flights the author had postulated as fatally compromised, how many were near misses, and how many just resulted in pilots landing in Milwaukee instead of Cleveland. He'd bring this information with him to Tucson, but there was something here that just didn't smell right, and it had nothing to do with the destroyed coffee maker. Randy looked at the table and had the depressing feeling that there were more stacks of paper still missing.

***

Chuck and his ferret-eyed sidekick sat through the Southern Command briefings at Rickman, and most had been quite interesting, though somewhat depressing. Southern Command monitored all activities in Central and South America that Homeland Security had deemed worthwhile to monitor, and the means for doing so were often as interesting as the actual information gathered. Satellites were the primary resource, but since 2010, a larger and larger number of unmanned aerial vehicles had been employed, and some of the smaller variety were being operated by some of Chuck's brethren with boots on the ground in some of the more sensitive areas. The imaging and intelligence gathered were remarkable, but the quantity of data was overwhelming, and the Air Force was looking to industrial partners and the Border Patrol to help process the flood of information. What they had processed was depressing enough in all truth. The cartels were stronger than ever, and were becoming bolder and bolder. They were running operations well into the United States, and in areas such as the San Bernardino Wildlife Refuge, were becoming increasingly comfortable with semi-permanent outposts within the U.S. itself. At the conclusion of the final pitch, Chuck and Randy thanked the colonel who had sponsored the briefings and headed out to the parking lot.

"Hang on just a second, Randy," said Chuck, pulling his phone from his pocket, "I just want to try a call."

Randy nodded, and leaned heavily against the car listening to the high pitched whistle of an A-10's engine as it took a training pass over the base's huge runway.

"Agent Munoz, U.S. Border Patrol," came the answer Chuck had hoped for.

"Munoz, hey, good to hear your voice! This is Chuck Johnson, we talked previously."

"Agent Johnson," the voice responded with considerably more enthusiasm, "good to hear from you. Man, this is a bad connection, though. You must be out of country or something."

"Actually, I'm close enough to hit your building with a rock. Blame effing cell phones. I'm at Rickman with my young Shao Lin apprentice Randy, wondering if you and or Kreski might have a minute to talk. By the way, it's Chuck."

"Formal or informal?"

"Oh, informal I'd say."

"Excellent. In that case, bein' as it's after five, and us BP guys don't get paid like you folks, I'd like to suggest a rendezvous at Conference Room N."

"Conference Room N? Uh, is that on your facility? You know I didn't pass a security visit request. That is, we're not expected at any meeting in that conference room."

Laughter on the other end of the line reassured Chuck. "It's an inside joke, Chuck. We call the local microbrewery, Nimbus, Conference Room N. It's located in an industrial area where the passing freight trains and the A-10s often interrupt a conversation. Kind of an unusual place. But the beer is cold and outstanding, and a couple guys can have a semi-private discussion pretty easily."

"Beer … conversation … beer. Sounds perfect."

"If you don't mind, I'll drag my boat anchor, Kreski, along."

"I heard that, you illegal piece of shit," came faintly through Chuck's cell.

"Perfect, so …"

"Simple," said Munoz. He rattled off directions that ended with, "… north on Dodge, east on 44th. Drive to the dead end. There's a big tank with a monkey on it out front."

"Got it. A monkey. And by the way, I'm buying."

"In that case, less talk, more motion. See you in 10."

"So, Grasshopper, let's roll. Dinner may have to wait for a bit."

***

The dazzling sun poured through the open loading dock door that separated the interior of Nimbus from the makeshift outdoor patio area which held random stools and tables. Munoz and Kreski had guided their guests to the inside table closest to this opening and were explaining the finer points of getting served at this establishment.

"It's simple," said Munoz, "you just get in line over there where the group is, at the center of the bar, and order. They've got a half-dozen truly excellent brews, great sandwiches, quesadillas, et cetera, but they don't have waiters. Being as how you're visiting, I'll get the first round. Let's see how you like Old Monkeyshine. By the way," he added looking at Randy, "you are old enough to drink, aren't you?" A strangled laugh from Chuck exposed that this was an inside job, as Munoz, laughing, headed off to the bar.

"Thanks, boss," Randy said sourly. "And I suppose you've already told these guys about my 'emergency row seating episode' on the airplane?"

"Had to, didn't I," laughed Chuck. "Good communication is the basis for trust."

"Not mine!" Randy snapped back. Randy sulked for a few minutes, but brightened perceptibly at his first sip of Old Monkeyshine. "Hey, not bad. This'd give 'Town Drunk'—that's our favorite microbrew in Oakland," he hastily explained—"well, this would give it a challenge. What is this, about 7.5 percent alcohol?"

"Eight point two, but who's counting?" answered Kreski, "And believe you me, after a couple of these, you won't be able to count, but you won't care."

A heavy freight train passed within a hundred feet of the loading dock, rumbling slowly along the well-traveled double track leading to the Tucson railroad yard. The westing sun cast nearly horizontal rays of golden light along the varied locomotives and the assortment of freight cars, shipping container cars, and auto carriers, reflecting brilliantly off the rails and making the scene almost beautiful; an image of industry and power; an image of man's resourcefulness and determination.

Chuck gave Eddie Munoz and Zach Kreski a brief and somewhat humorous account of his attempt to recreate the scene in the Arizona desert where Kreski and Munoz had come across the dead coyotes.

"And you were trying to see if one shooter could have handled all four of them?" Kreski asked, astonished.

"Yep," Randy replied. "The boss just got the notion that maybe it was all one shooter, and that maybe the drugs weren't the real cargo at all."

"Kind of a stretch isn't it?" asked Eddie. "But still, even for a far-fetched theory, there isn't any contradictory evidence."

"Of course, that's 'cause there isn't much evidence period," added Randy.

"Always the optimist," said Chuck.

Randy took another huge pull at the Monkeyshine and just shrugged his shoulders.

"So by the way," asked Chuck, "You guys both gave an estimate of the number of people, that is, the number of not-dead people, that were on the other side of the clearing. I think you both had it between eight and twelve." Kreski and Munoz both nodded in the affirmative. Chuck continued, "Couldn't have been fewer, could it? Maybe as few as four?"

Eddie and Zach exchanged glances, and Eddie spoke for them both. "No way, Jose. I'd say eight is even below the min."

"Concur," said Zach, "There was a lot of activity over there. Four guys? No way. Is that a big deal?"

"Only if you worry about bad guys being loose in the U.S. of A," Chuck replied.

Eddie gave him a quick questioning look, and Chuck said to his unspoken question and to the table in general, "I'm going out on a limb a little bit here, so what I'm saying never actually got said, OK?"

Eddie and Zach nodded. They got it.

"OK," Chuck continued. Randy got up to get another round at the bar. He knew this story.

"So," Chuck began, "I told you we found an ID at the toxic spill that matched your phony from the site. Somebody is, or was, trying to keep consistent with names and IDs. So, logically, the charmers at the lake were from the campsite you saw. But here's the bad news." Eddie and

Zach sat up straight and were focused on Chuck as Randy very carefully deposited four fresh beers at the table. Distracted thanks around the table. "There were only four dead bad guys. By your minimum estimate then, that leaves at least four others, maybe more, running around with bad notions."

"Fuck!" said Kreski.

"Yeah, well put by the Polish philosopher here. A gentleman would have said, 'Oh fornicate!'"

"Know any gentlemen, you wetback SOB?"

"Actually, no, including me," said Munoz without much humor.

"So we still have a tiny problem," said Chuck, pulling on his brew. The group sat in silence for a long while, watching another long, slow freight train roll by on the nearby tracks. The sun set, taking the sharp edge from the surrounding buildings, cars, and trees, but also leaving the area looking much like what it was, a small, modest microbrewery located at the end of a dusty road in a dingy industrial area in south Tucson.

"Shit, I believe this stuff is drilling into my cranium," said Chuck over the noise of the very full bar area. "Randy, can you still drive?"

"I can always use the Braille method, boss," Randy slurred.

"In that case, gentlemen, well, men anyway, I want to thank you for an outstanding evening of fine wine and entertainment. Come visit us in the garden spot that is Oakland, and we'll continue this teambuilding relationship. Also," he added seriously, "if you think of anything, or see anything, or smell anything, and I mean anything, that might bear on this little mystery, don't hesitate to call. Maybe not tomorrow, though. I believe I may need to pack my head in ice for a day."

Goodbyes were said, and Chuck and Randy, fighting a stiff headwind, made their way cautiously to the door and down the short flight of stairs to the parking lot.

"Uno más?" asked Eddie.

"Hey, why not," Zach replied. "I believe I'm familiar with that Braille method."

Chapter Twelve

Working Late is Dangerous

Jason's only remaining concern was the backbone of the three associates working with him on this assignment. They were as nervous as birds and he finally had to corral them in an empty conference room, give them each a set of unclassified, meaningless charts on cruise missile defense and tell them to pretend to be reading them. Jason had easily rolled them past the guard, each flashing a simply forged Alpha ID. It had been nearly five, but the group had been muttering about a "fucking proposal" and had been carrying several ripe-smelling pizzas, as if to confirm their dedication to the task and their commitment to a long night. The guard had barely looked at them. They weren't the only ones working proposals that night. The guards had recognized two of the more friendly and gregarious, Bart Wiley and Kevin Flahrety, who had Baggins subs, and were equally morose about a long night.

The two buildings Jason had targeted were considered to be "mobile buildings," meaning a large series of pre-fab building structures ("trailers" to most of the inhabitants), rolled in, placed on a perimeter foundation, and fastened together in a seemingly endless row. The raised floor would provide an excellent flow of oxygen once the fire had truly caught hold. A large transformer in the empty gap between the buildings was Jason's target. And that was where the raccoons came in. A study of the history at this plant showed that on more than one occasion, animals (feral cats, opossums, even bats) had gotten into the buildings or the surrounding infrastructure. A fried cat had once taken out power over half the plant site. In this case, the poor raccoons would have chewed through high voltage cabling at the junction of the transformer and the buildings. The raccoons and their "nest" had already been treated with an inflammable accelerant. Their extensive "nest" of papers and miscellaneous trash, also treated, would easily ignite the two buildings. Jason had walked casually through both of these buildings, had even flirted with two of the female admins that had found him attractive, and concluded that once the wooden flooring of the buildings was pierced, the paper within, fed by oxygen from below, would become an inferno. His associates would help place the raccoons, arrange a break in the floor of each building (those raccoons could absolutely rip through rotten old wood) and would help monitor the buildings, including watching to ensure that those who exited had left the scene. No casualties were necessary or anticipated, but there were several large proposal and program areas within one of the buildings, and Jason would ensure that the electrical short would fry the fire alarm systems, leaving them in a state of "green" until the actual smoke and flames became apparent. There was some minor risk that someone might discover that the fire wasn't accidental, but who, when provided with an obvious answer, seen before at this location, would question further? And what person would check a charred and carbonized raccoon carcass for accelerants? It would be a sad, regrettable accident, and the solution would be to install more animal traps (of the humane type, of course) around all critical buildings and infrastructure.

Jason's main concern was the state of mind of his minions, and he repeatedly provided them with trivial chores to keep them occupied. At last, as 11:00 p.m. approached, he sent the least jumpy of the three to cruise through the building one last time to check for employees, custodial staff, or random security patrols.

"Remember, Mamoud," he had said, looking into the man's eyes with calm, seriousness, "if someone spots you, just give them a smile and mumble, 'Fucking proposals!' Got it?" The man nodded silently and moved off. Jason then addressed the other two. "When Mamoud gets back with the thumbs up, you two move into the two buildings and get things ready. If by any chance someone spots you or tries to talk to you, you're the facilities maintenance crew, repairing hazardous floor tiles that have been reported as part of the initiative to reduce slips, trips, and falls. You just say that and I guarantee the people will move on. Now, radio check, test … test … test." The two repeated "test … test" and Stone nodded, the words crisp in his earpiece. "If you get harassed by anyone you can't shake, or anything crops up out of the ordinary, you say what?"

"I need to call my supervisor," they responded in unison.

"All right, now stay cool. We'll be out of here and smoking a Lucky in no time."

At that moment, Mamoud rounded the bend. "Well?" Jason asked.

"Both buildings seem empty."

"What does that mean, exactly?" Jason asked.

"I saw no one. But several rooms, what you call proposal rooms, were locked. I do not have access, but I do not believe they were occupied."

Jason considered for a moment. "Can't be helped. Okay you two, go. When you're done, contact me and head out. There's going to be zero delay before all hell breaks loose. You meet up with Mamoud at the water tower and exit the plant site. I'll observe until I can confirm our job is complete and then withdraw. Remember, once I get your affirmative messages," he pointed a finger at each of their chests, "get the hell out and do not forget your exit route. It's liable to get a little dark in those buildings and then very, very warm."

The two left, still looking like nervous high school students heading to their first dance, but after all, it was a simple enough assignment. "Gather up all this crap," said Stone, pointing to the bogus briefing packages. "I'll meet you at the transformer in four minutes," he added to the wide-eyed Mamoud, and left the conference room.

***

Bart yawned loudly and rubbed his blurry eyes. "Are you guys nearly done? I'm fucking whipped and I'd like to go and get me a hooker. But what I think I'll actually be doing is going home and going straight to bed."

"The wild, exciting life of an aerospace drone," said Gary Walkin, drily.

"Actually, you can just bite me," said Kevin, but without his usual sarcastic edge. He too yawned. "I guess I'm almost there, but we really ought to merge these files, burn a final disk, and print a hard copy before we go."

"Oh, are you fucking kidding me?" Bart snarled.

"We really should. This briefing is in the early a.m., and I don't want to be dealing with some printer fuck-up. Let's just do it and then get the hell out of here."

"You guys both suck, you know that don't you?" grumbled Bart, though he knew they were right. They had a briefing with a room full of vice-presidents scheduled in the morning, and all of them had been burned, at least once, by last-minute computer glitches that had been both embarrassing and career limiting. With the files merged, a disk burned, and plenty of hard copies to go around, they would be pretty well set.

"Bite me!"

"You know, one of these days, I'm gonna take you up on that Mr. 'I only have one joke line'!"

"C'mon, a little less BS, a little more of 'let's just get this shit done,'" said Gary.

"Fine, OK, fine! I figure that means about another half hour. Any of you losers want another cup of hot, dark-brown caffeine in a grubby ceramic cup with some glucose substitute and milk byproduct?"

Gary, staring blearily at a computer screen and not bothering to turn around just grunted and shook his head in the negative.

"Yeah," said Kevin, "if you're buying."

Bart silently left the room and headed towards the kitchen area. As the door snacked shut, he could hear Kevin's parting, "And then you can bite—" blocked by the door. Bart smiled. Though he'd never admit it to these clowns, if you had to work shitty hours on unrewarding projects and then get your ass chewed by unimpressed VPs, these guys were OK. He even missed that lucky old fart Logan. They had worked on some cool shit, and had more than once burned the midnight oil until sunup. Yeah, he'd miss these guys, assuming he was ever able to hide enough dough from the "ex" to allow him to retire and still indulge in at least a mixture of Ramen and dog food for the rest of his life.

As Bart walked down the deserted, partially darkened corridor towards the break area, his vision seemed obstinately blurred. Though he repeatedly rubbed his tired eyes, he simply couldn't get them to focus. *Man, if I keep working these hours I'm gonna need glasses or a seeing eye dog by the time I do get out of this joint.* Just at that moment, the smell hit him, and he briefly thought, *Damn, something's burning. Did I leave an empty pot on the burner?* But his nose quickly contradicted this theory, for it wasn't the rank odor of carbonized coffee that he was smelling. It smelled more like a campfire. No, not that exactly, more like when he would try to light his fireplace or his chimenea and the stubborn thing just wouldn't burn, and so he'd stuff it with more and more … PAPER. A thicker cloud of grey smoke billowed around the end of the corridor further obscuring his sight, and this cloud had an angry edge of orange. In an instant, Bart realized the seriousness of what was happening. A jolt of adrenaline brought his heart to racing and instantly cleared the cobwebs from his fatigued mind. He raced to the end of the hallway and looked down the intersecting aisle to his right. A terrifying, fierce blast of heat met him just as the building lighting flickered and went out.

In the locked program space, as the power sputtered and failed, Kevin slammed the desk top, cursing. "Shit, shit, shit, did you save? Damn it, hours of work. Please tell me that you saved?"

After a short pause, Gary replied dismally. "Yes, no, well, not in the last forty-five minutes or so."

"Oh FUCK!" Kevin yelled. "We are so screwed!"

The smoke, which had been a thin vapor only moments ago, now boiled from the massive blaze now engulfing the open, bullpen seating area to Bart's right. Emergency lighting, provided by a sparse sprinkling of battery-powered units located in the halls and office areas, was already being swallowed by the smoke. More light by far was being thrown off by the blaze. A few sprinklers had kicked on, but in the back of his mind, he wrote them off as hopeless.

Bart turned and dashed back down the hallway in the direction from which he'd come, coughing and spluttering now from the acrid fumes, his only thought to warn his friends and get the hell out. As he ran through the near blackness, he tripped over the foot of a chair and stumbled forward, cracking his head on the sharp edge of a desktop organizer. He felt a jagged cutting pain and stumbled to his knees. He put his hand to his aching head and felt a steady flow of liquid from above his left eye. The situation had changed drastically in the last few moments, and Bart realized that if he didn't get to his friends and get out soon, things could end very, very badly. He was breathing very rapidly now and was near panic. The blood was completely obscuring the vision in his left eye, but at least, down on the floor, the smoke wasn't as bad. He gave up trying to stop the flow of blood, took a few breaths, and began crawling down the hallway.

"Well, and how long do we wait for the power to come back on?" asked Kevin. "Man, we are going to have to redo everything since our last save, then merge the files, then burn the disk, et cetera, et cetera. This could be an all-nighter."

Just then a loud pounding sounded on the heavy door to the program area.

"Oh crap, just go let Bart in, will you," said Gary. "I'll bet the power for the cypher pad is out, too, even if he could see the keypad."

"Man, is he ever gonna have to bite me for this night," Kevin growled. He pulled the door open and a dark shape, about knee high, tumbled into the room. First shock, then anger raced through Kevin's mind. Here they were, totally screwed, and Bart was playing some kind of game. An instant later, the choking reek reached his nostrils just as Bart coughed out, "FIRE! The building is on fire! We've got to get out, now!"

"But what about our stuff? We've got to lock up the program material and ..."

"NOW!" Bart nearly shrieked. Smoke at head height was rolling into the room. "C'mon, get down, let's go!"

Both Kevin and Gary now experienced the same jolt of adrenaline-charged energy, and, crouching, sprang out the door and began to go down the main hallway towards the building entrance.

"Not that way!" Bart yelled, stumbling up and grabbing Gary's collar from behind. "Go left, past the restrooms ... emergency door!"

The relief as Kevin slammed into the crash bar and the door flew open into the cool night air was spectacular. All three were coughing now as they staggered down the short flight of stairs and headed away from the building and towards the parking lot. The parking lot lights were also out, but a near-full moon was shining in a cloudless desert sky, and it was in the relative safety of the parking lot that the three stopped to catch their breath and celebrate their escape. It was there that Gary got his first real look at Bart's face.

"Jesus Christ! Bart, what happened?"

Kevin spun around and was brought up stunned. The jagged gash above Bart's left eye was still bleeding steadily, half his face was covered with blood and his shirt was wet down to his waist.

"Holy shit! Sit down, man." Kevin quickly stripped off his shirt, grabbed the ends of the arms and twirled it around until it was a loose sausage of cotton. In this light, he couldn't be sure if Bart's head was bleeding, or if his eye had somehow been destroyed. To him, Bart's left eye socket seemed to be a dark hole flowing with blood. He felt he was going to be sick, but he mastered his fear and nausea and wrapped the shirt around Bart's head. A few minutes of wiping the blood from Bart's face, and the eye reappeared, easily seen now in the ruddy glow that seemed to be lighting up the night air all around them.

"Thank God, man, thank God." Kevin was almost sobbing and Gary was in near shock.

"Hey, it's OK, just some blood," said Bart, unconsciously patting Kevin's shoulder with a blood-soaked hand. "It's all right, man. Thanks. Hey, at least we're alive."

Suddenly, a frightened yell for help filled the night, coming from the adjacent building. In the glow of the flames, Gary's face turned deadly pale. "Jesus, someone is still in there!"

The three were frozen, terrified at the thought, until a second, more desperate cry was heard. At this, Kevin leaped to his feet as though he had been prodded. He turned to Gary. "Stay with Bart. I'm going to see what I can do." Before Gary or Bart could reply, he had sprinted back towards the second building.

Kevin immediately realized that the front entrance to the building was impassable. Flames filled the lobby entrance, and heat and smoke poured through the door and shattered windows. He ran frantically along the perimeter, but at every window he saw violent, hellish flames leaping within the structure. His last hope, an emergency exit door at the opposite corner from the front entrance, was painfully hot to the touch, and the nearby windows, most of which had burst outward from the heat, revealed an inferno just inside. Hot tar was now pouring from the roof, carrying heat and flame to the outside of the structure. He grabbed at the emergency exit door handle one last time, and pulled his hand back with a grunt of pain. Hopeless.

Kevin made his way back to his companions in the parking lot, and flopped down, silently shaking his head. At that instant a hideous, unearthly, animal scream bubbled up above the roar of the fire. The three men huddled in horror as the scream seemed to go on, and on, and on. Then it was suddenly extinguished. Gary leaned away from the other two and vomited violently, and Bart just kept repeating, "Oh my God, oh my God …"

***

A surprisingly short distance away, concealed in the hard shadows of another building and a clump of scrubby palo verdes, Jason Stone observed. The destruction of the two target buildings was now confirmed. He had watched the three engineers stagger from the flames of the building to the north and make their way to the parking lot. The scream had surprised him, but had not been totally unexpected. Mamoud had been unable to confirm that the buildings were empty. Someone had been trapped with no escape route. And Jason had witnessed one man's futile attempt to enter the second building; a brave act, but foolish.

It was unfortunate. Jason had not intended for there to be casualties, and he was never completely satisfied, never completely happy when things did no go exactly as he intended. But he had known that the chances were far from remote that injuries or deaths might result, and he consoled himself with that thought: it was a statistical probability and he couldn't control everything. He had known casualties throughout his military career. The important thing was that the mission had been accomplished. It was the mission that mattered. He moved noiselessly away as the eerie howl of emergency vehicles filled the silence, and an unearthly orange glow lit the sky.

Chapter Thirteen

Dinner at the Beach

Oceanside Restaurant was built on huge wooden pilings that stretched out over the rocky beach area below and past the water's edge. The brilliant orange of the setting sun was shattered into fragments by the ever-moving surface of the Pacific Ocean: broken, scattered, and reflected onto the patio seating area. A pleasant muted roar and hiss as the waves washed in among the weedy rocks and sand and then retreated seaward brought a sense of calm and relaxation and also a feeling of continuity. The perpetual repetition was a gentle reminder that this natural music had preceded man's intrusion here and would undoubtedly be here long after he was gone.

Several couples and groups, many in studied, semi-formal evening wear, sat at tables unevenly placed along the patio and enjoyed the spectacular sunset, the ocean's endless sonata, and the excellent wine and food. But one couple, who shared the place of honor, the most coveted table at the very edge of the patio, and who were silhouetted against the spectacular background of sun and sea, had caught the notice of many of the other patrons. The man was tall and handsome, ruggedly built, but with gentleness about the eyes and lips, especially when he smiled, which he did quite often while conversing with his gorgeous and exotic partner. And though he looked dignified and serious in his neat slacks and dark blue sport coat, she was simply stunning in a tight-fitting black dress, open at the back nearly to her waist, then flowing in shimmering folds to her ankles.

Luana sipped her Cosmo and nibbled on a crab cake looking alternately at the setting sun and at her intriguing partner.

"And what exactly is going through your mind right at this moment?" Jason asked, with a nearly boyish grin of mischievousness.

Luana smiled and nearly caused the collision of two busboys who were hopelessly distracted by her stunning beauty and were vying with one another to refill her already full water glass. Embarrassed apologies, followed by the undignified retreat of the two young men, still arguing over precedent at the coveted table, left both Luana and Jason amused.

"Well," Stone persisted, "and before that charming interlude, what was going through your mind?"

Luana smiled again, and this smile, while superficially the same as those she had used to dazzle hundreds of clients, was subtly different. Perhaps it was a certain gentleness about her cheeks and the corners of her mouth or a slightly more lively sparkle in her eyes. In any event, careful study of that look could only lead to the conclusion that this smile was real and the other, her perpetual façade, was just that. One could be confused, seeing each smile individually, and conclude that they were, in fact, the same. However, if placed side by side, there could be no doubt about which was the true reflection of the thoughts and emotions within.

"Well, aren't we inquisitive, Mr. Stone?" she began.

"Don't start with that 'Mr. Stone' moniker again, or it's back to 'Ms. Chu,' formal business relations, and sad disappointment for me."

"OK, Jason. It is a relief to be free from the forced formality for a change, and I would hate to disappoint you."

"And so …" he began teasingly.

"Persistent as well! Well then, I was thinking that Oceanside has met my expectations in every way: ambiance, quality, beauty, and service, our overzealous bus-people notwithstanding. But," she added thoughtfully, and with a sudden much more serious look clouding her face, "the company has not."

"I'm very sorry to hear that," Jason replied. But before he could continue, Luana interrupted him. "Don't be. You've exceeded every expectation I had for you Mister … Jason. Charming, witty, well-bred, funny, thoughtful, and obviously extraordinarily capable. I find it somewhat distracting."

The arrival of the couple's entrees briefly interrupted the conversation, along with the arrival, opening, and sampling of the wine, a fabulous Passagno Chardonnay that would have made even Logan Fletcher stare with envy.

"And did I mention superb taste in wine?" Luana added, continuing her thought process.

"Well, wow!" Jason said, smiling. "And I could say with perfect truth that you are the most stunning, sensual, disturbing woman I have ever met."

"And why disturbing, Jason?" Luana asked with surprise.

"Well, I suppose it's because in addition to being beautiful, highly intelligent, focused, determined and, if I might say," he continued, leaning across the table in a conspiratorial manner, "deadly, there is a pride about you, an unabashed and honest appreciation of your self-worth that is, well, the closest word I can come up with is 'regal.' If you were short, awkward, and plain looking, you would still be a formidable human being, and it wouldn't ever be wise to underestimate you or, God forbid, cross you."

Luana smiled back with an almost girlish shyness that she thought she had left behind her when she turned eight. For once, she had no answer to the bold and confident man sitting across from her.

"And incidentally," Jason added with another impish gleam in his eyes, "how would you know that I'm extraordinarily capable?"

***

Luana lay naked and exhausted on top of the sheets of the huge California King, a mild, jasmine-scented breeze gently whispering the sheen of perspiration from her body. Jason had once again exceeded her expectations, and in fact, even that wasn't true, he had shattered them. It wasn't that he was strong, masculine, and very adept. She had known this with many lovers before. And with many lovers before, she had always left their company feeling disappointed despite being physically manipulated to certain sexual satisfaction, while her partners had invariably seen to their own desires as well. Perhaps that had been the fundamental difference. Jason had been patient, gentle, and above all, considerate of her throughout.

The enigma that was Jason Stone troubled her in a pleasant way as she recalled the evening. They had driven a short distance from the restaurant to a small but spectacular house perched on the hillside above Malibu. The house projected out over the ocean-facing hillside, with huge glass walls and sliding glass doors on three sides, perfect solitude and privacy guaranteed by the steep drop-off. Jason had thrown the doors open when they arrived, and the warm fragrant sweet-smelling air and the muted "hish" of the surf on the rocks and beach far below had reminded Luana of home, her real home, the house of her mother and her mother's family for generations on the island of Maui. And when Jason had taken her in his arms and pulled her body against his, she had felt young again, young and happily naïve, a thought that was reinforced when he had gently pushed her back and asked with complete seriousness, "Are you sure this is what you want?" It was the last thing she expected to hear, her other lovers, having finally achieved their ideal circumstances, would have simply proceeded to satisfy their own desires, and hope that hers were satisfied as well. But that had never been their first concern any more than their pleasure had been hers. She had answered by rising up on her toes, crushing her body against his, clasping his head in both hands, and kissing him deeply.

Jason gently removed her clothes as she unbuttoned his shirt and kicked off her shoes. His fingertips traced the perfect curves of her body as her dress fell away and he took her in his arms once again, her firm breasts pressed against him, her warm mouth finding his. He easily lifted her and placed her on the bed, lying beside her and caressing the smooth skin of her legs, her stomach, her hips.

"You are beautiful," he said.

"But you can't see me," she teased.

"I see you more clearly in the dark," he said, cupping a smooth, soft breast in his hand.

The evening had taken on the illusion of a dream. The huge bed, the glass walls, the soft, scented breeze, and this man who seemed focused on bringing her pleasure. And Luana found herself reciprocating, not needing to be concerned with herself, and therefore free to do what would please him, instead. They talked much more during their lovemaking than she ever had before, and far from being distracting, it added surprisingly to the experience, not merely in the obvious expressions of what each other was feeling and in how to amplify that feeling, but just in an openness and communication that was far removed from the frantic race to orgasm that she had often experienced.

***

During the quiet interval that followed, as both lay breathing deeply, their blood coursing strongly, but their bodies relaxing, Luana had rolled next to Jason and wrapped a warm arm around his chest. "That was lovely, Jason, just, well, lovely." And he had surprised her once again by saying, "I always try to follow the advice my mother gave me about a job worth doing being a job worth doing right."

"Really, your mother? I would have thought that it would have been your father."

Jason's gentle laughter rippled through her body as he quietly replied, "Oh, my dad was more of an old school 'work hard, play hard' kind of guy. I still remember my first high school date, the girl all dressed up, pretty and nervous, and me looking more like a corpse in a coat and tie that I just couldn't get right. I had brought her over to say hi to my folks after picking her up, and as we're about to leave, my dad comes up to me and says in a whisper that I swear the neighbors could hear, 'Well, ride 'em cowboy!'"

"Really? That's awful!"

"Well, my date looked scared and I turned red, and we got out of there fast. That was the stiffest, most formal date I've ever had. I got her home before nine, shook her hand, and beat it. I swear, I would go lobster for a week every time I thought about it. It's funny, though, he didn't mean anything by it. At least, I can say that now, though I hated him for months after. It was just the way he was. He lived, worked hard, fought in combat, and then expected the rewards. There wasn't any malice in it, you know? It was just how he was wired, and I suppose most guys in a similar situation would be the same."

"Not you." It was a statement and not a question.

"No, not me. I guess I lean more towards my mom's philosophy."

"A job worth doing … How I appreciate that woman! Do you speak often?"

Jason paused, realizing that he had shared more of his personal life with Luana than he had with anyone before, with the exception of his mother. And he also realized just how much he had missed that comforting, trusting, reinforcing relationship. He shrugged mentally and replied. "She thinks I'm dead. Both my parents do. In fact everyone I ever knew before I left the army thinks I'm dead. It's the price I had to pay. I'm not sure it was worth it."

"Jason," Luana began, "I'm so, so …" She gave up on words at that point, pulled herself even closer to him, and slid her hand down his stomach and began to caress him.

"Oh, don't feel too sorry for me. I'm just not used to having someone who'll listen to my griping. And if you keep doing that, you'll spoil my concentration, and I have a very delicate procedure in mind."

"And what's that?" she laughed, releasing him as he slid down the bed, stroking her thighs open as he positioned himself.

"A job worth doing," were his last words, and a few moments later she arched her back off the bed in ecstasy.

***

And now, with the sun just beginning to creep around the hills to light the ocean with a deep phosphorescence, Luana turned a surprisingly tender face to Jason, who was awake and quietly watching her.

"Good morning," he said, smiling.

"Morning? It can't be already."

"I'm afraid so." He leaned towards her and gently kissed her forehead. "I'll just get some coffee going."

As Jason rose from the bed, Luana could see in the early light the scars along his back and legs, scars that she had felt in the night but which were harshly exposed in the unsubtle light of morning. It was a reminder that their business, her father's and Ivor's, often resulted in blood. After the attack at Alpha, both she and Jason had flown to LA, she to execute several days of legitimate work, once again dazzling prospective clients to her firm and more importantly, to meet with her father, and Jason to meet with Ivor. Luana and Jason's time together since had been pleasantly stolen from that reality.

Jason returned to the bed, standing naked at her side. "Are you getting up, or …"

"Or," she said firmly. "Lie down."

Jason rolled into bed on his back and Luana immediately pulled herself next to him, her warm breath tickling his chin. As she ran her hand over his body and began to touch him once again, she asked, hesitantly, "Did they … I mean, when you were wounded, did it …"

"Hurt?"

"Yes. It, it must have been very painful. Oh, I'm so sorry."

"Actually, I didn't feel a thing. Shock. Pretty common. And of course, I bled out quite a bit. I didn't feel anything the next day or the next either. The medevac got me out and to the base hospital pretty quick, and before I really knew what was going on, I had so much morphine pumping in my veins that the docs could have sawed off my arms and legs and I wouldn't have cared. It was on the third day, as they started reducing the dose that things really began to … sting." He laughed a humorless laugh. "I believe I questioned the birth status of more than one doctor that day. And then, of course, a couple of months of rehab that wasn't too fun."

"Oh my God, I'm so, so sorry."

"I'm glad you weren't there. I was more than a little rude. But the docs, they patched me up pretty good. Hey, I can still do this," he smiled, rolling onto her and entering her with one easy motion.

Luana let out an involuntary gasp and wrapped her arms around him, grasping his scarred shoulders and pulling him closer.

"Yes, by God, you can. Ohhh … God!"

***

Forty-five minutes later, she looked at her watch and sighed inwardly. In three hours, she'd be on the cattle car flight back to Tucson. Her grimace faded and a warm smile took its place as she heard Jason pouring coffee in the kitchen. Jason planned to return with her.

Chapter Fourteen

Golf Lessons

"No, Logan," the golf pro said irritably, "You're turning your wrist on the back swing! Yet again!"

"Jeez, Harv, I'm sorry. Mind must be elsewhere, way elsewhere. I guess since that fire at Alpha, I've been a little distracted, and in about," he glanced quickly at his watch, "in about thirty minutes I'll be meeting up with my friends to play a round and hoping to hear the latest buzz. I don't know whether I told you, these three guys were at the plant working late that night and they were lucky to get out of one of the buildings that went up. I think you know one of them … Bart Wiley?"

"Yeah, I do know him. He takes a lesson every now and then. And by the way, he doesn't turn his wrist on the backswing!"

"Yeah, well, Bart fell and hit his head trying to get out of the building. Got cut pretty bad above his left eye. The doc says it'll be fine, but Bart is kind of hoping for a scar, you know, sort of an ice breaker with the ladies on 'Cougar Nights.'"

"Sounds like Bart."

"Yeah, well, I also happen to know the guy that didn't make it out, Danny Kerrigan. Danny was always kind of a dick, but shit, I wouldn't wish that way out on anybody."

The golf pro heaved a sigh and tried to look properly mournful as someone only can when hearing about the tragedy of a complete stranger.

"Well, anyway," Harvey added a few moments later as he was leaving, "work on locking down that wrist motion. It's good for twenty yards. And I'm thinking you need it. You know, your original swing, the one you had when we first met, was more natural, more relaxed. Try and go back to that approach. Yeah," he finished, throwing in the only semi-technical jargon he could think of to try to snag Logan's memory, "go back to Rev Zero of your swing. It's a better starting point and we'll just work on it from there."

"Thanks." Logan tried a few more swings on his own, shook his head, and headed back to the pro shop. He entered from the course just as his friends came in through the main entrance.

"Logan, you lazy old fart," began Kevin, "it's been a while."

"Well, if it isn't my favorite trio of ass-clowns. Bart, you look like shit, fella. You can't possibly hope to pick up something looking like you lost the brawl at a hockey game."

"Kevin, if you would, please," replied Bart.

"Bite me!" Kevin instantly responded on Bart's behalf.

"Actually," Gary said, "he fancies himself the rugged, manly type now. I believe there is an entire series of exceptionally creative pick-up lines that he's been working on. I'm pretty sure one involves ninjas."

"Truthfully," said Bart with uncharacteristic seriousness, "I still can't get that sound out of my head. You know, the roar of the flames and that God-awful scream. Poor fuckin' Danny!"

"He was a dick, but shit crackers, man, what an awful way to go," Kevin said as he hauled his clubs past the other two and headed for the cart area.

"Funny," said Logan, without much humor, "I guess we've established that he was a dick and that it was a hell of a way to go, but do you guys have any intel on what happened? The radio didn't say much other than two buildings went whoosh. I presume you guys were in 931, right?"

"Right," replied Gary. "The other was 932, where Danny was."

"Yeah," said Logan, "That makes sense. He had that lab there, the one with the cool frequency synthesizer. That was a sweet toy."

"Was, brother, was," said Bart, as he and Logan loaded their clubs, got seated in the cart, and headed off to the first tee. "Nothing left. I mean, you knew those buildings; the world's biggest trailer park is what Otto Greeves used to call them. Crappy old tinderboxes as it turned out."

"Did they figure out a cause? I mean, shit, somebody died, not to mention you becoming so much less pretty."

"Rugged looking, rugged looking. Did you know I was attacked by ninjas?"

"Yeah, Gary mentioned it," Logan replied with a bland, dismissive tone. "The cause … what was the cause?

"Turns out it was sabotage. Yep," Bart continued in response to Logan's extremely quizzical look, "the work of evil geniuses. Too bad the culprits didn't make it out alive. The CIA could have tortured them for information."

"Bart," Logan continued, with some exasperation, "are you ever going to tell me what happened?"

"Well," said Bart, pausing for effect, "it was a fucking family of raccoons. No, listen, I am not shitting you," he added to Logan's look of frustration. "Raccoons. Swear to God. They got into the transformers, gnawed on some wiring, which by the way, took out the alarm system, finally bit a very high-voltage line, which fried their furry little asses, and took the buildings down with them." He paused as if searching his memory, then said brightly, "Hey, you remember that old Bill Cosby routine, where Cosby is talking about the guy that rolls his car down a steep hill and into the Frisco Bay 'cause he's no fuckin' good with a clutch, and when he tells Saint Peter what happened, old Saint Pete says, 'You go to hell!' Can you imagine that dick Danny telling Saint Pete that he died in a blaze caused by a family of raccoons?"

"You go to hell," Logan finished, but without a humorous edge.

"Don't mind me, Logan," Bart said with a somewhat guilty expression as they pulled up to the first tee. "If I don't laugh a little about it, it really fucks me up. Haven't slept for shit the last couple weeks. I plan to fix that tonight, though. Cougars beware!"

"Ninjas, you say?"

"Ninjas!"

It wasn't until the fifth hole where Logan, trying desperately to remember what his Rev Zero swing had been like, and so far failing badly, recalled something else that he wanted to ask the guys, something that Harv's words had triggered in his mind.

"So, did they ever move the two big classified servers out of those buildings? I know there was some talk about it 'cause they were overloading the cooling capacity."

"Nope," Gary replied, slightly louder than was necessary during Kevin's backswing.

The ball made a graceful hook into some very prickly desert rough, and Kevin turned with an accusatory, "Dude! Really?"

Gary, who was two strokes behind Kevin, muttered an apologetic, "Sorry. Hey, Logan asked me the question!"

Logan gave him a surly look and muttered, "Threw me right under the bus."

Gary ignored him while busily calculating that he could pick up at least one stroke on Kevin on this hole, maybe more if the ball was unplayable and Kevin had to take a drop. He remembered one of Kevin's favorite fighter pilot sayings, "If you aren't cheating, you aren't trying," and smiled a satisfied smile.

"So," Logan continued, "the servers?"

"Both still there, both flambéed back to their base elements of hydrocarbons and silicon."

"Shit, did they still have the latest revs of tactical code for, like, most of our systems on them?"

"Yep. The estimate was that 80 percent of the fielded and development programs were on those two machines. The product line bosses are screaming mad. If it wasn't just paranoia, I'd swear those raccoons knew exactly where to hit us to make it hurt."

"Backups?"

"Naturally. They're working three shifts with … what the hell was that company we outsourced to a couple years back? It had a cool name."

"ISG. Infinity Services Group," said Logan.

"Nice! Sounds like heavenly angels looking after the fate of the world."

"Speaking of heavenly angels, did you ever get a load of their CEO?" added Bart. "Man! I wouldn't toss her out of bed for an entire wildlife preserve full of cougars!"

"And how do you happen to know this?" Logan asked.

"Dude, it's my corporate duty to follow all the latest developments in the tech world." Logan snorted his disbelief. "And as I am a slave to corporate duty," Bart continued, unperturbed, "I just happened to find a photo of the young woman in a highly technical journal."

"Her picture's in the latest Aviation Week," Kevin said. "Duh! Seems like her company was the hero after that cyber-attack took out some major Pentagon and prime contractor servers. Infinity to the rescue! I imagine her company is going to be rolling in business from now on, and she'll be rolling in dough."

"Yeah, well, I just wish her picture had been a fold-out, if you know what I mean," Bart concluded with a salacious grin. "And as for rolling . . . !"

"So when do you think they'll have everything back to something like normal?" Logan asked, badly interrupting Bart's sensual fantasy.

"What? Oh, who the hell cares?" Bart said with a frustrated look on his face. Logan said nothing, but continued to stare at his friend, one eyebrow raised expectantly.

"Oh well, hell, I heard they're going to stumble and bumble along with temporary servers for a while. But the big plan now is to use the fire as the excuse to finally construct the dedicated building that they've needed for years. Rumor has it they're paying off the county inspectors to hustle things along. The plan is to have the new server farm ready for a big reload by next April. Happy? Now, can we please get back to discussing beautiful women? I've got to be in the right frame of mind for tonight."

***

"How I ever let you guys talk me into this, I'll never know," Logan said, as he took his place at a large table in the bar area of Skybox with his three friends, who were already executing highly sophisticated search algorithms in the cougar-rich environment of the bar and restaurant. "Target acquired, two o'clock, switching to Single Target Track," murmured Gary, indicating a tall, professional-looking blonde who had just entered the restaurant and was moving towards a table where an equally sophisticated looking brunette was waving her over.

"Clustered targets. Employing hair color resolution to break out separate tracks," added Kevin.

"You guys are like juveniles," grumbled Logan.

"Hey, just 'cause you have something at home, don't grudge us our little fun!" Bart responded.

"Not at home. At least, not tonight, or I wouldn't be able to get away with this."

"You mean to say that if I sent an e-mail to Cathie that just happened to include a picture of you getting sloppy drunk with a couple of babes draped all over you, she might get a tad upset?" Bart needled.

"Possibly," Logan said drily, "But then it might be hard for you to operate your little black box with two broken thumbs."

"Excellent point. Think I'll just sidle up to the bar and see if that lovely lady in green needs a drink. Ta, ta, you old fart."

Before long, Bart was deep in conversation with the woman at the bar. At one point, it appeared that Bart was gesturing towards his face and looking at the woman with a pained expression. Over the general rumble of conversation, TV noise, and clinking glass, Logan would have sworn he heard the word "ninjas."

"Switching to Track While Scan," Kevin commented. And while keeping the two earlier women, the blonde and the brunette, carefully located, he proceeded to survey the rest of the building, occasionally commenting to Gary. After a few minutes, he looked at Gary, who nodded. "Hey, Logan, mind keeping the table warm? We're just going to …"

"I know," Logan interrupted, "You're just going to see if the two lovely felines over there need a drink."

Kevin gave Logan a friendly slap on the back as he and Gary moved off, causing Logan to spill a few drops of beer on the table. Before he was aware, an attractive woman with short, dark hair leaned near to his ear and said, "That's alcohol abuse, you know."

Logan turned a startled face in the direction of the voice and was surprised to see a familiar face. "You probably don't remember me," she began. "My name is …"

"Becky," Logan interjected, "Becky Amhurst, Software Center, right?"

"Guilty," she replied. "And you're Mr. Fletcher, the very serious, very upright Program Manager from Advanced Development."

"Now there I think you must have me confused with someone else," Logan laughed. "Anyway, I'm retired now, so I've become a lot less serious lately."

"And less upright? No, I'm just teasing. It's just that seeing you with these guys, semi-regulars if you know what I mean, made me wonder."

"A moment of weakness. Cathie's not home this evening and these guys can be pretty entertaining. Anyway, I guess my manners haven't improved much with age. Please sit down. Would you like something?"

"Quite definitely," she said, with a sly look at Logan, "but I'll settle for a drink."

Occasionally one or more of Logan's friends would make a brief return to home base, before venturing out once again, and at one point later in the evening, Bart came by the table and said, "Well, I'm taking off, Fletcher. Enjoy the rest of the evening." Logan took a quick glance towards the exit and noticed the very attractive lady in green, looking both somewhat embarrassed and impatient, staring in Bart's direction. "Hey, Becky, see you next week," Bart added as he left.

"So I don't get it," Logan asked with genuine curiosity. "I mean, here you are and here they are …"

"So why am I not hooking up with one of your friends. Well it could be personal preference, but actually it's a bit of an unwritten rule. We avoid people we know from work. It's a good rule, in general. Avoids a lot of unpleasantness down the road. Ahh," she added a moment later, "I see a couple of my friends rolling in. Promised to meet them here. Thanks for the drink and the company, Mr. Serious and Upright, more's the pity," she laughed as she moved off.

A few minutes later, Kevin and Gary sank into chairs back at Logan's table. "Well, I see Mr. Bart had some luck," Gary said. "I wouldn't have thought that ninja thing would work."

"It's a joke, moron," Kevin put in glumly. "Ladies like a sense of humor."

"Guess that explains why you're sitting here with us," was Gary's rejoinder.

"Oh, bite me!"

"Logan seemed to be doing OK with Ms. Becky. You know, you just might be a natural at this."

"I hope I don't need to remind you that this little adventure is top secret, need to know, eyes only, compartmentalized, etc, etc. Besides, you guys dragged me here. As you know, I am very happily married."

"So was I, at one time," Gary continued. "So, one more round?"

"Seriously, you guys giving up already?"

Kevin gave Logan a pitying look as to one of profound naiveté. "You may have noticed that as the evening progresses, the, what shall I call it, the younger crowd begins to arrive. It kind of becomes an unfair fight at that point."

"Well, well. That's a shame."

"So, one more round?"

"No, I'm out," said Logan. "Got to go home and do a little research in the technical journals."

"What?" asked Gary.

"Bite me," said Kevin.

Logan moved towards the door and caught a final glimpse of Becky, who waved to him as he left. Her two companions, as if enjoying a good joke, also waved. As Logan opened his car door, he realized that although he was retired, he really wasn't that old or hideously out of shape. The fact that he might actually be attractive to someone, that is, someone other than his wife, hadn't really crossed his mind for years.

"Easy there, big fella," he said aloud to himself as he drove off.

Chapter Fifteen

Dinner with the Wife

Logan poured himself a glass of port, and settled down to the piano, running through a respectable set of major 7th chords and then a few pieces from an improvisation Method book he had bought online a month before. The fingering was getting easier, and he played perhaps better than he ever had before. It cleared his mind, and he continued playing for nearly an hour. When he finally rose from the piano bench it was with a certain pride. Those hours of practice, a priceless commodity when he was working but now available in droves, were paying off, and he was very pleased with his progress.

It was as he was refilling his glass that he remembered Bart's comment about the hot CEO from Infinity Services Group. Strolling over to the coffee table, he picked up the latest addition of Aviation Week and hadn't flipped through more than a few pages before he came upon the article that Bart had been referring to, a large color picture of the attractive CEO surrounded by Pentagon General Officers and corporate VPs, all grinning at her in an undoubtedly grateful but seemingly lascivious way.

Logan placed his drink on a coaster and looked more closely. Luana Chu, President and CEO of Infinity Services Group. "Holy shit!" exclaimed Logan, aloud. "Ms. Blue Hawaii!"

***

The next day, with a somewhat undeserved guilty conscience, Logan had invited his lovely bride to dine with him at Tony's, an outstanding restaurant located in the foothills of the Catalina Mountains, and offering a beautiful view over the city of Tucson. At first Cathie had bridled. It was short notice, she had a lot of work to do, etc. In the end, she relented. (She truly loved Tony's steak and seafood.) The only gloomy aspect was her insistence that she be allowed to keep her cell phone and Blackberry discreetly with her to use, as she promised, only for extreme emergencies. *Damn*, thought Logan. *And why am I doing this exactly, anyway?* he pondered. *Because I bought Becky Amhurst a drink and enjoyed her company for ten minutes? No*, his subconscious clarified, *because you enjoyed her company, and you had the illusion, if only for a few minutes, that you were a virile young stud again, on the prowl. True enough*, Logan mused, *So this dinner is for Cathie, and if she wants to carry her electronic leashes, well, so be it.*

Logan sipped his scotch and stared out the huge windows towards the twilight gently blanketing the town. It had a cool, grey look to it, especially with the sun still burning orange patches on the taller peaks of the Rincon Mountains to the southeast, while the Tucson Mountains to the west cast their long, grey shadows out across the valley. Cathie had barely touched her drink as yet, and Logan could see her look of intense concentration as she stared into her lap, her arms making small, rapid movements as she typed on her poorly concealed Blackberry. *So be it*, Logan repeated to himself, as he sat quietly.

His gaze had returned to the window and the rapidly crowding lights in the city below when a reflection in the glass caught his eye; the hostess seating a couple at another table. Logan's eyes adjusted their focus from the distant sparkles to the much nearer reflection as the two advanced towards the table, and it was as though he were seeing them through shallow, crystal-clear water, an illusion that added to the overall sense of surreal fantasy that struck him at that moment. It was all Logan could do to prevent himself from swinging around in his seat and staring gape-mouthed like a college freshman at his first strip club. Could it be her? The picture from the Av Week was still stuck in his mind. Could it be Ms. Blue Hawaii?

With as much nonchalance as he could command, Logan leaned across the table and said, "Just going to the little boy's room. I'll be right back." Cathie nodded absently, her primary focus remaining on the glow coming from her lap. Logan carefully kept eyes front as he moved off towards the restroom, feeling stiff, uncomfortable, and obvious, like an extremely poor spy whose every attempt at natural behavior is revealed as false simply because he is trying too hard to be natural. On the return trip, it was easier to let his eyes roam around the restaurant, and he stole a quick glance at the table where the couple had been seated. No doubt about it! Ms. Blue Hawaii—that is, Ms. Luana Chu—was the woman at the table. The temptation was to enjoy the scenery and stare at her during his entire trip back to the table, and in this Logan would not have appeared in false behavior since, as always, most of the male eyes within a thirty-foot radius were locked on the stunning woman. But Logan had wanted to see which Alpha wheel was wining and dining the young woman, since he assumed that her presence in the backwaters of southern Arizona must be related to the fire and her company's backup system. So Logan reluctantly tore his eyes away from Luana and took a quick glance at the man. He was large, handsome, and younger than Logan had expected. Logan quickly determined that he wasn't one of the Alpha VPs, nor was he even one of the senior directors, most of whom were well-known to Logan. In an instant, his time was up and he was forced to reseat himself. The only possible view now was the dim, semi-transparent reflection, which at this angle gave a decent view of Luana, but only showed the back of her male companion's head.

***

Randy reached for another slice of now-cold pizza in the oily cardboard delivery box. It drooped sadly as he lifted it and a mushroom slid off onto the conference room table. Unperturbed, he raised the pizza well above his head and positioned his mouth under the tip and took a large bite. Chewing, he reached for his coffee, thankfully still hot. It chased the pizza down his throat leaving an aftertaste that wasn't too revolting.

Once again, the conference room table was crowded with Post-its. These were in two distinct clusters this time. The first was interspersed with photos, some excellent, and some mere caricatures, of professional gunmen. These were the skilled executioners that he and Chuck had pulled from an Interpol database that might possibly have the expertise to be the single shooter that Chuck was becoming more and more convinced was responsible for the massacre at the wildlife refuge. It was an odd, international collection of A-player assassins: professional killers that, like the highest-class hookers, were in constant demand and could command extraordinary wages for their services. Many of the worst killers were unknown by sight, and hence the caricatures or sketches included with their probable records. And some of the records were quite impressive. Victims included police chiefs, military leaders, ministers, ambassadors, and multiple politicians, one a former dictator of a West African country. These kills were attributed to the men in question; men who had never been apprehended or who had escaped. Randy had quickly sorted out those incarcerated during the time of the border killings.

The other pile, which Randy considered to be more fun to work on, fun being somewhat loosely defined as work he was more willing to do at 11:30 p.m. in a drab, deserted office in a less than ideal Oakland neighborhood, consisted of notes and potential scenarios for poisoning C-squared F's next novel.

But while "fun" by Randy's standards, it was also frustrating and extraordinarily complex, for Randy realized that he needed to not only invent a terrorist act that would be adopted, but that it must also allow the capture of major players in the terrorist organization and, of course, stay believably within the overall context of Cathie's novels. Randy had summarized the basic points of his operation:

1. Plan must be an extremely tempting operation in terms of political and economic impact that would justify both resources and potential risk

2. Plan must remain believably within the context of Cathie's books

3. Plan must be of sufficient magnitude to expose high level leadership or lieutenants

4. Plan must incorporate a known missing link (material or intel) if attempting a "sting" operation

5. The plan MUST NOT succeed

Randy had given a lot of thought to this last point. History was strewn with clever operations for catching criminals or terrorists that had backfired in spectacular ways, ways that had actually allowed the bad guys to succeed in exactly the way that the operation had been intended to prevent. The horribly botched gun-walking operation run by the Department of Justice circa 2010 was a case in point. While attempting to trace the flow of illegal weapons to Mexican cartels, the DOJ had allowed hundreds of them to "walk" into criminal hands. With no apparent plan to actually trace the weapons, the guns had simply become a part of the large arsenal of cartel weapons, resulting in the murders of many Mexican citizens and a few Americans, including BP agents, as well. And so, the brilliant plan to stop the flow of guns had, in fact, opened the floodgates, resulting in extremely sad and tragic results. Randy knew that this last point would need to be ironclad before Chuck would take any proposed operation to his superiors.

Randy had come up with a few ideas that satisfied points one and two, though he was unconvinced that they addressed three, and he was internally struggling with four versus five, while six just hung like a black cloud over everything he considered. Based upon the notes Logan had provided for Cathie's next novel, he could see that she was considering some sort of primitive cruise missile attack from an offshore platform, such as a moderate to large freighter. There was a string of scribbled notes discussing the potential payload including a suitcase nuke, a dirty bomb, a chemical agent, or a biological weapon. This was all major league stuff, certainly the type of thing that kept Homeland Security anxious. But an attack of this kind would require resources and funding that dwarfed those of the 9/11 attack. Judging by the small-ball stuff that had, presumptively, been lifted from her books to date, this would be quite a leap. Still, the terrorists weren't required to rip pages from her book and use them as a tactical roadmap. All that was necessary was for them to become sufficiently interested in the critical piece and to be given enough information to allow them to believe they could succeed. Randy found himself leaning towards the dirty bomb approach. It was highly believable considering all of the poorly stored and guarded waste material scattered throughout the former Soviet Union. Some sort of "clearing out" operation could be orchestrated with a friendly ... Randy smiled at this one. *Well, if not actually a friendly government, then at least a poor one that will do business with us*, he thought. "We'd need State behind us, and that's going to take Chuck's boss, minimum. Complicated! Still and all, the dirty bomb sounds like a possibility," he added aloud to the empty conference room. He took a quick look at his watch and at the squalid array of notes, coffee cups, greasy plates, used napkins, and the congealing oil in the pizza box. "Looks like a bomb went off in here, too! And a dirty one at that. I'm starting to feel like used dog shit. Better clean up while I can still think straight, and then, to complete the abuse on my body, I think I'll go to Murphy's and get a 'Drunk' on the way home. Yep, sounds like a plan."

***

As Randy forced himself through the cleanup process, his mind kept wandering back to the poisoning of the book. It would be much, much more difficult than he had first envisioned when he had suggested it, bright-eyed and enthusiastic, to a more practical and less enthusiastic Chuck. But Chuck had authorized him to try to turn his notion into something with a little flesh on the bones. Yes, Randy thought, this was becoming much more real and work-like, with a myriad of details to resolve. And then too, if they were to even begin executing such a plan, they would need the full cooperation of Ms. Cathie Clarke Fletcher. Chuck and Randy had discussed this at great length, and it was decided that the only way that she would allow them to co-opt her novel was to convince her of the importance of the operation. And of course, they would need her full and willing cooperation to actually turn their suggestions into the consistent storyline dictated by point two. To this end, Chuck had discussed the matter with Logan, an acceptable first step, since Logan still held an active Top Secret clearance.

***

After laying out the outline of the plan, Logan had responded with an emphatic, "You're going to have to clear her, Chuck. I mean, you're asking an awful lot, and even if she was willing to do it with just your word that it was for national security, and believe me, that would take some convincing, you'll never be able to have the interaction with her you'll need to get the right product, which is an unmistakably C.C. Fletcher storyline, with your poison pill baked in. And by the way, I'm guessing that a simple TS isn't going to do the trick."

"A 'simple TS'? Do you have any idea what the backlog on clearances is these days?"

"Fourteen months average from the time of submittal," Logan replied instantly. "I still have friends in security, Chuck."

Chuck had grunted and nodded his concurrence.

"And I know that you know that fourteen months isn't going to cut it. So, what can you actually get it down to?"

"If I pull enough strings, threaten, badger, plead, and sell my kids into slavery I reckon I can manage six weeks, five absolute best case."

"Well, I'd be getting my knee pads out, it I were you," Logan responded.

"Hey, brudda, don't forget you have a part in this, too. You've got to get Cathie to sit down with thirty pages of forms and instructions and get it done, and I mean pronto. Oh, and don't forget, there'll be more to follow. She's going to need some additional information."

"And?" Logan questioned, hinting broadly.

"Yeah, fuck, I guess you're gonna need it too. Shit, I'm going to have to get some top cover for this, and soon. Hell, if we can't come up with a really solid plan, this whole exercise will be for naught and I'll be cleanin' toilets at the Pentagon to close out my illustrious career!"

"It's easier to get forgiveness than permission," Logan quoted back to Chuck. This had been a common philosophy when Logan was working, usually espoused when attempting to secure research money, facilities, or staff, and Logan had used it very effectively after having discovered that a lot of yelling by his bosses, sometimes in public, usually did not result in his unblessed actions being overruled. But the beating, private or public, was the necessary and expected outcome of using this tactic.

"Yeah, well right now I'm skating on thin ice, man. Lucky for me, Randy is out ahead and he doesn't weigh as much," Chuck concluded, the double meaning of the word "weigh" not lost on Logan. Often, a more junior person who went too far, a "lightweight," could evoke more sympathy and tolerance in an irate boss, and it was clear that Chuck intended to use Randy as a human shield if necessary.

***

When Logan first casually suggested that Cathie should "just fill out a little paperwork for Chuck" because he needed her expertise to help him with a few problems, she had been incredulous. "If he needs my expertise, he's really screwed," she'd said, bluntly; and then, seeing the actual "little" stack, was adamant in her refusal. "No, and that's final. I don't have the time!" Several days of pleading, cajoling, expensive dinners, and promises of lovely and exotic vacations had finally brought a grudging acquiescence, and Logan was sitting at the piano, playing something that he hoped would mellow the mood, when a rumble from Cathie's office preceded her entry into the music room and her third (or was it fourth?) eruption since she had begun filling out the forms.

"No!" she began without preamble. "They simply cannot need to know what high school I went to! And three references that knew me well when I was in college! Logan, this is insane! No wonder the government is broke. 'What was the dorm address at school?' And why do they need this kind of information, anyway? Nosy, busybody, Big Brother bastards! No! They can just go to hell."

Logan patiently waited for her to complete venting, and then silently went to the bar area and, sighing, pulled his most prized bottle of Merlot, the one he had been keeping for a VERY special occasion, opened it, mumbling to himself, "Frickin' Chuck owes me!" and poured two glasses. He offered up the glass and waited while Cathie's internal reactor cooled a bit. He considered using the argument that he had been forced to fill out similar paperwork at regular five-year intervals through the course of his career, plus innumerable other stacks of paper as well, but quickly dismissed this approach. He knew with certainty that the immediate rejoinder would be, "Well you picked your own stupid career, so that's just what you get." And in fairness, after the first time someone filled out this particularly hideous form, assuming he or she kept a copy safely stored for future reference, refreshing it in subsequent years amounted to no more than reviewing and updating the original information. Annoying, certainly, but not at this initial level, which necessitated dredging up rather ancient information. With luck, she would not need a five-year update nor, he hoped, too much additional information.

"Look, honey," he began tentatively, "I think Chuck wouldn't have asked if he didn't think it was important."

"Important? Is it as important as missing a deadline with my publisher? That's going to cost us money, you know! Not to mention the fact that I've never missed a deadline before, and that little wiener Geoffrey has been beating on my guilty conscience like a damn snare drum. Is it that important?"

"Babe, Chuck knows what you do for a living, and he knows, 'cause I told him, that this is a huge sacrifice. You know Chuck. He wouldn't just ask for no reason."

"But that's just the point," Cathie exclaimed, beginning to boil again, "Why won't he just tell me so I can at least understand, so that I can make my own judgment on whether this is worth it or not?"

Logan sighed inwardly. He knew it would come to this, and he knew that his only explanation wasn't a good one, at least not if you hadn't lived for thirty years in the business.

"Sweetie," he tried, gently, "it doesn't work that way. You can't have access to the information, any of the information, until you get cleared. I know, I know, it seems like Chuck doesn't trust you, but that's not it at all. It's just the way it works in the real world." Logan regretted this last phrase as soon as it passed his lips, for he knew Cathie would resent it as a criticism of the authenticity of her novels, where the heroine would invariably disclose critical information to secure help or receive reciprocal information, based on her "gut feel" towards someone. Logan was correct. Cathie drained the rest of her wine, slapped the fragile wineglass down on the bar's granite countertop, and returned to her study.

Blew it, Logan thought, but with a slight edge of resentment. *Her and her damn books are driving me batshit! You'd think that just this once, she could trust me and Chuck and just fucking do the paperwork! It's not like every fucking kid with a wet nose coming out of college doesn't have to do exactly the same thing if they want to work government programs*! Logan poured himself another glass of wine. Getting thoroughly pissed wasn't going to help. He wandered back to the piano and began playing. As always, the smooth jazz, now coupled with his more proficient delivery, quickly restored his equanimity. He continued to play. *Guess I'll just have to try again*, he thought as the music floated around him.

So it was more than a little shocking when, nearly two hours later, Cathie emerged from her study bearing a stack of papers and a sheepish look. "I'm sorry I went off, Logan," she said, kissing the brow of his upturned face. "Here, it's done. I guess when I finally just accepted the fact that I'd have to answer all those, well, stupid questions, and just went back to my old records, well, it wasn't all that bad. Truce?"

By way of an answer, Logan stood and wrapped her in his arms.

Chapter Sixteen

Looking for a Plan B

On the other side of the world, both physically and culturally, Ivor Vachenko waited nervously to be shown in to see Hasim bin Wazari. As he waited, Ivor chastised himself for thinking how easy, how simple it would be to develop a relationship with a new sponsor after many years, marginally rewarding, with Wan Chu. He had spoken bravely to his nephew of a new alliance, an alliance with a believer, a man of their faith and culture, and one with exceptional resources. His nephew's chief delight had been in anticipating the day when the arrogant Stone could be brutally dealt with. On this score, Ivor had relented, though he would regret the loss of their pet scorpion. However, Vachenko had told Hamid to put any thoughts of revenge against Wan Chu's daughter out of his mind, and he prayed that his nephew had listened, for a man as powerful as Wan Chu could be expected to exact painful, bloody revenge. And this brought Ivor back to his apprehension regarding bin Wazari. Could Elaya, a longtime confederate, truly be expected to smooth this pathway for him? Would bin Wazari be resentful of their long-standing relationship? Ivor sighed. In the end, it would be a difficult, sensitive introduction. Bin Wazari was another powerful man; another powerful man to fear.

He had not been waiting long, in fact, before he was escorted into a large, lavishly furnished room with an adjoining patio that looked down from bin Wazari's enormous hilltop home onto the city of Rabat. The heat of the day was declining and the cool blue and violet shades of evening were creeping steadily along the dun-colored streets below, enveloping the city house by house in a near liquid bathing of twilight.

Ivor approached with marked deference, bowed low, with his eyes to the ground, and remained silent, waiting for bin Wazari to speak first.

"Allah, the great and merciful be praised," bin Wazari began in a deep, melodious voice. "Our meeting has been too long postponed, my brother," he continued, laying a friendly hand on Ivor's shoulder and raising him up to face him directly. "Come, sit. Accept the hospitality of my home and be refreshed."

Hasim bin Wazari was a large man, tall, stout and heavy without giving the impression of being fat or in any way soft. His meticulously trimmed black beard had only a few traces of grey; his eyebrows were thick and dark. For a large man, he moved with surprising grace and silence, and as he motioned Ivor to take a seat, Vachenko caught a glimpse of large but perfectly manicured hands. Dressed in Saudi garb, but of a quality unmatched in the city below, Hasim gave an air of overt, unapologetic opulence, quite at ease in his lavish house or in the palaces of his cousins, the royal family.

Ivor seated himself in a large, cushion-covered wicker chair across from bin Wazari that afforded an unobstructed view of the city. He politely accepted a cup of tea and a date offered to him by a house servant from an ornate silver serving tray. "You have had a long and tiring journey, I am sure," said bin Wazari. "Relax a moment. We will dine soon, and then I am very eager to hear how you and your people are progressing in your service to Allah, all praise to his name!"

As Ivor sat nibbling dates, drinking his tea, and listening to bin Wazari carry on a pleasant and unhurried monologue of his life, his wives, children, and business, Vachenko was struck by the contrast between this gracious man, who surely must know of both his successes and his failures, and the stern, hard, Chinese man who had treated him with such cold disrespect. Both were wealthy and powerful, and both detested the West and wished to see its ruin. But here, the hatred was driven by a deep religious loathing of the West's decadence, by its pollution of the purity of Islam and the Holy Lands through occupation and a cancerous, pervasive undermining of its culture and traditions. It was what Ivor himself felt, and though still cautious, he found himself much more comfortable in the presence of this man than he had with the arrogant Wan Chu, who was driven by base political motives and a desire for worldly dominance. Still, Ivor had to remind himself to proceed with caution for this man too had a bite that was worthy of his bark.

Ivor also, quite naturally, harbored a deep jealousy and resentment towards this large, self-confident man. And though he had prepared his mind for this meeting and had repeatedly cautioned himself to show nothing in his words or behavior that might betray his emotions, he struggled to maintain an icy, impersonal control. So much time had passed, and yet the feelings threatened to burst from him. He mastered them, and smiled.

Dinner was a sumptuous and lengthy affair, with courses of saffron lamb, seasoned rice, dates and cheeses, and a tepid, custard-like dessert. Nearly two hours had passed in extreme comfort and relaxation and Ivor now found himself on the patio with his host, overlooking the now-sparkling city. The air had cooled pleasantly and Hasim's huge manservant and, Ivor assumed, personal bodyguard, had deposited a fresh pot of tea and honey-sesame cakes before withdrawing noiselessly. Hasim swung one leg comfortably over the other as he settled back into a large, cushioned chair.

"So, you are perhaps less weary and hungry, praise Allah for his gracious generosity? Perhaps we may now speak briefly of business?"

"Yes," Ivor replied. Hasim smiled a godfatherly smile and created a silence in which Ivor could continue. "As you know, Excellency, I have established a small organization within the United States. Within this organization are numerous believers, eager to do Allah's works, and another man, a very interesting and capable man, loyal to our cause though not of our faith."

"Sadly, it is often unwise to place full trust in a nonbeliever. You have proofs of his loyalty and dedication?"

Ivor broke from his planned narrative and proceeded to relate the history and service of Jason Stone: his recruitment, his careful monitoring, and his subsequent successes, omitting the specifics of the brutal conflict with his nephew. "However, as you have so wisely stated, no one who is not of the true faith can ever fully understand our cause or be completely trusted." Hasim raised a questioning eyebrow and Ivor continued with a shrug, "There have been certain disagreements, misunderstandings between Stone and my other followers, easily managed. But we will be ever vigilant in watching him, with both eyes. Still … a useful man."

Hasim smiled pleasantly and nodded without committing himself to the certainty to Ivor's conclusion. "Please, go on."

"I have been operating somewhat under the patronage of a certain man …" Vachenko hesitated. But Hasim merely smiled more broadly and waved for him to continue as he said, "Names are of no importance to me, for now. Please, continue." And in the interval that followed, Ivor explained his working relationship with Wan Chu, being careful to never be overtly critical or disparaging, but nonetheless conveying his sense of constraint, his inability to fully pursue the will of Allah while under obligation to this man.

Hasim waited patiently for Ivor to complete his narrative, sipping thoughtfully at his tea, and when he was certain that Ivor had said all he had planned to say, he sat forward in his chair and began, "I believe that you and your people may be able to do me an essential service in the immediate future, which, if Allah smiles upon your success, could lead to a very valuable partnership. Your relationship with this other man is an unfortunate complication, though perhaps it may yield advantages that we do not yet see. Do I understand that you would like to sever ties with him at some point in the future?"

"Indeed, that would be best."

"Though perhaps not immediately practical?"

"It would be unwise to act precipitously."

"And so we must deal with this complication, for now. And yet, since by your current arrangement, you have autonomy to carry out your own actions, then perhaps an immediate solution presents itself. For it would be surprising, perhaps shocking, if our desires did not coincide, so that your actions, taken upon your own authority, may simply be those which suit both of our purposes. No constraint was placed by this man on the actions, merely a notification, and you were wise not to allow this constraint. As for my, let us say, cooperation and participation in any of your private actions, why, I am sure this man would rather not even know of it."

"I understand completely, Hasim."

"Excellent." Hasim clapped his hands and servants entered, some to clear the tea things and the large manservant standing by for instructions.

"Ivor Vachenko, please accept the hospitality of my home this evening. We have much more to discuss, but the day is spent. Rest tonight by the grace of Allah, and we will speak again in the morning."

With Vachenko safely escorted off to bed, Hasim strolled down a long corridor in his home and entered the apartments of his third, and most useful, wife. "Hasim," she said, bowing gracefully as he entered, "are you pleased with your new associate?"

"Very much so Elaya, my love. And has Colonel Zareb conveyed to you his needs regarding our plan?"

"His scientists have completed their test of the electronics, and the hardware appears to be functioning. It is the algorithms that give his people concern. The tactical fire control and missile software appears to lack full functionality and we must acquire newer versions."

Hasim waved an impatient hand. "I do not need details, but details we must have, and quite soon if we are to meet our timetable. I believe our new friend may be able to help."

"And what of the aircraft requested by the Colonel?"

"Ah, once again Allah has smiled upon us, for our new friend has himself associates that may serve our needs. But I must arrange to have the colonel meet with our Ivor Vachenko tomorrow." Hasim reached a thick-fingered hand out and caressed his wife's cheek. "I will return in an hour."

***

Elaya smiled him out of her rooms and then sat on the edge of her bed. Hasim was a boor and somewhat of a pig, but his needs were minimal and infrequent and she tremendously enjoyed the life of power, luxury, international travel, and intrigue. Hasim was blissfully unaware of her long-standing relationship with Ivor, and both had agreed on the fiction that allowed her to make the introduction based upon distant and casual family acquaintance. In most things, Hasim trusted Elaya implicitly, a state of affairs that she had been eager to cultivate and reinforce. The trust was not returned, and Elaya often wondered how long she would need this man.

Her aspirations went well beyond the anonymous manipulation of trivial events, and bloody political statements. Well beyond. They involved a staggering ambition on her part. For her desire was for nothing less than to become the first female leader in a revitalized, secularized Iran; to see the ayatollahs and mullahs stripped of their power and sent back to their filthy mosques to pray and see to the people's spiritual needs. Spiritual needs were nowhere on her list of objectives, whose items could be neatly summarized by the one heading: acquisition of power.

For years Elaya had nurtured her plans. The painful sting of exile from Iran, the need for her to court favor among the decadent men and women of the West, and the passionless marriage to bin Wazari in order to acquire wealth and power grated upon her daily. Yet, she sensed, her web was nearing completion. She would act, soon, and be rewarded with supreme success … or devastating failure.

For a short while longer, her husband's path and hers ran parallel courses, and she would use her influence, her Western connections, and her jihadi acquaintances to support his goals, always keeping in mind that in the end, particularly if her coup was successful, a well-placed phone call or e-mail could put Hasim in the crosshairs of a Reaper drone. She smiled at the thought that he would die a martyr.

Chapter Seventeen

Rewrite the Story

This time, Logan had agreed that they would have to meet at the CIA's LA offices with both Chuck and Randy. Cathie's paperwork had been rapidly processed through an enormous expenditure of time and effort by both Chuck and Randy in shepherding the documents through the many staged investigation. And while this process which might seem like an amorphous mass to an outsider, Chuck, with his many years working clearances from the government side, knew it involved real people at specific key junctures of the clearance labyrinth. These people all had names, were invariably overworked and underpaid, and received at least fifty stacks of paperwork each day marked HOT, with a request or demand for immediate priority processing. Between Chuck and Logan, the names of those key individuals were well known. Markers were called in, leverage was applied, and, as Randy put it, "I personally wore out three sets of knee pads." Four weeks and two days after Cathie submitted her paperwork, she and Logan were on a United regional jet headed for Los Angeles to be briefed.

***

At the LA office, Cathie was escorted into the anteroom reserved for security in-briefs. For the next half hour, Cathie received a very abbreviated presentation outlining her personal responsibilities in preserving the confidentiality of everything she was about to see. More paperwork was signed, and she was given a badge with a green stripe and the words "Cathie C. Fletcher, Interim TS."

"Well," said Chuck, when she was finished, "wasn't that just fun? Welcome to the 'I Can't Say A Damn Thing About What I Do At Work' club, Cathie. This will give you a little bit of empathy for what Logan went through for thirty years, but I know that wouldn't make this worth the hassle. So, let me just say personally, thank you so much. My young sidekick, Grasshopper, will fill you in on what we have in mind."

Randy went up to Cathie and shook her hand. "Actually, my name's Randy, Ms. Fletcher, and I've got a couple of slides to flip through, but mostly I'll be talking and looking forward to your feedback, good, bad, or indifferent. Any comments or questions before we start?"

"Well," said Cathie with a lopsided smile, "your office here is kind of a dump, isn't it? I don't believe I've ever seen so many walls painted grey. And when were they painted, actually? I'd say no less than 15 years ago. As for your furniture, well, it's a wonderful, eclectic mix of unpopular styles from the fifties and sixties and it smells moldy. On the other hand, this cup of dark brown, caffeine-infused water may taste like motor oil, but at least it's hot! You gentlemen should get hazardous duty pay to work in a place like this."

Randy turned to Chuck in mock surprise. "We get paid, too, boss?"

Chuck and Logan were laughing, and Chuck responded with complete truthfulness, "These are palatial quarters compared to our Oakland office, Cathie. I'm going to recommend that you never visit us there."

"I solemnly swear," she replied.

"Take it away, Randy. And remember, brevity is the soul of wit, although if you try to get witty, I may have to dock you a week's pay, which I believe would be around thirty dollars."

"When did I get a raise?" Randy muttered, as he approached the head of the table and clicked the remote to display his first slide. Only the left half side of the slide contained writing, and Cathie was astounded to see that it was the titles of her first three novels, with a bullet point under each. The title of the slide was "Critical Elements in CCF Novels." The first novel, *Address Unknown,* contained the sub-bullet—Sabotage of GPS software in commercial aircraft to trigger confusion and loss of life at a predetermined time. The second, *A Little Local Color,* gave a one-line summary of a cyber-attack to shut down military and commercial servers, and the third, *A Tangled Web,* had a sub-bullet that described the poisoning of a town's water supply.

Cathie stared at the list. "Well, I'm impressed that you got the titles of my books correct, but I would take exception to referring to those sub-bullets as 'Critical Elements.' Certainly the GPS sabotage was central to *Address Unknown*. Even the title is a little play on the confusion that would result if you honked up everyone's precious, and might I add, extremely taken-for-granted global navigation system. But the other two were very minor elements, not critical at all."

"Ah," said Randy, "but that's because what you assume by 'Critical' is that they are critical to the plot of the books. Our definition of 'Critical' is a little different." As he spoke, Randy replaced the slide with another whose left hand column was identical to the first, but which contained a second column which matched up to the first under the heading "Known Terrorist Attacks," which contained a brief description, a location, and a date. The main title of the second slide had also changed to "Cases of Copycat Terrorist Attacks."

Cathie's mouth hung slightly open as she studied the slide, and Logan, who already had some inkling of the events in question, leaned forward with intensity, absorbing details previously unknown.

"And you're telling me ..." Cathie began incredulously.

"That someone is sifting through your novels and plucking out some very nasty ideas. The next three slides go into detail on each of the specific attacks. In the case of the first," he began, clicking to the slide, "only the testing stage was implemented, and there is a small army of software engineers trying to unravel the worm in the code so that we can determine if it's already lurking in the commercial airline fleet. A warning has already been issued to all the major carriers to instruct pilots to use a little old school navigation to cross-check and we're pondering a recommendation to revert to earlier code."

"That'll cost the airlines a fortune," Logan interjected, "as well as causing a configuration management nightmare."

"You got that right, brudda," said Chuck. "Right now we need to walk like 'Grasshopper' on rice paper."

"Hey, I actually rented the entire first season of *Kung Fu,* so I get the whole 'Grasshopper' thing now. That show was kind of entertaining in a camp, cheesy sort of way, assuming you bought the entire premise of Shao Lin priests with superhuman skills, which I didn't. Actually, in truth, I thought it was crap. But still, nice cultural reference there, boss!"

"Randy, you are on the verge of being witty. Don't make me come over there and smack you!"

"And so," Randy continued in his bland, professional voice as though the entire most recent exchange had never happened, "we continue with the cyber-attack. It was publicly acknowledged at a very basic, that is vague, level with a happy ending to calm the eight people of the general populace who gave enough of a shit to turn off *American Idol* for ten minutes and watch the news."

"Randy … witty?" Chuck warned.

"Except that the vague, basic stuff can't even begin to describe the cost in time, manpower, and money to retrieve, install, and baseline backups," Logan added. "Hell, that fire down at Alpha is causing exactly the same kind of scrambling as a kid kicking an ant hill."

"Right you are," said Randy, "not to mention the embarrassment and necessary head rolling that went on both in the commercial and the military side to punish the innocent, nor the future safeguards that are being mandated for all military and defense cyber-systems to prevent this kind of shit happening again. The estimated cost is one arm and two legs. Ooops, sorry boss," Randy added quickly, "I mean, uh, the costs are substantial."

"So, I don't get it," asked Cathie pointing at the screen. "Why does it say 'Specific Purpose Unknown'? It seems like a pretty effective attack in terms of the annoyance it caused."

"That's just it," said Chuck. "Annoyance is not what the bad guys are about. I mean, Randy is right. I'll bet ninety-five out of one hundred people out there don't even know what happened, and if they did, they wouldn't give a shit any more than the five that did know. The other two attacks create fear at a minimum and more likely, some serious casualties if they are pulled off successfully. This one just doesn't smell right," Chuck concluded.

"How did it go down in your book, babe?" Logan asked his wife.

Cathie gave him a withering look that said, *You'd know if you'd read it!* But it was Randy who answered. "The attack resulted in the theft of critical strategic data involving major weapon systems, specifically the vulnerability of weapon systems and sensors to 'airborne attack.' Sorry," he added, seeing the look of confusion on Cathie's face, "through wireless hacking. There was damage to national security, though reparable, but it's still not really terrorist style."

"In the book, there was a foreign government behind that attack. That kind of information could only be exploited by a major military power looking for a real strategic edge," Cathie added. "But you didn't say information was lost in the actual attacks."

"It wasn't," Randy added. "The firewalls did their job to that extent, at least. The only known problem was corrupted servers, forcing use of backups. An annoying pain in the ass, but not much more. That's not the M.O. of terrorists or major powers."

At this Logan said, "Unless the attack isn't complete." Puzzled looks converged on Logan.

"Brudda?" Chuck queried.

"Oh, hell, I've got nothing specific, just a gut feeling that we're missing something here, like that damned attack of ninja raccoons at Alpha. Something just doesn't add up."

"Ninja raccoons?" Randy asked, astounded. He was beginning to feel that he was losing control of this briefing.

"Never mind," said Logan. "Just me trying to be witty," he added, with a grin at Chuck.

"Yeah, well, five minutes in the penalty box for you. If you would, Randolph, please continue. Book three."

"Right, book three. In your novel, Ms. Fletcher, a village well is poisoned with a tasteless chemical …"

"A nerve agent," Cathie interrupted.

"Yes, and the results were spectacular. Hundreds died in the novel before someone began to suspect the root cause. Well, here, fortunately for us, a band of true incompetents planned to dump hundreds of gallons of a nasty, toxic cocktail into a fair-sized mountain lake, the water supply for two local mountain towns. However, our intrepid band of murderers either incorrectly calculated the dilution ratio for the rather sizable volume of the lake, or they couldn't be bothered to even try. The resulting mix wouldn't have been particularly harmful, let alone lethal."

“Wouldn’t have been?” Cathie asked. “What do you mean?”

“Well, unfortunately for our would-be terrorists, they failed to exercise proper precautions in handling such a murderous mess.”

“What?”

“They used very poorly sealed 55-gallon drums to transport the stuff on a bumpy road. The stuff just leaked out and all four bad guys died a pretty gruesome death. A cover story of attempted unlawful industrial dumping satisfied the locals, including the local PD, and that would have wrapped things up except for one little oddity.”

“Which was?”

“Well, shockingly, the men in those trucks weren’t U.S. citizens of Hispanic descent, as their IDs indicated.”

“And that was a surprise?” Cathie asked in astonishment.

“No, no, that wasn’t it. Without getting into too many weeds, it turned out that we got a positive ID on one of the guys. He had been brought into the U.S. through the San Bernardino Wildlife Refuge. The story is a little complicated, but a couple of Border Patrol agents …”

“A couple of awesome BP agents,” corrected Chuck.

“Well, they came on the scene in southern Arizona and helped us figure out that a group of guys …”

Chuck coughed with some irritation.

“… or maybe just one very competent man, was herding about ten or twelve recruits into the U.S. with the help of four coyotes. At some point—for instance at the scene the BP agents came upon—they, or he, must’ve decided they, or he, didn’t need the coyotes and wasted them and then moved off with his band of potential bad guys.”

“And the man you ID’d at the lake?”

“He was one of the men at the San Bernardino kill site. Can’t prove the other three at the lake were with the same group, but it kind of makes sense.”

“So, there is still a large group of these men in the U.S. and a good possibility that they may want to borrow another idea from one of my books.” Randy nodded and Cathie looked at her husband to gauge his reaction to this information. To her surprise and irritation, he seemed uninterested in the conversation and was perusing the original summary chart of book incidents and terrorist acts, printed as a handout.

"So, Logan," she asked pointedly, her brow furrowed in an invariable sign of displeasure, "what do you think?"

"What? Oh, sorry. It's just ..." he paused with a quick glance at the hardcopy slide. "Never mind, just something bugging me, something that should be obvious."

Cathie turned back to Randy with a scowl. "He's like this at home, you know."

"Hmm," Randy responded without committing himself. "So the last thread to this tangled web," he continued, using Cathie's book title for deliberate emphasis, "is that we've been trying to determine the identity of the shooter, given the capability that he displayed. There are probably fewer guys like this in the world than there are pro quarterbacks in the NFL, and they're not nearly as well known."

"Which reminds me, Randy, did you bring down the folder with the resumés and mug shots?" asked Chuck.

Randy patted a black, unlabeled three-ring binder at his elbow. "Right here, boss."

"Fine. I want to look at that later but we won't have to keep Logan and Cathie around for that."

There was a brief silence, and then Cathie spoke up briskly. "Well, you seem to have evidence to support a theory that someone is using my novels for ideas on terrorist attacks. And I'm sure you'll agree with 'theory' rather than 'fact' and 'evidence' rather than 'proof.' Now, Chuck, while I was wading through that awful paperwork, both you and Logan repeatedly emphasized that you somehow needed *my* help. So far, I haven't seen how. So Randy, I think it's time for the other shoe to drop, don't you?"

"And gentlemen," said Logan with a grin, "she is definitely like this at home!"

Randy, who all along had been thinking that this would be the more interesting and fun part of the briefing, was now clearly hesitant to go to the next chart under the stern, somewhat impatient gaze of this very formidable woman. However, there was no escape, so he reluctantly clicked "forward," saying nothing and making a great show of fussing with the projector's focus and elevation. The title read, "Options for Poisoning C-squared F's Next Novel."

Cathie stared at the slide as though it were some extinct life form—perhaps a dodo—that Randy had somehow conjured back into existence and deposited before her for her examination. The men remained silent as they watched the muscles of her face tighten and her eyes scan down a list of potential options. At last, Cathie shook her head in utter disbelief and managed to force the words, "Are you fucking kidding me?" in a measured, barely constrained growl.

"Language, dear," said Logan. "I believe Randy may still be a minor." And turning to Chuck, he said with a distinctly patronizing touch, "I told you she'd take it well."

In the silence that followed, Randy did his best to stand very still and try to blend in with the furniture. He immediately sensed that this discussion might become quite emotional, and he, being the outsider, neither a spouse nor a friend, was liable to get trampled if he stepped out into this fracas. "Look, Cathie," Chuck began with the smoothest, most endearing tone he could muster.

"Look here yourself," Cathie interrupted, rolling over his opening with force, "I do this thing … it's called writing. I have ideas, I develop characters, I tell a story. If people like it, I sell books; if people don't, we live off of Logan's pension and I become very, very irritated. Just which one of you two geniuses thought I could just dribble in a little terrorist-tempting gibberish, somehow integrate it into the storyline and then get my publisher, not to mention my readers, to accept it?" she demanded, looking angrily from Chuck to Logan.

Randy was trapped. Though neither Chuck nor Logan threw him under the bus, they did wait patiently for Randy to do the honorable thing and throw himself under. "That would be me, Ms. Fletcher," he said at last.

"You?" Cathie asked, amazed, staring at Randy as though he had just materialized in the room by magical invocation.

"Yep. Guilty, I'm afraid. It's just that, well, I've read your novels and I believe I understand your main characters: who they are, how they might be expected to behave. I also believe that some of the recommendations on the slide, that is, some of the possibilities for baiting a would-be terrorist, aren't that much of a stretch, given that someone with your talent and experience would be the one to work them into the plot. It's a lot to ask from someone who takes pride in her own creativity, but I, we, could be extremely flexible. In fact, if you could come up with something better, well, really all we care about is nailing the guys who have been stealing your ideas."

Cathie paused a moment, and the angry look, the tightened lips, the narrowed eyes, the signs Logan had known of an impending eruption, melted miraculously from her face to be replaced by a half smile and a much softened demeanor that seemed to combine barely stifled amusement and a near approach to respect.

"Well," Cathie began again, turning back towards Chuck and Logan, "I suppose you two bozos would have abused my ears with appeals to patriotism and the good of the nation. Thankfully, your young genius here appealed to my foolish weakness, the soft underbelly of every creative person … her ego! Well done, Grasshopper!" she smiled back towards him. "You have learned! All right," she said, "no promises, but I'll listen. I just want you to know that if this novel is a best seller, you don't get a cut!"

"Understood," Randy said, breathing normally for the first time since his briefing had begun. "And also, Ms. Fletcher …"

"OK, fine, and can you please stop calling me Ms. Fletcher as though I were your third grade teacher, Randy. It's Cathie, OK?"

"Cathie, you've got it. Well, uh, Cathie, I, well, we also know you have a relationship with a woman named Elaya who seems quite interested in your next novel. And we know that you are aware that she is married to one Hasim bin Wazari. Perhaps you may not be aware that he has a rather poor reputation. In fact, he may have no connection with the events taken from your books, but …"

"That's enough, Grasshopper," Chuck said with a firm, quiet delivery.

Randy looked puzzled, and Logan jumped in, "Just tell her, Chuck. She's going to figure it out if she hasn't already."

"Jeez, Logan, you really want me to walk the plank, don't you? Some of this info is going to get tucked away, and when that happens …"

"Look, Chuck, you know you'll have to get her briefed on all the material she's going to need. C'mon, man, in for a penny in for a pound.

Besides, 'going to get tucked away' just means that you can use your discretion for now and beg forgiveness later, yes?"

Chuck gave his friend a serious, professional stare, while he tried to search within his own mind and guarantee that he wasn't making a foolish decision based on friendship rather than on a serious need that would justify a liberal interpretation of the rules. In the end, his features relaxed to a neutral state and he gave Randy a curt nod.

"Well, without getting into the realm of pure speculation, there's at least a chance that this bin Wazari is involved. He's got big cash, lots of people resources, and has a strong, traditional Wahhabi religious background, meaning plenty of disdain for the West, Jews, and all other Muslim sects."

"Disdain? Really?" asked Cathie, sarcastically.

Randy shot a quick glance at Logan, who just shrugged noncommittally. "Yes, indeed," Randy continued, "he wants them all dead. Also," he added, "might it be possible to slip a little advance copy to Ms. Elaya?"

"Doubt it," Cathie shook her head emphatically. "It would be out of character for me to contact her, especially after I practically had to scrape her off me at my college reunion. On the other hand," she considered thoughtfully, "if she were to contact me, or if we just happened to meet again … maybe not a good possibility, but a possibility."

Chuck glanced at his watch. "And there may just be a possibility that lunch has arrived, courtesy of the U.S. government." Cathie winced and he quickly added, "Actually, Rosa's Barbecue ain't bad at all. Let's take a break."

Randy propped the conference room door open and proceeded to help his administrator bring in a few aluminum containers that gave off a very pleasant aroma of smoked meats. Plates, plastic utensils, napkins, sodas, and a bowl full of ice followed.

"Hey, Randy, mind if I take a look at this?" Logan asked, holding up the unlabeled notebook containing the potential shooter profiles.

"Go ahead. Not much to go on, unfortunately."

Logan flipped through the notebook. Randy was right. The information on professional killers and firearm virtuosos was thin, at least for those identified as Russian, Chinese, probable Chechen, Central

American, or unknown. But towards the back, under a separate sub-tab labeled U.S. Special Forces, was a larger set of bios including photos and complete historical data: birth place, branch of service, personality profile, etc.

"So why the U.S. servicemen, Randy?"

Randy turned back from the table where he was digging into the brisket. "Well, it wouldn't be the first time someone in our armed forces went rogue, Logan. Chuck had me chasing down the location of all of these guys during the time of the border killing as well. Took me two weeks to eliminate them. C'mon," he added, "food's getting cold. Rosa's Barbecue is one of the few good things around here. You don't want to miss it while it's hot!"

Logan idly flipped through the final pages of the folder. Two weeks chasing down the locations of potential U.S. shooters. He had to admire Randy's perseverance and Chuck's thoroughness. Logan's hands had begun to close the book as the last pages fluttered by, but in an instant he was bolt upright in his seat, staring at a photo with the text, "James Kulwicki, honorable discharge, deceased," directly below.

"Hey, I've seen this guy! Hey, Randy, Chuck, I've seen this guy."

Randy took a quick glance. "Afraid not, Logan. He's been dead for years. Killed, murdered actually, while working for a security company after he left the service."

"But I'd swear …" Logan began. Chuck came over, balancing his plate, a drink, and a dessert, looked over Logan's shoulder and turned grey.

"You OK, boss? I thought you liked Rosa's?"

"Yeah, fine, just sit down and eat, Randy. Where'd you say you think you saw this guy, Logan?" Chuck asked, exercising a firm control over his voice.

"At a restaurant in Tucson, with the most beautiful, well hell, you remember her, Ms. Blue Hawaii, aka Luana Chu, CEO of Infinity Services Group."

"Not possible, brudda. He's dead."

"I'm telling you, it looked just like him."

"And I'm telling you he's dead. I actually saw the remains. Not a pretty sight. C'mon, man, you can't tell me you were actually staring at this guy while Ms. Chu was in the vicinity?"

"Well, I guess I didn't actually focus on him, and it was just a glance, but still …"

"Well, there you have it," Chuck said much more cheerfully. "You were blinded by the light. Besides, a lot of people look like this guy. C'mon, get some lunch."

Logan reluctantly rose from the table and headed for the food, wondering why Chuck should be so insistent that the man he had seen was dead. But it wasn't really "insistent" as much as anxious; anxious to crush the conversation; anxious to prove Logan wrong. I suppose seeing someone's murdered corpse could make you a little emotional, but still … As he was filling his plate, Logan couldn't help noticing that Chuck had hastily grabbed the notebook and left the room. Chuck returned a moment later, empty-handed.

Logan ate his food in silence. Randy was deeply involved in a straw-man discussion of plot lines with Cathie, while Chuck would occasionally jump in with a comment or question. It was clear that Randy had made a good impression on Cathie and not simply because he had read and retained much from her previous novels. Randy was a straight-up guy who spoke his mind, wasn't afraid to be wrong or even ridiculed to some degree, and maintained a healthy respect for Cathie (they were, after all, asking a lot) while not fawning over her or simply agreeing with everything she said.

Logan sat quietly wondering why Chuck had handled him so roughly regarding Ms. Blue Hawaii's date. It was that hangnail feeling again, that feeling that he was at the edge of understanding something but that his conclusion kept snagging just before he could pull his thoughts into clear focus. He picked at his food and his hands, deprived of the book of assassin bios, took up Randy's second chart once again. He stared at item two from *A Little Local Color*, the cyber-attack to shut down servers, and at Randy's comment in the margin: "Specific Purpose Unknown." Chuck had said that no data was lost, the primary damage being the pain of having to reload terabytes of tactical and sim code from backup systems. And he considered his own seemingly random comment about the attack being incomplete. Even he hadn't known what he had meant by that choice remark, but the whole thing just didn't seem right. It was as odd, in a way, as the thought of ninja raccoons; or as odd as Alpha having to go to backups just as though their systems had been hacked … by ninja raccoons. This time, the image in Logan's mind was one from his childhood where, as a budding young engineer, he had pushed two magnets closer and closer together, a tiny fraction of an inch at each adjustment, until the magnetic force of attraction had overcome the friction of the table surface and the magnets had leaped together with a satisfying "clack."

"What if it wasn't an accident, what if the two events were related?" he blurted out suddenly.

"I presume you're referring to the first two times when we met," said Cathie, the first to respond to Logan's seemingly random outburst. "I always suspected that you manipulated events to have me alone with you. I mean that Ferris wheel at the fair stopped with us at the very top for over a half hour. I vaguely remember you kissing me. And then the picnic date where the perfectly good rental car fails to start, but you suddenly realize you can fix it after another three hours. I have to admit, it was a beautiful afternoon, and the company wasn't all bad, though I believe you took unfair advantage of the situation. Oh my," said Cathie with a sweet, playful look, "I think I'm making Grasshopper blush." She turned back to Logan with a look of mock sternness on her face. "I was always pretty sure you somehow arranged that last one. Don't tell me you're confessing to both, now," Cathie finished, with a smile.

"What? Oh yeah," Logan said with a nervous laugh, "actually I did set up both. My bad. But, uh, what I meant this time was the Alpha fire and the cyber-attack. They both have the same consequence, forcing a painstaking reload from backups."

"Are you serious?" asked Chuck with some annoyance. "So someone carries out an overt attack in one case and then somehow manages to execute a completely covert op and they both result in what? A pain in everybody's ass, a lot of overtime pay, and about a three-month setback at most. That's fucking pinot, man!"

"Unless …" Randy interjected, but then stopped suddenly, a puzzled look on his face. "Pinot? What?"

"Just shut the fuck up, OK?" Chuck said, with surprising vehemence.

Randy gave Chuck an astonished look and remained silent, but sent a quick glance towards Logan, who finished for him "... the attack isn't complete. And don't mind him," Logan added, with a serious, somewhat disapproving scowl at Chuck, "we're just 'wining.' I'll explain later over several stiff drinks."

"I think I see," Cathie nodded. "And we'll talk about how you tricked me into falling in love with you later."

"Well, am I the only one in this room still baffled?" asked Chuck in annoyance.

Randy's eyes shifted around the room from person to person, counting silently with his lips: one, two, three. One.

"Do NOT open your mouth and say a word, or you're gonna be one very squashed grasshopper!"

Randy's lips clamped shut, but Cathie felt no constraint whatsoever, and, grinning, shot back, "Well, Chuck, you had some good years, but they're apparently all behind you now. Yes. Yes, I am afraid that you're the only one that still doesn't get it."

"Oh well, hell. I swear this job isn't worth it anyway. Enlighten me, would you?"

"What does one do with backups? One loads them onto every sensitive server used by the military and by defense contractors. And what if one were to add a little something special, like a bug in the GPS software? The applications are classified, the GPS code isn't. You insert it during servicing the off-site backups, a whole hell of a lot easier than attacking the actual servers, and you do it completely covertly."

"So wait," Chuck began, "you're telling me that, even though your novel postulated an attack on GPS systems of commercial ships and planes, the real targets here are U.S. military systems? Ships, aircraft and missiles?"

"Why not?" asked Cathie.

"Well, I'll tell you why not," Chuck began, but he faltered as he was collecting his thoughts, and rather than the withering argument he had been contemplating, what finally came out was, "C'mon, that's not an act of terrorism, not like that amateurish poisoning attempt with the trucks, this is, this is ..."

"It's a coordinated attack by a major foreign power, designed to cripple most of our tactical weapon systems," Logan finished for him.

"Oh c'mon, seriously? And we're going to leap to this to explain why raccoons took out the servers at Alpha? They found the little fried bodies, you know."

"I think it might not do any harm to re-investigate that fire," Logan began. "Of course, there isn't going to be much to investigate. I imagine once the Tucson and Alpha fire departments concurred on an accidental cause, it was all over. Those buildings were leveled and the sites cleared in two weeks. I don't suppose somebody kept the raccoons?"

"Yeah," said Chuck with scorn, "the CSI unit of the Tucson PD has them in cryogenic storage right next to a little grey space alien and that notorious parakeet that murdered four people on the south side."

"Funny!" Logan said drily.

Randy leaned over and whispered to Logan, "And he's like that all the time."

"Did you say something, Randy?" Chuck asked, glaring angrily in Randy's direction.

"No, nothing boss."

"That's right, you didn't!"

"Oh all right, Chuck, dial down the testosterone for a minute," Cathie interjected.

"Why does this seem so unlikely to you?" Logan quickly added.

"Logan, you've been playing with Randy's chart for the last half hour. Why don't you put it up on the projector?" Randy clicked to the corresponding slide, and Chuck continued. "Here's what's bugging me. We have three instances of ideas being stolen from Cathie, and even if we take your assumption that the GPS and the cyber-attack were connected, we still have the odd duck, the poisoning attempt." —

"To be honest, boss, we had an odd duck before: the cyber-attack. Now the groupings have changed, two for a national threat, one for terrorists, kind of stupid ones."

"Hey, if they can't follow directions that's not my fault," Cathie joked.

"Yeah, and thank God they didn't. OK, Logan, you started this hare, what do you say?"

"Well," Logan replied cautiously, "here are the possibilities as I see it. The GPS being correlated with the cyber-attack seems more logically a national action, the poisoning not."

"Obviously," Chuck replied with some impatience.

"There are a couple of explanations for that," Logan continued, ignoring Chuck's irritability, but at the same time wondering what was bothering his friend. "The first is that two distinct groups are stealing material from the novels. I sort of think of that one as the 'lightning strikes twice' theory. Doesn't seem likely. The second is that one or more of these incidents is nothing but coincidence, and if so I'd vote for the lake poisoning. Terror by poisoning a water supply isn't exactly all that creative." Logan regretted the words as soon as they had left his mouth, and he could sense rather than see the waves of anger rolling off Cathie and the scowl on her face as he concentrated on the projector. *How, how do I keep putting my big foot in my mouth?* he thought to himself. Chuck shuffled nervously and Logan decided to press on. Damage done. "The third, which I really don't like at all, is that there is a connection, not so much a connection by a common goal, more likely a connection of shared interest—maybe only temporarily—and shared resources; some sort of weird alliance, but with a single leadership structure."

"That's good, logical thinking, Logan," Chuck said sarcastically, "but it gets us exactly nowhere!"

Randy had known his boss long enough to realize something was wrong. Something had drastically changed in his demeanor since just before lunch. Chuck was clearly irritated with his friend and was openly ridiculing him even though the entire purpose of this meeting had been to secure the help of Cathie and Logan. If this kept up, the entire effort would blow up right here. He would need to get to the bottom of Chuck's irritation at some point, but for now it would have to wait. He needed to diffuse the tension and get everybody re-focused. As the junior partner here, that would mean he'd have to use cleverness rather than a heavy hand. He sighed inwardly. Being clever was always more tiring than being autocratic.

"Well, maybe not exactly nowhere, boss," he began cautiously. "You're right, the poisoning is the odd duck," he began, throwing Chuck a deliberate bone, "and the correlation of the cyber-attack and the GPS is just speculation. But, we can get some techno-geeks digging into some of the backups that were reloaded, let's say at Boeing or Northrop, and do the same with Alpha. If we find something, that would prove the theory AND pretty much prove that the Alpha fire was no accident. And if that's the case, we've got our poison pill!"

"I think I see," said Cathie. "If we can determine that someone has a means of getting into weapon system software through the backup process, we can throw out another notion for them to exploit that entree and use that as the bait. I think I see a couple of ways we could make that very attractive, but we'd have to be really certain we could prevent a data loss. We'd really be dropping our shorts on this one."

"Crude, but well put, dear," Logan smiled.

"And the lake poisoning?" Chuck asked.

"Well, boss, if the bad guys are connected at the head, we take off the head. If they really are uncorrelated, well … we've got nothing on that piece. But still, we have something, right?"

Chuck considered, trying to shove his own internal anxiety down and think clearly. At last he gave a tight nod of agreement. "All right, Randy, you'd better hit the local Target for some more underwear and toothpaste, you'll be heading off to Tucson with these two. I'll have a room at Rickman made available for the duration. You three have some work to do."

"What about you, boss?"

"I've got something to take care of in Oakland. I'll join you later."

As the three men began to rise, Cathie remained stubbornly seated and said to Chuck, "Aren't we forgetting something?"

"Umm, well, thanks for your support, Cathie," Chuck said weakly.

"Nice try, Chief, but I'm talking about more tangible compensation." Chuck seemed puzzled and Randy looked nervously from Cathie to Chuck. Only Logan remained calm. This, he felt, would be interesting.

"Uh, sure, Cathie, uh, time and material, plus travel expenses. I'm not sure what kind of rate I can get, but I'll try to …"

"Oh, don't be silly, Chuck, I'm not trying to extort money from our prostrate federal budget. What I want won't cost you a penny. Look, if I have to rewrite my novel to work in our little poison pill, it'll take time.

You'll need to call my publisher and apply a little pressure. Tell him I need full creative license with the plot, including material he previously rejected." At Randy's puzzled look, Cathie added, "That would be the love story between the heroine and her ex-Navy RIO. Very key to throwing the bad guys off the track. A little bit of a white lie," she grinned. She paused for a moment, and the grin faded.

"What's the problem, babe?" Logan asked immediately.

"Well, it's the timeline. I mean, we've got some serious work to do before we can even go to the first proofs, let alone full pubs to meet a Christmas deadline. We can press hard, but we'll need some help compressing the pubs timeline."

"I'll talk to the director," said Chuck, still with a glum look on his face. "We've, ummm, used the same publisher before. You might say they've gotten a lot of business from the agency for years. If my boss buys in to this scheme, he can discuss priorities with the publisher. It wouldn't surprise me if they could speed things up for us."

"OK," Cathie agreed, with apprehension still clouding her face, "but as for my love story, that is, the mandatory inclusion of my love story, I want him to make the call!" she exclaimed, pointing an emphatic finger at Randy. "It'll take a silver-tongued devil like Grasshopper and not a ham-handed sourpuss like you to convince Geoffrey."

Logan chuckled quietly and Randy did his best to hide a disloyal grin. At last, Chuck forced a smile and replied, "Deal!"

Chapter Eighteen

Strategic Considerations

For the first time in many years, Hasim bin Wazari had been unable to rest peacefully. Despite his luxurious surroundings, his hedonistic comforts, and his choice of sensual gratification, he had lain awake thinking back to the pivotal event in his early life. In hindsight, he had been no more than a foolish, zealous boy, risking his life for adventure in an obscure service to Allah. He had, as the fates allowed, played a not-insignificant role in taking the prize. But with such a prize came blood. Intrigue, assassination, blackmail, and a feud within the royal house itself followed the device for years. But by Allah's divine grace, the power and the responsibility had ultimately fallen to him.

Years of careful planning had followed, and then more years of patient waiting, waiting for the precise confluence of political events on a global scale. No biblical prophet could have shown more faith and forbearance. But bin Wazari knew full well that only one wish was allowed from this genie's lamp and that there would be only one opportunity to use the precious gift he had acquired.

Hasim bin Wazari had grown in wealth, power, and girth through those decades of waiting. During that time, he had demonstrated a calm demeanor worthy of a servant of Allah. What was written was written. Hasim would act when it was time, and would follow the will of God. Success would follow.

In recent days, however, as it became apparent that the time of waiting was soon to end, the burden of responsibility had begun to press upon him like an unseen weight. He could no longer simply smile and pontificate on Allah's will. He was now required to act, and his decisions in the next weeks would either lead to a great victory or a hideous disaster. While it was true that what was written was written, it appeared that Allah had handed Hasim bin Wazari the pen. No man of true worth could lightly undertake what must now be done, and Hasim felt the burden. However, he concealed his doubts as well as he could. He must show no outward signs of anxiety during the meeting that was about to take place.

***

Ivor joined his host on the patio once again, where the fragrance of saffron rice, boiled eggs, toast, and coffee filled the still morning air. The sun, already up for several hours, was warming the eastern walls of the city below, the reflected intensity felt even at this distance and the warming air portending a brutally hot day to come. Another man, seated at the patio table, rose as Ivor approached.

"My dear Colonel Zareb," said bin Wazari, "let me introduce our new associate, Mr. Ivor Vachenko, thanks to Allah for his kindness." The colonel rose and bowed slightly before extending his hand to Vachenko, who took it, smiling.

"A pleasure, Colonel," said Vachenko.

"Sit, please," Hasim continued. A servant quickly stood at Ivor's side to fill his water glass. Ivor continued to smile as he performed a quick assessment on the colonel. He was a short man, somewhat barrel-shaped, but with a neatly tailored uniform, a meticulously groomed short, black beard, thick eyebrows, and brilliant and intelligent dark eyes. He wore an expression of polite noncommittal wariness, neither hostile nor completely trusting in spite of Hasim's gracious introduction. A capable man, Vachenko supposed, though perhaps rather dull. But he would be careful to withhold judgment for now. He smiled amiably at the colonel as he reached for the toast.

"I was just informing Colonel Zareb of our accord, our commitment of mutual support, and when I spoke to him of your relationship with your unnamed benefactor, he became nearly giddy with excitement at the opportunity to immediately put our friendship to use."

Ivor turned a questioning face to the colonel, and though he could not by any means imagine this blank-faced man as being giddy about anything, he asked politely, "I am fully at the service of Hasim bin Wazari, and therefore completely at yours. How can I or my associates be of assistance?"

"Ah, well," began the colonel, seeming somewhat embarrassed as to how to begin. "There are several things that we … need to acquire. My researchers are still investigating some rather technical aspects of, well, let us just say, we will need some tactical weapon system software, several Alpha products, rather outdated. When we are fully certain of their description, I will inform you."

"You will have this information tomorrow before you leave," Hasim said firmly to Ivor, but with his eyes focused harshly on Zareb.

"Yes, Excellency, tomorrow," the colonel repeated.

Hasim smiled a crocodile smile. "The next item is something where your fortuitous relationship with your, hmm, other benefactor may be a blessing from Allah. Continue, Colonel."

The colonel, clearly ill at ease, forced a smile in Vachenko's direction. "We require, that is, we believe we may need several, well, two, MiG-29s, of the type currently in service in the Iranian air force. His Excellency believes your unnamed benefactor may have access to such equipment. They are older, of course, but completely serviceable for our needs."

Ivor sat astonished. Never had he expected such a request. It was true that the aircraft Zareb was seeking was an older model, but still, a MIG-29! Two, no less! Could Wan Chu really make such an arrangement? And the cost? How to approach Wan Chu with such a request? Through Stone and hence through Luana? Yes, that would be possible. A delicate, tentative feeler. Stone would know how to be discreet. And the transaction. How could he arrange such an exchange? This was much, much more than Ivor had ever anticipated, beyond anything he had ever attempted.

His confused and troubled look seemed to amuse bin Wazari, who eyed him appraisingly and chuckled aloud. "All things are possible, my friend, by the good will of Allah! There are many details to be considered and much work to be done. For now, simply contacting your business associate and determining if any such arrangement is possible will suffice. That is all: a simple question. However," Hasim added harshly, his jovial façade banished in an instant, "time is a luxury which is not ours to enjoy. Colonel Zareb will provide you with the information that you will need for all of our transactions before you depart tomorrow. May I rely upon you to make your discreet inquiry no later than, say, the following day?"

"Yes, of course, Hasim, and I will press for an immediate response."

"But gently, gently, yes? We would not want to alarm our potential ally in the great work of Allah."

Vachenko nodded and continued, "When I speak with him, he may ask, he may desire me to provide an offer or respond to the proposal of a fee. I must confess, I have never arranged a purchase of such magnitude and I feel my ignorance deeply. What amount might I assume would be favorable to you in this arrangement?"

"Calm yourself, Ivor," replied bin Wazari. "Even this small detail has been considered." The colonel nodded silently. "We will not haggle. We believe that twenty-five million U.S. will be more than adequate; per aircraft, of course. It is an older model. We will also expect delivery to an unobtrusive location. The colonel has three possibilities from which to choose. And Ivor, for your efforts, when successful, I propose a small commission. Shall we say ten percent?"

Ivor's mouth hung open. Five million dollars! It was a spectacular amount that beggared the miserly stipends from Wan Chu. What he could accomplish with five million! "Hasim, your Excellency, I shall do as you ask."

"Good, good," bin Wazari smiled, the harmless, jovial persona once again upon his face. "By the will of Allah, all shall move forward to our mutual benefit!"

***

And yet, another restless night followed. The following day, after Ivor's departure, bin Wazari had sat in close conference with Colonel Zareb.

"Can it be done, Massoud?" bin Wazari finally asked.

The colonel fidgeted in his chair and sat thoughtfully for several minutes, and then recited, as though to himself: "The device itself has been preserved as though it were the jeweled sword of the great prophet. Every test has been done to ensure that it will function. It will fit within the great missile, but the components that Ivor Vachenko must acquire are crucial. The launch aircraft has been kept with nearly the same care as the device itself, and it will perform its function, provided again that Vachenko can provide the necessary computer circuitry and algorithms. Even the aircraft transponder has been verified. Like a ghost from the past, it will shout its Iranian origin. The MiGs will fly as a most plausible escort." Zareb was silent for another period of time, then added, "Yes, Excellency. It can be done. Iran will proceed with an unprovoked nuclear attack on the Zionists. Israel will respond in kind. Once the dust has dispersed …"

"The great Kingdom of Saud will be the dominant power in all the Middle East!" Bin Wazari finished, with a satisfied smile. "My friend, I will sleep well tonight!"

***

Chuck had rarely been so angry with himself. His first blunder had been overreacting to Logan's alleged recognition of James Kulwicki, a man known to be dead for years. Chuck had badly mishandled the situation, only recovering slightly and barely managing to cover his gaffe with his rationale, and a good rationale, that in the presence of Ms. Chu, Ms. Blue Hawaii as Logan still referred to her, any man could make an honest mistake in identification. But he continued to mentally kick himself, for he had allowed that one incident to completely rattle him, as evidenced by his angry, unproductive, and argumentative behavior during the rest of the meeting in LA. Cathie was probably right. His best years were behind him. Yet he still couldn't believe how his professional demeanor had been shattered by that one photograph and by Logan's assertion that this one man that he thought he had buried had sprung back to life. *Damn it, damn it, damn it!* Chuck growled to himself.

And now, Chuck sat at a computer terminal in the downtown Oakland library, wearing a pair of dirty jeans, worn Converse tennis shoes, and a faded Raiders T-shirt, surrounded, he presumed, by sex offenders, child predators, underage teens surfing porn, and perhaps one or two legitimate students too poor to own computers.

As he logged onto his Facebook account—just another anonymous man with a fictional identity sending small, sadly unimportant messages to a handful of equally fictional "friends"—he took careful stock of his current mental state. A mistake here would make the blunder in Los Angeles seem like a flake of snow compared to a blizzard. He thought very carefully and wrote: "You'll never guess who turned up at the friends of LGBT meeting last month. Our old friend Shirley Donaldson! At least, that's what Agnes told me. What a rotten time for me to miss a meeting! But now that Shirley's back in town, I'm determined to renew our acquaintance. Can you believe it after all this time? I'll keep you all updated on her if I can get in touch. Really, who'd have guessed? Our old pal Shirley!"

Of the eight total friends belonging to "Alex," Chuck's online persona, only one mattered, only one was real: Sean Carlos DeFranco. Chuck had always hated this name and wondered why someone in this man's position would so abuse common sense and insist on this "clever" scrambled acronym rather than a perfectly random name such as Sammy Watson, or Ingred Ehlmendorf. Chuck supposed it was ego combined with years as a career political hack, years during which one could get a badly overinflated estimate of one's own intelligence. Still, it grated annoyingly on Chuck. However, he reminded himself, for all his professionalism, he had still stepped in a pile of shit in LA, a mess he himself would still need to clean up. He put aside his misgivings about Sean Carlos and re-read his note. Clear, concise, with no interpretation or postulation; a simple statement of fact. And what if Logan really were wrong? What if "Ms. Blue Hawaii's date" just resembled Kulwicki? Well, in that case he'd be throwing "Agnes" under the bus for her stupid misinformation. In the meantime, he'd be attempting to contact Shirley, using a dusty line of communication that had been dormant for years and was a bit more old-school. He wondered if he could still find a pay phone.

Chuck hit "enter," updating his account with his latest giddy news. Sean Carlos DeFranco, Chuck sniffed. Stupid, stupid, stupid. Sean Carlos DeFranco. Sec Def! Of course, there was at least a little stirring of professional pride within Chuck that the only other actual friend on "Alex's" account was the Secretary of Defense.

Chapter Nineteen

Local Distractions

Chuck was MIA. Randy, Logan, and Cathie had been ensconced in a windowless, cell-like office at Rickman Air Force Base for over two weeks, or rather, Randy and Logan had. Cathie had lasted exactly three days and then had simply refused to try to work in, what she called, "this supermax prison environment." "Honestly," she had added, "it's no wonder that every defense contract is over budget and late to delivery. I would think mass suicides would thin out the engineering staff pretty quickly." In the end, she had agreed to come in each day and work for two hours on what now seemed a plausible story line. To make it believable—that had been the goal—all three, with Chuck's approval, had agreed that some classified information would need to be spilled. With Logan's background and Cathie and Logan's wide set of friends in the aerospace business, it made sense that a few unguarded fragments would drop, to be vacuumed up by the human black hole that was Cathie Clarke Fletcher. And now that Cathie was looking to a publish date in November or December at the latest, she was working twelve hour days: details of classified bait approved for release discussed in the morning, writing and editing from ten to four, an early dinner, then a re-read from four to six, then at least a forty-five minute call with Geoffrey to discuss status.

Logan's and Randy's days were equally long, though duller; the primary creative impetus being Cathie's. They continued to work details, Logan often harassing Bart, Kevin, or Gary who had received a soft brief—basically a license to cooperate with Logan—that had brought surprised and resentful comments from Bart, including, "How come you get to have all the fun and we still have to work for a living?"

"Because you're still getting paid!" Logan had replied. "Now, tell me about the schedule for the computer reload."

Gary had remained silent, but Logan guessed, uncomfortably, that Gary had probably discerned more than he should have, while Kevin summarized the feelings of the three with his universal comment, "Bite me!"

Ironically, as the days passed, it was Cathie who became the driving force in the group, prodding them all towards an aggressive publishing date. The date had been part of the agreement with Geoffrey that had also allowed the inclusion of Cathie's love story. When the others complained, Cathie pointed an accusatory finger at Randy. "Blame Grasshopper! He's the one that agreed to the November release!"

In truth, the timetable had been driven from the start by the projected April software reload at Alpha. It was essential that the book should have several months of circulation prior to that reload. This event offered a unique opportunity for a terrorist cyber-attack, such as the insertion of a complex worm that would snatch the critical encryption of the next generation of tactical weapon datalinks. But … there must be enough time to allow their adversary to sift through Cathie Fletcher's novel, discover the golden opening, and devise a method to exploit it.

The temptation was more than sufficient. The ability to crack a U.S. tactical datalink would allow a foreign adversary to "subscribe" into the information network of aircraft, ships, and weapons; to redirect attacks, to cause weapons to become ineffective, or worse, to be directed towards friendly forces. Next generation weapons had, for years, been envisioned to operate and communicate on a common secure network. The subsequent ability to develop situational awareness from multiple platforms, to re-target in flight, to share advanced reconnaissance information from previously launched weapons, resulted in a substantial probability-of-kill improvement factor. But here was the rub: it required a secure link, a rock solid, guaranteed, unimpeachably secure network. Disrupt the network, or better still, infiltrate the network, and every tactical weapon employed in combat would become worse than useless. The risk to national security was stupendous.

Alpha was the key. The fire that had destroyed the servers containing the tactical code for nearly all of their deployed or development weapons had created one, and only one, opportunity for a spectacular data-poaching coup: the scheduled April boot of the new servers and the massive software reload. The scope of this effort, the necessary utilization of the backup systems, the anticipated time pressure, conflicting priorities, and chaos created by the large numbers of people and the huge quantities of data to be restored, provided a fabulous opportunity to introduce a "hunter" worm. The worm would replicate and devour the encryption into its own structure, and then be extracted in the obscuring cloud of hectic activity. With the information stolen and the system sterilized, leaving no trace of the intrusion, the multi-billion dollar inventory of United States tactical weapons would be rendered … useless.

Logan and Randy felt the pressure both from Cathie, who Logan realized, was as tenacious as a terrier when it came to a release date for one of her novels, and from the slightly less intense pressure of preserving the security of the U.S. tactical weapons while baiting a would-be state-sponsored terrorist organization.

"Well," said Randy, one late Wednesday evening, "that's why we get paid the big bucks!"

"Speak for yourself, Grasshopper. I don't get paid shit! Plus overtime which is … well, more shit!"

A long time later, when Logan glanced at his watch, he abruptly exclaimed, "Crap! Listen … it's 7:20! No más, no más! Cathie will have given up on me long ago. Why don't we get a sandwich and a beer? And I'll tell you what, no start 'til eight, no, nine tomorrow. This saving-the-free-world shit is wearing me out!"

Randy yawned and seemed about to argue, thought better of it, and nodded. "Man, Logan, I'm beat. And it's not just the long hours, it's just, you know, just …"

"Being 'on' every single minute we're here. I know! I've been on a few ball-busting proposals over the years that have been like this. It's not just the hours, it's that you can't take a quiet piss while you're working on them. C'mon, my friend," he said, with a pat on Randy's back. Let's call it. "I know this place …"

***

Randy and Logan were seated in the Skybox outdoor balcony, kicking back their second beer and looking out over the flickering lights of Tucson. Far to the southeast, lightning flashes lit the Rincon Mountains, huge rolling thunderheads briefly visible then vanishing to uniform blackness. Nearly a minute later, an extended rumble reached their comfortable perch, where a late-summer breeze brought at least a pleasant flow of the still-too-humid air. A group of women, laughing and talking over each other, were seated at the table next to theirs.

Logan looked up and recognized one of the women, Becky Amhurst, who smiled and waved at him. Logan smiled and returned the wave. "You know them, Logan?" Randy asked. Logan looked back and was surprised to see that all the fatigue and lethargy had vanished from Randy, who was smiling at the group of women. Logan followed his gaze, clearly directed towards a petite, dark-haired young woman that he didn't recognize, who now seemed to be blushing and looking down at her place setting.

"No, well, I know the one nearest to the railing. An acquaintance from my working days, that is, from my working days when I still got paid. Can't say I know the one you're staring at."

"What, staring, I was just …"

"Staring, Randy. Can't say I blame you. She's cute. Not exactly my type, well, my type thirty years ago! You know, hanging around you young folks is just plain irritating. However, there is at least one advantage that us oldsters have," he said, rising from his seat.

"Logan, what the hell are you doing? Oh, Jesus Christ!"

"Hey, Becky, good to see you," Logan said, as he strolled comfortably up to the table of women.

"Logan, not traveling with your usual band of Neanderthals? And who is the lovely young lad?"

"That would be Grasshopper, the young apprentice to my old CIA bud Chuck; here in town to do some unbelievably dull training at Rickman. And who might your friends be?" he asked with a winning smile. Becky introduced her first two friends, Jane Kramer and Stacy

Michaels, both women of about Becky's age, late forties or early fifties, senior engineers within Becky's software center. Logan smiled amiably and then looked questioningly at the young woman who had attracted Randy's attention.

"And this would be our 'Grasshopper' equivalent, Gail Kamenchek, just one year out of UW-Madison with a master's in computer science."

"And probably has an IQ equal to the sum of the rest of ours," added Jane. Gail blushed still further and briefly glanced up at Logan to say hello before dropping her eyes again.

"Well listen," Logan continued, "I wouldn't mind sitting down and maybe buying a round of drinks, but you seem to be out of seats." Randy, straining to hear every word, sat with an embarrassed and nervous look and tried to pretend he was staring out over the city, but kept irresistibly glancing in Logan's direction.

Becky smiled, sensing where Logan was going. "Well look, Gail, Logan and I are old friends. Would you mind keeping the other Grasshopper company for just a minute? Besides he looks a little lonely."

Jane and Stacy were both giggling uncontrollably as Gail rose with an accusatory look, straightened up, and then stepped over to the table where Randy was now unambiguously staring, his mouth hanging open slightly.

"Hi," Gail said, pulling her gaze upward to meet Randy's incredulous eyes. "I've just been thrown out so your friend can join our group. Do you mind?" she asked, motioning to Logan's abandoned chair. To Logan's astonishment and delight, and much to the amusement of the three older women, Randy leaped to his feet, losing his napkin and upsetting his water glass, thankfully, nearly empty.

"Please," Randy said, with a glance at Logan that caught a flickering wink before Logan turned his attention to the table of women and his back to Randy.

"Thank you. My name is Gail."

"Mine's Randy," he said, returning with embarrassment to his seat. "Would you like a drink?"

"Love one. Maybe that will get this sixteen-year-old girl's blush off my face. And then, maybe you can explain why we're both being called Grasshopper."

***

"Well, I guess that was a little mean," Logan whispered with a slightly guilty look on his face.

"It was entertainment, and we come here to be entertained, right?" she asked, eyeing each of her companions in turn. Both nodded and smiled, trying to suppress their giggles as they continued to glance towards Gail and Randy, hoping to be further amused.

"There, you see: entertained," Becky concluded.

"We'll see how it works out. I'm not sure Randy has ever been out on a date." Logan darted a quick look back towards him and barely suppressed an outburst of laughter. Becky and her friends were not as controlled, and they stared and laughed in amusement. Both Gail and Randy were being asked to show their IDs.

***

"I'm sure glad Logan and your friends are having a good time at my expense," Randy began, with the somewhat sour look he reserved for people that made fun of his boyish looks.

"Our expense," Gail corrected. "I've gone out with this bunch a few times now. You'd think they'd get tired of the joke, but they never do." Gail paused and looked towards the city, watching the distant lightning flashes. It gave Randy a minute to look more closely at this woman who had suddenly appeared at his table. Despite looking younger, she was probably in her mid-twenties. She had long, thick brown hair that she wore in a style that might seem old fashioned if it had not perfectly complemented her oval face and slender build. She had high cheekbones, large eyes of a color Randy had yet to determine, a narrow mouth that widened wonderfully when she smiled, and a soft chin. As she looked out over the city, Randy was able to catch the glow of lights reflected in those eyes. Green, he was certain of it.

***

After a while, Jane and Stacy seemed to have had their fill of watching the young couple, and with mutual nods of agreement, rose to head towards the bar.

"Well, Becky, you and the child woman seem to be the only ones with an available man," said Jane. "We'll be back. Maybe. Depending!" she smiled.

"Hey, I'm not exactly an available man!" Logan protested.

Becky just laughed. "No, I suppose you're not, Mr. Proper," she said, patting his hand, "but you are pretty good company. So tell me all about your lazy days of retirement, and I'll just sit here and fantasize," she said, with thinly veiled ambiguity.

***

"So after I graduated from UW, I came out here for an interview. The job seemed interesting right from the start. Not just applying what I had learned about computer systems and servers, but a chance to really work networked systems, encryption, secure links—all things that fascinated me when I was at school," Gail continued, responding to Randy's questioning. "The field is changing so fast, and I can actually see a really exciting future, maybe a career for me. Of course, when I came out to Tucson it was kind of a shock. As the airplane was coming down, it looked as though we were flying over a wasteland. Everything was so brown! I guess I was used to Madison where there are beautiful, huge, green trees just everywhere, lots of little lakes, streams, parks with acres of thick grass. At least," she added with a crooked smile, "when it's not all covered in three feet of snow. I still miss it though, I guess, but I've actually grown to love it here. It's beautiful, but in a different way. I like to hike the trails in the Catalinas; that's the mountains just north of here."

Gail suddenly stopped and lowered her eyes, a bit of her former blush returning to her face. "You're very polite to listen. I hope I'm not boring you. You could tell me a little about yourself, you know."

"Well, you're not boring me, and if you aren't, well, seeing anyone that would object, I'd like join you on one of those hikes, sometime. I mean, only if you wanted to," he added quickly. "As far as me, I guess it's a little-known fact that most three-letter-agency guys are pretty dull. Most of what I do is background research for my boss, and if I ever do get to go out on an assignment that's a little more interesting (Randy thought of the melted corpses in the trucks near Adams Lake), well, I can't talk about it. It makes us quite poor company as far as conversation, but we do often make good listeners. So tell me more about your experiences in Madison. I've been to Milwaukee a few times, done a little fishing in the local lakes, without much success, I might add, but never made it as far west as Madison."

Gail looked up and smiled, the light catching the translucent glow of her eyes. Definitely green. "OK, but stop me when you've had enough!"

***

"Well, Logan, your friend seems to have really hit it off with our Gail. Amazing. The one or two times we've coaxed her into going out with us, she has usually sat quietly at the table perusing her napkin and occasionally giving us a look of mild disgust."

"Randy's exceptional. And I don't just mean the lean, dark-haired, youthful good looks. He's smart, creative, and a pretty good communicator. Better than I was at his age."

"So you didn't become the eloquent devil capable of talking the VPs out of millions in precious research dollars until later in your career?"

"Hmm, not so much, and then mostly out of necessity."

"Not what I've heard, Logan. If only your wife would foolishly leave you for a younger man. So what are you doing with Randy?"

Logan's look of discomfort, brought on by some of Becky's openly covetous comments, didn't decrease at the sudden change of topic. He furrowed his brow, then tried to look relaxed, took a sip of his drink, and then letting out what was meant to be a lighthearted laugh, replied, "Well, just some really dull training at Rickman, just like I said."

"So … can't talk about it."

"No, I just …"

"Logan," Becky said, patting his hand again, "Don't try to kid someone who lives in that world. I get it."

Logan visibly relaxed. "Thanks. After decades of stumbling and bumbling around questions like that at cocktail parties with Cathie, it's kind of a relief to just say, 'I can't talk about it.'"

"However, you're not entirely off the hook. You need to buy me another drink and keep me company for a while longer. As she spoke, Logan could see the fatigue and stress on her face.

"So tell me about it," he said. "That is, tell me everything you can. I can be a pretty good listener."

"You know, I believe that. But do you really want to hear this shit?"

"Absolutely. I'm immune to this stress, remember?"

"Well, you asked for it." She paused, collecting her thoughts. "It's hard to know where to begin. Do you remember when we acquired CyberSecure?"

"I was packing my office when that was still in process. So I take it the deal went through."

"Yes. It's an interesting company with excellent credentials. You know, at a demo, they took three random laptops from our area and hacked into all three in no more than five minutes, I swear. Kind of embarrassing since all three were owned by good boys and girls who used all the recommended protocols for passwords and encryption. Actually, it was a little creepy. If you ever thought you had privacy, let alone anonymity, forget it!"

"Amen," said Logan seriously. He knew.

"We have the pleasure of working with them for the reload. Every scrap of code has to go through their scrubber as part of the process. It's some super-trick error-check software that uses … what do they call it? … pseudo-stochastic, heuristic, artificial intelligence algorithms. Hmmmm, try to say that five times, fast! And of course, we have a small army of people from ISG there, since they hold the backups for us. So imagine three organizations with three sets of intelligent, arrogant, hyper people all trying to meet a bullet-to-the-brain deadline."

"Sounds like monkeys and a football," Logan said, shaking his head.

"Delicately put, but yes, that pretty much says it," said Becky, with a tired, stress-tinged grin.

"Well," said Logan, seriously, clumsily patting her hand, "I believe if anyone can pull this off, you can. Sounds like you've got the lead, and you know the old saying, 'When you're in command, command!'"

"Will do." A moment later her face brightened. "Have a look at that," she spoke softly, inclining her head in the direction of the table where Gail and Randy were in quiet conversation, looking both happy and anxious, focused entirely on each other. "Ah, youth!" she said, with a light laugh.

***

As they left the restaurant, Logan had a tremendous amount to think about, and a fair bit of nagging guilt to deal with. Once again, he had truly enjoyed the time spent with Becky: her humorous work anecdotes, her constant rapid touching of his arm, his hand, his shoulder, and her well developed, non-stop flirtation. But the guilt was a natural consequence of allowing her to behave in that way, or certainly not discouraging it, in order to keep her talking. Because of her intimate involvement with the process and her somewhat casual concern for total security, at least with a known former employee, she had given him a tremendous amount of detail regarding the new buildings, servers, and the massive software reload and checkout scheduled for next April. It was information that he and Randy would be able to filter and provide to Cathie; the juicy bait on the hook that they hoped would tempt someone, presumably the same someone responsible for the earlier cyber-attacks, to venture upon the grand heist: the capture of the encryption code for the next generation of tactical datalinks. The information regarding CyberSecure, in particular, would need to be integrated into the book, exposing just enough vulnerability while leveraging their company's ability to prevent an unintentional leak. It could be done, but it would be tricky, and he and Randy would need to work like mules to get it done in time. Logan's shoulders ached with the thought.

***

Logan's impatience to confirm what he was already certain of—that the GPS code reloaded into the servers of aerospace companies around the country contained a sophisticated worm—had been steadily growing. He was also convinced that this code was designed to disrupt navigation systems of military aircraft and ships, and to seriously degrade the midcourse guidance of many tactical weapons, eroding their effectiveness significantly. But the process was going slowly, and the preliminary assessment was that there was no such infiltration. As for Alpha, no resources had yet been spared even to examine the backup code. Most everyone, including Chuck, was still convinced of the accidental nature of the fire that had destroyed the servers. Becky had helped him with that as well, agreeing to have one of her junior staff who was waiting for clearances, quite possibly Gail, review the unclassified GPS code, map older and newer versions, and look for any anomalies. Recalling Becky's eagerness to help had brought Logan's thoughts once again back to his primary source of guilt. He frowned and tried to explain it away, but in fact, he did enjoy that woman's company.

To clear his conscience, or at least to override it, he turned to Randy as he drove and related some of the information he had been able to glean from his conversation with Becky. "So, tomorrow, let's review and document all of this. By Friday, we can sift through it all, select the critical items to incorporate, and by Saturday, build a strawman outline as to where it can be inserted in the novel …"

"Can't do it Saturday. At least not in the a.m."

"What?" asked Logan. "Well, why not?"

"I'm gonna be hiking … with Gail. Some trail called Esperito or Espinoza … wait, Esperero, that's it!"

"Well, Grasshopper, you might want to consult the third season of Kung Fu. It deals with the pitfalls of love when you're in the wandering-Shao-Lin-monk profession."

"It's a hike, Logan, not love!" Randy replied with some embarrassment, looking and sounding much more like the twenty-four-year-old man than the budding CIA operative.

"I'm just sayin'! And here's a thought. If your young lady friend is the one that Becky assigns to grind through the GPS code, having a relationship might give you a little more access to information, that is, information with some detail."

"That's a pretty damned cynical thing to say!" Randy rejoined, with surprising seriousness, as though he were defending not only his honor, but the honor of the young lady in question.

"C'mon, man, isn't that what you guys do in your business? Develop contacts, relationships, and exploit them?" Logan persisted.

"Not this time. Anyway, it seems you've got that information conduit pretty well open with your friend Becky." Touché, thought Logan, who pondered a reply, but thought better of it and just shrugged, as he silently re-chewed the guilt that had just been thrown back in his face.

Chapter Twenty

Light Dawns on Stonehenge

Jason and Luana sat on the outdoor patio of the Red Sails Inn on Shelter Island, San Diego, waiting for their entrées while drinking margaritas and nibbling on fried calamari. The atmosphere was extremely casual, and both wore shorts, T-shirts, and dark glasses against the brilliant light of the late afternoon sun, a light that danced off the nearby dock, sailboats and fishing craft, and sparkled off the water of Shelter Island's inner harbor. A few other groups, dressed in a similar manner and giving every appearance of being tourists, were also seated. The tinkling of a large fountain in this small, secluded courtyard behind the restaurant added an aquatic treble to the soothing lapping of water against the boats and pilings, and to the oddly melodic hollow clang of rigging and running lines against masts and spars. The relative solitude, the random and appealing sounds, and the relaxed atmosphere were perfect for obscuring, by sight and sound, the private conversations of the people on the patio, including those of Jason and Luana, whose discussion had taken a serious turn.

"The I-man seemed extremely nervous when he first approached me with the request. Of course, his hyena nephew was nowhere in sight, but I have no doubt that the little reptile was skulking nearby and heard every word. Eventually, I suppose I'll have to deal with him. It's fairly obvious that neither he nor Ivor really trust me completely, but then, maybe they never did." Stone paused, dipped a ring of calamari into cocktail sauce and popped it into his mouth. "Still," he went on a minute later, "I can be useful to them, especially regarding this rather odd request."

"Yes, quite," Luana replied, sipping her drink. "And so you were sent to approach me, discreetly, rather than him contacting me directly."

"Yes. I suppose that he realized that, given our cordial friendship,"—Luana smiled and Stone continued—"this request would be more likely to be received positively, or at least not rejected out of hand."

"Of course."

A small fishing boat maneuvered towards the dock, and its engine rumbled and grumbled as the captain expertly brought it kissing up against the large, dirty-white fenders.

"Two rather old aircraft, though far from obsolete. I'm sure my father can arrange such a purchase, but it will arouse his curiosity. He'll want to know …"

"Why Ivor needs them," Stone finished. "And I would have asked Ivor, but it was clear that he really didn't know."

"He told you this?"

"What … admit his ignorance? No, it was just that he overplayed his role as the confident, informed insider. You know … giving a significant look or saying 'ah, just so' whenever he was out of ammo. He just oozed stupidity. I was tempted to challenge him just for the entertainment value, but no need to put him on alert. As it was, I played the dutiful professional and took the assignment."

"You are a professional, and a very capable one at that," Luana said with a flirtatious smile.

"The thing is," Stone continued, after returning her smile in kind, "it was the rest of the request that seemed even odder, some central computer processing boards from a true museum-piece aircraft: an F-14A! And then too, he wants the umbilical interface card and data processor from a Phoenix missile. It's as though he was planning to fight some kind of time-warp combat."

Luana was silent for a while, looking out over the harbor, watching a family—two adults and two children—clumsily maneuver their rented kayaks into the harbor, crossing the exiting path of a small sailboat. Angry words and gestures were exchanged, but a collision was avoided. By the time the kayakers had maneuvered out beyond the end of the dock and back into clear water, dinner had arrived.

Stone looked thoughtfully at Luana and went on as though no interruption had occurred. "I don't suppose Ivor would have wanted me to mention that last part of his request. I've got a line on the bits and pieces already. But I've been puzzling over it ever since he asked. It's just too damned odd. And then too, I guess …" he trailed off, but continued to stare fixedly at Luana.

"What do you guess, Jason?"

A mixture of puzzlement and uncertainty fluttered across his features until he finally shrugged and smiled. "I guess I've come to trust you. It's usually deadly in our line of work."

"It is," Luana said seriously. "Yet how often do we feel the need to unburden ourselves to someone. I have my father, somewhat. My mother doesn't care to hear of it. Yet, with you, I feel … a mutual trust. As you say, often a deadly flaw."

Jason held up his wineglass and Luana raised hers as well. "To deadly flaws," he said.

"To trust," she replied, as their glasses touched.

Towards the end of the meal, Luana spoke again regarding the age of the aircraft and their specific types. "Have you considered which government militaries fly or have flown these aircraft types? Or the nationality of Ivor's mysterious buyer?"

"Yes, though to no real end. It's fairly clear from Ivor's somewhat clumsy description of, as you say, his mystery buyer, and a little checking of Ivor's travel itinerary, that his man is a Saudi, with high probability. They certainly met there. I've dead-ended on a name, at least for now."

"Perhaps I may be able to apply some of my resources to help. It will almost certainly be needed to satisfy my father."

Stone nodded. "Well, the Saudis never flew F-14As or MIG-29s, at least not overtly. The rumor is they might have snatched some aircraft during the eighties Iran-Iraq war when their owners were otherwise occupied."

Luana gave Stone a questioning look.

"No idea, really," Stone responded. "If I had to guess, it'd be so they would know what they might be facing if they ever found themselves in a shooting war with Iran; you know, by disassembly and reverse engineering the jets."

"Iran still flies MiG-29s," Luana said with certainty.

"Yes, they do. Not at the top of their fighter inventory, but damned close. Quite serviceable. Quite deadly. But why the F-14? And why a Phoenix?"

"The Phoenix missile was a large, long range air-to-air missile; heavy warhead—well over one hundred pounds; sophisticated radar, at least for its day."

"So an ideal standoff weapon," Stone mused.

"And adaptable. There were several variants in development that never reached production."

Key words of their conversation were now revolving rapidly in Stone's mind: long range, heavy warhead, standoff weapon, adaptable. And a tiny glimmer of resolution began to peek through his clouds of confusion. Iranian aircraft, Saudi buyer. And there was the one bit of priceless information that Stone had that he would never share except with one other individual, and that was not Luana. Right now, he had no more than a hunch. Despite all of his desensitizing years in special ops and his life as a terrorist operational leader, and despite his near constant exposure to danger, to sudden calamity and death, his heart was pounding. Was it possible that after such a long span of time plumbing the depths of a dark well, some light was beginning to shine? Was it possible that he might be able to complete his mission?

Jason's face was unnaturally tightened and he stared blindly past Luana and out over the harbor, oblivious to all around him, his mind transported back to a conversation that was over five years old when he, as a newly resurrected man, had received his final instructions in a dirty hut stuck to a crumbling hillside in Afghanistan. The man had no name, at least none that Stone had cared to know. He'd spoken to Jason first, with an economy of words, while Jason had been recovering in the hospital; while the morphine dulled his confused thoughts of chaos, shattering noise, emptiness, foggy consciousness, disdain, re-birth, admiration, self-worth, and above all, independence. Stone's third revelation had evolved from the sparse but convincing words of the man at his bedside. And this revelation had stitched his torn consciousness, and knit his shattered beliefs just as the sutures and restraining casts were doing for his ripped skin and broken bones.

The nameless man had returned on occasion over the months that followed, but it was his original words that had been the foundation. And it was the words of the nameless man that had sent him off months later into the dusty, Afghan night, on his lonely, hope-starved mission.

***

"You're on your own, Stonehenge. You've got your assignment; you've got your instructions. Do whatever you need to do to find this thing and destroy it. Remember: No good guys, no bad guys, just you and the mission. Right?"

"Right, sir."

"Wrong! There is no sir! There's just you and the mission. If I get in the way of the mission ..."

"I'm authorized to kill you or anyone that jeopardizes the mission. There is only one priority. Complete the mission."

"There you go. Check your voicemail when you can. I will as well; as will our friend Sean. The phone number will sequence as we discussed. If we hear nothing for over one year, we will assume that you have failed and will pursue other options. Those options may involve your death if that will move the mission forward. Understood?"

"Yes."

The man concluded that he had now covered every necessary point, and softened slightly. He extended his hand. "God speed, Stonehenge."

The man that was now Jason Stone shook his hand in an iron grip. "Thanks."

Jason had never seen him again.

***

"Jason?" asked Luana. "Are you all right?"

He shook his head and gave what he hoped was an unforced smile. "Sorry, just gathering wool as my mother used to say."

"I'd say you must have gathered enough for a wardrobe full of sweaters."

"Sorry again," said Stone, finally banishing his excited thoughts and returning to the present. He looked at their empty dinner plates. "Would you like some dessert?"

"Oh no. Perhaps a walk around the island for a bit. And then you can explain to me the origins of this 'wool gathering' reference."

***

"Blackett's Ridge, not Esperero? A night hike?" Randy had asked.

"Sure," said Gail. "There's a full moon Saturday night and there will be fewer people. Well, there'll be exactly nobody except for us, and it's a spectacular view."

"And do you take all your first dates on moonlight strolls up the mountains?"

"Oh yes," Gail replied. "Those that can't keep up are eaten by mountain lions, gored by javelinas, or fatally bitten by rattlesnakes. I'll point out their bleached bones lying on either side of the trail on the way up … if you can keep up, that is," she said with mock grimness. Quiet laughter on the phone followed, and then, "I've always gone alone. Consider it a privilege that you get to accompany me, and I'll consider an honor that you do. Besides, I'll have a little surprise for you at the top."

"A surprise at the top? Well, now I suppose I must go."

"Also, you'll be able to do whatever it is you're doing with Logan all day Saturday."

"Now that's a buzz kill!" said Randy. "But I suppose you're right. Work first, then pleasure."

***

Randy's quads were beginning to scream and he was seriously rethinking the "pleasure" assessment of his phone conversation. He continued following Gail, who seemed to be entirely fresh, full backpack and all, as they finally appeared to be nearing the top of Blackett's Ridge. But before his hopes had even begun to take root, she had turned pleasantly back to him and said, "That's the first false peak. There's only one more behind that, one more false peak that is, and then we'll be almost there. You doing OK?"

Randy smiled bravely and lied boldly, "Doing just fine! Lead on, you female version of Sir Edmund Hillary!"

A slight lift in one corner of Gail's mouth indicated that she wasn't buying it, but she turned and resumed her steady pace.

But Randy had to admit that she had been correct about having the mountain to themselves and also regarding the spectacular beauty of the moon-drenched landscape. The dull and dusty tans of rock and sand and the pale greens of palo verde, saguaro, brittle bush and creosote, deprived of daylight, seemed to have shed their earthly coarseness and their savage desert beauty and had become ethereal objects of black and silver, casting hard shadows that amplified their spectacular shapes to bizarre dimensions. The silence of the night had also required an adjustment by Randy who was never far from the noisy traffic and street sounds of a major city. For the last hour and a half, the only sound other than the crunching of their boots had been the occasional "woo, woo, woo" of hunting owls or the chirr of desert insects. And then there had been the sky. Randy realized early in the hike—owing to trips and stumbles—that he really needed to concentrate on his foot placements rather than gawking at the impossibly huge night sky. It was cluttered with more stars than he had ever seen in his life; the unmistakable band of the Milky Way making a noble swath across the dome overhead, and he planned to gawk aplenty when they reached the summit. Lastly, Randy had to admit to himself that the moonlight reflecting off Gail's thick, auburn hair was fascinating, distracting, and lovely.

Ten minutes later, Gail and Randy were seated comfortably on convenient rocks at the summit, the trickle of sweat down Randy's back drying in the pleasant night breeze. Their view was unobstructed in all directions. To the north was the floor of the deeply-carved Sabino Canyon, over a thousand feet below, seen with perfect clarity by the light of the brilliant moon. Silver flashes indicated the path of the creek which originated in the mountains to the northeast and ran, intertwined with the tram road, along the canyon's four-mile length. Taller mountains to the north were silhouetted against the diamond-studded night sky, and to the east, Thimble Peak reared up, seeming close enough to touch, but in fact separated by a deep chasm from their perch. To the south, the city of Tucson twinkled against the backdrop of the Rincon and Santa Rita Mountains, many miles distant, and to the west, the Tucson Mountains closed the valley in which the Old Pueblo quietly rested.

"You couldn't have been more right. This is beautiful," said Randy, with feeling, "and worth every step," *especially with you here*, he thought, but before he could force the words from bashful lips, Gail had dropped her eyes. "I'm glad you like it. Most of the people I work with won't go to the trouble to get here. Now," she said with girlish mischievousness, "you have to turn around while I get out the surprise. Promise not to look."

Randy complied and focused his attentions solely on the lights of the city south and west, picking out the runway at Rickman Air Force Base, but no other identifiable features. There was the noise of things being pulled from the backpack, shuffled around, set down, moved a bit more, a sound like the clink of glass, and finally a distinctive popping sound as Gail said, "OK, you can turn around."

When he did, he saw Gail holding a wine bottle that she had just uncorked. Spread on a flat rock in front of her was a white cloth, a plate of sliced cheese and crackers, two wine glasses, and a subtle, battery-powered LED light in the center.

Randy stood with his mouth hanging open, and then looked at Gail with an expression somewhere between wonder and affection. "My God, this is fantastic! There can't be any two people alive having wine and cheese with a view like this on a night like this in the middle of God's universe!" Randy had a somewhat poetical nature that was of no value to him at work, but that served him well here. "Gail Kamenchek, you are one in a million!"

Gail's eyes dropped and her blush was hidden by the conspiratorial moon. "Glass of wine?" she asked at last.

***

The same late-August evening, Jason Stone checked messages on a phone whose number had recently changed and was surprised to find a veiled warning. He in turn called back, but left, after years of dull gloom, a truly hopeful message: "Light is dawning on Stonehenge."

***

They drained the last of their wine and began repacking Gail's backpack. "Are you sure you don't want me to carry this on the way back?" Randy asked.

"I've got it, no problem," laughed Gail. "Besides, it's all downhill."

Randy took one last look at the canyon, the mountains, the city lights, and finally at the brilliant stars and the huge moon, now heading westward, lazily following the impatient sun. When his eyes finally drew down, he met the very intense gaze of Gail, who seemed torn between shyness and expectation. Randy looked at her and smiled. "Thanks, for a wonderful, magical night." And almost without thinking, he added, with only a moment's hesitation, "You have such beautiful eyes." Gail immediately dropped her gaze in embarrassment, but quickly brought her eyes back up to look again with expectation into Randy's face. Though not entirely sure of himself, Randy hesitantly moved towards her, gently wrapped his arms around her, and kissed her deeply.

Chapter Twenty-One

Deadlines and Romance

With Luana occupied with briefings to high-level military and corporate leadership, Stone found himself oddly at loose ends. He spent many long hours alone, usually at the beach, listening to the endless crash of surf on the shore. To him, it had a certain familiar language that spoke of a task unfinished, a mission never accomplished; an endless refrain that never reached a crescendo, a symphony that never reached its climax; a play that contained no final act. Jason was surprisingly well read for someone in his profession—mercenary, assassin, terrorist cell leader—and he had once read a long, plodding, painful novel by Franz Kafka called *The Castle*. It seemed as though the story would never reach a satisfactory conclusion, and then, as the remaining pages grew thinner and thinner in his hands, it had abruptly ended with a statement that, at this point, the author had died, but that according to his friends and confidantes, he intended it to end in the following way. Several paragraphs of narrative brought the sad novel to a bizarre close. As Jason listened to the endless story of the waves, he wondered if perhaps his most important mission might end in the same way.

It was a fruitless path of thought, and one that he felt his mother would not approve. He wondered whether she would approve of anything he had done over the past five years. Perhaps not. But, he reminded himself, she would probably approve of his personal handling of himself. She would be proud of his self-confidence, his independence, his unfailing dedication to that which was pure and right. He hoped she would approve of what he had made of himself. Of course, all of this was an illusion. To her, he had been dead these many years, and in his own mind, his doubts outweighed his certainty: a deadly weakness.

And yet, if he were right … Moreover, if Luana and her father's intelligence network could confirm that Hasim bin Wazari was Ivor's latest customer, then perhaps his intuition was correct, perhaps he could bring his mission to a successful close. He thought again back to the man who had recruited him, the man who refused to be "sir'd."

***

"Let me be plain," said the man, "this weapon represents the greatest threat to world peace since Hitler started the Blitz. How it slipped out of the Soviets' hands is almost irrelevant. While we were celebrating the collapse of the 'Evil Empire,' while we were growing giddy over the tearing down of the Berlin Wall, while we were celebrating ourselves as the only remaining superpower, they were trying to stop the flow of the tide with their fingers. They did pretty well, but for all their efforts, they failed. We think there's only one. We pray to God that only one got loose. Your mission is very, very simple. One: find it. Two: destroy it. There are no other constraints, no other guidelines, no other rules, no other laws. Do you understand?"

The man who was now Jason had taken his time to answer this question. He had pondered; he had considered asking for clarification, certainty. For what this sounded like was madness, anarchy, authorized murder. He wondered whether the IV drip—the continued doses of painkillers, antibiotics, and sedatives—was distorting his thought process. To him, the words were very clear, and perhaps he was the only man alive—well, barely alive—who could take on such an assignment. The man had studied his background carefully. This mission was made for him. His mother would agree.

"Yes," he said at last.

"Good. Now listen very carefully. I won't repeat anything. You should know that good men died to acquire the information that I'm

now entrusting to you. They would want you to succeed. Here is what we know."

***

The words that followed had guided Jason's existence for over five years. They had allowed him to ascertain the current lords of the weapon, solidly confirmed by his own painful efforts. As to their intentions, well that had been somewhat more difficult to ferret out. He had several hypotheses: it would be used as no more than leverage, the possessors being too timid to use it directly; it would be sold to surrogates—zealous, religious madmen—who would in fact, use it, but in such a way as to benefit the now-anonymous puppet masters. It was only this latest assignment from Ivor that had caused him to see a third possibility, but for that to become a hypothesis, he must know who Ivor's mysterious buyer was. He was confident that Luana and her father would provide the answer. As for his own instinct? His mother would nod her silent approval, for he was certain.

***

Randy continued to spend long hours closeted with Logan, working the extremely delicate details that they had chosen to weave into Cathie's novel. Cathie came by on occasion, mostly because of feelings of guilt for avoiding the dreary work conditions that the two men still found necessary. During those times, she would review their progress, discuss the status of the release of specific information, and provide them with the latest draft of her work. She had made remarkable progress. By virtue of these planning sessions, she was able to take the essence of the plan and incorporate it into the novel, barely hindered by the lack of specific details that had yet to be approved for release. This had been Chuck's area of focus. He had remained in Oakland, filtering through the material created by Randy and Logan and sent to him through secure channels along with the succession of drafts from Cathie.

Chuck had been right in assuming that the release of sensitive information would require approval at extremely high levels, and he often found himself stuffed uncomfortably into his one business suit, (it had grown oddly tight around the middle) and briefing the local director, Homeland Security staffers, or DoD representatives. When the need arose, he would fly to the Langley, Virginia, headquarters, usually on a red-eye, brief in the morning and be back in Oakland that evening. On those occasions, he would generally arrive back home rumpled, fatigued, depressed, and grumpy. After his latest trip, he had hauled his suitcase into the house, thrown off his suit coat, and flopped into a chair, not even acknowledging Joy other than to comment, "Did I ever tell you that anyone who thinks business travel is exciting or romantic is a damn fool?"

"Yes, dear," she had replied, "about a hundred times."

"Damn right!"

On his latest trip, he had been granted a very brief moment alone with the Defense Secretary which had done nothing to relieve the stress of the last several months. "Chuck," the secretary had said, "this business with Stonehenge is the absolute highest priority. If you can't focus on that, I can have you ordered off this other bird-hunting expedition."

"Not necessary. Nearly all of that work is being done by my deputy, Randy O'Neil, and a couple of private contractors. As for Stonehenge, well, it doesn't take much to monitor one lousy answering machine and a Facebook page. Hell, I've got time to burn!"

"Don't try to bullshit me, Chuck. I'm not kidding. If this thing gets out of hand, we'll both be wishing we were pulling guard duty at Guantanamo. You've got your priorities. Just don't fuck up."

"Yes sir, excellent advice sir."

The Secretary of Defense gave him one last long, piercing look, then reached out a hand and shook Chuck's firmly. Before he had even released him, he turned and called over his shoulder towards the partially open door that led to his administrator's cube. "Madeline, Mr. Johnson will be leaving now. Please send in my next appointment." The entire meeting had lasted less than three minutes.

***

There is a popular saying, often used in the military and the defense industry: "Shit flows downhill." Logically, therefore, being at the bottom of the hill was a highly undesirable location. But that was the precise location where Randy now found himself. Twelve-hour days for Randy and Logan had now become routine. The pressure being applied by Chuck was tremendous, but no less crushing than that being applied from the book publisher through Cathie, who reminded them that the proof draft needed to be complete by mid-October in order to meet the publisher's desire for a pre-Christmas release.

Logan carefully watched Randy for signs of stress and fatigue. He himself had worked brutal proposals and development efforts many times over his thirty-five-year career. Age didn't seem to be as much of a factor as some internal stamina that could tolerate day after day of intense focus, pressure by superiors, demands by customers, and the near suspension of any kind of private life. It could be not only mentally exhausting, but clinically depressing to arrive home at 11:00 p.m., microwave a cup of noodles or a hot dog, drink three or four scotches or a bottle of wine within an hour, collapse into bed, and be woken again at five so as to arrive at work on time for a daily six-thirty planning meeting. And while Logan had grown genuinely fond of Randy, his main concern wasn't so much for Randy's health (mental or physical) as it was his concern that being stressed, exhausted, and stupid would cause Randy to make mistakes. There was no margin for any major screw-up at this point, and he prayed that Randy had that internal resiliency to withstand this environment.

So far, he had been holding up well enough. Logan had been insistent that Randy take at least a little time each weekend for himself, and he was delighted that he did not need to press this point, since a much greater motivation than his urging existed in the physical presence of Gail Kamenchek. To say that she and Randy seemed to have hit it off would have been a gross understatement, and when Randy would roll in on Mondays for another brutal week's work with a refreshed attitude and a hopeful, if not too energetic smile, Logan would marvel at the change this woman seemed to have made in him over their short time together.

It was the second week of October that Cathie rejoined Logan and Randy in the Air Force base conference room that had been their near home. She was carrying what she hoped was the final draft of their combined Opus Deluxe which she was eager to deliver to her nervous publisher. The weeks of work carefully selecting the bait material, the endless reviews and iterations with Chuck and his superiors, a string of approvals as information was released piecemeal, and Cathie's integration of the critical elements into her manuscript had all boiled down to this. She flopped her five hundred page draft manuscript on the conference-room table with a solid thud.

"So that's the latest?" asked a tired, hollow-eyed Randy, glancing at the distilled product of thousands of hours of combined effort.

"The latest and the last, I hope!" said Cathie. "I wrote 'Fin' on the last page, and I sure hope it is 'Fin.' What else is left to do before we can green-light the publisher, who, by the way, is approaching a coronary with anxiety?"

"At this point, I think I'd trade that for a total physical collapse from exhaustion, which is where I'm headed right now," said Logan, rubbing his eyes and then rasping his hand along a stubbly chin. "I'm not as young as I used to be."

"Who are you kidding?" asked Randy. "You're holding up better than me. I think if someone took a blood sample from me right now it would be two parts Folgers and two parts Red Bull. I feel like ten pounds of shit in a five-pound bag!"

"Well, neither of you will win any beauty contest at the moment, plus I think you both need to be aired out for a day or two. But still. Are we done?"

"Well," said Randy wearily, "I have one more thing that I need to do, which is to take a copy of your draft, annotated for our special information, along with a briefing on how this all might go down, with us as the winners in the end, and fly up to Oakland to brief my new 'Mr. Hyde' boss."

"Yeah, what is up with Chuck, anyway?" asked Cathie. "I've talked to Joy and she says she hardly recognizes him; that he hasn't been the same since our first meeting in LA over two months ago. I mean, we're all feeling the pressure, but he seems to have really taken it to heart, in a bad way. Most days, when he's not traveling that is, she says she just avoids him. That won't work for very long," Cathie added shaking her head.

"I know what you mean," said Logan. "When I talk to him it's usually a series of grunts and snarls, and poor Grasshopper here just gets abused pretty much nonstop. I don't get it. Knowing what he's been through, what he's seen, I can't believe that the pressure of this project would set him off this much. It's almost like there's something else, something more that's bugging him, tearing him apart." Logan too shook his head. "It just doesn't make sense."

"Well, you're not the only one that has a few more miles of wear on you." Cathie shrugged. "Maybe it's just getting to him more than it would have a few years ago."

"I doubt it," said Randy, stifling a yawn. "I think Logan is right, there's something else, and it must be big and maybe not going well. And before you even ask, I don't have any kind of clue. Seriously, I may be his faithful sidekick, and I've gotten kicked a few times lately, but I believe he's handling this, whatever it is, solo."

"So when is this briefing?" asked Cathie.

"I don't know. What day is it today?" asked Randy, with no hint of humor.

"Thursday, Grasshopper," answered Logan. "And I talked with Chuck last night. He'd like you out next week. He wanted Monday, but I argued him into Wednesday. So, here's what I think you should do. Go home, call Gail and make some plans for the weekend. Sleep all day tomorrow, have a little R & R on the weekend, and polish up your briefing Monday and Tuesday."

"Polish it? There isn't any 'it' yet."

Logan smiled and put a fatherly hand on Randy's slumped shoulder. "Yes, there is. I started it three days ago. There should be a hell-of-a-solid draft for you on Monday. Hey," he added to the astonished look on Randy's face, "I may be old, but I'm not completely useless!"

"That's the truth, love," said Cathie, giving Logan a kiss on the cheek.

"No, listen, I'm fine, I'll come in tomorrow and we can …" Randy argued.

"Randy," said Logan firmly, "Go home! Don't make me get security to change the cypher code. Just go. You earned it!"

Randy, still protesting ineffectually, was hustled by Logan towards the door and forcibly ejected from the room, with his final comment, "Well, I'll be in first thing Monday morn …" cut off as the heavy door latched shut.

"You're such a sweetheart, dear," said Cathie, "and it's a shame you won't get the reward you deserve, at least not for a couple of days."

"So you're definitely going to Dallas? Tonight?"

"Last flight out, which is in about an hour and a half. Geoffrey insisted we meet and discuss the cover layout, et cetera … et cetera. We're behind the power curve as it is and he's right. Besides, you need to keep herding the Grasshopper until his trip to Oakland. Are you going with?"

Logan paused for a moment in thought, then shook his head in the negative. "No, probably not. I mean, I should, if for no other reason than to keep Chuck from dragging Randy over the coals, but then, that's the whole problem. If Chuck was in a better frame of mind, he'd want me there, hell, he'd insist. But something is definitely going on with him and I think I'd do more harm than good. I'll just have to make sure that the Grasshopper is very, very well prepared and doesn't give Chuck a reason to bite his head off."

"Well, I should be off or I'll miss my lovely flight to DFW. Come here you handsome old techno-stud," and she wrapped her arms around Logan and kissed him gently on the lips. "I can see there could be an advantage to working in these little locked rooms," she said when she finally drew back.

"Don't you believe it! I could tell you stories, and they all ended very badly!"

Cathie was halfway to the door when she turned back to him with a look of concern that had completely obliterated her affectionate expression of moments earlier. "There's one last thing. I … well, maybe I was bad to not say it when Randy was here, but he looked so damn beat and I didn't want to pile on."

Logan, catching the tone of seriousness that reinforced her expression, stopped shuffling the stack of papers in his hand. “What is it, babe?”

“Well, maybe nothing, but, well, I got a call from Elaya today.”

Logan tossed the papers on the desk and focused intently on Cathie.

“Well?” he asked.

“Well, at first she was just talking about visiting, in LA; wanted to know if I could come out for the weekend to watch her do some very expensive shopping, although she didn’t put it exactly like that.”

“Girls’ weekend out?”

“Something like. I told her I couldn’t, that I had this trip to see Geoffrey—that we were getting close to publication. Logan,” she continued, her eyes widening with nervousness, “she pounced all over it. Was dying, just dying to read the new novel; couldn’t wait; could I give her a few more tidbits. She went on and on.” Cathie shook her head to clear the memory, and then looked intently at Logan. “It was clear that was why she called, that was why she wanted me to come out to LA. Oh, Logan, when we started this I knew, intellectually, that she might be involved, but somehow I just never really believed it. I’m scared. I’m scared because I *am* beginning to believe it!”

Logan held her tightly and tried to murmur soothing words, and Cathie allowed herself to be held, to briefly release the overpowering feeling of responsibility that had flooded over her.

“Anyway,” she continued, still leaning comfortably into her husband’s shoulder, “I don’t think I, you know, acted too weird or anything. In fact, I drowned out my feelings of, well, of being deceitful by profuse thanks for her loyalty as a reader, and I promised to send her a signed copy, pre-release, in November. Jeez, Logan, I hope I did the right thing. The thought that she might be … well it just makes me sick to my stomach.”

“You did good, babe. I’ll let Randy know Monday and he can pass it on to Chuck. You did great. But now,” he said, releasing her and looking at his watch, “you’d better head out or you’ll miss that flight.”

“Jesus!” Cathie exclaimed, glancing at her watch. “I must go. You’re a dear. Take care of the ’hopper!” And she rapidly left the conference room.

Logan sighed as he took a look at the scattered papers, coffee cups, sticky notes and miscellaneous flotsam that he'd need to put into some order before he left. "I thought I'd retired!" he said aloud, and began cleaning up.

***

Guilt fought a losing battle with Randy on the following day when he slept to the ungodly hour of seven thirty before dragging himself up and into a hot shower that he allowed to pound on his cramped back and shoulders for nearly twenty minutes, an unspeakable luxury. And then another treat, a breakfast that consisted of more than caffeine in a hot, liquid solution: actual eggs with toast and orange juice. He made coffee just because he liked the taste. And then the treat of all treats, he put in a CD that Logan had given him of smooth-jazz piano, pulled a random book from his bookshelf—it happened to be Larry McMurtry's *Lonesome Dove*—flopped back into bed and read until exhaustion. The full stomach, book, and music took him back to a pleasant near-sleeping state until nearly ten. When something close to consciousness returned to him, Randy realized the extent to which he had been drained over the last months and he blessed Logan and his gift of some R & R.

"Hey, Grasshopper girl, it's Grasshopper boy. How are you doing?" asked Randy over the phone. Randy and Gail had grown fond of the name that had been thrust upon them at the Skybox, and as their mutual affection had grown, had adopted it as a pet name for each other, along with several pleasant variations that seemed to spring from nowhere and be accepted immediately. Though they had not yet spent a night together, it hadn't been from any sense of reluctance or resistance on either's part, but more from a feeling of wanting to make that occasion, well, special. Their mutually hectic and wearing work schedules had driven them to often postpone their plans and push their desires to the back. It was a sad trial, often driven by simple exhaustion.

"G-man?" asked Gail, incredulously. "Are you on a break or something? It's like eleven o'clock, and not in the p.m. Are you OK?"

"Better than. My true friend and blessed mentor Logan is holding the fort today whilst I recoup from Grasshopper duties. And, get this, I have been granted a weekend leave of absence! Both days! No kidding! Soooooo, I was just wondering. Could I interest you in a little offbeat weekend with *moi*? Perhaps a surprise destination; interesting places, a large comfy, umm, well, sleeping quarters, which maybe you'd be willing to share. A large bottle of wine, and by that I mean a 1.5 liter of the finest vintage Ripple that money can buy, oh hell, what's the rest of that … 'A book of verses underneath the bough, a 1.5 liter of Ripple, a loaf of bread, and thou'?"

"That's close, Shakespeare, or should I say Omar?" she laughed. "Well, my social calendar is pretty full."

"Grasshopper!" he implored.

"Oh, well, OK," Gail teased. "When?"

"How about noon tomorrow? We'll hit a couple of vineyards south of this burg and then … well, I may have to blindfold you. I insist on the surprise. It's a little, ummm, place, I discovered kind of, sort of, well OK, it's in Bisbee, but I refuse to tell you more. You can pull out my fingernails and I'll never tell. Please say yes."

Gail hesitated in mock consideration for a moment, then answered with a smile that Randy could sense over the phone line, "Yes!"

***

It was mid-afternoon when Gail and Randy left the Kief-Joshua Vineyards with two bottles of Chenin Blanc that Randy assured her would come in handy later. Though she had been in Tucson for many months now, Gail had not done much sightseeing nearby and she and Randy were taking in their first views of the rugged, reddish-tan mountains along Highway 80 for the first time. Their first sight of Bisbee had left them both impressed, not so much by its size or magnificence, but as a demonstration of the tenacity of the men and women that had constructed this mining town of wood and brick, perched at many levels along the steep seams and valleys that flowed downward from the mountain peaks nearby. The mining operations had long ceased, and the town had become an art haven and tourist destination that included a tour of the deep underground copper mine and the huge open-pit mine south of town.

The town itself was almost entirely located north of the highway and ended abruptly just as the huge open-pit mine gaped enormously to the south. Gail stared for a few moments at the massive, layered excavation, unable to see, from the road, to its ultimate depth. Finally she turned to Randy. "Did we miss our turnoff? We seem to be out of Bisbee already."

"Not on your life. We're close, very close. And now I think I'll insist that you close your eyes and wait for the surprise."

"Oh really! I thought you were joking," she said.

"Grasshopper humor? Never heard of it! Now close your eyes, just like I had to on our very first crazy adventure."

"Technically, I just made you look the other way."

"Now!"

Gail smiled and closed her eyes, and in a moment she felt the car navigate a near complete loop. "Not lost, are we? It feels like we just turned around." In fact, Randy had just completely changed direction on a large roundabout and was now heading north, back the way they had come. But he was also now on the correct side of the road for the entrance to the Shady Dell, a rather unique motel.

A few more turns and Gail heard the crunch of gravel under the wheels of their car, and then they were stopped. "Eyes closed!" Randy insisted, as he leaped out of the car to meet her on the opposite side. He carefully guided her out of the vehicle, walked her a few steps to the other side, turned her slightly and then said, "OK, open!"

Gail stared for a moment, her mouth hanging open slightly and a very puzzled look on her face. She had been expecting a hotel or a cabin, or maybe even an old western saloon and bunkhouse but what she saw was … she looked to the left and to the right … nothing other than what seemed to be the derelict remains of old travel trailers, albeit in a very neat and nicely landscaped junk yard. Randy said nothing, and gradually Gail's eyes returned to the scene directly in front of her. There she saw a large old pale-blue-and-white bus, a streak of stainless steel along its side. On a raised wooden porch directly in front of the bus was a brightly polished, long wooden table made to look like a South Pacific outrigger canoe, the outriggers doubling as seats, with wooden paddle blades at their backs. A few brightly colored metal lawn chairs completed the scene, with a pole structure at the corners holding up a palm-frond covering to provide shade. Nailed to the framework holding the fronds was a sign that read "Tiki Bar," and on the side of the bus near the door, within the glass-covered marquee that might at one time contained the bus's destination or the name of the organization which owned it, were the lettered words, "Randy's White Elephant."

Gail continued to stare while Randy stood at her side with an enormous grin on his face. Gail finally turned to him and said, blankly, "It's a bus."

"Oh, it's not just any bus. It's the Tiki Bus!" said Randy, as though that explained everything. "C'mon," he said, taking her hand. "Let's look inside." With the exception of the driver's seat, which was more or less intact, and the surrounding gauges, pedals, steering wheel, and the worn handle of the mechanism the driver used to open and close the door, the interior had been gutted and replaced with a small sink and stove, a breakfast area with grotesque turquoise vinyl benches, and a bedroom and shower at the rear. In totality, it looked like a camper that had been built in the '50s. The effect of having traveled backward in time was emphasized by light fixtures, an old turntable and half a dozen LPs, the kitchenware, and decorations, all with a Polynesian theme that were true to the period. The clincher was the music playing softly from a battered old radio, also of the same throwback vintage. She recognized Bing Crosby crooning away.

When Gail was finally able to wrap her mind around the bizarre surroundings that Randy seemed to have conjured from the rugged countryside; when she finally realized that this would be their special place for the weekend, she smiled a happy, contented smile, dropping her eyes in some confusion as she had often done in the earlier days of their relationship when Randy would say something complimentary or gallant. Without looking up, she took a half step forward and wrapped her arms around him. "It's wonderful. It's magical. And 'Randy's White Elephant'! How on earth did you manage that?"

"That, my lovely 'hopper, was the intervention of a benevolent God." She looked up at him questioningly with her lovely green eyes, causing him to nearly forget where he was and what he had been thinking.

"Umm, it was just a wild coincidence. When I saw that picture online, I decided on the Tiki Bus rather than the boat."

"They have a boat?"

"Yes. We should take a look around."

"We should, maybe later. Let's get checked in, and then, well …" she looked down again, flushed slightly, and pointed towards the large swinging door of the bus. "Do you suppose that locks?"

Chapter Twenty-Two

A Dose of Reality

Randy was still in a haze of pleasantly befuddled euphoria as he boarded the jet bound for Oakland. His weekend with Gail had been an unbelievable escape from a hard reality into a fantasy of perfume-scented softness and warmth. They had made love twice on Saturday; once as soon as their suitcases were in the bus. They had shaken off the pleasant, but poorly timed, solicitude of the proprietor, telling them the lengthy genesis and history of the Shady Dell. And they had found that the bus's front door did lock.

Later that evening, the sun setting purple behind the western hills, they had eaten a romantic, candlelit dinner on the outdoor patio of the Copper Queen Hotel's restaurant. To Randy and Gail, surrounded by the glow of their own happiness, the hostess and waiters had all seemed to be especially friendly and considerate. Afterwards, they had briefly strolled through the narrow streets of the old mining town, browsed a few stores, and then by silent, mutual consent, returned to their steel retreat to make love once again. The late evening found them sitting at the Tiki canoe, drinking wine, talking and laughing, their faces alive with joy and contentment.

"So, Randy," Gail had asked, "how did you end up in the CIA?"

Randy had laughed. "Oh, actually it's kind of funny. When I got within a semester of graduation, I started looking around for jobs. I did the usual: filled out applications, sent resumés, made a few phone calls. One day, on the way into the student union cafeteria, I saw this eight-and-a-half-by-eleven posting on the bulletin board outside the entrance—definitely low budget, a little dusty, and hung slightly crooked. Well, it was a job notice for the CIA; for analysts. My schooling wasn't a perfect fit, but I figured 'what the hell, I've applied for thirty jobs already, why not make it thirty-one.' So I did. A couple of weeks later I'm sitting in this dingy office in this dingy building in a very sketchy part of Oakland listening to one of the most persuasive men I've ever met."

"Would that be your legendary boss, Mister Johnson?" Gail asked with a smile.

"Indeed," laughed Randy, "my now somewhat-schizophrenic boss. Funny," he added, with a complete lack of humor, "he seems so different now."

"I suppose all bosses get that way. So," she had continued, after a short pause, "do you like it, your work I mean, notwithstanding Mister Johnson's current behavior? I guess, I mean, are you planning to stay there, in Oakland?" Gail had dropped her eyes and blushed slightly as she said the last words.

Her actions made Randy somewhat embarrassed—he had wondered about the continuation of their relationship as well—but he answered quite truthfully, "Oh, I joined up because it was different; interesting and different. I guess I'm an OK analyst. I've done a little field work, but I'll never be able to match up with Chuck, even though …" he hesitated, then added, with some reluctance, "… I guess I'm a pretty good shot. But still … no … my plan was always to spend a few years with the agency, learn some lessons, maybe make a few connections, and then make a dash for private industry. You know … the big money, a nice office … lots of techno-groupies."

Gail hit him on the arm, none too gently, for that one.

"I can't believe you said that!" she laughed. "And I don't suppose that maybe, just perhaps, one of those companies might be within the same time zone as Alpha?"

"Oh, I wouldn't be too surprised. But then, a young lady with your talent can practically write her own ticket. Would someone like you ever consider relocating, say to San Diego or DC?"

"Oh, it would take something very compelling to make me leave the garden spot that is Tucson, Arizona," she joked. "But yes, perhaps I might."

Randy smiled and held up the wine bottle. Gail nodded, and Randy refilled her glass and then his.

The night concluded with a deep, deep, restful sleep in each other's arms. Passion once again in the morning, followed by the true climax of the entire trip for Randy, as he kissed the top of Gail's head and whispered, "I love you, Gail," for which he received a warm squeeze, and the words tickling his chin, "I love you back, Grasshopper."

***

Two "short," fourteen-hour days with Logan, polishing the briefing, then rehearsing it, with Logan acting as the Dr. Hyde version of his friend Chuck—interrupting, questioning, and challenging every assertion with a snide comment—had produced, to Logan's mind, the most exceptional briefing and the most well-prepared briefer that he had seen in his thirty-five-year career. He told Randy this, and he also told him that it probably wouldn't save him from a skewering.

"I talked to the old Grinch over the weekend, Randy. I don't know what's going on, but don't expect any kudos from him at the end of your brief. But I will tell you, all false modesty aside, that it's outstanding. Are you OK? You seem way too calm."

"Chalk it up to being in love, Logan."

"Ahh, love. It is pretty awesome, isn't it?"

"Yes, it is!"

"Well, listen, and I mean this seriously: Chuck realizes you're a gem. I don't know what's gotten into him lately, but he'll remember it someday, Randy. And don't you forget it, yes?"

"Thanks, Logan. I won't. And," he stopped and looked at the older man, the man with thirty-five years of scars and creds and hard earned wisdom, "well, just thanks! And … this is a little hard for me … thanks for pushing me and Gail together, that first night!"

"Go catch your jet," Logan said, with a smile.

***

Randy felt distinctly out of place in a coat and tie within the dingy walls of his home office, but Chuck had invited his boss, the local director, as well as several other senior agents from the surrounding districts to this briefing, and he wasn't about to get abused for being "out of uniform" before he even began. As it was, everyone was dressed casually and Chuck had started off the introductions with the unwelcome comment, "You look like you're out on a job interview, Randy," to the chuckles of the others. Randy merely smiled. It looked like today was going to be tough on the ego. Good thing Logan had warned him.

"Yes, sir," Randy had replied.

"All right, let's go," Chuck said tersely.

"Well, first a little background," Randy began, "regarding the novels of Catherine Clarke Fletcher."

"Jesus Christ, Randy, we've all been briefed on this before, can we get to it?"

"Easy, Chuck," said the director, "I for one wouldn't mind a little background review. To quote a former infamous Vice President, 'This is a big fucking deal.' We can take a few minutes and all get re-calibrated."

Chuck nodded tensely and motioned for Randy to continue. And Randy gave a succinct, crisp account of Cathie Fletcher's previous novels and the ideas that seemed to have been stolen by terrorists and put into effect, some more successfully than others. "And so," he continued, eyeing his boss carefully, "it was determined that it would be reasonable to assume that an idea, given life through Ms. Fletcher's next book, would provide us with an opportunity to create a sting and potentially get access to the head of this snake."

Randy paused to see if Chuck would remind the director that it had been his, Randy's, idea to create this operation, but Chuck remained grim faced, in surly silence. *What the hell is eating him?* thought Randy. And he once again blessed Logan's advice which had suggested that Randy treat the entire audience, including Chuck, as skeptical if not hostile, and to brief in the dullest, most professional, detached way possible. Randy proceeded, although he hadn't thought it would be this hard; this hard to treat Chuck, his mentor, his friend, as someone wishing him ill.

"So, the basic premise is this," Randy said, changing slides. "The adversary clearly knows that Ms. Fletcher has access to information through her husband and his friends, perhaps all unclassified, but information that is still unique. She has used it in the past, perhaps flying in the face of good OPSEC, to embellish her novels. And it has, on occasion, exposed certain vulnerabilities. We play on that here. The recent cyber-attacks on Pentagon and defense industry systems, but more importantly, the fire at Alpha, provided an unusual opportunity for cyber-terrorists."

"Alpha will be rebuilding all of their data bases on their new servers in their new facility in April of next year," Randy continued. "Cathie's fictional company, obvious as Alpha to those familiar with her, her husband, and the more than suspicious fires this past July, will be using backups from Infinity Services Group in a massive restore process. There will be dozens of Alpha employees and dozens of contractors involved, and while security will be present, the size, scope, and confusion of a job of this type will be an unmatchable opportunity to hack into the system."

"And why would they do that, son?" asked the director.

"As I'm sure Mr. Johnson has told you, the bait is extraordinarily tempting. Alpha, that is, the corporate Alpha and not just the Tactical Weapons Division, has been deeply engaged in the development of the next generation of secure, tactical datalinks. These links are highly flexible, allowing multiple ground and airborne systems to direct, redirect, or abort every air, surface, or ground-launched weapon in the current inventory or planned for initial operational capability for the next thirty years. Through Ms. Fletcher's book, we have made it known that the algorithms for generating the crypto-codes for these links will be in the software to be reloaded."

"Because of the recent attacks on server systems all through the defense industry that we've already discussed, certain protocols have been put in place to prevent this type of code hijack. In Ms. Fletcher's novel, she alluded to these procedures and made it very clear that this would be the one, best, and possibly last, opportunity to recover the datalink cypher algorithms."

"I presume that the actual algorithms are not in the software that is being loaded?" asked the director.

Randy glanced at Chuck who remained stonily silent. This was the key point, the point where the actual risk of exposure of TS information was so acute. Randy couldn't believe that Chuck had never briefed the director on this. It was an unfathomable omission. Randy swallowed hard and licked his lips that now seemed as dry as desert stone. "Sir, the actual algorithms are there, in fact."

"Let me guess," the director began sourly. "To tamper with them would be to risk exposing the operation. What the fuck, Johnson. You'd better have a solid-gold, leak-proof method for ensuring no escape."

"Randy," said Chuck, with an almost sarcastic tone, "explain it to the boss."

At this point, Randy was lost. Was this some sort of bizarre test, some sort of proving ground for him? It seemed impossible. There was way, way too much at risk. Of course there was a plan, as solid and hermetic as they could devise, but why had Chuck not pre-briefed the boss? Randy's sense of solid reality seemed to be vanishing. But as he stood there, baffled for the moment as to how to proceed, Logan's words rose up once again in his mind.

***

"Look, Randy, and I say this with a lot of hesitation because Chuck is a friend, a really good friend, but he's been acting irrational the last couple of months. Expect the unexpected, and above all, don't doubt the plan and don't doubt yourself. It has risks, but it's solid, trust me. If you were the last man standing you could defend it alone, so don't lose faith in yourself."

***

Randy swallowed painfully and tried to clear the dust from his throat. "Well, sir," he said, "the majority of the reload takes place at night so as to minimize interference with ongoing work during the day. Understand that prep work for this will have been going on for several days in advance. Every individual working for Alpha or their subs has been identified and security will know them by sight. There will be no substitutions allowed during the final week of the reload. RF monitors will be installed in key locations surrounding the new facility, and a jamming protocol will be activated if any RF transmission is detected."

"Meaning they have to physically remove the media on a disk or drive," the director put in.

"Yes, sir. An unannounced search of every individual working that night, immediately as they leave the facility, should discover any media that is leaving in that manner."

"And you think they'll be carrying it? Just like that?" The director once again looked at Chuck as he spoke the words.

"Actually, sir," Randy continued, "that is a possibility, though the media may be small enough to be swallowed. But there are really only two possibilities. The first, that it is on them, will be eliminated by subjecting each individual to an RF scan on exit."

"Their civil rights? Unlawful search and seizure?"

Once again, Randy was amazed that Chuck had not already cleared this through the director. "Sir, they've signed paperwork that, umm, voluntarily allows this procedure. It's in the fine print, sir, but 'legal' assures us that we are within our rights."

"Right," replied the director, "until one of them hires Johnnie Cochran to defend them."

"Long before that, we have the media, and the individual is removed, quickly and quietly. Our techniques for rendition and subsequent extraction of information have improved over the years, and within days we'll have the information that we need," Chuck said grimly.

Randy was once again shocked by Chuck's brutal demeanor, but the director nodded tersely, turning to Randy. "And if it isn't on anyone?"

"We sweep the room. And then we sweep it again, just to be sure someone hasn't left behind a gift package. Of course, no one leaves until this procedure is complete."

"And that's it?" the director asked again.

Randy looked directly at Chuck with questioning eyes before giving up. He turned back to the director. "No, sir. We said we didn't remove the code, but we did add a little something. Anyone attempting to access it will find their hard drives infected with a pathological bug that not only crashes servers, but will attempt to transmit its location to, well, to us, sir."

The director nodded, and rose. "Nice work, Johnson. You know what they say. 'Don't fuck up!' Thanks for the brief, Randy. Oh, and of course …"

"There will be agents there, including me and Randy," said Chuck, "to be sure there aren't any hitches."

The director nodded again and left the room.

***

With the meeting over at last, Randy checked himself for fatal wounds … none. Minor bleeding would cease eventually. It was now or never.

"Boss, can I have one more minute?"

"What?" asked Chuck, the harsh edge still in his voice.

Randy took a deep breath and looked directly at his mentor. "Permission to speak freely, sir."

Chuck narrowed his eyes in a hard face, and after a moment said, "Granted."

Randy took another breath like a high diver attempting his first triple, and plunged in. "What the fuck is the matter with you, boss? You've always been tough, capable, and somewhat inscrutable, but the last couple of months, since our meeting with the Fletchers in LA, you've had a stick up your ass the size of a sequoia. I don't mind being on the wrong end of the shit-shoot for a good cause, but I'm not going to get fucked up the ass for no good reason. So, how 'bout sharing just what the hell is going on?"

Randy had expected an immediate response: possibly a considered one, most likely a blow-up that might just end Randy's career, but he had not anticipated the thoughtful silence followed by the quiet, measured words, "Is that all?"

Randy blinked and swallowed hard, but accepted the opening. "No, actually," he continued, his voice a tone lower, but his intensity undiminished. "You've really hurt your friend. He's no fool. Hell, he's probably smarter than both of us combined, and you've been wiping your feet on him like he's a doormat. As for his wife, if it weren't for Logan, she'd have ripped your balls off and stuffed them down your throat."

This image seemed amusing to Chuck and he smiled and rubbed his stubbly chin, his invariable sign of thoughtfulness. "Boy, are you ever right about that, Grasshopper." It was the first time in months that Chuck had used the name. "And where'd you learn that language? I didn't think you'd ever been in the military."

"College," said Randy. "I imagine it's changed over the years, sir. If you don't say 'fuck' every other word now, people think you're strange."

"Well, that just beats shit!" said Chuck, with a tired smile.

"Boss, let me help! You know I will. You know I can."

"Randy," said Chuck, all the edge gone from his voice, his features and body language once again the man Randy had known drinking "Old Monkeyshine" at Nimbus Brewery, "do you know what I want, for you that is?" Randy said nothing and Chuck continued. "I want you to stay alive. I've been good as dead three … four times over the years. I don't want that for my son, and I don't want that for you. You think there's something else on my mind? You're right. You think you can help?" Chuck paused for a long, long time. "You can't. I'd say I wish you could, 'cause you could, but this is not something I want you involved in. Trust me on this, Randy, don't get yourself dead."

***

"You look beat, Randy," Gail said, as they strolled along Golden Gate Promenade later that afternoon. The wind was chilly and damp, but there was no heavy marine layer and they were able to enjoy a very clear view of the stately Golden Gate Bridge as they moved west along the bay.

"Beat? Maybe … yeah … I guess so. Actually more than beat, I'm confused."

"Did you talk to your friend Logan after the meeting?"

"I did. Gave him a full dump … well … he already knew the content of the brief, so it was more a dump of the reactions of the group, mostly Chuck."

Gail hesitated a moment and then continued, “I know you can’t really talk about the information, but can you tell me about your boss? Did you get any kind of an idea what was bothering him?”

“Well, there is definitely something on his mind that has nothing to do with anything I’m working on. He told me that straight up. But then he slammed the door, hard. Seems to think, well, anyway, he said I couldn’t help. Well, he didn’t say exactly that, in fact he said I would be able to help, but he didn’t want me to.”

“And hence the confusion,” Gail sighed. “Maybe he’ll come around.” She moved closer to Randy and shivered slightly in the steady wind as he automatically wrapped an arm around her shoulder.

“Well, that bridge is an awesome sight, but I was thinking maybe a nice bottle of Chardonnay and a chargrilled grouper on steamed rice at Scoma’s,” said Randy. “What do you say, Grasshopper?”

“Scoma’s?”

“It’s a nice restaurant along Fisherman’s Wharf.”

“I think you must get out more than you let on, Mr. G. I guess working in Oakland, you’d have access to all of the fancy restaurants and beautiful women in the Bay Area,” she teased.

Randy laughed, and the tension in his shoulders seemed to ease for the first time since his briefing. “Actually, I can see the restaurant from the top floor of my building in Oakland, and that’s as close as I’ve ever been. My friend Cesar recommended it. And by the way,” he added, stopping and turning Gail towards him and peering into her inquisitive, expectant, green eyes, “there is no treasure on Treasure Island! That is,” he added with some confusion, “there would be, I mean, if you … if you were there.”

Gail didn’t reply, but leaned forward and kissed him for a long, long while. When she finally released him, she stood back a half step and studied his face for a moment. “How did I ever get so lucky?” she asked. “Remind me to send Logan a ‘Thank You’ card on the anniversary of meeting you.”

“Hmmm,” said Randy, smiling contentedly back at her. “I’ll get us a cab.”

***

The same day, Logan returned home, still puzzling over Randy's feedback on the briefing. It was at least something to know that there was a reason for Chuck's upsetting behavior, and Randy had shared a little more with Logan than he had dared to with Gail, particularly the thinly veiled warning from Chuck to stay clear of whatever he was engaged in. Whatever was going on had to be significant. This wasn't Chuck's first dance, and he was a tough, tough guy. The more Logan pondered it, the more he worried. What the hell was Chuck involved in that would overwhelm the operation they were all working on together? What could put that kind of pressure on him?

Logan tossed down his keys and hit the message button on his phone.

"Hey, babe," came the voice of Cathie, "I'm really sorry to tell you that I need to stay over in the Big D a couple more days. Some PR work with Geoffrey, you know, and setting up some book signings around the holidays. Oh hell, that probably isn't what you wanted to hear either. But I'll be back in a couple of days, I promise. I hope the little Grasshopper survived his meeting with Mr. Hyde. Give me a call and let me know how it went and that you still love me. Talk to you soon. Bye."

Logan sighed. He had more than half expected that Cathie's schedule between now and the New Year would be hectic if not insane. *The price of success,* he thought grimly. And with Randy out of town, he felt at loose ends for the first time in weeks. Strolling over to the bar, he selected an extremely mellow Tobin James Merlot, popped the cork, and emptied it into the decanter close at hand. He swirled the velvety liquid in the container and applied a sensitive nose to the opening: a lovely, mildly plummy smell with some very nice woody overtones. He poured himself a glass and strolled over to the piano. He hadn't played much during the last crushingly busy weeks and he cracked his knuckles gingerly before trying a few phrases of the well-known "Jazz Blues Etude." Before he realized it, he was completely immersed in the music, stopping only to sip and refill his wine glass at intervals, playing a new book of great jazz arrangements including "On Green Dolphin Street," "Misty," and "Watermelon Man" well enough that, perhaps, the original artists would not object to his rendition.

An hour and a half later, Logan pushed back the bench, drained the last drops from his glass, and stood up, unconsciously smiling. The music and the wine had acted in an almost magical way to unfetter both the rational and intuitive parts of his mind; to relax them to the point where thought and decision-making seemed almost effortless; to allow them to blend and to work in harmony while he remained almost a spectator to the process itself.

And as Logan rinsed the glass at the bar, several distinct conclusions, all children of this one relaxing interlude, came clearly to his mind. The first was that Chuck, distracted as he was, would need all of his help, and Randy's, to pull off their sting. Brutally put, he needed to be watched and corrected if he erred. The second, and Logan was certain of this by a leap of intuition that he could never have explained, was that whatever was going on with Chuck was not going to stay bottled up for long. And when it spilled, he knew that Randy and he might get splashed. But was it connected with the sting in any way? There his intuition left him hanging. The third thing, which brought a smile to Logan's face, was that Randy and Gail were in love. It was too, too easy to see in Randy's actions and hear in his voice. He wondered how they'd deal with a four-hundred-mile separation once the current task was complete. And finally, Logan realized he was hungry and in the mood for some company. And he knew exactly who to call. When the cell phone picked up, Logan could hear the loud, disjointed chatter of multiple conversations and the clink of glasses and silverware that confirmed his suspicions.

"Logan, you old coot, what's up?" asked Bart loudly over the background noise.

"Bart, you pathetic excuse for an engineer. It sounds like you're having another quiet evening at home. I was just wondering if I could join you for a baloney sandwich and a game of gin rummy."

Bart laughed a hearty laugh. "How about a nice Philly Cheesesteak, a game of darts, and I believe we can find some gin, or rum, or even a single malt scotch. Say hello to Logan, guys," he added, holding the phone out towards his two invariable companions, Gary and Kevin.

"Hello to Logan, guys," they both bellowed into the phone.

"Just like trained monkeys, those two," said Bart, "except without the training. So come on down. We're at McGuire's. Cougar night, my friend! Hell, even Gary might get laid."

"Heard that," Gary's voice responded faintly.

"Sounds good. I'll see you in about 20 minutes."

"Oh, and Logan, if I'm not mistaken, your lady friend Becky Amhurst and her posse are here as well."

***

"Becky, great to see you again," said Logan as he walked up to her table after circulating through McGuire's and touching base with his friends. "Bart said you might be here."

"And if that was the main reason you came tonight, I'd be completely and totally delighted," she said smiling. "As it is, I'm still happy to see you. Take a seat. We have plenty of spares tonight."

Logan pulled up a chair. In fact, only Becky was currently seated at the table, though he thought he recognized at least one of her friends from Skybox seated at the bar and talking animatedly to the gentleman seated next to her.

Becky caught his look and turned a tired smile to Logan. "Pathetic, isn't it! No, don't say anything. I know you'd make up a polite lie. It's one of the things I love about you. I'm actually too worn out to be here tonight, so don't mind me."

"Things that busy at work?" Logan asked.

"Bees aren't in it! Busy, crazy, chaotic, like a nonstop proposal. And it's going to stay that way until we finally reload the new servers. Honestly, I wish I could kill those raccoons a second time for all the trouble they've caused." Logan squirmed slightly, but said nothing. "Oh, and I've had Gail looking over that GPS code, as promised, even though I'd kill to have her working the servers."

"I thought she was waiting on clearances."

"Was, she was. She sailed through the process so quickly I'm beginning to think she really is pure as the driven snow. I'll bet she never even cheated on an algebra exam in high school."

"That's 'cause everyone was probably cheating off of her," Logan laughed.

"Oh, and speaking of things that you owe me, I might be able to get a little overtime from her on weekends if it wasn't for that young cicada you introduced to her."

"Grasshopper. It was a grasshopper. But, yeah, I understand. You never know. It could be love."

"Well, let's drink to love, then," said Becky, raising her glass and staring with a certain unveiled desire at Logan. He clinked her glass, and took a sip, looking the whole while like an embarrassed schoolboy.

"Don't worry. I'm just a little less subtle than most people. But I got it. Married, happily. Besides," she said, taking his hand gently, "I really do value your friendship and I wouldn't spoil that for a futile attempt at something more."

"You're OK, Becky. You're a whole lot more than OK. Another time and place, maybe?"

Becky shrugged. "If it wasn't for that silly clearance that I still need, I might have been tempted to use recreational drugs. Probably better this way." She took another drink and looked around at the bustling crowd as a sudden thought occurred to Logan.

"Umm, Becky, so did she, you know, find anything?"

"Did who find what?" Becky responded, with such a deadpan delivery that Logan nearly bought it, but then smiled.

"I suppose I shouldn't ask, at least not here, but …"

"The ungoverned inquisitiveness of the feline brought about his premature demise, my friend."

"Oh, to hell with the cat!" said Logan, with feeling. And both laughed.

Becky looked around the room, considered the heavy, blanketing amalgamation of sounds, and said, quietly, "I really shouldn't say, but, well, maybe. Now keep your shirt on," she added quickly, seeing the look of excitement on Logan's face. "Or," she added, reconsidering, "you can take it off, if you really want to! Sorry, my bad. Look," she continued, "our friend Gail is a girl genius, and she may, and I emphasize, may, have found something. When I can spare someone more senior to double check her work, or maybe even give it a look myself, then I'll let you know, I promise."

"Becky, I hate to press, but it is kind of important."

"I don't suppose you'd have anything to trade? Oh, dammit, I just have to stop that," she said, shaking her head in negation, and then turning to Logan with a serious concentration in her eyes. "I do wish you could tell me a little more. It would help, you know."

"I'm working it, Becky," said Logan, who, in fact, had pressured Chuck into starting paperwork for Becky. "In the meantime, trust me, OK?"

Becky nodded, the look of fatigue settling back onto her features. "So at least buy us another round?"

"That, I can do."

Chapter Twenty-Three

Nightmares

Stone slept uneasily on the flight from LA to Honolulu. He had been delighted to be on his way, knowing that Luana would be waiting to meet him on Maui for a long weekend of sun, relaxation, and surf. Alone for the past few weeks, without the companion that he had grown used to trusting, Stone found his anxiety had grown overwhelmingly. So much was at stake. Images of his early days in the employ of Ivor Vachenko blended irrationally with horrendous images of his solo pursuit of the mission—the mission from the man with no name—and with images of his mother and of his childhood. He rustled nervously in the airline seat in a state nearer to dreaming than to consciousness.

***

"Kerry McPherson got expelled from school today, Mom," he had burst out, as soon as he had entered the kitchen where his mother was preparing dinner.

"Oh?" asked Mrs. Kulwicki. "Was she being very bad?"

"She argued with the teacher, Mom."

"Well that's not always bad. Was she rude?"

"No, she just argued back, and the teacher didn't like it."

Mrs. Kulwicki sniffed and then asked, "What were they arguing about?"

"Well," said James, pulling up a kitchen chair, and snatching a carrot slice from the pile his mother had chopped for their salad, "we

were talking about the end of World War II, and how we dropped a nuke on Japan."

"Two nukes, dear."

"That's right, Hiroshima and Nagasaki," said James, eager to demonstrate to his mother that this bit of history was known to him.

"Very good, James."

"Well, and the teacher was trying to say that we didn't need to drop those bombs, that we would have won anyway."

"Rubbish. Tens of thousands of lives would have been lost; many of them our soldiers."

"That's right. And that's what Kerry said."

"And so that's why she got expelled?"

"No, not exactly. It's just that Kerry said that 'the end justifies the means.' And Mrs. Donnely said, 'That's just stupid. The end never justifies the means.' And then Kerry said she was wrong 'cause her dad taught her and he was always right, and then they were just yelling at each other, and then that's when she got expelled."

Mrs. Kulwicki nodded sagely, but continued to tear up lettuce in silence.

"So Mom, who was right?"

"They were both right and both wrong, son."

"I don't understand. When does the end justify the means, Mom?"

"You alone are the judge of that, son. Don't be afraid to make a decision. I'm sure you'll choose well."

***

Stone's drifting consciousness dissolved from his mother's kitchen, where a cool breeze had been rustling the curtains. There was no cool breeze here, only brutal, endless heat.

***

The man that was now Jason Stone had been working with Ivor Vachenko—he would not internally acknowledge "working for"—for over a year now and he had proved his worth, perhaps even his loyalty. His intel and tactical planning were beyond question, an uninterrupted series of successes following the first two missions that he had directed while under the threat of his life. Additional attacks, usually on poorly deployed NATO outposts, supply convoys, and maintenance facilities—all relatively soft targets, but as much as Jason felt his new colleagues could handle—had gone very well. And though he had been certain that neither Ivor nor the younger, arrogant man whom Stone had discovered was his nephew (how foolish was this man to believe he could hide this from him?) had fully trusted him at first, that had changed nearly three months ago when the nephew had encouraged his uncle to allow a night attack on an armored infantry column. Jason had vehemently objected, the plan requiring not only luck but relying upon additional fighters—unskilled to Stone's professional eye—who had only recently joined their cadre. Under the angry protestations of Vachenko's nephew, who had openly challenged Stone's loyalty in front of the entire group, the operation had gone forward. Stone had refused to rise to the bait of Ivor's nephew, and Ivor, overruling his nephew in this alone, had insisted that Stone accompany them.

The mission had gone poorly from the start. They had expected four vehicles on this black, deserted road, when in fact there were six that were approaching. Stone had silently waited to see if the nephew would display rational judgment and call off the attack. Under Stone's cold gaze, he had insisted that they proceed. Only one of the three IEDs had functioned, taking out the first vehicle, but allowing the others to form a protective group, and the young U.S. commander had been able to gather his soldiers between his remaining HMMVs and MRAPs and put up a bristling, withering fire. Precious minutes passed in a futile stalemate, minutes that Stone knew would soon bring down the Apache gunships or possibly an AC-130 that would put a bloody end to this feeble attack. A fighter with an RPG rose up from behind a crumbling stone wall where he, Stone, and several others had taken refuge. The sharp staccato burst of a fifty-caliber ripped the air; the rounds exploded the man's head and his body tumbled lifelessly to the ground amid his terrified fellows. Stone seized the man's RPG and slid to the end of the wall. He seized a grenade from his belt, pulled the pin and threw it in an arc over the wall, back in the direction from which the man with the RPG had been killed. It was a pointless waste, the grenade exploding near an MRAP and rattling dirt, rocks, and shrapnel off its sides like so many BBs. Pointless, that is, except that it drew the attention of the defending men for, perhaps, two seconds, and temporarily blinded those wearing night vision equipment. Stone rolled from behind the wall, targeted the HMMV at the center of the defensive position, and fired. The shot entered the cab with a violent explosion and a secondary fire immediately erupted.

Stone rolled back behind the wall and signaled for the three men remaining there to follow him. They were more than eager as he led them directly away from the road and the fighting that had intensified once more. When not more than fifty yards from the road, Stone turned parallel to it and proceeded nearly seventy-five yards past where the vehicles had formed their protective semicircle. Then, heading back towards the road, he passed unseen directly across it and into a stony culvert on the opposite side. Crouched and semi-running, he led the three men to a position behind the defenders.

Stone was amazed that there was no rear guard of any kind: an awful, unprofessional disposition of forces. He motioned for the man nearest him to pass him his rifle, a battered AK of dubious origin. Stone checked the magazine, waited for an eruption of shots from the opposite side of the road, sighted quickly, and fired. One man was down, unnoticed. Two others went the same way before the defenders realized they had been outflanked. The man on the .50-cal went down next, and now Stone's three companions began to fire, hitting nothing, but providing a noisy, frightening distraction. Stone lost count of the countrymen he killed that night, wondering if the mission, his mission, could bear the weight of all this blood. But the most significant result of the night's work did not occur until Ivor's nephew, realizing that they had somehow won, came upon the scene, firing his gun in the air, looking to loot and spoil, and perhaps take a human trophy. He approached the young U.S. commander and reached out a knife to take an ear when the young man, mortally wounded, but not yet dead, had jammed his .45 right into Ivor's nephew's gut. Ivor's nephew had looked into the man's flickering eyes, the last spark nearly gone, and had turned white with fear and despair, eyes wide, expecting the sharp crack of the .45 and expecting his own immediate death. The .45 barked out, a single shot, and Ivor's nephew stood, stiff as a stone, waiting for the pain and the oblivion. Instead, he saw the spark flee from the young commander's eyes, a neat hole appearing in his temple and his head turning to the side as though rolling over in sleep. The nephew slowly turned in the direction of the shot and saw Stone silently holstering his own H&K.

"We ought to get the fuck out of here, don't you think?" Stone asked, calmly.

That night's work had resulted in embarrassed gratitude from the nephew, from Ivor, and naked praise from the three men, now heroes, whom Stone had brought with him. Embellishments, truly unnecessary to the fact, were fabricated and piled upon the man who had brought them victory against odds, and the fetters of doubt were broken at last. Certainly there was resentment, at least by the nephew who, once having realized he was still alive, insisted in his own mind that he had the situation under control at all times, and was jealous of the praise that his men heaped on Stone. But though resentment still remained, the fear of disloyalty had vanished. Stone had killed U.S. soldiers with apparent unconcern. He was a viper, but he was their viper.

***

A jarring transition within Stone's consciousness and a soft groan escaped his sleeping lips.

***

Three months after the attack that had shaken off the manacles of mistrust, Stone had been able to return to his true mission, seeking those whom the man had implied might be able to help him. They were a scurrilous lot: ignorant, brutal, greedy, and untrustworthy;

and yet, possibly able to confirm and improve on the man's information, which was growing stale with the passage of time.

The village in which he met them—there were five in all—had no name; in fact, it barely qualified as a village. It was a collection of dirty huts and buildings that had, in the past, housed the shepherds who fought a losing battle with the elements and thieves, trying to protect their malnourished flocks. Now, it was used as a resting area by the poppy dealers who traversed these mountains bearing their crops in jeeps, carts, or on the backs of asses or human slaves.

In the months since he had been allowed to move more freely, he had made contact with a mixed band of Uzbeks and Iranians who claimed to have knowledge of a valuable prize, taken through Uzbekistan at the fall of the Soviet Union. As his informant had told Stone, the "prize" had been destined for Iran, but betrayal and murder in Turkmenistan had brought confusion, fear, and uncertainty as to whether the prize had survived, and if so, who held custody. The man's intel, gathered over years of spying, bribery, theft, and killing, had pointed an odd finger in the direction of Saudi Arabia and to a strong, intensely loyal family not directly linked to the government.

The leader of the group that Stone met that night, a former member of the Iranian elite guard and a man of now uncertain loyalty, had offered to assist Stone, for a price. Over the course of weeks, this group had isolated an individual, a Saudi national, who was reportedly a conduit for information, a communication drone and courier for sensitive information between the royal house and the custodian. The courier's family had been captured and sequentially beheaded until the courier had surrendered—a humane gunshot to the head had replaced beheading for the remainder of the family, which had included several children. The courier had then been brought to this location for questioning as Stone had wished.

Stone ducked his head to pass through the low door into the dimly lit room where the prisoner was being held and received his first shock. The courier was not a man, but a woman, an attractive Saudi woman perhaps not more than twenty-five years old. It was clear that she had been handled roughly. Her long dark hair, tangled and dirty, framed a lovely face spoiled only by a dried trickle of blood from the corner of her gagged mouth and a dark bruise above her forehead. Her dress was equally dirty and torn in several places and she had no shoes. One ankle seemed to have been injured, and more dried blood was apparent on her foot. Stone quickly recovered from his shock as the woman's huge, terrified eyes registered a tiny flicker of hope at the sight of this large man. English? American? Perhaps he might be a friend. The flicker of hope died quickly as Stone asked, "You speak English?" Hesitation, and the Iranian slapped her hard across the face, starting a flow of tears and sobs. "You speak English?" Stone asked again, quietly. This time the woman nodded rapidly in the affirmative. "Remove the gag," Stone ordered.

The woman licked her lips and tried to mouth words, to beg for help. "Water," said Stone, and a metal cup was placed to her parched lips. She drank greedily, the water running down her chin and neck. "Please, I ..." she began, but a hard slap silenced her and she hung her head, crying softly.

"I need information," said Stone, "So please listen carefully. When you have given me this information, all this will end," by which he meant a swift, painless death. The Iranian only smirked and stared greedily at the woman. "Who has custody? What are the plans for its use? Where is it kept? How is it guarded? That is all I need." In a snake-like movement, the Iranian grabbed the woman's hair and jerked her head back and waved a huge knife in front of her eyes. "Speak," he hissed.

Despite her fear, the woman said nothing. The silence hung in the room like a death sentence. Stone motioned to the Iranian and they left the room, the woman watched by the four remaining men.

"Does she know?" asked Stone.

"She knows who. As for the rest ..." and he shrugged.

"Find out." Stone said in a voice of steel.

The man grinned an evil grin and turned back into the room. At a word of command, two men raised her to a standing position and sliced and tore the remaining clothes from her body. There was no door between the two rooms, and Stone listened to the yells of the men and the terrified screams as the woman was thrown onto a small table in the room. Sounds of pleading, blows and another agonized scream as the Iranian brutally began raping her. What followed: screams, begging for relief, crying out to the large, pale man, the American, for help; more struggling and more beating as each man in the room savagely took his turn with the young woman. Nearly an hour passed and near silence came from the room, followed by a splash of water and the cursing of the Iranian, followed by another string of orders to his followers.

Glancing in the room, Stone could see the woman, still pinned to the table, blood running from between her legs to a small pool on the floor. Her breathing came in rough gasps as the water the Iranian had thrown into her face to bring her back to painful consciousness, mixed with her tears and made a pool of another kind around her head. One man grabbed her wrist and brought her hand out in front of her face and a second man grasped her little finger and bent it back, back, slowly, until a dull snap was heard followed by a blood-curdling shriek of agony, the woman's body arching off the table and writhing, squirming, with an energy renewed, but to no purpose. The Iranian repeated his question, waited but a moment, and nodded again. A second snap was heard and the screaming became incessant. Time lost meaning. There were only the questions, the dull snap or the flash of a knife and the screams that went on and on. And yet, surprisingly, Stone had been able to think during the hours of torture that followed, and he had reached a satisfactory decision.

At last, the Iranian left the room, his own sadistic needs sated for now. "Only one answer," he said. "It is all she knows, but it should be worth very much, no?"

"The name?" Stone asked.

"Hasim bin Wazari," the Iranian said with a grin.

Stone and the Iranian reentered the room. It was a scene from a butcher shop. Nearly all of the young woman's fingers had been broken, several completely sliced from her hands, and cuts along her legs, belly, and breasts had painted the table red, with dripping still to be heard into the puddles soaking into the dirt floor. Though breathing and apparently conscious, it was uncertain whether she was truly still in this world. The conversation with his mother repeated with startling clarity in Stone's mind.

***

"I don't understand. When does the end justify the means, Mom?"

"You alone are the judge of that, son. Don't be afraid to make a decision. I'm sure you'll choose well."

***

Stone silently pulled his handgun, and without the slightest hesitation, placed one clean shot in the girl's forehead, and she quickly passed beyond all pain. With equal rapidity, Stone whipped the gun upward and in an easy arc around the room. Five other shots rang out in rapid succession and echoed in the enclosed space and the five men dropped like sacks of meal—human garbage, now just something for him to dispose of. The decision Stone had reached while the woman had been tortured was a simple one: leave no loose ends. It was a policy that would serve him well over the years.

***

Stone woke from a restless, disturbing sleep as the aircraft touched down in Honolulu. And he woke full of doubt.

***

Some of Stone's disgust, if not his doubt, was wiped away a few hours later as he and Luana drove up Highway 30, on Maui, in a meticulously restored 1968 Jaguar XKE convertible. The ocean flashed in and out of view as they headed up the coast towards Kaanapali, and the steady trade winds added to the self-generated flow of air as the big cat's six-cylinder flung them effortlessly along the road. Stone had been unusually silent after a warm welcome at the Kahului Airport, and Luana had allowed him to sort through his own thoughts, or, as it seemed to her, to internally resolve some problem that clearly manifested itself in the tenseness of his body and in every facial feature from his slightly furrowed brow, to his narrowed eyes, or the firm set of his jaw.

***

When at last they were comfortably seated on the veranda of her parents' home, sipping champagne and nibbling at appetizers, Stone broke the silence. Gazing down the gentle green slopes upon the gleaming, toy-like coastline and the town of Lahaina, all bathed in the gold-orange, horizontal rays of the setting sun, he began. "I'm sorry if I've been rude. Remember that wool gathering we talked about in San Diego? Well, I've been loading up a few truckloads full."

"You did seem, well, preoccupied."

"And for that, I sincerely apologize. I've missed you," he said, taking her hand in his.

"And I you," Luana returned, with the faintest of blushes that only this man could still coax from her cheeks.

"It was generous of your parents to let us use their home."

Luana laughed. "Well, it is my home as well! And, of course, they are traveling in China, together for a rare wonder, for several weeks."

"It's unfortunate we can't spend that time here, together."

"Yes," Luana frowned slightly. "Our respective duties call us away much, much too soon." She sighed, but then a smile brightened her face. "And yet, we have the weekend to ourselves. Two precious days! And so," she began after a moment's thought, "let me dispense with one last matter of business, after which I propose we banish all thoughts of any cares, demands, or responsibilities beyond the boundaries of this island."

"To which I wholeheartedly agree," said Stone, raising his glass and delicately tapping hers. "In fact, I must confess to a fantasy of swimming naked with you in that pool at moonrise," he said, indicating with his glass the huge, pristine pool that seemed to depart from the edge of the veranda and extend out into space, perched as it was on the very edge of the sloping hillside.

Luana laughed and said, "And what if there is no moon tonight, Jason?"

He in turn laughed and gave her a knowing look. "Oh, in my former line of work, we did a lot of things at night, and it was a necessity to know the phase of the moon. Trust me! Nearly full tonight. Moonrise around ten thirty."

"I bow to your superior celestial skills, sir," she laughed again. "And so, back to business for a brief moment, for my news will only take a moment. Then the anticipation of dinner and a lovely swim." She paused, as the news seemed oddly out of place, oddly disjointed with the reality of beauty and relaxation that surrounded them. "Well, it really is quite simple," she began in a tone of voice which seemed as discordant to their previous dialog as the subject was to her previous thoughts. "My father has found the identity of Ivor's mysterious buyer of fighter aircraft. He is a Saudi, a very wealthy cousin to the royal house and a man of rather bad repute."

Stone sat up in his seat, and the tense eagerness upon his face made Luana hesitate. At last, she shrugged inwardly and continued. "His name is Hasim bin Wazari. Do you know him?"

It took every fiber of self-control that he possessed for Stone to answer in what sounded like a calm voice. "Yes, by reputation only. He is, as you say, a man of rather bad repute."

Luana hesitated a while to see if Stone would say more. There was clearly an enormous amount of thought taking place behind the rigid mask of his face. When it was clear that no more was imminent, she reached out a hand and took his shoulder. "Jason, I hope this information hasn't upset you, but if it has, you must know that you can share, well, your thoughts or your concerns with me."

By a titanic effort of willpower, Stone pushed the thoughts of his mission, the years of deception, brutality, and near hopelessness aside. He was even able to force the bloody image of the young Saudi courier from his mind, and the words of the Iranian pig, "Hasim bin Wazari," that Luana had just echoed. He captured his thoughts, locked them away for a later time, and returned to the present, leaning across the table and kissing Luana gratefully.

"Thanks," he said with a more relaxed smile than Luana had expected. "I may take you up on that. But for now, this is our weekend." And he kissed her again. The last thoughts that still haunted him before fleeing for the weekend were the words spoken with his mother so long ago, repeated once again, faintly, in his mind.

***

"I don't understand. When does the end justify the means, Mom?"

"You alone are the judge of that, son. Don't be afraid to make a decision. I'm sure you'll choose well."

***

Perhaps she had been right after all.

Chapter Twenty-Four

The Illusion of Normalcy

Fall moved towards winter and the passage of time, unburdened with anxiety, fatigue, or fear, seemed almost dream-like. Logan sat at the piano playing a mellow "Days of Wine and Roses" and enjoying the scent of the spiced-pumpkin candles that burned all around the room. It had been a truly lovely Thanksgiving. His daughter, Kelly, and her boyfriend, Scott, had spent the day and would be here for the remainder of the long weekend. Randy had also returned to Tucson for this gathering and, at Logan's insistence, had invited Gail. Both now were out on the patio seated within the warm, orange glow of the brightly burning chimenea. As Logan played, he looked out and watched them, remembering the days when he had first been in love, and still feeling the sweet feeling of emptiness, the feeling that there was no way to get close enough to this one special person, but enjoying the preciousness of the attempt. He smiled as he saw Gail feeding Randy bites from her own slice of apple pie, a specialty that was Logan's only contribution to this meal, a secret family recipe handed down from his mother, and always the finale to Thanksgiving dinner.

Logan transitioned to "I've Got it Bad (And that Ain't Good)," and played on. His daughter and boyfriend, cradling a second piece of pie, had joined Gail and Randy on the patio and were also enjoying the music as well as the warm, golden light.

The stress of the past months was momentarily forgotten; a calm interlude following the frantic labor, exhaustion, and anxiety. A FedEx delivery the previous day had included a note of congratulations from Geoffrey, and a dozen pre-release copies of Cathie's new novel,

Flashback. Without hesitation, Cathie had signed one, "To Elaya, my friend and gracious reader of my works. Happy Holidays!" She had wrapped and mailed it before the day was over, concluding, she believed, her last contribution to the sordid scheme that she could still hardly believe had so absorbed her and dominated her life. As she released custody of the package, a feeling of relief and finality flowed over her, as well as, oddly enough, a sense of emptiness. It was a feeling she always endured at the completion of a novel, though in the past she had always felt the thrill, excitement, and adventurous discovery of her next work teasing her towards the future. She felt that again, of course, for she had several quite fascinating ideas outlined on paper, or in her mind. However, the added element—the involvement with Chuck, Randy, and Logan in an actual, clandestine operation—was over, and there was no subsequent event of equal consequence to fill the void.

She was still puzzling over this unexpected sense of loss when she strolled into the family room and placed her hands lightly on Logan's shoulders. Logan smiled and tilted his head slightly to acknowledge her presence and continued to play. The candle smell wafted into Logan's nose along with the mixed fragrance of the apple pie and Cathie's perfume. It was a day to relax; to relax and be thankful. Tomorrow would bring what it would.

***

Black Friday brought a shopping blitz by the ladies, while the men remained home, smoking cigars and playing pool or darts and letting another lazy day pass by. A late return from shopping by three exhausted ladies, who, shattered nerves restored by a trio of Cosmopolitans, insisted upon displaying every item purchased to the somewhat less enthusiastic men, who nevertheless ooh'd and ahh'd at intervals sufficient to prevent abuse.

The late evening meal was a chaotic free-for-all among the leftovers—pots, pans, plates, dishes and utensils everywhere. It was, if anything, more satisfying than the previous day's. Even the cleanup of what had appeared to be an explosion of foodstuffs in the kitchen went well, and the after-dinner entertainment—Logan, Kelly, and Gail taking turns at the piano playing jazz, blues, and folk tunes respectively—brought the evening to a pleasant close. Only one disturbance during the day, a quick call from Geoffrey, had resulted in a relaxed smile from Cathie and the announcement, "The first shipment of *Flashback* is on its way to the retailers. Amazon will start filling pre-release orders on Monday, and, unfortunately darling," she said, putting a hand on Logan's shoulder, "I'll be doing a little traveling and wearing out my signing hand for the next couple of weeks. Back for Christmas though, I promise!"

"And I hope you all are too," Logan said with much sincerity, looking around the room.

"Wouldn't miss it," said Scott, enthusiastically.

Logan noticed a glance exchanged between Gail and Randy, and an immediate understanding and concurrence.

"We'd love to, Mr. Fletcher," Gail spoke, for the two of them.

"Oh for heaven's sake, darling," said Cathie, smiling, "Logan feels old enough as it is. If you don't call us by our first names, particularly him, he'll sink into a purple funk for days, maybe weeks."

"Well, then, thanks Logan … Cathie. We'll be here!"

Logan's mouth had opened to suggest that perhaps Chuck and Joy might like to attend also, but thought better of it, covering his mouth and faking a cough instead.

"Well look," Cathie teased. "He's all choked up!" A quick glance at his eyes told her that more was afoot, best discussed at a later time, and she continued smiling as she said, "I believe one more nightcap will do it for me. Any other takers?" A confused gabble of consent followed.

***

Later that evening as Logan prepared to turn off the lights, Cathie said, with uncanny intuition, "So what was bothering you?"

"That is so bizarre," Logan said, a look of pleased astonishment on his face, "like you're reading my mind." He paused and shook his head slowly, the smile fading from his lips.

"I was about to wonder out loud whether we should invite Chuck and his family. I mean, it would make sense since he already knows Randy pretty well, and then I suddenly choked it off because lately …"

"Chuck has been a gigantic dick!" Cathie finished for him. "But, yes, I had entertained the same thought. It would be wonderful to have him and Joy, their son maybe, but … I mean, it could really spoil things if he wasn't in a better mood than he is now. No sign of improvement, I suppose?"

Logan shook his head. "I haven't talked to him in a long while, but according to Randy, things have gotten even worse. Apparently, he isn't harassing Randy so much, but he's gotten distant … cold … extremely impersonal; no sign of the trust they used to share, let alone the friendship. No, according to Randy, it's a strictly professional relationship, but with the added stress that Randy knows something else is going on and Chuck knows that he knows."

"Does Randy have any idea when this might, well, resolve itself?"

Again, Logan's head wagged from side to side. "No. And he says it's clear that Chuck would NOT welcome any more questions, and so no more information is coming, period."

"Well," Cathie began. "It's a damned shame, but … well, we'll stick with the youngsters for Christmas. I'll be dragging by the time I finish this little tour, and I can use their youth and energy to help cook and clean and cook again."

"And I'm going to extort a little decorating help before they all leave Sunday. Early is good!"

"And early to bed is also good. Get the light, will you love?"

***

The same Friday evening, Chuck sat dismally alone nursing a "Town Drunk" at Murphy's. It was his third, and he recognized that the effects of the first two had impaired his judgment sufficiently so that he had ordered this one, and that the third would undoubtedly lead to a fourth. *Well fuck it, anyway,* he thought grimly.

Glen, the bartender, and a long-time acquaintance of Chuck's, had considered asking him directly what was wrong. It was rare, though not unknown, for Chuck to come in alone; no friends from work crowding in boisterously with him. But it was unusual for Chuck to have a third "Town Drunk," and when the request for a fourth was made, Glen sensed that some type of intervention was necessary.

"So," Glen began hesitantly, "fight with the spousal unit, Chuck?"

"What? Oh no," he said, automatically, before adding, "Well, yeah, actually. She said … what was it exactly? Oh, yeah, she said I had turned into a grumpy old shit, and that if I kept it up she just might change the locks on the house. That was yesterday, over that big fuckin' bird. I mean, why do the two of us need a twenty-pound turkey, anyway?"

"Uh, Chuck, you didn't actually say that, did you?"

Chuck rubbed the stubble on his chin. "Actually, I did."

"Dude, I'm surprised you lived to tell the tale. If I had said that to my wife, it would have gone something like the game of 'Clue,' you know, Glen, murdered in the dining room, by his wife, with a turkey leg. Yep, beat to death with the turkey leg. So I take it you're persona non grata today? I mean, she told you to take a hike?"

"No, actually, she tried to figure out what was bothering me, 'cause she is the absolute best, and I just confirmed to her that I am a grumpy old shit. No, I'm here voluntarily, hoping to not do any more damage."

"Yeah, well," said Glen, dubiously eyeing the fourth "Drunk," now half empty, "you might want to slow it down just a bit or your liver might be getting the damage. By the way," he said, leaning closer to Chuck in a conspiratorial manner, "I'd appreciate it if you wouldn't tell the owner I said that. It's my professional duty to get you loaded, you know."

Chuck looked at Glen, and chuckled slightly, a tiny smile fighting for purchase on his face. "First laugh I've had in weeks, my friend."

"So you know what they say, Chuck, barbers and bartenders. We're better people to talk to than shrinks. We cost less, listen better, don't judge, never tell the wife and, something I know you'll appreciate, we forget everything said to us by the next morning. So I know you can't talk about the business, but you can talk about the business behind the business. So how about it?"

Chuck's spontaneous decline froze on his lips. "The business behind the business." Well put. And why not? Fuck, the business had been painfully, brutally slow. He had exchanged e-mails with Sean, most of Sean's feedback extolling Chuck to "not fuck up." Helpful. And the messages on that crusty old answering machine had been maddening on so many levels. First, they were unbelievably sparse. Well, that was probably good as long as your gut wasn't in knots, waiting for information that might be available tomorrow, or never! And second, the information that Chuck had received told him of an ever growing certainty … an ever growing conviction that events, dormant for so many years, were about to erupt like a brooding, long-silent volcano. And if they did …

Chuck tried to remain calm, tried to convince himself that Shirley was up to this task, though he could not even begin to fathom the mind-breaking stress this man must be feeling considering what he himself was enduring, though so far removed. It wasn't as though there were anything at stake if things went wrong, Chuck reminded himself, with massive sarcasm. Oh, no, probably no more than a regional conflict. A regional conflict with WMDs, that is! And of course, he was certain that all the world's powers and superpowers would calmly sit back and counsel the parties to settle things peacefully. There was hardly any chance that things would get really out-of-hand and that the world would destroy itself in a radioactive inferno. Oh no, hardly any chance at all!

Chuck realized that his eyes had been staring blindly at the bar behind Glen and tried to refocus on the present. What had Glen said? "The business behind the business."

"Yeah, that," Chuck spoke at last. "Aw, man, I just wish … but listen, here's what it is." Chuck considered for a moment. "I've … I've got this assignment, and I think it's too much for me, you know, the stress, the pressure, whatever, and because of that I've been a gigantic grumpy old shit extraordinaire; and not just to Joy, but to Randy, that brilliant fuckin' kid, and to my best friend Logan. God I've been a shit. But you know, I guess I have discovered my limits—not of being a shit, there may be more potential there—but of what I can handle on the job. Man, I must be getting old, or something."

"Or, you're working on something big." Chuck started and shot a questioning glare at Glen. "Don't worry. That was just a wild guess, well kind of, oh well, the truth be told, Randy's been in here. Hey it's OK," Glen added quickly, noting Chuck's stiffened posture, "He didn't say shit. But look, Chuck, the man is worried about you. That much is clear. And he wants to help but knows he can't. And that's all. He just cares."

Chuck sat silently for a while, his angry words, the words that had no cause, melting away. "Like I told you, Glen," he said at last, taking a long pull and draining his glass, "I've been a galactic shit. And half, maybe more than half, of what's got me down is my reaction to being so fuckin' overwhelmed."

"You know, Chuck, when I've been a grumpy old shit, you know, on those rare occasions, especially with my lovely bride, I've used a technique that I discovered is infallible to get back in their good graces. It's kind of a secret, but if you want, I guess I could tell you."

Chuck had visions of flowers, candy, a romantic dinner with at least three bills involved, but asked, "So, how?"

"Apologize. Just tell her, tell Randy, tell Logan, that you're sorry. They'll get it, man. They know you. And tell them why. Not the details, just the plain facts."

"Yeah, but …"

"I got it, man, and warn them that you're likely to be a little, well, a little off until things settle down. I swear, it will work."

Chuck considered and then nodded. "Barbers and bartenders, huh?"

"In my opinion, bartenders are at the top. I'm just sayin'."

"And I might just have to agree with you," said Chuck.

***

Cathie, exhausted but happy, had returned from her whirlwind book signing tour a week before Christmas. The phone call from Geoffrey, two days later, had informed her that *Flashback* was now selling extremely well. The other factoid which he had been loath to admit was that the addition of the love story between her heroine and the former F-14 Radar Intercept Officer had not brought a wave of negative responses from readers. To the contrary, reactions to this part of the novel leaned heavily to the positive. Whenever Cathie recalled Geoffrey's forced meal of crow, a tiny smile crept to the corner of her mouth.

The addition of Chuck and Joy at the Christmas festivities, which had seemed impossible a month before, also brought smiles to both Cathie's and Logan's faces. The unexpected apology not only to the two of them but to Randy had brought a sense of reconciliation and normalcy that had been painfully necessary. In Randy's case, the verbal apology had been followed by a blind copy of a letter from Chuck to the director in which Chuck had given Randy (and the Fletchers) proper credit for their contribution to the hoped-for sting and had very graciously shouldered all of the responsibility for the communication breakdown prior to Randy's briefing. Chuck had also accepted all responsibility for the disharmony that was apparent at the meeting itself. It was an unexpected and nearly unprecedented act by Chuck, and the director, in turn, had heaped praise on Randy for his creativity, and Chuck for his candor and his obvious and successful mentorship of his young apprentice.

Nevertheless, the first meeting at the Fletchers' home on Christmas Day had been somewhat awkward, with Randy being unsure to what extent his previous relationship with Chuck had actually been reinstated versus only the establishment of a tenuous truce. However, when all of the family and friends, including Logan's daughter, Kelly, and Gail, were gathered in the same room, Chuck had raised a glass of wine in a toast.

"To my family and friends," he began, pausing for a long, long interval, "Well, what can I say. No excuses. I've been a real dick, and I'm truly sorry, and … and that's about it, I guess."

When everyone had drunk, Joy raised her glass again and looked with love and admiration at her husband, and said with a misty sparkle in her eyes, "And to my husband, the dick, and a brave man."

"Hear, hear," Logan said, draining his glass. "Now," he continued with a grin, "Who needs a drink?"

Chapter Twenty-Five

Heading for the Windmill

Wan Chu was unused to dealing directly with Ivor, having delegated this responsibility to his daughter with success. However, Ivor's request had been suitably deferential, promising also information of extraordinary value and timeliness. Ivor had also offered to meet Wan Chu at any location convenient to him at the earliest possible time. Wan Chu had considered this offer, and then accepted, under the condition that Luana also be present. Had he expected any resistance to this part of the arrangement from Ivor, he was disappointed. What had followed was an unqualified flow of praise for Luana—her intelligence, strategic acumen and leadership—that left Wan Chu absurdly pleased, beneath a layer of troubling suspicion.

A thick marine layer and a steady drizzle ruined the view from the penthouse of Wan Chu's Marina Del Rey hotel, but did not detract from the luxury. Beautifully furnished, carpeted, and decorated rooms extended out in every direction, covering the top floor of the building. Candles lit throughout gave more the impression of a Buddhist Temple than the rendezvous of a terrorist leader and his wealthy, rabidly anti-Western accomplice. Ivor was shown in and led to a table in a glass-walled dining area with views in three directions that spoke only of the dreary weather, far from unusual in Southern California in January. The scene did nothing to lower Ivor's spirits, however. Though he retained a certain anxiety, as appropriate when dealing with Wan Chu, he was confident that the information he possessed would be of exceptional value.

Once again, Ivor blessed his long-standing relationship with Elaya as well as hers with the foolish and gullible American author. Ivor had met Elaya years before in England, where he was developing his first contacts for a jihad that he hoped would spread across Europe. Elaya had only recently arrived to begin her graduate studies at Oxford, and the wild streak that Cathie Fletcher had observed in her friend in California had flamed into brilliance, and many a lost weekend was spent in the London metropolis seeking excitement and pleasure. Ivor, a handsome, enthusiastic, and bold man, with radical views on the role of the Middle East in world politics and the forceful tactics required to achieve his goals, had captivated Elaya, body and spirit. From his radical politics to his forceful lovemaking, she became enthralled. She had fantasized with Ivor of a revitalized Iran as the single dominant power in the region; enlightened and more liberal than the fanatical ayatollahs and mullahs would allow, and more powerful than even in the glory days of the Shah. It could be done! By controlling and subordinating the weaker countries in the region, and using Iran's military might and strategic location, it could become a dominant global player through control of the one substance which quite literally ran the machinery of the world: oil.

As both had grown, some of the fire and enthusiasm had left their veins, and both had taken a more practical approach, and confined the scope of their activities to what was practically achievable. For Elaya, marrying the pig of a Saudi princeling had allowed her to maintain a lavish lifestyle, circulate among friends around the globe, and maintain a shadowy hope that one day her grander schemes might still be realized. Her association with bin Wazari had also yielded an unanticipated and spectacular opportunity. And while she secretly laughed at his foolish notions of Saudi hegemony, she delicately and discreetly tailored his plans to align more fully with her own revitalized dream.

Ivor had carried on in a much smaller way with his jihad, enlisting the help of Wan Chu to bankroll his operations at a cost in forced humility and submission that had finally begun to rankle. Age had made Ivor more cautious, Elaya somewhat so, and their liaisons became few and discreet. Yet they remained, to some degree, the passionate lovers and starry-eyed zealots, still faithful to each other and their mutual cause, in an oddly muted and distorted way.

It was Elaya's relationship with Cathie Fletcher and her recognition that perhaps Cathie's fictional stories might contain ideas, if not actual sensitive information, which Ivor might find valuable. Her assessment had been correct, and though not every opportunity had been successfully exploited—Ivor still reddened with shame thinking of the wretchedly bungled lake poisoning—still, many had, and Wan Chu and his daughter had been able to severely embarrass the Pentagon and their military suppliers by their hacking operation, inspired by the intelligence he had provided. It was true that the breach had been discovered and that no real damage had been done, but still …

Wan Chu and Luana entered the room and Ivor quickly rose to greet them. "Luana, a distinct pleasure to see you, as always," he said, with a lowered head and a slight bow, which she silently returned. "And Wan Chu, my friend of long duration, it is a pleasure to see you as well. I hope all of your endeavors run as smoothly as you might wish?"

Wan Chu gave a courteous nod to Ivor and motioned for him to sit. "Some well, some less so," he replied, revealing nothing. "But perhaps this information that you bring will be the prelude to a future success. Please take water, tea, juice. Help yourself to fruit or pastry. No?" he asked, as Ivor politely declined, "Then please proceed."

Good, thought Ivor. *No silly small talk. No polite, banal pleasantries.* For as much as he might have denied it, Ivor's nervous tension had increased dramatically once Wan Chu and a completely mute Luana had entered the room. However, his confidence was still high, high enough to risk putting his proposition to Wan Chu as a rhetorical question. "Wan Chu," he began, "Would you like to acquire the ability to disrupt all U.S. tactical weapons? To interfere with their communication with their launch platforms and fire control systems? To override their targeting instructions? To, in fact, redirect them to targets of your choosing?" Ivor paused to let the words fully sink in. Luana's face took on a highly skeptical look, but Wan Chu's remained impassive, apparently unaffected.

"If such a thing were possible," Wan Chu began, at last, "its value would be beyond measure. American doctrine has always relied upon superior technology to counter superior numbers. A capability such as you describe would emasculate their tactical forces, which would then be pitifully outnumbered should a conflict arise." He paused again, and only the continuous patter of rain invaded the pure, thoughtful silence in the room. "*If* such a thing were possible," he finally repeated.

Ivor accepted the opening, and began to relate, as Elaya had done for him, the details exposed in Cathie Clarke Fletcher's latest book that indicated a once-in-a-lifetime vulnerability to the encrypted datalink network that wove so many future weapon systems together, a network like an entwining rope that, if grasped, could drag them all down together. Wan Chu listened phlegmatically, but Ivor thought he noticed a slight brightening of his eye, a slight involuntary opening of his irises, a fatal tell that a man in a high stakes poker tournament might make, and so tip off an opponent to a strong hand. Ivor finished his monologue and looked questioningly from Wan Chu to Luana.

At last, Wan Chu also directed his gaze at Luana. "Daughter, could this be accomplished?"

Luana had rarely been asked a more pointed or more significant question. She considered carefully under the silent stare of her father, and then began, cautiously. "If the information were presumed to be accurate, and this could be confirmed, in time, then the opportunity does exist to extract these critical algorithms … with proper planning."

"Ahh," said Ivor, looking pleased, and relaxing considerably.

"But planning is critical. There will be safeguards, certainly, and even in the confusion of rebuilding the server network of Alpha Defense, even though ISG already has a defined role and will have critical people present, there would be much work needed. It will take time."

"But the servers will be rebuilt by April!" blurted Ivor. "It is barely three-month's time!"

Wan Chu held up a hand. "Please forgive the interruption," said Ivor, hastily, though his own impatience at this tone of cautious deliberation was growing quite evident.

"And then," Luana began, "to fully exploit this vulnerability, to use it reliably in a combat environment, to achieve, as Ivor suggests, the capability to actually re-target weapons, will be the work of years and of many talented scientists." Ivor squirmed uncomfortably in his seat, but held his objections and his plausible counterarguments behind clenched teeth. "However," Luana continued, "the likelihood is that, in time, the capability to neutralize many tactical weapons, if not actually retarget them, could be achieved."

"We have no immediate need of this capability. There is time available to exploit such information," said Wan Chu, at last. "But, is there sufficient time to plan the information capture, daughter?"

This question, the true issue of consequence at this meeting, hung in the air for long moments. At last, Luana answered with a slight lowering of her head, a sign to her father that she understood the seriousness of her next words and the events that might spin forward beyond the control of them both. "Perhaps." Ivor choked back an exclamation of impatience. "I will need to consult with one or two experts whom I trust, and develop a tentative plan," she continued, her eyes commanding Ivor to remain silent. "In the meantime, I will lose no time in reassigning ISG staff so that, should such a plan prove feasible, the most skilled individuals will already be on site and poised to act at the word of command."

Wan Chu nodded, and a tight-lipped smile of approval made a brief appearance upon his face. He would have been disappointed in his daughter, a rare state indeed, had she answered in any other way.

Ivor looked from one to the other and realized that this was the best outcome he could have hoped for. He shrugged his shoulders in poorly affected nonchalance. "I only hoped that this small bit of information might prove useful," he said, rising from the table.

Wan Chu also rose and took Ivor's hand. "You as well as I know the significance of this information. It will not be overlooked, regardless of whether we choose to act upon it or not. Nor will your efforts be unacknowledged. Luana will make the arrangements."

Ivor murmured words of thanks, gratitude, and respect, and was shown to the door.

***

Later that evening, Wan Chu sat puzzling over the possibility that this unbelievable coup could actually succeed. The contract to acquire the two MIG-29 aircraft was already being executed, and seemed an unrelated issue entirely; Luana had made the request on behalf of Ivor prior to this meeting. But the notion of exploiting the reload of Alpha's servers to ferret out the encryption of the new tactical datalink system seemed too much of a gift. To think that every weapon launched would not only fail, but could be manipulated in flight; all midcourse information subverted, all terminal sensors made useless at a minimum, or redirected to track their own launch points! He forced himself to think more calmly. He would await his daughter's assessment, but it was possible, just, that his life would be justified, completed, with this one last dagger to the heart of imperialism.

Had he been able to penetrate the mind of his daughter, he would have been less pleased. She had grown accustomed to Ivor Vachenko's braggart ways and his poorly trained and boorish minions, but she no longer wished to work with him. She would follow her father's wishes, for now, but she had begun to wonder why he would put faith in this man, this charlatan. Luana, of course, exempted Jason Stone from her contempt. This was partially due to having first grown to respect him for his skills, and then … Trust! It was a fleeting substance. How long would it last with Jason? She had, in fact, begun to distrust her father. His judgment of late seemed clouded, his repeated faith in Vachenko, unwise. And if Wan Chu was losing his ability to lead, what then? Luana had often thought of the succession plan for her father. It was a dangerous and bloody path.

***

Joy ran a hand across her husband's stubbly cheek. "What's bothering you, babe," she asked quietly.

Chuck's inner strife, quieted somewhat by the Fletcher's gracious Christmas celebration, had returned, and he felt the pressure of failure more strongly than before. He was so, so close to simply saying …

"Oh, lover, I, I wish … I wish I were a better man, a man who actually deserved the likes of you!"

"Sweet, dear," Joy replied, kissing his forehead. "But that didn't tell me shit. Can you really not share it, just a little bit?"

"Oh, babe, I wish," he stopped entirely. "Joy," he began again. He so seldom used her name now—preferring other teasing, loving expressions—that she turned swiftly to him, more frightened than before.

"Joy, keep your passport handy. Oh babe, just pray that when the dung hits the windmill, it doesn't splatter on us."

***

Randy held Gail in his arms and listened to the rain pounding the roof of his Oakland apartment. By her soft, rhythmic breathing, Randy knew she was asleep. He moved slightly, and she tightened her grasp around his chest. What the hell had happened in the last five months? She meant more to him now than his work, his life. He puzzled over it for long minutes, and finally reached a conclusion. He wondered if Logan would laugh.

***

"Randy's in love, you know," Cathie said, as she placed both of her hands on Logan's shoulders. Logan turned his head slightly and continued to play a somewhat sad rendition of "My Funny Valentine."

"Of course he is," said Logan. "She is too … Gail I mean."

"And so …" Cathie offered.

"So, I have no specific information, like whether he has bought her a ring. He'd be a fool not to, though, just as I would have been a fool to not buy one for you."

"Tiny historical correction, dear," Cathie said, "I believe I asked if you would like to get married. The ring came a little later."

"So I let you think," Logan added with a laugh. "I bought that ring months before. I was just too chicken to ask you right out, I guess."

"No! And you tell me this after," she thought quietly and then gave up the effort, "after all these years of marriage?"

"Had to, didn't I?" said Logan, as he continued to play.

"Lucky me," she said. "C'mon, love. Finish that and come to bed."

***

Less than a month had elapsed since Ivor's meeting with Wan Chu, but the wheels had begun to spin rapidly. Stone had said goodbye to

Luana in Los Angeles before boarding a nonstop to Paris, from thence to Riyadh to meet with Ivor and to discuss the details of the critical acquisition of the equipment, the strangely archaic equipment, which seemed to be such a priority. Hasim bin Wazari had insisted upon this meeting with Stone, as Ivor had informed him that tactical control of the operation would be in Stone's hands. And Stone had for once blessed the years living the life he had lived, spilling the blood he had spilled, for this opportunity seemed like a gift. There would not be a better chance to confirm his already firmly settled suspicions, gain priceless intel on bin Wazari's plans, and begin to develop his own strategy. April was getting too damn close!

Stone felt extremely confident in his ability to move about Riyadh. He had a few contacts, was fluent enough in the lingua franca of the region, and knew the city well. His only concern was that Ivor was going to keep him within arm's reach the entire time. And why not? He was being brought here at bin Wazari's behest, more to display himself than to actually describe his plan, which was childishly simple and extremely low risk. With that as the primary goal, when would he be able to free himself from Vachenko, and how much time would he have? Stone had concocted several stratagems, including a feigned illness and possible hospital stay, if no other better opportunity arose. He hadn't begun to realize that the odds were already heavily in his favor, for Ivor was wondering how to free himself from Stone.

***

The business with bin Wazari went by quickly, but not without some theatrical excitement. Stone would have normally been on his guard in the strange home of a powerful, unpredictable man. Since Stone had already concluded that the meeting had been arranged more to display him than anything else, he was doubly so. As Ivor and he walked down a narrow corridor towards the room where they were to meet bin Wazari, Stone noticed that Ivor had begun to hang back, glancing, it appeared, at some extremely interesting fourth century urns that decorated the hallway. *So Ivor is in on this little puppet show*, thought Stone. *Just as well. He'll have to offer a stupid, unbelievable denial later, which will put him at a disadvantage.* He smiled inwardly, for Stone was always looking for an edge. In this event, in fact, he held all the cards, for he knew exactly what to expect.

As he entered the large sitting room where they were to meet bin Wazari, the escort suddenly spun around and produced a knife, which he meant to wave in Stone's direction. Stone, fully anticipating the attack, grabbed his arm and, using the man's own momentum, brought both knife and arm harmlessly in front of his body and into the shoulder of one of the two men who had been positioned on either side of the hallway's entrance into the room. As he did so, Stone leaned and pivoted on one leg, driving his other foot into the chest of the man on the opposite side, sending him crashing into a small table. Stone then spun and planted his elbow in the escort's windpipe, easily acquiring the knife as the man collapsed to the floor. He re-gripped the knife in an effortless but blinding motion, drawing back and throwing with deadly accuracy, the blade whistling across the room to plant firmly in the hardwood floor between bin Wazari's feet. It was over.

Hasim bin Wazari recovered from his shock, glanced at the knife at his feet and at the man at the opposite end of the room who had thrown it, and politely applauded. He then motioned Stone to enter and take a seat. "Most impressive, Mr. Stone," he said, in perfect English. "Most impressive indeed." He gave a frown in the direction of his injured men, and made a curt motion with his head for them to leave the room. "My good friend Ivor has repeatedly told me of your great skill. I confess a part of me was disinclined to believe him entirely. I see now that he spoke no more than the truth, perhaps even understating your abilities. Allah be praised that such a man as yourself should be serving Him." Stone made no comment, and bin Wazari pried the knife from the floor, laid it on the table and seated himself. Ivor, already wearing a somewhat sheepish look, joined the two at the table.

"Excellency," Ivor began, "We are fortunate indeed to have the likes of Mr. Stone as our ally in a righteous cause." Ivor smiled a winning smile at Stone, who only thought, *You owe me one, my friend. Advantage—Kulwicki!* His internal use of his own name, his true name, nearly forgotten over the years, pleased him, and he smiled back at Ivor.

The rest of the meeting went as Stone had expected. Bin Wazari seemed more interested in making small talk with his guests and urging them to try a fig, a sugared date, an exceptionally delicate pastry, than in Stone's bland, and quite brief, explanation of the operation. Hasim took note primarily of the date, mid-April, and the clever way Stone planned to use the airshow to gain access to the necessary F-14 while simultaneously extracting the missile components from an extremely well-preserved Phoenix missile located a very short distance away, at the Southern Arizona Aerospace Museum. A single operation on a single night, with all material acquired and no loose ends. Stone estimated a twenty-seven minute execution time for the entire plan. His risk assessment: extremely low.

"Wonderful, wonderful, Mr. Stone. Another cake, please," he continued, holding out the plate. Stone politely declined, and the meeting ended with the three rising and bowing graciously to each other. A somewhat cowed and resentful escort led them to the gates of bin Wazari's compound.

It was then that the second half of Stone's extraordinary fortune became apparent, as Ivor turned to him with the same sheepish expression he had displayed in the home of bin Wazari. Stone was expecting the beginning of a lame excuse when Vachenko shocked him with the words, "Jason, with great regret, I must leave you. A former business acquaintance of long standing has engaged me for the evening. Our talk will be mostly reminiscence of old times and old friends, which would be sadly boring to an outsider. The hotel offers many diversions which would please you more, I am certain. You will forgive me, I trust?"

Stone gave him a penetrating look, as though somewhat angered by this sudden abandonment, then shrugged his shoulders in mock resignation. "Of course, Ivor. Enjoy the time with your friend. I plan on having a lovely dinner and then perhaps a walk in the square; possibly see if I can find a quiet, discreet location for an adult beverage, if you know what I mean."

"Yes, yes," Ivor brightened. "I may be able to recommend one or two possibilities."

***

Jason's plans had changed dramatically from the moment Ivor announced that he had another engagement for the evening. He still intended to re-enter bin Wazari's compound and look around. There had been far too many men, well-armed men, lingering around a decrepit old building near the south wall. And there had been guards posted along the parapet of that wall as well; not so on the others. Stone knew he would not be able to get too close, but he felt that a vantage point from the roof of the main building, which looked down upon the mysterious relic to the south, along with a parabolic microphone and a few hours of monitoring discussions between the guards, might prove instructive. He had intended to wait until at least 2:00 a.m. before returning, which still gave him plenty of time to follow through on the new element of his plan: tracking Ivor Vachenko.

Ivor had left the hotel with extreme caution, carefully looking about before entering a cab. Stone left shortly thereafter on a rented moped, dressed so as to be entirely unrecognizable; resembling more a robed and hooded street peddler than his mother would have thought appropriate. The taxi wound through the city by a circuitous route clearly meant to deceive an observer. Stone followed innocuously less than half a block behind until the cab turned down a small alley behind a row of moderately sized, walled houses. Vachenko stepped out of the cab, paid the driver, and was left standing behind a tall stone-and-plaster wall with a small, olive-colored door at its base. From the shade of a brushy palm tree at the end of the alley, Stone watched as Ivor produced a key and let himself in. Jason motioned to a group of small boys, begging on the nearby street corner. He pointed to the bike, said a few words, and produced a handful of coins. He distributed half of them evenly among the group, showed the other half once again, and then deposited them into his pocket. He was quite certain that his moped would be safe.

Stone first entered the neighboring house's yard. It was quiet and deserted. From the alley, he had noticed a large sycamore tree, growing in an ancient tangle from this yard, tightly pressed against the wall that separated this yard from the one Ivor had entered. The tree stretched out with large, gnarled branches that disappeared into a thick cloud of foliage. Stone climbed the tree silently, checking carefully at each pause for visual or auditory warnings. There were none. He waited patiently, comfortably situated in the tree's sturdy branches, for dusk was near. As the shadows deepened, he edged himself along the wall until he came to the house and a frosted and thickly curtained window; very likely a bathroom. Reaching within his robes, he pulled out a small packet which resembled an iPod. In fact, Stone had over two thousand songs on this unit, a unit that had also been slightly modified. He pressed a small microphone nestled in a rubber suction cup against the glass, and plugged the jack into the iPod, situated his ear-buds comfortably, and selected Classic Rock 2 from his playlists.

At first Stone smiled. Then he frowned. He smiled because the first sounds he heard, resonated off the glass and amplified to clarity within his earpiece, were clearly the sounds of two people making love: panting, rustling of sheets, endearing words, creaking of springs, cries of pleasure. He frowned because he felt himself a fool for following Ivor to a tryst and for being the depraved idiot at the window. *Hell*, he thought angrily, *all old Ivor had to say was that he was going off to get laid. I wouldn't have cared and he'd have known it.* But that was the thing. Ivor did know it. Why the dissimulation? Why the subterfuge? Perhaps it was worth listening a while longer. Stone listened on, feeling he was an altogether distasteful human being; this eavesdropping seeming somehow dirtier and more ignoble than all of the violence and killing he had taken part in previously. The end was close, the voices grew louder, and Jason reached for the microphone with distaste. His fingers were prepared to pull the device when he heard Ivor clearly: "Elaya, Elaya, my love, oh, my love."

Stone froze. Elaya? Certainly not! *Oh, Ivor*, Stone thought, *are you banging bin Wazari's third wife? Really? You're a brave man. Your life wouldn't be worth shit if he found out. No wonder at the secrecy! Vachenko, you're a fool.*

The sounds grew confused and violent, and then lapsed into near silence, heavy breathing gradually slowing.

Long minutes passed by until, at last, the rustling and creaking of the bed indicated that one or both had risen; sounds of clothes being pulled on, the scrape of chairs. A subtle "pop" was followed by the sound of liquid being poured into glasses. A few more quiet minutes passed before Elaya, her voice unmistakable, spoke in a hushed tone.

"Ivor, my love, we mustn't, not again, not here."

"You wish me to leave?"

"I wish you to be with me, always, but not here. Soon. Very soon."

"Always soon! Always the future!" said Vachenko, angrily. "Why? What is in the future?"

"My love, do not be angry. It is our chance. It is our hope from so, so long ago, here at last!"

"Tell me, Elaya! As you love me. These things which Hasim has demanded. The aircraft, the foolish bits of old weapons and jets. Why?"

"As I love you, so I will tell you. Oh my Ivor, you must not fail him, you must not fail us."

"I will not, I swear."

"Ivor, as I love you, he … he has a … device." A long, deathly silence ensued. "A device from long ago, lost by the Soviets, taken by loyal forces. It is here! He has it! And at last, there is a plan. The old aircraft, the old jet, was once part of the Iranian air force; its electronics, not functional, the weapons old and of little use. For a decade Saudi scientists have examined how to make these weapons work again."

"Speak plainly!" Vachenko said, harshly.

"We will take the device, it is quite small, and put it into the weapon. The electronics that you and your man will deliver will allow us to launch it, as though from an old, though recognizable, Iranian fighter."

"The target?" asked Vachenko, grimly.

Elaya hesitated. Though above all she desired power within a secular and dominant Iran, and was willing to do much to achieve it, she realized the extreme risks, and somehow speaking the name brought the reality, and the risk, into the immediate present. "Jerusalem," she whispered.

"What!" cried Vachenko. "What insanity is this? They will retaliate! They will destroy Tehran, all of Iran!"

"No, no, no, my love, listen. That is the plan of my husband, my husband the fat fool! Israel crippled, Iran destroyed, and only Saudi Arabia left as a dominant power in the region, with control of all oil exports in the region, a dominant power in the world."

"This is madness! How can you stand by and …"

"Hush," she said, placing a finger to his lips. "The fool will not succeed. The weapon will destroy Jerusalem, but the ayatollahs will be indicted, immediately. Iran will fall upon the mercy of the world community, slaying the ayatollahs, slaying the mullahs, and a new, enlightened regime will be in place before there is certainty, before the Israelis can retaliate. It is all in train, my love. And then, and then our dream will be achieved: a free and powerful Iran. Soon after, we will implicate the imperialist dogs of the house of Saud as the true instigators of the attack. No more than truth! And the swine bin Wazari will crawl and beg and die. And we, *we* will *be*, still and forever! My love, the dream will be reality!"

Stone listened for a while longer. He imagined what was going through Ivor's mind. The foolishness of Elaya's argument was beyond belief, but perhaps Ivor might be persuaded. At bottom, Ivor was weak; a pawn, a man to be manipulated by more powerful men. Or women!

The game was on. Stone would return to bin Wazari's compound this evening, but there was really nothing to be gained. Stone was as certain as he could be that the device, a small nuke, was hidden there. Stone himself would procure the final pieces that would allow Hasim bin Wazari's people to complete the weapon. And it would fly, it would be launched at Jerusalem, and a fireball, an inferno, would light the night sky!

***

Thousands of miles distant, in a quiet house on a quiet morning, James Kulwicki's mother smiled for no reason.

Chapter Twenty-Six

Spring Skiing

James Kulwicki dreamed uncomfortable dreams as the Boeing 777 jet flew through black night towards Dallas's DFW International Airport. In his dreams, James was alone. Of course, he had been alone for so many years through every waking hour of every day. But then, during those years, he hadn't been James Kulwicki. He had been Jason Stone. He had one mission only, and he had been allowed to exercise complete autonomy and discretion to fulfill that mission. His mother would have been so proud. He himself was proud. It was the assignment he had always prayed for: no incompetent superior officers making foolish, tardy decisions, no rules of engagement preventing obvious and logical tactical decisions and actions, no politically shifting strategic goals that wavered like a reed in a storm. It was a solo, well-defined mission governed by self-direction and self-reliance.

There was only one problem, and that was that Jason Stone had no mother, and James Kulwicki had no mission. Why this was, he couldn't at first discern. He had been born, he was fairly certain of that, and he had grown up as James Kulwicki, with a doting mother and a rather simple, even foolish, father. But he had somehow evolved, somehow transformed. It was like the caterpillar to a butterfly transition if only the chrysalis had been a concussive explosion that had torn his body and rattled his brain. And he was now like the butterfly if butterflies were brutal, heartless, single-focused killers. But above all, he was alone.

The man who was now Jason Stone smiled briefly in his sleep, for his subconscious mind had made a decision long before it would be spoken or even acknowledged in his waking mind. He would no longer be alone! A part of him would argue that it was required that he forgo being alone in order to complete his mission, and a part of his mind would counter that the mission could rot in hell. James Kulwicki had been raised as a Christian, and this much of his upbringing had transferred to the man Jason Stone. James or Jason was damned. For what he had done, there was no forgiveness. And so, to hell with the mission! Yet he must clutch the only thing that was now accessible to him in the world which would surely be his last. Could she, would she help? And to the question, "Help with the mission or help with salvaging my soul?" the man who was two men had no answer. And so James Kulwicki dreamed uncomfortable dreams.

The next flight was much shorter—to Denver, Colorado, where he would meet Luana. It had long been arranged that they would meet for some late-winter skiing. Jason had struggled in his mind with their last conversation regarding trust. Both of them, it seemed, were heartily worn and disgusted with the continuous dissimulation. Part of Jason's mind cautioned him against this trust, when trust at this juncture might jeopardize the mission he had suffered so much to complete. But a fully rational and logical part of his mind was certain that the only sure means of success was to engage Luana's help. He was at the edge of a cliff, with a leap of faith the only option. He little realized that Luana found herself at the brink of the same dangerous precipice.

***

Both were unusually silent as they drove along the interstate, past Idaho Springs and Georgetown, through the Eisenhower Tunnel at the Continental Divide, past the icy Dillon Reservoir, and finally turned south on Highway 9 towards the town of Breckenridge. It was Luana who broke the silence with a perceptively intuitive comment.

"It seems that we both have very much to say, and so we are silent."

Stone thought for a long moment about the wisdom of that statement, and then nodded. "Yes, I suppose that's so. At least, I need to talk to you and risk that rather deadly trust that we've discussed previously."

"As I must do, as well. It seems odd that we both have come to the same need at the same time."

"Maybe not so odd," said Jason. He thought for another long minute. "Look," he began. "We have three days together. I have an idea. What do you say that we take tonight and tomorrow and just enjoy it; pretend that the fate of the world really doesn't rest with either of us." Stone gave a lighthearted laugh as he said this, but Luana cast a piercing look in his direction. "And then," he continued, "well, we get back to the business that's distracting us both. Do you trust me?"

"I do, Jason."

"And I trust you."

The car crunched along the plowed but icy roads through the town and they pulled up, a few minutes later, at the Grand Lodge. The evening found them at a candlelit table watching a gentle fall of snow powdering the ski slopes west of the lodge. They drank several bottles of wine with a filet and lobster main course, talking of common, inconsequential things: the extraordinarily clear and icy air; the laughable, inexpert skiing of the couples they observed, perhaps attempting night-skiing for the first time; of snowfalls Luana had seen on Mount Haleakala. That night, they made love slowly, with very few words spoken, but gently, appreciatively, as a married couple might on their first anniversary, or as two lovers might when they fear they may soon be parted forever; and so capturing and savoring the moment, living perfectly in the present. Afterwards, they slept deeply, untroubled by dreams of an uncertain future.

***

The exhilaration of skiing, and the concentration that was necessary, overwhelmed their thoughts the following day. Luana and Jason were both capable, though inexpert, skiers. Yet they tackled increasingly difficult runs throughout the day, plunging down steep gaps or carving the slopes with graceful curves, racing along and then changing direction suddenly, fountains of snow shooting up from the edges of their skis. The brilliant sun turned the powder they tore from the hillsides into cloudbursts of dazzling micro-diamonds that arced gracefully through the chill air, drifting at first, and then settling like a silver blanket on the slopes as they raced on. Though the sun was dazzling in the clear air, it delivered no warmth, and the two would meet repeatedly at the base of the runs, near the lodge, exhaling rapid little clouds of breath, cheeks rosy with the chill and the pumping of their blood. More than one tumble left them laughing and teasing each other for their ineptness. And before they were aware, the sun had hidden itself behind the mountains to the west, which cast huge, hard shadows across the ground, finally reaching out and shrouding the lodge. Their holiday was nearly over.

***

They had agreed to enjoy their dinner first, however, and they sat in the spectacular, glass-walled enclosure of the Packed Powder restaurant, which afforded a near 360 degree view of the moonlit mountains. Brilliantly lit ski runs were scattered all about the steep slopes, and a few skiers continued to brave the rapidly falling temperatures. As Jason and Luana sat at their ease, they relived their day's escapades, greatly exaggerating each other's slips and falls, as well as their own skills on the slopes; unwilling to relinquish what seemed like such normal pleasures to the crowds of people throughout the resort town, but which, to them, were a precious commodity, stolen from a life that both had begun to see as morbidly brutal, anxious, and unsatisfying. Luana at last spoke quietly, masked by the happy buzz all around them.

"I sometimes feel, Jason, that all of my resentment, ambition, hatred, and …" she hesitated, "frankly, disgusting behavior, dedicated to some largely hypothetical purpose, has robbed me of my life. Perhaps this," she said, looking about the room at the people, enjoying a simple luxury, talking, laughing, relaxing, "has not been so worthy of my scorn and derision as I once thought."

Jason looked at her with hard, unblinking eyes, and finally shrugged. "I guess we grow," he said, simply.

Luana smiled. "Well, at least you didn't say we grow *old*."

Stone laughed. "Oh, I reckon that will happen pretty much whether we want it to or not." But a cloud passed over his face as he thought of all of the people he had known who had not grown old, who had left life early, often in pain, always in regret. Images flashed before his eyes: his partner's face as the IED ripped him apart, the young commander of the armored column, the light fading from his eyes, and the beautiful woman, screaming as she told him all she could of Hasim bin Wazari.

Stone turned his face away from Luana's for a moment. Nothing could change what he had done, and nothing could possibly justify all of the evil in which he had played such a significant part. What he could do was to remain true to the reason for it all: he could complete the mission. And once that mission was complete, what then? Oddly, it was a question that neither Jason Stone nor James Kulwicki had ever asked himself. Perhaps, he thought, it was because in his heart he had never believed in the possibility of success; he had never actually believed that he would accomplish the mission. The man had implied as much. If Jason Stone failed, he would be replaced, if he interfered, he would be swept aside. Jason wondered if the man had ever for an instant believed that Jason could succeed.

***

Not so very far distant, in a small home in the hills above Oakland, Chuck Johnson coughed and gagged, spitting phlegm and blood into his toilet.

"Are you all right, babe?" Joy called through the door.

"Yeah, fine," Chuck lied. "Just a little, you know, indigestion or something."

"Are you sure?"

Chuck's self-reliance was at its lowest ebb. He had received a message from Shirley today. Another simple, banal, information-packed note. "To all my friends, I'll be visiting the sunny Southwest, Tucson area, looking for work. That might just prepare me for a little more extreme heat when I go to Israel and points beyond. Perhaps it won't be quite so hot in spring. Wish me luck in all things. Your dearest friend, Shirley." What the message meant in simplest terms was that Shirley would be in Tucson, on the job, with bloodshed likely. He would then proceed to the Middle East (talk of Israel was a blind) and the reference to extreme heat meant an action, perhaps the culminating action to conclude his assignment. An exploding nuke was as hot as the sun.

Chuck was terrified, for this conclusion would put many things at risk. He prayed that the splash wouldn't reach the shores of the United States. Chuck was desperate to share the stress he was feeling with someone other than the seemingly brass-balled Sean Carlos DeFranco, and his wife's question hung in the air, a soft, tantalizing, temptation.

In the end, he reverted to something his mother had told him after he joined the navy and had been so, so discouraged. "You take one day at a time. Don't worry about tomorrow or the next day or the day after. You get by *this* day, and do you know what happens? You get one more day closer to success, and you never, never give up. That's the secret. You just hold out for one more day."

"Yeah, babe, I'm fine. I … I'll be right out and we can hit the sack."

Chuck wiped the blood from his lips and flushed the toilet, but as he grasped the knob to exit, he had a sudden thought that seemed to appear from nowhere. He realized that he had never really expected Shirley to get so far; he had never really expected her to succeed.

***

"You seem to be gathering wool again, Jason, wool of the very blackest kind," Luana said, with a worried smile.

Jason sat silently staring out the glass wall of the restaurant, and then turned weary, troubled eyes back to her. "It's starting to snow." He paused and then answered her implied query, "Yes, wool of the very blackest kind. And I'm tired of it. The time has come to talk, at least for me, and to take the biggest risk of my life."

"For me as well." She reached out and took his hand. "I want my life to change. I want it to be with you. Is there a way that this can be?"

"I have a bottle of cognac stashed in our room for just such an emergency," Stone continued, the touch of a playful smile returning to his mouth, "What do you say we continue this conversation back there?"

As the two left the restaurant, hand in hand, more than one table buzzed about the tall, handsome man and his beautiful date, obviously so much in love, and spending a romantic ski weekend in Breckenridge, Colorado.

***

Both Jason and Luana were sipping their cognac, both desperately wanting to speak, and both reluctant to begin. Jason plugged his iPod into the radio/dock and selected a playlist. Much to Luana's surprise, a vintage Simon and Garfunkel tune, "The Sounds of Silence," began.

Luana listened and smiled. "In fact, that is one of the most beautiful and haunting melodies that I've ever heard."

Stone smiled, and then began, as though to himself, "I will not work with Vachenko any longer. There are several reasons. One is that he is a fool. He is in league with Elaya Andoori, wife of bin Wazari."

"You mean with Hasim bin Wazari?"

"Not with bin Wazari, and twice the fool on him. Ivor intends to double-cross Hasim; he is in league with Hasim's wife, Elaya, only. A relationship of long duration, if I'm not mistaken, and far from platonic! Luana, do you have any idea what that fool Hasim has in his possession?"

"My dear Jason," she said, placing her drink on a table, and crossing the room to place a hand on his shoulder, "it would seem we have more than one fool here, and you must speak to me more slowly, or I will become confused."

Jason heard the teasing note in Luana's voice, and saw the twinkle in her eye. He laughed aloud, relaxing somewhat.

"Perhaps I had better begin at the beginning," he said. "But first," he added, pulling his concealed weapon, a very professional looking H&K compact, from the holster at his armpit and placing it on the table, the grip facing Luana. "I am now going to trust you as I haven't trusted another human in years. If my trust is misplaced," he hesitated only a moment, "then, kill me. I bet my life that my trust in you, that my love for you, is on solid ground."

Luana seemed shocked, but touched the butt of the gun, edging it back towards him. "Your trust is secure."

Stone stared at her with the eyes of granite that he had often used to penetrate deception in others. He saw none. He stroked her hair, grasped his glass, and sank into a chair, staring out the window at the now steady snowfall. "Fresh powder tomorrow. That's lucky."

"Luana," he continued, turning back to her, "I've been searching for years for a stray nuke that the Soviets let slip through their hands when their empire collapsed. I found its location years ago in the physical custody of one Hasim bin Wazari. I've been searching for evidence as to how it might be used or transferred to others who might use it, and I've trodden a path of bodies to learn what I know now. But I don't just want to track it, I want to destroy it! That's proven to be a bit harder, but it looks like there may be a possibility, now. Bin Wazari is the key. And after years of violence, betrayal, and blood, he's finally concocted a plan to use the thing. I know the plan or, I should say, the plans. Bin Wazari intends to destroy Jerusalem, to frame Iran, and so bring the Saudis to regional hegemony. By the way, did you know his wife, Elaya, is Iranian?" Stone asked, interrupting his narrative. Luana shook her head, a sense of the surreal creeping into the room, and a look of horror crossing her face. "Yeah," Stone said, "that complicates things. Her plan is a bit more convoluted: allow Jerusalem to be destroyed, but blame the ayatollahs and mullahs, lead a popular uprising in Iran and seize control, begging the world for forgiveness and begging the Israelis not to annihilate them."

"Jason," Luana began, "this is madness, sheer madness! Once the genie is released, there will be no stopping. It will mean a regional war, growing to a …" she stopped, unable to speak the words. "Jason, they are all fools! There can be only one end! My father would not wish it. I do not wish it! It can only mean destruction!"

"I mean to stop it," Stone said. "But, Luana, I need your help."

Luana stretched out a burgundy-nailed finger and rotated the butt of the gun back in Stone's direction. "And now I will trust you."

Stone waited, tensely. Luana poured herself another drink, and seated herself as well. In the background, the music whispered on.

"I have served my father and my mother for years, seeking their recognition and approval as they pursued their dreams: my father's, that China should take her rightful place in the world, my mother's that the haole should pay for their arrogance and brutality. And my dream … my dream … Jason, I no longer have any dream but to somehow …" Luana halted, allowing bitter, resentful tears to run down her cheeks. "My father's judgment is … no longer my own. His dream has turned to blind obsession and his judgment has waned with his growing bitterness. Vachenko and his men are fools, pigs! I will be free! I will choose to live … as I see fit!"

"This insanity must not occur," she continued passionately. "There must be no war in the Middle East. I will no longer deal with these puppets. Vachenko must pay! This I can easily accomplish." She looked at Stone with blurred eyes, and he nodded. "As for Hasim and Elaya … how may I help?" she asked.

Stone explained and Luana blinked incredulous tears from wide, terrified eyes.

***

Stone waited patiently for Luana to completely absorb what he had said. As she became calmer, it was clear that the analytical part of her mind was performing an assessment of his plan. When at last she spoke, it was in a soft, thoughtful voice. "When will you acquire the parts for the old aircraft and missile?"

"April 17th, the night before the airshow begins."

"And when must you deliver them to Hasim? Or will you be turning them over to Ivor?"

"My intention was to deliver them myself, one week later."

"That leaves very little time." Stone waited and watched Luana's face. An internal calculation, perhaps more than one, was in process. "I must act now," she continued. "In order to have the equipment, I will need to discover if it still exists, obtain the necessary documentation, and find among my staff one or more persons with the necessary skills. The software is extremely old, the language, I am sure, is assembly language. Its use is a forgotten art except by those who cherish an understanding of the history of computers. There are still a few who can perform the task. But the interface hardware must be located and acquired soon. Can this be done?"

"You tell me where," said Stone, "I'll get it. Being as old as you say, I can't imagine it will be kept under much security."

"No indeed. In fact, my greatest fear is in locating a working, or at least, reparable, set of equipment. I have ISG staff that can do so, discreetly."

"Then it is possible?"

Luana thought a while longer, but only for the sake of form. She had already made up her mind. "Yes," she said, "technically quite feasible. But Jason, the risk, once the missile has been modified and loaded onto the aircraft, is absolutely enormous." She struggled for an appropriate analogy. "Perhaps like juggling loaded weapons with their safeties off." She shrugged. It seemed woefully inadequate.

"Yes," Stone acknowledged. "And yet it seems the only sure way. Can you think of another?"

Luana had thought hard on this subject over the last hour since Jason had first opened his mind to her. "No. I can think of no better way. As you say, it must be destroyed or the fools will simply try again." She paused. "No, it seems the only way."

"Then we'd better hope our juggling skills are up to the task!" he said, with a humorless smile.

"Indeed," Luana quietly replied, with a tense nod.

Stone thought a moment longer, then continued on a topic he had intended to broach once they had completed this discussion. "Luana, you mentioned that you could deal with Vachenko. How?"

Luana actually smiled. "What would be the reaction of Wan Chu or Hasim bin Wazari if they felt Ivor had somehow deceived them both and planned to break their deal for the purchase of the two aircraft?"

"They'd be a trifle put out," Stone replied—a spectacular understatement. "I take it you could set up Ivor to take a fall?"

"Yes. Fifty million dollars will need to be exchanged. Ivor is the conduit for this exchange. What if that conduit should prove ... porous? What if, at the crucial moment of transfer, the money should disappear?"

"Both bin Wazari and your father would be livid, and they'd naturally assume that Ivor's sticky fingers had snagged the cash. His life wouldn't be worth spit, and it would be a race to see whose people killed him first." Jason considered. "Luana, can you actually intercept the money en route?"

"With a little information that I hope you can provide, borrowed, let us say, from Ivor, I can do even more! Jason, with fifty million dollars, our lives can become whatever we wish!"

"You're serious?"

"Oh, yes. Quite serious."

Stone looked out the window and stared for a long while. Snow was still falling gently on a deepening night. He could almost taste it: success at last; the end of the deception, the end of the filth, and the end of the bloodshed, if … if they could do it. He himself felt stronger and more confident than he had in months, and he realized that some, perhaps much, of this was due to the abandonment of his solitary loneliness; his willingness to trust. Ah! That perhaps was the key. Jason had an ally for the first time since he had spoken to that forceful man in the hospital room, so long ago. He had opened himself up to tremendous risk, and he was certain that the man would not approve. And yet, the man had given him the mission, trusting entirely to Jason's skill and judgment, and this decision, though perhaps the most dangerous gamble of his life, seemed … right! Stone applied his usual litmus test to this decision as he had to countless others of lesser importance throughout his life. What would his mother think? Jason considered as he continued to stare out at the peaceful scene. In his mind's eye, he could see her nodding and smiling. He had done well. Stone made one other critical decision that night. He had put his life and his mission in Luana's hands, but he would withhold one tiny bit of information until the successful conclusion of their plans. He would wait until all was accomplished to tell her his real name.

Stone turned his face back to Luana, a face clear of doubt and full of confidence, and he smiled.

Luana returned the smile, and then by a leap of intuition said, "There is something more on your mind, Jason. Will you tell me?"

Stone smiled more broadly and pointed to the Jacuzzi on the patio of their suite, a three-inch blanket of snow on its cover, steadily deepening. "How about it?" he asked. "We're going to be pretty busy for the next couple of months. How about we finish this vacation with a little midnight hot-tubbing? Just you, me, the snowy night, and the rest of the Courvousier?"

"That would be lovely!"

Chapter Twenty-Seven

Contact

April in Tucson brought the first hint of the brutal, intolerable heat of the summer. A white sun shone down from a cloudless sky, parching the last of the winter's moisture from the soil and air, and threatening even harsher days to come. Though still well below one hundred degrees, the intensity of the sun's rays along with the extremely low humidity could combine to fool a careless hiker, and the local mountain rescues were actually more numerous during this time of year. Rapid evaporation tended to provide temporary cooling, and a lack of sweat-saturated clothes a false impression that one wasn't really working that hard, seemingly not even sweating at all. Extreme dehydration and heat stroke were the common results. Randy and Gail, Logan knew, had restricted their occasional hikes to early mornings, leaving at sunrise, and returning by 10:00 a.m. at the latest.

Logan smiled when thinking of the two. They were expending unconscionable amounts of money traveling back and forth to each other's homes, but seemed happy enough about it. The smile left his face, however, as he fumbled through a jazz etude for the tenth time running. For some reason, his combined left hand and right hand fingering simultaneously failed at this point, an unusual double failure that seemed unconquerable. *Two simultaneous failures*, he thought, sourly. It just didn't seem fair.

Logan stared out the window at a cactus wren, working busily on a hole in an old, tall saguaro just outside, and thought about multiple simultaneous failures that had plagued him over the years. His first recollection brought a return of his smile as he pictured himself, a boy of no more than seven, crawling under the Christmas tree and sequentially replacing light bulbs in the string around the pot-like base. In this early period of his engineering career, therefore, Logan learned the meaning of "series" versus "parallel" when it came to wiring. Unlike all the rest of the light sets on the tree, these oldies were wired in series. When one burned out, the entire string went black. And how to fix them? Well, the only method was to remove each bulb in turn and try a new one. When the string returned to life, you had discovered the burned-out bulb!

The technique worked well enough, in a slow, steady, brute-force sort of way. But on more than one occasion, two bulbs had chosen to give up the ghost simultaneously! Oh the frustration of trying to find the correct combination! In his later days, Logan had calculated the relative complexity of discovering a single point failure versus a multiple. It was maddening. With a single bulb out, it took at most six attempts to find the problem. With the possibility of two out, it took twenty-one total combinations to guarantee success.

Several times throughout his professional career, multiple coding errors in tactical software or multiple simultaneous hardware failures had plagued him. The level of complexity had often caused major delays—weeks to months—troubleshooting and correcting these problems. In the end, none had beaten him, but he felt that at least half of his grey hair had its origins in these sticky, multiple failures.

And so here he was, staring at the piano keyboard and his two hands, carefully placing his fingers, and moving slowly, slowly through the passage. It was no good. Every time he attempted to play at the appropriate tempo, his hands would betray him. He put the piece aside in frustration, and stared out the window. There was something else, something else troubling him, and he was taken mentally back to the meeting in LA where he and Randy had argued with a grumpy and pigheaded Chuck regarding the odd connection of terrorist events, and how no hypothesis seemed to entirely satisfy the observations. In the end, they had made a conscious decision to act based on an incomplete understanding. And this was what was now troubling Logan. Certainly, their plan seemed to encompass all logical possibilities. But what if their logic was flawed? What if there were, in fact, two burned-out bulbs? The analogy helped Logan to focus the question, but brought him no nearer to an answer. He kept thinking about Cathie's discussion with Elaya, and how Elaya had shown such a ridiculous interest in the love story, involving her heroine and the former F-14 RIO. Yet Elaya was the prime target of their poisoning. Did any of this make sense? Logan saw himself in his mind's eye, cramped beneath a Christmas tree, testing bulbs. What if two were burned out? He decided that he'd better re-read his wife's latest novel.

***

Chuck felt he had no choice. According to Shirley, very important things were soon to happen in her life. She had mentioned an exciting visit to the desert Southwest, with the hopes of a successful job interview in Tucson. She was zealous, giddy with the chance to close this deal. Chuck had been alarmed, and his ulcer had worsened. Against his doctor's advice, he had not taken time off from work, and he was drinking very heavily. His drinking and his anxious irritability had been a heavy burden to Joy, who had long since given up trying to get him to share his problems and had settled into a basic avoidance mode. This was easy enough, since the number of daylight or evening hours when Chuck was at home had shrunk to zero. And when, completely frustrated at last, Joy had announced that she was going to travel to visit some cousins in Los Angeles, Chuck had only grunted noncommittally. Joy had stormed out of the room, packed, and left the next day.

The pressure only increased when a comment from Sean Carlos DeFranco on his Facebook page strongly hinted that Alex should "get off his lazy butt, and get back in touch with Shirley." What was he waiting for? Chuck had spent that evening vomiting blood into his toilet. Chuck's only feeling was gratitude that Joy hadn't been around to patronize him, but no, that wasn't it, to witness the physical manifestations of his weakness. *Damn Sean Carlos and damn Shirley!* thought Alex/Chuck.

There was a protocol for contacting Shirley more directly, and Chuck was ashamed at his lack of faith when he internally acknowledged that he had never expected to use it. At one point he picked up the phone to call Logan to just … and that was the problem, to just what? Chuck realized he was lonely, tired of carrying the burden of secrecy alone, not needing to disclose content, but just to share his awful, solitary burden. And then he thought of Stone: the unique man who had been more alone over the years than Chuck could even imagine. How had Chuck dared to give this man such an assignment? "The safety of the Middle East, the safety of the world," was the knee-jerk response. Chuck could have laughed; the words were so hollow, so childish. He coughed again, and automatically brought up the stained handkerchief to catch the blood. Damn it! This needed to stop. According to Shirley, events were coming to a conclusion. Chuck must re-establish contact.

***

Cathie waved and smiled at Logan as he sat in his backyard, a warm fire in their small chimenea, a glass of "Cab" at his elbow, and her novel in his hand. Logan smiled back, took a sip of wine, and read, for the fourth (or was it the fifth?) time, the dialogue of the lovers from her novel.

***

"I don't understand, Frank. You're telling me you can't say a thing about that mission: when you left, when you returned, whether there was any danger. You know you can trust me."

"Please don't ask me to explain. It, it was ..." Words failed, and he took her in his arms. "Listen, babe, it ... it wasn't pretty ... never mind."

"What was it?" she insisted. "What did you do?"

And time spun backwards towards a very, very bad day.

Expo, Frankenstein, and six others had left the carrier with a full load. It had been a slow, clumsy climb from the deck. The Phoenix missile was no lightweight, and they had a load of six on each aircraft! Their mission was unacknowledged; the missiles modified to exclusively suit this unique situation. The Radar Intercept Officers had given them their targeting: a convoy of extremely high value targets, moving along a desert road in the blackness of the night. Coordinates were passed, and an intercept vector was calculated. At extreme range, they launched. Twenty-four weapons bound for a convoy of six high-value targets. Midcourse was easy. A highly improvised and experimental terminal guidance had been incorporated into these unique missiles, and hence the redundancy in weapons. They needn't have worried. Coming in at close to Mach 2, the kinetic energy was nearly enough to wipe out any target they struck, and the large warhead easily compensated for a near miss. It was shooting fish in a barrel. Six high members of a rogue government and their entire entourage were obliterated; not a trace was left to identify the United States as being responsible. In fact, no acknowledged U.S. weapon had the capability to do what they had just done; and hence, the beauty and elegance of the operation.

It had been long ago, and Frank just hugged Liz warmly. "Sorry, babe. You don't have a need to know."

***

Logan put the book aside, reached for a metal poker, and prodded the wood within the chimenea. Sparks floated from its top and drifted, flickering, into the night, while the pleasant smell of mesquite filled the air. What was wrong? Why couldn't Logan put the pieces together? In Logan's opinion, the love story itself was predictable and uninteresting. The use of the missiles, well, somewhat of a stretch, though Logan had seen more unlikely things in his long career. But, so, so, so …

"You seem to be in a brown study, love," Cathie remarked, as she came up behind him and placed both of her hands affectionately upon his shoulders.

Logan turned his head and smiled up into her smiling face. "Come and sit for a while, would you?"

"Oh, I was hoping you'd ask," she teased, pulling a chair closer and offering an empty wine glass, seemingly produced from nowhere, for him to fill. Logan did so.

"So," he began carefully, "where did you get the idea for modifying the Phoenix missile … for your book that is? It's really a very interesting concept," he added, with sincerity.

After a first suspicious glance, wondering if this was just a tease, Cathie shrugged her shoulders and said, "Oh, I just pick up all those old

Aviation Week magazines that you leave lying all over the house. There's a lot of interesting information."

Logan nodded sourly. *Perhaps a bit too much interesting information*, he thought. "And so …" he encouraged.

"Well," she continued, cautious once again, for she had had her book's technical underpinnings ripped out on more than one occasion by her husband, "it just seemed logical, or at least possible, based on what I've read."

"Hmmm," Logan replied, as he refilled his glass.

"Come on, darling," she persisted, "Is there something bothering you?"

Logan snapped out of his musings, and turned what he hoped was a relaxed, content visage to his wife. "No, not really. It's just, well, quite interesting. And quite logical, as you said." He paused for a moment, and then said, with sincerity, "I like your book. I really do. And the love story that Geoffrey objected to really seems to work well. I like the character, Frank, too."

"You mean it?" Cathie asked, as she might have after handing in her first high school writing assignment and receiving praise.

"I do, babe, I really do."

"You're a dear," she replied, leaning across the small gap between their chairs and resting her head on Logan's shoulder.

Logan smiled, but continued to stare at the flickering flames within the chimenea. What the hell was he missing?

***

They had been Stone's first spoken words to Chuck in over five years, transmitted over a throwaway cell phone that was now at the bottom of the Oakland Harbor. Those words, brief, measured, and cautious, had told Chuck all he needed to know. Stone was on the very brink, so he felt, of being able to complete his mission, the mission that had dominated his life since Chuck's hospital visit in Germany.

Despite the reopening of verbal communications, Chuck and Stone had immediately understood and approved the need to keep specific information to a minimum. Chuck's primary concern, prodded by Sean

Carlos, had been to confirm Stone's hopeful messages, to encourage him to proceed (Chuck realized how ludicrous encouragement now was to a man like Stone, but provided it for form's sake), and, most importantly, to understand where Stone would be operating in Tucson. This concern was purely logistical, to confirm that his own operations at Alpha did not in any way interfere, and to be sure that no inadvertent steps of any of his agents would intersect with Stone. Above all, it was critical to provide Stone with an open field, and allow him to proceed as he saw fit. Stone had expected nothing less from this mysterious father of his assignment, and he had expressed his gratitude with a simple, "Thanks."

"Listen," the man said, before hanging up, "we need to have a way to communicate directly in case of any problems. Get a backup soup can (he meant another throwaway cell phone). I'll have a new one as well. Alex and Shirley can communicate the details."

Though Stone was certain that this would not be necessary, he knew he could count on the discretion of Alex and Shirley. It was an important decision, and one of the few that Chuck could later look back upon with, if not pride, then with at least the satisfaction of having saved a few lives.

***

Luana listened to the soothing rattle of palm fronds, waving steadily in the seemingly immortal trade winds; ever steady, mild, and reliable. She had requested a meeting with her father, a rather brash act and a direct result of her discussions with Stone. Luana knew her own worth, had known it for years; but deference to age, acknowledgement of experience, and above all filial duty, constrained her from putting herself forward, from offering her own opinion un-asked. For reasons that she could not fully have expressed, a change—small, but growing—had taken place after her last weekend with Stone. A certain independence of spirit, a bridling at the perpetual casting down of her eyes and offering silent concurrence even when she believed she was right, had gained entry to her spirit. It would not be easily dislodged.

"Daughter," Wan Chu said, as he walked out onto the patio of their gorgeous Maui estate, "you wished to speak directly with me, and so we have both come here." And though he spoke with outward kindness,

Luana could sense the barely concealed irritation. She herself had flown from Los Angeles; her father, cutting short several days of meetings, from Hong Kong. It was unusual in the extreme, and Luana felt the burden upon her. She had inconvenienced her father. But the small part of her that had forever cast off her childish bonds spoke harshly within her mind. This was important, more important than his meetings, and she intended to make this stubborn old man understand.

"Come," he began again, "we have both traveled a long journey. It is late, and I must return to Hong Kong tomorrow. What do you wish me to know?" The huge Hawaiian who was invariably with Wan Chu when he visited the Islands moved on nearly-silent feet to the extreme end of the patio, to afford them solitude. Luana watched him glide away gracefully—an amazing feat for one of his size—and stand quietly, staring down the now darkened slope of grassy hillside to the twinkle of lights in the small town, far below.

"Luana?" her father repeated, and now there was an undeniable edge of impatience in his voice. For some reason, it infuriated Luana, but she suppressed her emotions and turned to Wan Chu with as much equanimity as she could summon. *Fine*, she thought. *He wishes me to be brief and blunt, and I will oblige him.*

"Father, I believe we should not proceed with the mission at Alpha Defense Electronics." The surprise and irritation on his face was unmistakable, and Luana decided to not allow him to interject comments or questions until she had had her full say. She pressed on, rapidly. "I do not trust Ivor. I do not trust his sources of intelligence. There is a feeling of …" The word "trap" had formed on her lips, but she bit it back. "… of uncertainty. It is too convenient … far too easy."

"And so," began Wan Chu, a cold light in his eyes, "because of this 'feeling' we must abandon this project, a project that you yourself concluded was feasible?"

"Based upon the information available," Luana interjected, "and based upon implicit trust of Ivor and his sources."

"May I remind you that we have two enterprises in train with Ivor Vachenko: this attack on Alpha Defense, in which he plays no other role other than providing us with information, and the exchange of two aircraft for a large sum of cash. In both cases, my colleagues and superiors are heavily invested in time, energy, and resources. There are now expectations of success in both arenas, very high expectations. Of course, the attack on Alpha is of primary interest. Again, as you yourself have said, acquiring the encryption codes will provide a massive tactical advantage." Wan Chu's patience was nearly spent, and he added peevishly, "You had time to evaluate the plan and to voice your objections. That time is past! We will proceed with the plan!"

"But, father ..." Luana began.

With startling suddenness and violence, Wan Chu brought the flat of his hand down upon the patio table. "NO! I will hear no more! It is decided!"

At the sound of the crash on the table and the loud, anger-laced tone in Wan Chu's voice, the large Hawaiian turned his head slowly, a movement as majestic and determined as the flow of molten lava down a shallow slope. He quickly evaluated the situation and saw there was no need for him at present. With an equally phlegmatic counter-rotation, he returned his gaze to the twinkling lights at the ocean's edge.

Wan Chu kept a hard gaze focused upon his daughter until she reluctantly nodded her head in submission. Without any further comment, he turned away, motioned for the Hawaiian to follow, and left the patio.

Luana watched him leave, no parting words on her lips, and only bitter frustration and resentment in her heart. She stared out over the Pacific, and was startled to feel a warm tear trickling down her cheek. She brushed it away with irritation, vowing that it would be the last she ever shed for shame caused by the stubborn old man who was her father. And as she straightened her back, a proud, aristocratic look took hold of her features. She was free; she would decide. She and Stone would break with Ivor Vachenko, the fool. And as she continued to stare, her jaw hardened with resolution, she also quietly vowed that there would be no operation at Alpha Defense.

Chapter Twenty-Eight

Encounter at the Air Force Base

Tucson

When Logan confirmed that Randy was coming to town to support the surveillance of the multi-night server rebuild, he had invited both Gail and him to dinner. It was an early dinner, since Gail was expected at Alpha to help support the first night of the rebuild, and Randy planned to join Chuck at the facility as well. Though several agents were already embedded in the IT organization, and all of the electronic listening equipment was in place, Chuck had declined the dinner invitation to spend a few more hours quietly walking the facility and convincing himself that all was well before he disappeared to a listening area in Building 12. "Listen, Randy," Logan had advised, when it seemed that Randy too would decline the dinner to be with his boss, "I've known Chuck a lot longer than you. He's so hyper he's about to explode, though he tries so hard to hide it. Just let him do his thing … alone, and meet him at 9 p.m., per the plan."

Battered by the persistent badgering of Logan, Cathie, and Gail, who was also due at the plant by nine, Randy had given in, simply insisting on soft drinks rather than any wine or liquor. In a spirit of solidarity, Logan and Cathie went along with the other two, who had a four-hour shift coming up. So at five thirty, Logan found himself sipping Coke and flipping burgers on his patio. It was a pleasant evening, no hotter than eighty-five during the day; and the westing sun seemed to have run out of venom, as a decidedly cooler breeze carried the heat rapidly away.

"Nice," Randy said, joining Logan at the grill. "You know, I might not mind living here at some point."

Logan grinned. "And is that a likely plan?"

Randy flushed slightly. "Well, we've talked possibilities, of course," he began.

"But you have the look of a man who is still dealing in hypotheticals. I take it you haven't asked yet?"

Randy shook his head in the negative. "No, though I'm going to, Logan. It's just, well, my … that is … both of our jobs right now have been crazy. This is the most relaxed I've been in a long time, except for those rare hikes we've taken. It always seems that we have to steal the time to do things, to be together, and both of us want our current assignments completed. Then we'll have time."

"I don't mean to burst your bubble, but there'll always be another assignment, another load of pressure, until you get lucky, like me. Though I've got to admit, this particular project you're working now is extraordinarily rough. Hell, I even had to haul my anxiety out of retirement for the duration, and even though I'm not invested like you are, I'll be glad when it's over as well. And so will she," Logan added, with a nod in the direction of Cathie, who was bringing out salads and placing them on their patio table.

"Oh, man, Logan, don't underestimate your value or your investment on this job. It's pretty clear that without you, and Cathie of course, there'd be no project. And have I ever said thanks?"

"About a thousand times!" Logan laughed.

"Still not enough," said Randy.

After a comfortable silence, Logan flipped the burgers and turned to Randy with the ghost of a frown. "You know," he began, "there's still something bugging me. All of the, you know, bad-guy activities, Cathie's nosy friend Elaya, the weird mix of amateurism and stone-cold professionalism. I don't know. I tell you, it bugged me so much I actually went back and reread the love story part of Cathie's book three times."

Randy gave Logan a very odd look, and Logan, with a spatula wielding gesture, quickly added, "If you tell her that I will seriously murder you!"

Randy smiled and nodded. "It's like money in the bank!" he said. "But if you don't mind my asking, why specifically that part of the book?

I mean, so what if Elaya bugged Cathie about it? That seems like, well, normal girly conversation. And do NOT mention that to Gail."

"You've got my word," Logan smiled in turn. "But basically, that was it. Why would Elaya be so damned particular? Do you remember ... but no, you may never have heard the details. Cathie told me how Elaya had shown an interest in the love story even at her college reunion."

"Yeah?" Randy asked, unconvinced.

"Listen, Cathie remembered a lot about that conversation, and it wasn't all about the love story. Elaya had some very specific questions about the F-14 and the Phoenix missile. Very specific. Stuff I'm sure Cathie didn't even know or care to know herself."

Randy set his glass down, and looked at Logan with increased interest, but then shook his head. "Still and all, what would be the point? It's an old jet, long since out of service, and if memory serves, it was the only aircraft that could carry and launch Phoenixes," he frowned slightly, "Phoeni? Phoenicies? Whatever."

"Your memory serves you well. But the fact that they're both museum pieces now doesn't entirely satisfy me. You know, the U.S. felt pretty uncomfortable about Iran potentially using them if we ever got into a squabble. The missile is relatively slow, but it has a hell of a range, and a pretty sophisticated guidance system."

"Wait," asked Randy, with a curious grin, "you didn't actually work on that old dinosaur, did you?"

Logan seemed somewhat put out, but reluctantly answered, "Maybe, possibly, when I was very young ... I might have, you know, worked on a tech support subcontract through Alpha, possibly ..." But by now, Randy was laughing uncontrollably.

"Fine," said Logan, "I'm old."

"I'm sure you boys are having fun," called Cathie, "but are you planning to serve those burgers or just let them cook to cinders and then order a pizza?"

"Hell's kitchen," muttered Logan to himself. "Coming, dear," he called, aloud.

***

Dinner itself passed pleasantly enough, but as eight o'clock approached, it became clear that Randy and Gail were becoming restless and eager to be off. As planned, Logan would drive the two of them down to the plant site, where Gail had left her car earlier in the day, and she and Randy would go home together. Gail was still giving her thanks to Cathie while Randy made a quick call to Chuck. When he hung up, Randy turned to Logan with an anxious, but knowing look. "Man, he's like a live frog in a hot skillet. I'll be glad when this is over."

Logan nodded. "Well, you can't finish until you begin. I guess we should go."

The last afterglow of the evening was vanishing in shades of green and blue in the far west as Logan headed south on Henning Boulevard, down a long, gentle slope from the foothills of the Catalinas towards the valley below. As they drove, a flash lit up the sky, quite near to the airport. A few long minutes later, a faint rumble reached their ears. At the same location, it seemed, tongues of yellow and red now wavered skyward.

"Now what in the hell was that?" Logan asked aloud. "Randy, give the boss a call, see if he knows what's going on." Logan then tuned his radio to a local station in the hopes of a bulletin, which arrived almost immediately, stating that an explosion had taken place at the Southern Arizona Aerospace Museum, and that fire crews from the city of Tucson, as well as Rickman Air Force Base, were en route. Randy listened with one ear while carrying on a hurried conversation with Chuck. When he was done, he turned to Logan and Gail. "Just like the news said, an explosion and fire at the museum. The boss seemed somewhat insistent that we just keep on coming to the plant and not worry about it."

"Right," said Logan, "as though we'd just chase the fire trucks and try to get a closer look. That makes no sense at all." Logan stopped talking suddenly, and turned quickly to Randy with a look of confusion and disbelief. "Randy that really doesn't make any kind of sense at all. What the hell is going on?"

"Maybe he thinks it could be some sort of, you know, diversion, to draw focus away from Alpha, from some activity there," he said, but seemed unconvinced.

The look on Logan's face—a look that his co-workers would recognize over many years that signaled that he had somehow made a breakthrough, had somehow made a connection—told an urgent story. "What building, Randy? Did he say what building had blown up?"

"Well, yeah, he did. He said it was the Modern Weapons Building. Odd that he'd know that, isn't it?"

"Shit!" said Logan. "The Phoenix! Why, why was I so slow in figuring this out?"

"What the hell are you talking about, Logan? Is it a diversion? Should we drive straight over there?"

"Yes! No!" Logan said. "It *is* meant to be a diversion, sort of, after they got whatever they needed from the Phoenix missile that's on display in the Modern Weapons Building. And I'll bet I know where they're headed now: to the one place where they can lay their hands on a working F-14, the one that flew in for the air show. Damn it, how could I be so stupid! Old age and a failing mind. Damn it! We've got to get over to Rickman right now!"

"Logan, I really don't understand. What's going on?" asked Gail.

"Don't sweat it, Grasshopper," said Randy with as much calm confidence as he could muster. He himself, however, was far from certain what Logan was driving at.

"Gail," Logan said, "we need to get you to Alpha," Logan stated, as he sped their SUV south.

"Logan," said Randy, "I've got the town layout pretty well down, and that'll take at least another twenty minutes, round trip."

"Twenty-five," said Logan, grimly, jabbing the accelerator. "Shit, I'm stupid."

"Look, never mind, I'll come with you," said Gail, with a frightened look that she couldn't quite prevent from creeping onto her face. "I'll stay out of the way, I promise."

"Randy, are you packing?" Logan asked, grimly.

"Always," Randy replied, patting the shoulder holster concealed under his light jacket.

"Good. Open the glove box and get my Glock out, carefully."

"Holy shit, Logan, this really is the Wild West."

"Oh hell," he replied, with a hint of a laugh, "Cathie had her concealed carry permit years before I got mine, and she's a better shot. Listen, Gail, once we're on the base, if we have to split up, stick close to Randy. Randy, you'd better call the boss-man and tell him 'change of plans.' He might want to get his bony ass over there, but even so, we'll be there first." *If I don't get pulled over for speeding*, he thought to himself.

***

Stone was pleased, with qualifications. He and the men with him had easily penetrated the museum's perimeter, disabled the alarm system, and entered the building containing the Phoenix missile. Their information had been accurate, and it was only a matter of minutes before the missile was opened at a major joint just aft of the guidance section, the electronics slid out of the missile's skin, and the required circuit cards removed. At Stone's insistence, the missile had been reassembled. In Stone's mind, there was no reason to leave clues lying about, and he was hopeful that the theft might never become known. It wasn't critical to his subsequent plans, of course, but Stone was a perfectionist.

With the circuit cards secure, a gas line for a building heater had been pierced and a detonator placed. He and his men had gotten cleanly away, only a minute or two behind their optimal timeline, and as they had driven off, blending into the evening traffic on Santa Cruz Boulevard, a flick of a toggle on the remote control device resulted in a thunderous bang, a half mile behind them, and a huge fireball that drifted lazily into the night sky. Within minutes, the wail of sirens filled the air. Now, off to the Air Force base, where Stone was to meet with Ivor's nephew and complete the night's work.

***

Sound carried from the speaker on Randy's phone: loud, angry, authoritative words, interspersed with Randy's calm, determined replies, conveyed a bizarre conversation in progress. A few moments later,

Randy turned a baffled and anxious face towards Logan. "What?" Logan asked.

"Well," Randy began, "Jesus, Logan, I'm really beginning to worry about Chuck. It was weird. When I told him our plans, he sounded furious, at first; he yelled at me, ordered me to come straight on to the Alpha plant site. I heard adjectives used in ways I never dreamed of before! He was literally screaming at me."

"Yeah, kind of got that part," Logan said.

"Well," Randy began again, as if unable to fully comprehend what had just occurred, "then he just stopped … snapped off … went dead silent. I thought he had hung up at first, but then he went on in a voice that didn't seem like his at all. He told me to carry on but to watch my ass, and then, after another pause, he just said, 'Get the hell off my line' or something like that, and hung up. What the hell does that mean?" asked Randy.

"It means we'd better fucking hurry," answered Logan.

***

Chuck coughed and spit more blood into the handkerchief at his mouth. *Damn fucking ulcer!* he thought. *Damn old age*. It was the fourth in a sequence of discrete thoughts that had rushed through Chuck's mind in the last few minutes like floodwater through a broken levee. The first, after Randy announced his intentions to go to Rickman with Logan and Gail, was primordial fear that his promising young co-worker Randy, Randy's girlfriend, and Logan Fletcher were in mortal danger. Stone's mission left no room for subtle distinctions between friend and foe. If they should cross paths with Jason this night, they were dead. And so Chuck had erupted: a wasteful, illogical, and above all futile outpouring of emotion. Randy had a mission as well as Stone, and Chuck's insistence that he ignore it was pointless. His second thought had been simply to encourage Randy to extreme caution; perhaps helpful, probably not.

The third thought, which Chuck pursued now, frantically jamming the bloody cloth back into his pocket, was to warn Stone. Stone was more than capable of dealing with Randy, Logan, and Gail. Perhaps, if forewarned, and most importantly, if the mission didn't require it, he might allow them to survive the night. Though Chuck was bursting to sprint to his car and race off to the Air Force base, he controlled himself and made the call.

***

Many long working nights at Rickman, entering and leaving the base at improbable times, had resulted in Logan and Randy becoming quite familiar and friendly with the guards who worked these evening shifts. They checked Logan's and Randy's badges, as well as Gail's ID, but mostly for form's sake, waving them through the gate. Logan glanced back in his rearview mirror and saw that both had already settled back into comfortable positions around the guard gate, resuming a conversation that had been briefly interrupted by Logan's arrival.

"Where to?" asked Randy.

Good question, thought Logan. But as his mind sluggishly dealt with the question, his hands and feet took over, directing the vehicle towards the flight line where he could already make out some of the Air Show aircraft parked along the tarmac. He drove slowly along the road, but did not see an F-14. As he considered his next move, he spotted several enlisted men walking along the pathway bordering the road, and slowed until he was alongside.

"Excuse me, fellows," he yelled out the open window. "I was just wondering where they're keeping the old Tomcat for tomorrow's show. I'm an old carrier grunt and was hoping for a sneak peak."

"What's that?" one asked. "Oh, yeah, the F-14 and a couple of the other oldies are being stored in Hangar 3. You know, that old Navy stuff can't deal with the rough Tucson weather," he joked, as his friends laughed appreciatively.

"Old Navy stuff," Logan said, forcing a laugh. "Got that right. Thanks, guys," Logan added, with a wave.

***

Beyond all reason, beyond all protocol, beyond all logical sense, Stone received the astonishing call from the person he only thought of as "the man," warning him of the imminent intrusion of another CIA agent and two others, interlopers of no real consequence. Stone had puzzled over this for what seemed an eternity, but was in fact only moments. He had his mission. He had followed his mission, obeyed his objectives, had murdered, betrayed, and sacrificed beyond all understanding, and now this call! At first, deep anger surfaced within him. These fools had no understanding of what he had been through, what he had sacrificed. For in Stone's quietest, loneliest moments, he felt himself lost. He had given, was still giving, all for the mission. He understood its consequences, perhaps better than any other. Why now should he care, why now should he jeopardize it for a trio of people that he didn't even know? But the mission had come from the man on the other end of the phone, and he had accepted it. Perhaps, just perhaps, there was a reason now to … to care. He thought of Luana and of what she would say. He thought of his mother and what she would say, and her words were clear in his mind. The end would justify the means for only as long as he believed it was so.

***

Redemption. It had crossed his mind more than once. Was there still some way to redeem his lost soul? Perhaps, just perhaps, he would do what the man asked … if … if it did not threaten the mission. He would have to hurry. Ivor's fool of a nephew had been delegated to retrieve the control computer from the Tomcat. If the man's friends interfered? The thought took him aback. If the man's friends were caught in the middle? *Friends*, thought Jason. *I've had none for so, so long. And now? Perhaps one. What would she want?* He would have to hurry.

***

"Randy," said Logan, "I'll take the south entrance. We've got to assume that they're already there. God I wish you were safe back at home!" he aimed at Gail.

"I'm fine," she lied. "I'll be safe with Randy. Go on! Let's get this over with!"

Logan nodded jerkily and headed towards the south entrance.

The hangar was huge. Logan ran alongside the building, feeling his age in the shortness of his breath and the pain in his knees. *Growing old sucks!* he thought, as he forced himself on. At the south entrance he hesitated, then entered through a side door of the hangar, and slowly, cautiously worked his way north along the interior wall, trying to remember all he had been taught in the advanced concealed-carry class he had taken years ago.

The hangar's cavern-like space was in near darkness; only a few lights hanging from the arched roof, high above, were lit. These gave an eerie feel to the collection of old aircraft gathered within: period pieces from World War II, Korea, Vietnam, and Desert Storm. It resembled a reunion of ghosts, waiting in the dim recesses of a dream; waiting for their pilots, many surely dead by now, to take them into combat once again. The few lights cast surprising shadows that distorted and elongated the shapes of the aircraft, and Logan would not have been too surprised if men in aged flight suits had stepped out from the dim, uncertain light to board their airplanes. He shook his head. Sometimes a lively imagination was actually no help at all. He wondered how Randy was getting on, and moved cautiously forward.

***

Stone had hurried, and he was now concealed in the hard shadows at the north end of the hangar, observing. His forty-five was drawn, and he automatically tapped the left pocket of his jacket lightly. Two full mags. Another in his right pocket. More than enough. He quietly twisted his silencer onto the end of the weapon. If only there were no foolish behavior, he might both fulfill his obligation to the mission and satisfy the man's request. If only …

***

As Logan approached the north end of the hangar, he nearly stumbled on the body of the airman, throat cut, blood in a pool around his body. Logan doubled over and wretched involuntarily. When he had regained a measure of composure, he took a second look, but there was no helping this man. Logan stepped away, carefully avoiding the pool that looked black in the dim light. When he looked up, a far more terrifying sight met his eyes. In the shadows not far ahead, two men had Randy pinned to the ground, struggling helplessly, while a third held a savage eight-inch knife to Gail's throat.

"Drop the gun, pig," shouted the man holding Gail.

Randy struggled violently, until a brutal gun butt struck his head and he lay there, dazed. Gail let out a faint shriek, but the man holding her only tightened his grip and laughed. A trickle of blood ran down her throat in a dark rivulet, dampening her shirt.

Logan gently placed the Glock on the ground and very slowly straightened to his full height.

"Good, very good," the man laughed with a nervous energy and an intoxicated sense of victory. "Over there," he commanded, and Logan walked silently over to where Randy, still partially dazed, was held down.

"Very good," he repeated. "And why do you fools bring your whores with you at such times," he said, stroking Gail's hair with his free hand. "Yet we thank you. We have earned the right, and you will watch. He reached his hand around and began to grope and fondle Gail, the knife firmly against her throat.

Randy had regained his senses and was planning a desperate lunge, possibly hopeless, and Logan contemplated how he might help, when a large man, with the calmness one might exhibit when entering a shopping mall, having no particular purchase in mind, stepped from the shadows.

"Stone," Ivor's nephew hissed. "Come and join us. We have the hardware," he nodded in the direction of a large backpack, "the computer cards from the old aircraft. And now we will have a small payment for our efforts."

Gail struggled and let out a terrified yelp as Ivor's nephew ran his free hand over her, the knife never leaving her throat.

"Are you a fool?" asked Stone. "We have no time. Kill her if you plan to, and then we must go."

"NO!" Ivor's nephew cried. "No longer do I take orders from you, infidel son of a whore! I will have this woman, this bitch, in payment for all of the dead in the Katyastan! For my mother, my sisters, my friends, and for Allah!"

He threw Gail roughly to the ground, knelt quickly down beside her, reached out a hand and pulled her skirt up to her waist.

***

The situation had changed dramatically, and Logan pondered what to do. Supporting Randy in a desperate rush now seemed ridiculous. Logan had read the resumé of this man, Stone, or Kulwicki, or whoever he really was. And in Logan's logical mind, they were all dead. And yet …

"Didn't I tell you there was no time?" Stone exclaimed with a tone of irritation. He directed his next words to the men holding Randy. "It's time to go." Ivor's nephew looked up, a snarl of anger and hatred on his lips, and with tremendous satisfaction, Stone raised his H&K and put Ivor's nephew's forehead directly above the triple sights. He squeezed once. A muffled "thud" disturbed the night's silence, and he turned the sights on Gail. A second "thud" and confusion ensued. Gail screamed, rolling to the side. Ivor's men released Randy and began running for the door. Randy, free at last, jerked up abruptly, intending to rush Stone, tackle him, beat him to death for the murder of his love. Logan lunged at Randy and brought him down, Logan's full two-hundred-twenty pounds restraining him effectively. Logan looked up from his uncomfortable position, crushing his friend and preventing his attempt at vengeance, and caught the faintest smile on Stone's face. And then the big man was gone, following his drones out the north entrance into the black night.

"I'll fucking kill you, you fucking bastard!" Randy screamed. "I'll fucking rip your heart out you son-of-a-bitch!" he yelled, an insane, suicidal light in his eyes. "Logan, you motherfucker, let me go! He murdered her! I'll fucking kill him!"

"Randy!" Gail cried. "I'm here. Oh God, Randy!"

Logan released Randy, who rushed to Gail's side. "Oh God, oh God, Gail, Grasshopper! Oh, Jesus God. Are you okay? Oh my God."

Gail winced and let out a yelp as Randy grabbed her, crushing her bleeding upper arm. And he kissed her and held her, his tears of love mixed with tears of rage and anger. "Oh my God," he whispered, "you're going to be okay. The bastard missed. I'll fucking kill him, that piece of shit!"

Randy gently released Gail and sprang for his sidearm, dropped and forgotten by his assailants. "I'll fucking kill them all!" he yelled.

It was almost a dream, a shadowy illusion, in which Logan stepped in front of Randy, reached out and grabbed his shoulders with both hands in a solid, unyielding grip. "Stop!" was all he said.

Randy's eyes refocused on Logan, the insane fire still blazing. "He tried to kill her!" Randy yelled. "He tried to murder her. And I'm going to fucking kill him!"

Logan gradually relaxed his grip, and looked Randy in the eyes, with a penetrating stare. "Don't be a moron," he whispered at last. "Look at that SOB," he added, quietly, motioning towards Ivor's nephew.

Randy's breathing came down half a notch from hysterical as he registered the small, round entry hole centered neatly between the dead man's eyes. "He hit EXACTLY what he was aiming at!" Logan said, emphasizing the word.

Randy cast another look at Gail, sitting now, eyes still wide with fear, the blood oozing from a minor wound in her upper arm, but smiling bravely back at him. "Randy?" she asked, as though he would explain all.

"Jesus Christ!" said Randy, glancing again at the dead man and back to Gail, understanding filling him at last.

"Yeah, that's it, Grasshopper. I think you've got it. And we deserve a little explanation from that man," Logan added, directing a steely gaze in the direction of Chuck, who had just emerged from the shadows.

***

Chuck, Logan, and Randy sat in the waiting area of the base hospital with three very different currents of thought running through their minds.

Chuck sat with his head hanging down, glum and uncommunicative. The feeling that he had betrayed his friends and nearly cost them their lives hung over him like a pall. Yet by a miracle and the incredible skill of Stone, here they were. The doctors would see to Gail, he was certain, and the mental trauma was liable to last longer than her physical injuries.

Another part of Chuck's mind condemned his own weakness in interfering with Stone's plans. It could have cost them everything, everything that he had prayed for and that Stone had sacrificed, innocent lives included, for years. Chuck's weakness in making an exception because he knew these people was an absurd, unprofessional, unpardonable sin. But could he have sacrificed people, that is, people he knew—his friends—for a larger cause? It was one thing when they were anonymous entities, practically fictional characters. Chuck choked down his self-disgust. Stone was a better man. He had seen the light fade from the eyes of men and women who had died to … to what? For every time Chuck logically argued that the prevention of a global, nuclear conflict was worth these sacrifices, he was faced with his own weakness and failure once again. If Stone ultimately succeeded, it was due to him alone. Chuck sank his head lower still. He had failed on all levels.

Randy sat nervously, staring almost continuously at the door leading into the examination room. Though he had pleaded to be allowed in, the doctor had firmly insisted that he remain outside. In the end, Gail's assurance that she would be fine had pacified him, and he had dropped into a chair, focused almost exclusively on that door. When his eyes did glance around the room, he would see Logan, gazing blankly ahead, his mind obviously lost in internal cogitations. Logically, Randy knew that Logan had done well, that all of them had very likely been saved by Logan's refusal to let Randy make a rash move in a clearly hopeless situation. And though Randy's ego argued vehemently with his logical mind, insisting that a properly timed lunge, a determined pursuit, would have been successful, a quiet internal wisdom knew otherwise. And so, Randy was deprived of Logan as an object upon which to vent his anger and his still boiling energy. And that left Chuck.

If Chuck felt he had betrayed his friends, then Randy would gladly agree with him. When Randy's occasional wandering eye met the image of Chuck, silent and slumped, Randy had to exercise every bit of self-control he still possessed to prevent himself from violently attacking his one-time friend and mentor. Had there been the least doubt of Gail's ultimate welfare, he would not have been able to resist. And, in fact, if Stone's shot had proven fatal to Gail, Randy felt things might have been settled back in the hangar, Logan's restraining hand on his arm notwithstanding. Randy seethed quietly. There was still a long score to settle, and he wouldn't wait forever.

Logan felt totally destroyed. He shared some of the double-edged guilt that Chuck himself felt: guilt that he had not solved this mystery sooner, but then again, guilt that, in solving it, he had still nearly gotten himself, Gail, and Randy killed. Logan and Randy had both seen Chuck emerge from the shadows only moments after Stone had left. Clearly, he had been there. Clearly he had chosen not to act. And while that fact in itself was enough to infuriate Randy (the hesitation was inexplicable and unforgivable in his eyes), Logan suspected something much, much deeper. He had only a very tenuous, intuitive sense that Chuck had wanted Stone to succeed and was relying on Stone to manage the situation. If this were the case, then he doubted that any explanation by Chuck would prevent Randy from a violent act, let alone reconcile the two in any way. And if his sense was correct, then they had all been played, used like pawns in a game of much higher stakes. And Logan felt not only anger but disgust at the thought. When the truth finally came out, and Logan would demand it of Chuck or it was "quits" to their decades old friendship, Logan would need all of his physical and persuasive strength to restrain Randy from a rash act. Logan was left to wonder—and it was this thought that had painted the confused look on his face—who would restrain him.

***

In less than forty minutes, the doctor re-entered the waiting area. Randy leaped from his chair and the doctor held up a comforting hand, saying, "She's going to be fine. She's resting and you can go in and see her." Randy hurried past the doctor with brief but heartfelt thanks and pushed through the door.

"How is she, doc?" asked Logan.

"Oh, she'll be fine, as I said. The wound in the arm was only a light graze. Incredibly lucky, I'd say."

Logan nodded, silently. He had no inclination to correct the doctor's mistaken characterization.

"Now, the neck wound," the doctor continued. "Well, it was pretty minor also, but it was much, much too near the carotid. I'd say another half-pound of pressure and she might not still be here with us. Oh, and I didn't tell the young lady that, so I'd appreciate it if you wouldn't either, at least not until some time has passed and she's had a chance to recover completely." The doctor seemed thoughtful, and then added, "I wouldn't mention it to the young man, either … possibly ever." This brought a slight smile to the Logan's face, and he nodded.

A staff sergeant entered the room and said, "Mr. Johnson?"

Chuck, who had remained gloomily seated, looked up.

"The base commander asked to see you once you were satisfied as to the lady's condition. If you'd like, I'll take you there now."

Chuck nodded and rose heavily. "I'll take care of this," he said, to the silent inquiry in Logan's eyes, "and I'll be back. Can Gail travel?"

"I'd strongly advise against it, at least until tomorrow, which is actually right about now," the doctor quipped, checking his watch. "No," he continued, seriously, "maybe after a night's rest. She's under light sedation. The young man is welcome to stay here," he said, pointing to a worn couch in the waiting area. "I doubt he'd leave anyway."

***

Chuck re-entered the waiting room at nearly the same instant that Randy was gently, but forcibly, exiled there as well, still sending words of endearment through the closing door. Logan looked at Chuck, questioningly.

"I need both of you to join me, right now, in the commander's briefing room," he said, with a leaden delivery.

"No!" Randy replied, immediately. "I'm staying here, just in case she needs …" Randy never finished, as Logan placed an easy hand upon his shoulder.

"Randy," he began, "She's safe; she's going to be fine, and you can be back here in," he looked significantly at Chuck, "ten minutes, max." Chuck nodded his concurrence.

A long, dismal silence followed, and then Randy turned to Chuck. "Ten minutes." Chuck nodded once again.

In the briefing room, Chuck began, "I've had to un-fuck everything that has just happened: Unauthorized weapons on the base, no contact to the commander, unlawful pursuit …" Randy snorted his disbelief, his expression of "couldn't care less" unmistakable. Logan prodded him gently in the arm, and Chuck continued.

"We're all okay. The base commander was seriously pissed, not just at the fact that the two of you came roaring onto his base, loaded for bear, like a couple of fucking cowboys, but because I still have no permission to brief him to what I'm about to brief to you. In the end, the Sec Def had to talk directly to him. Do you think that's going to help his attitude, 'cause I sure fucking don't!"

"The Sec Def?" Randy asked, in disbelief.

Chuck just looked into Randy's eyes, registered the undisguised hatred there, and continued. "Yeah, the Sec Def." He paused, glanced at both Logan and Randy, then continued. "I have authorization, strictly as a defensive measure, to brief you on a project that has been ongoing for over five years. By briefing the two of you, I will be nearly doubling the number of individuals that know about this operation: the Sec Def, of course, myself, a man called Jason Stone, and now you two." Chuck took a sip from a Styrofoam cup that might have contained hot coffee three-quarters of an hour ago, grimaced, set the cup on the table, and proceeded to explain the unlikely recruitment of one James Kulwicki, an independent, some would say arrogant, and uncontrollable special operator. Chuck explained his mission: to locate and destroy a stray nuclear device the Russians had let slip as their empire collapsed. He explained Kulwicki's, that is, Stone's constraints in fulfilling this mission: none.

"You bastard!" Randy hissed, angrily. "And Gail might have, could have died if it moved his mission forward, not to mention Logan and me!"

"That's right, Randy!" Chuck responded forcefully. "What do you think? That your life, her life, Logan's life, my life is worth a shit to stop a fucking nuclear war? Are you fucking nuts? These people that control the weapon are insane. They think they've got a fucking leash on the genie. They're as stupid as you two! Don't you fuckin' get it ..." Chuck was unable to finish and began an uncontrollable coughing. He pulled out the soiled hanky, adding to its bloody quota. Logan reached out a hand, but Chuck slapped it away. "I'm fine, I'm just fucking fine!"

"So what was Stone, or Kulwicki doing here? Why the hell was he scavenging that old Tomcat?"

Chuck wiped the last of the blood from his lips. "This is a defensive brief. You don't have a need to know."

"Don't have a ..." Randy began, incredulously. "She almost died! She almost, she ... You know what, boss?" Randy said, savagely, "Fuck you and the fucking horse you rode in on!"

"Randy," Logan began, gently.

"No!" Randy yelled. "Fuck you, fuck Stone, and fuck the agency! I'm done." Randy leaped from his chair, daggering a look at Chuck. "I'm going back to the waiting room," he rasped, slowly regaining control of his anger. "I just want you to know that you're a worthless piece of shit. Also, I'm going to kill Kulwicki. I'm going to personally kill the motherfucker, and if you try to interfere, I'll fucking kill you too!" Randy stormed from the room, slamming the door with enough force that it failed to close properly as it swung back.

Chuck rose, as if to pursue Randy, but Logan placed a firm hand on his shoulder. When Chuck turned to face him, Logan said quietly, "You've lost him. Just let him go."

Chuck struggled, torn for a long moment, and then sank back in his chair, a look of total defeat on his face. "And have I lost you, too?"

Logan considered his response for a long time, and then shook his head. "Not just yet. Let's just say, you're on probation." And when Chuck looked gratefully up at his friend, he thought he might have possibly caught the shadowy hint of a smile.

Chapter Twenty-Nine

On a Collision Course

Stone had expected a geeky individual—Luana's expert on the old weapon system technology—but was somewhat surprised at what seemed more a caricature of a man than a real human being. The man was aged. Stone guessed he was in his late seventies, with a half-bald scalp surrounded by a brushy confusion of white hair, a pale, somewhat jowly face, and thick glasses that magnified his moist eyes. He must have been about medium height, but a perpetual stoop brought on by decades hunched over computer screens and test stations, made him seem shorter. His loose-fitting clothes spoke of a time when he must have weighed considerably more, and they also spoke, quite clearly, of his disdain for considerations of personal appearance, as did his three-day growth of dirty-grey beard.

Stone gave Luana a questioning look, but she only smiled. "Jason," she began, this is Mr. Richard Crandall." Stone reached out a tentative hand, but Crandall simply reached past it to take the backpack from Stone's other hand. He unzipped a flap and peered myopically into its interior, and then a smile lit his face. "Oh, how lovely! One so rarely sees such a perfect example of late '70s electronics. Oh, yes, young man. Quite state of the art in its day. Quite special!"

"And you can really work on this?" asked Stone. "You can actually reprogram it?" Crandall shot a quick, contemptuous glance at Stone and addressed Luana. "I have the TE that you sent me as well as all of the interface cards already checked out, and I can begin now … given a little privacy," he added, rather rudely.

"Thank you, Richard. You are completely aware of all that we need?"

"Yes, yes, you've explained it three times already!"

"Very well. And your estimate of completion?"

"Unchanged. By this time tomorrow, it will be reprogrammed, tested, and ready to ship. It really is quite simple, you know. As always, the test results will be available for your evaluation, or for whomever else you can find that would even understand them," he said, with a skeptical glance towards Stone.

"I trust you confirmed the transfer of funds to your account?"

"Yes, of course. Quite adequate, thank you."

"Richard, I realize you took this assignment on short notice. If you complete according to schedule, there will be a small bonus, let us say, 30 percent, added to the agreed upon amount."

"Oh, that would be lovely. Thank you Luana. Now, goodbye. I must start to earn that bonus."

***

"So what's TE?" Stone asked, as they left the small lab building, and walked through the grey, damp evening towards the entrance to the Tube.

"Test Equipment," Luana said with a smile. "Part of the collection of hardware and firmware Richard will need to talk to the electronics on the circuit boards. Back in the day, TE could take up huge amounts of space, maybe the size of a couple of refrigerators, to test and integrate electronics a tiny fraction of the size. Fortunately, this equipment easily shipped in two crates. It is amazing that the United States ever got to the moon in 1969 and throughout the next decade. A teenager's smart phone has a hundred times the computing power of the computers that flew back then."

Stone shrugged. "There's more to it than the machines," was all he offered. "Look," he added, "I shouldn't even ask, but ..."

"Jason, the equipment is perfectly safe. ISG keeps that laboratory here in London for the exclusive use of Mr. Crandall. It's well protected by surveillance and alarms, as I'm sure you noticed, but its real protection is its anonymity: just one small, grey building in a row of other small, grey buildings in a modern industrial park on the outskirts of London. A decent if boring neighborhood."

"And Crandall?"

"Reliable and faithful through no weakness of his own. He is given jobs of this nature: highly technical, usually unique by virtue of age or unconventional design. The man has two vices: one is his love for the technology, the other a more shadowy love for, let us say, rather eclectic pleasures, pleasures that he finds easier to satisfy here in London than in the US. I accommodate both of these vices by virtue of a stream of challenging assignments and the very large salary he earns as a result. He is completely apolitical. In fact, he is truly uninterested in humanity, at least, beyond what he requires for his personal enjoyment."

They reached the entrance to the Tube, and followed a sparse group of individuals down the steps towards the gates.

"Does he know what he has there?"

"Yes. He would have to, of course. But trust me, Jason, he has no more interest in our purpose for the modified modules than an ant drinking sweetened water would have in understanding the workings of a sugar plantation." Luana smiled at her own analogy. She herself knew quite a bit about the workings of a sugar plantation; her family owning quite a large one on the big island of Hawaii. "But to be doubly sure, I will make the final changes after he has demonstrated his modifications and left us alone, fully content with his bonus."

"I'm amazed that you know this stuff well enough."

"Well enough is correct. Not 'well,' but well enough." She smiled her true smile. "Trust me."

"You know I do," Jason smiled back.

***

Twenty minutes later, they emerged from the Underground at the Green Park Station, a short walk from the Ritz, where they were staying. A late evening sun had sunk just below the level of the low clouds in the west, bathing the park and Buckingham Palace in an unearthly, yellow-orange light, instantly transforming a scene of pervasive greys to one of a jubilant gold and green.

Luana and Jason exchanged a look, a silent communication passing between them, and they turned from the hotel, walking instead into the long, tree-lined corridor of the park. They walked somewhat at random, looking occasionally across the Thames towards the London Eye, glinting in the setting sun, or towards the Palace, gazing at ancient oaks, or the dense, verdant willows crowding the water's edge of St. James's Park Lake. Ducks, geese, and endless pigeons gabbled or cooed all along the pathway, and once, an ancient, grey heron strode across the green with solemn dignity, like some stately old butler from a fading past.

The sun did set, at last, and a veil of moist fog seemed to descend in an instant as the couple turned back towards their hotel. If all went well, they would have only this night to themselves. Tomorrow evening, Jason was bound for Saudi Arabia to personally deliver the package to bin Wazari, Luana to Los Angeles to begin the preparations for the transfer of funds for the delivery of the two jet fighters. Of course, those funds would never reach her father. But that now was the plan … her plan, and Jason's.

The unfortunate death of Ivor's nephew—unfortunate, that is, to him, less so to his uncle, and of no consequence to Jason—had not overly strained the relationship between Stone and Ivor. In Ivor's heart, he had known that his nephew was a fool, and the fool had chosen the wrong moment to challenge Jason Stone, and over a woman! Well, he had paid the price. But now, there was much too much at stake. Stone was still the man to get the job done, and Ivor would settle with him when he was ready to do so. Stone was central to both plans: the purchase of the aircraft and the acquisition of the parts needed by Hasim.

The funding-transfer account numbers and passwords had been entrusted to Stone. He would arrange with Luana to see to it that the funds were moved into her father's account two days prior to the execution of Hasim's plans. The aircraft would be flown to the abandoned base recommended by Colonel Zareb, with Saudi pilots taking over upon confirmation of the transfer of funds. The three-ship mission would go forward the next day. Stone and Luana had wondered whether Hasim would proceed without the two cover aircraft, should the need arise. At no time had they seemed critical to the plan, other than as insurance. Well, Stone had his own delicate tasks and Luana had hers. Both were risky, but well within acceptable bounds. He was certain he and Luana would succeed.

Stone glanced over at Luana, and was not surprised to find her gaze fixed firmly on him, as though trying to enter into his thoughts. He leaned over and kissed her, and they both smiled. This evening there was time: time to make love, to shower and dress, to attend a revival of *Les Miserables* in a theater less than two blocks from their hotel, and then a lovely, late dinner, a long night's sleep, and then … Tomorrow would come, as always, and they both had their tasks.

Later, in their suite, as Stone removed Luana's dress, he whispered into her ear, "Soon, here, again … free!"

"Free!" she said.

***

Crandall had been as good as his word, crowing over the ease with which he had carried out Luana's wishes. With his bonus firmly secured, he patiently explained all of the modifications he had made, running multiple simulations to demonstrate their effectiveness. Luana soaked up the information, asking intelligent, pointed questions. At last, she smiled at him and said, "Richard, you have done extremely well, and your *40* percent bonus (she emphasized the number, while Crandall chuckled his approval) has already been deposited to your account. You are a genius, my friend. Now, please," she said, graciously indicating the door, "we will finish up here and secure the lab. You have done very, very well, indeed!"

If Crandall had the least hesitation, the least inclination to balk, to insist that he should be the one to secure the lab, he did not show it. In fact, he had an appointment this evening with a very entertaining, very young, man and woman. He would have more time to prepare. Perhaps he might shave. He smiled at Luana, ignored Stone, and left the building.

"And now, I must work for a bit, Jason."

"Can I help at all?"

"Perhaps a pot of coffee," she replied, motioning to the pot nearby. "It is slow, tedious work. When I am complete, then you can help evaluate the simulations, to be sure all is as you would wish."

Several hours later, Luana repeated the sixth and last simulation, with 500 Monte Carlo runs, simulating random inputs: variable geometries, noise levels, and other temporal and spatial factors. The result: 100 percent success.

"My God, this is astonishing!" Stone exclaimed.

"Jason, you realize, of course, that this cannot guarantee success. It is based on many random factors, including the likelihood of poor or unanticipated modifications made to the rest of the processor and warhead assembly by bin Wazari's men. But, as you see, there are three automatic processes which will detonate the bomb, as planned, and," she added, with some pride, "a fourth, wholly within your control." She hesitated, frowning. "Jason, you will be ..."

"Safely out of range," he finished for her. "It's a little thing: five kiloton yield. I'll be behind some very large rocks, thirty-five miles away from the likely launch point."

She shook her head. "The *likely* launch point! It seems so near, so near to such a thing. Oh Jason, please ... please take all care!"

"Luana," he said, pulling her close, "I have more to live for now than I've had for five years. I'll be careful."

***

London ... Cairo ... Riyadh: a long, annoying, uncomfortable journey for such a relatively short distance. And yet Stone was here. He mentally calculated where Luana would be: nearly to Los Angeles with her blessed direct flight. Soon, soon, he would be with her again. How soon would depend on the day of the mission, which he still needed to determine.

He was welcomed to bin Wazari's palatial home once again, though this time, without the theatrics. Ivor was there, tension unmistakably marking his features, as was bin Wazari, a childish look of excitement on his face, and a woman, well dressed in western attire, certainly bin

Wazari's wife ... certainly Ivor's lover. Stone smiled at her, thoughts of approval running through his mind. This was, perhaps, a woman for whom much might be risked. *Ivor, you old hound dog!* thought Stone.

"Is this it?" bin Wazari asked, pointing to the backpack, impatience and excitement in his voice. "Please, may I see it?" he asked, forgetting that it was, in fact, his property, paid for with many dollars and much blood. Stone handed over the backpack and bin Wazari carefully removed two circuit cards in anti-static pouches as well as a much larger unit in a metal container with several interface connectors along its perimeter. The cards were destined for the missile, the larger box for the F-14.

"So small!" bin Wazari exclaimed, referring to the circuit cards. "My men must have them, and the box, for testing and ... installation. Mr. Stone, you are quite an amazing man. The items delivered as promised. Really quite amazing!" Hasim rang a small bell and two men entered the room. "Take these treasures to the lab, and ask Colonel Zareb to step in." The men bowed deeply and carried the electronics from the room as though they were carrying eggs of the most fragile, thin-shelled sort. Stone had no doubt they were heading for the rather dilapidated but heavily guarded building at the end of the compound. Somewhere, probably in that same building, they would complete final assembly of the missile; the interface box would replace an older, highly constrained cousin in the jet, which Stone assumed was in a nearby air base. As he had heard Ivor discuss with Elaya, the missile would be launched from a point that would seem to indicate that the strike had originated in Iran. Of course, the Tomcat's transponder would declare the aircraft to be an aged Iranian F-14, a relic from the last days of the Shah, reinforcing that impression.

A few moments later, Colonel Zareb entered the room. "Colonel, all of the equipment is now here. When should Ivor arrange for the delivery of the MiGs?"

The colonel looked around the room with a sense of nervous irritation. Why was this other man, this large American here?

Bin Wazari caught his eye and frowned. "Mr. Stone will undoubtedly be the one to finalize the arrangements with the daughter of our generous benefactor." Vachenko silently nodded his agreement. "So please, Colonel, you may speak freely to Mr. Stone."

The colonel considered. "In forty-eight hours we will have verified the functioning of the electronics. Assuming there are no issues, the date should be two weeks from today."

"Mr. Stone," said bin Wazari, "please finalize arrangements for two weeks from today. The colonel will provide you with specifics. And once again, you have our thanks."

Elaya watched as Jason and the colonel left the room. *A very remarkable man, indeed*, she thought. *He may prove quite useful in the future.*

With the delivery date of the MiGs now established, Stone knew within a day or so when the launch would take place; it was clear that events would move very swiftly once all of the pieces were in place. He would have to do a little camping, but a few nights in the desert did not seem like much of an inconvenience. He would need to scout a location and supply it with water and rations for, say, four days, just to be safe, and he would need to proceed there very quickly after the two MiG aircraft were transferred to Saudi custody. It was very clear that Hasim feared the risk of exposure for every minute of delay once all of the pieces were in place. This suited Stone extremely well. He'd be able to give a rendezvous date to Luana quite soon.

***

Stone still needed to know where to set up his camp, though he already had a pretty good notion. Later that night, in a dusty hotel room nearly two miles from the bin Wazari compound, Stone repositioned a very special antenna attached to a highly sensitive wireless receiver and set to work hacking into bin Wazari's home network. The encryption gave way quite easily to an algorithm that Luana had provided. It actually caused Stone to frown in disbelief. He knew that wireless networks were soft targets, and he never relied on them himself, but this had been spectacularly easy. "Note to self," Stone whispered, as another algorithm hunted through bin Wazari's files, "never use a credit card online!"

Once again, Stone was surprised with the ease in which the needed files were found. He glanced quickly at several graphics that showed flight path alternatives for the mission. One was highlighted differently than the others, but he intended to not rely upon this. There were at least three potential locations for his camp that would cover all of the alternatives. Stone downloaded the files onto a small tablet for later study, and began shutting down his equipment.

***

Colonel Zareb reported no issues with the hardware, so with a firm date for the aircraft delivery in mind, Stone departed Riyadh with a request to finalize all of the transfer plans. Stone had a considerable amount of travel to accomplish in a short period of time, so he contacted Luana from the airport in Kuwait City. "This is Eton Simonson from International Home Sales Services. I'm sorry Shirley wasn't able to call, but she's feeling a bit under the weather. She asked me to request that you please tell your father that the buyers wish to close on the house on May first. Funding transfer as already specified. Shirley will be in touch as soon as she's feeling better." But before Stone boarded his flight, the first of a series that would ultimately take him through Amman, Jordan; Tbilisi, Georgia; Ashgabat, Turkmenistan, and back to Amman, he entered another breathless post on Shirley's webpage. The contents spoke of a long delayed family reunion at the beginning of May, specific dates and times to follow, but definitely "on," at long last. Sean read the message and asked his admin to get him a secure line to the Oakland CIA office. Chuck, returning from the men's room after a violent session of retching bloody phlegm, reached his desk as the phone began to ring.

"So, we're coming to it, at last," said the Secretary.

"Yes," replied Chuck, in what he hoped sounded like a firm, confident voice.

"And in two weeks, give or take, we may be out of a job," the Secretary continued, "and a lot of people may be dead."

"No," said Chuck, with real confidence. "He'll do it. I know he will."

The Secretary was silent for a long while. "God, I hope you're right, Johnson. I hope to God this doesn't get out of hand. We're as prepared here as we can be with denials, accusations, threats; that is, as prepared as we can be without knowing exactly how he plans to proceed."

"It's clear from his messages that he means to destroy it, beyond salvaging," said Chuck.

"You don't think ..." began the Secretary, "he wouldn't actually ..." but he was unable to finish.

Chuck knew precisely what the Secretary wanted to ask, but he knew that the only answer he could possibly give would be of no comfort. Stone would do exactly what he believed best fulfilled the mission. Chuck remained silent.

At last, the Secretary spoke again. "Well, then there's the bright side." He stopped. "Yeah, that's a little fuzzy right now. Either way, Johnson, stay in touch."

"Yes sir," Chuck replied, but before the phone clicked dead he could hear the Secretary's voice telling his admin to send in his next appointment.

***

Stone had often traveled the Middle East as a free-lance geologist: a native of Ottawa, Canada, working for a variety of companies exploring for oil, copper, tungsten, and even uranium. In this capacity, he was able to fly into small, regional airports in extremely out-of-the-way places, lease or purchase rugged off-road vehicles, and with the proper licenses (often acquired through large exchanges of cash), drive off into obscure areas of countries openly hostile to America. His first stop, Amman, Jordan, was dictated by the planned flight path of the aircraft that was to launch the weapon on Jerusalem. The flight path was logical, passing through northern Saudi airspace, but on a direct line that pointed to a launch point in southwestern Iran. Part of the northwestern border of Saudi plunged, like a dagger, into the guts of Jordan. At this point, Jerusalem was less than ninety miles away. The plan called for launching the weapon just inside Jordan's airspace, possibly twenty miles in or less, with the weapon easily flying the remaining distance.

This region of Jordan consisted of a web of dry rivers and streams, originating along the backbone of hills that ran from north to south through the central part of the country, and draining to the parched plains of the east. Stone found two locations among deserted rock piles along two such dusty streams, and provisioned both. When he returned, he would leave the vehicle a safe distance, perhaps five miles, equidistant from either, and hike in; two hours at most. He planned to leave the area and head for Al Haditha, in Saudi, once the mission was complete. For now, he was satisfied. Either location would suffice. They were sufficiently distant from the flight path, but not so far that his last resort could not be employed … if necessary.

***

Four days later found Stone in Ashgabat, a surprisingly large and thriving city in southern Turkmenistan. The tall Kopet Dag Mountains to the south brought water and life to the city, while to the north were thousands of square miles of barren, hell-on-earth desert, barely above sea level, with rippling sands, scrubby brush, and dunes. A Soviet-era airfield sat abandoned, nearly seventy-five miles to the north. That night, Stone looked out from the balcony of his suite at the five-star Sofitel Oguzkent, his Land Rover parked in the garage below. He silently sipped cognac and watched as the long shadows from the hotel reached across the spectacular park to the east. He must return here, he thought, with Luana, when all was over. And for what seemed a brief instant, he forgot about his plans for the next week: more violence, more dry and desolate nights alone. Instead, he looked to the future, and to something that might be considered a normal life. He smiled. His own normal, childhood life was a thing of the past, never to be recaptured. But a more normal life cushioned by wealth, luxury, and the freedom to travel was nearly within reach. He hoped it would also be free from the daily fear and the pervasive stench of death that had become routine. Time passed swiftly as he thought of a life with Luana once his mission was complete. The sky had gone a deep purple and the heat had ceased to ripple from the ground below when he shook off his musings, and lay down in his deliciously comfortable bed to sleep. It would be the last bed he would enjoy for quite a while.

Chapter Thirty

Not the Way it was Supposed to Go Down

As facilitator of the transfer of the MiG aircraft, and as one who had made a powerful impression on both Hasim and Elaya, Stone had been requested to ensure that the physical transfer of the jets to Saudi pilots proceeded smoothly. It was a request that Stone was only too happy to fulfill. As with comedy, timing would be everything, and he had intended to be at the transfer whether welcome or not. There would be not only the two Chinese pilots to deal with should the timing be less than perfect, but an unknown number of "support personnel" on the transport aircraft that was to return them to China. In addition to his usual weapons, Stone's Land Rover was packed with a sizable quantity of C-4 explosive. Stone intended that this transfer would take place.

***

Jason Stone checked his watch—nearly 12:30 a.m.—and once again scanned the skies with a set of powerful binoculars. At last, the transport became visible; the much smaller fighter aircraft appeared a few minutes later. The funds transfer was set for 1:00 a.m., local time, and Stone knew that Luana, nearly 7,500 miles away, in her private office in Los Angeles, was preparing to execute the convoluted funds transfer that would leave Hasim bin Wazari $50 million poorer, and she and himself that much richer. The other side effect, of course, was that it would leave her father furious; beyond furious, and in very much of a killing mood.

The landing strip had been sparsely lined with sputtering, fifty-five gallon drums burning a smoky mixture of jet fuel and waste oil. They had only several hours of life in them, and by morning would just be empty vessels of no interest whatsoever. The transport landed first as the MiGs continued to fly cover; a wise precaution, thought Stone with approval. After landing, two men left the aircraft, walking down the ladder from its side. Stone preferred to stay anonymous, and stood well off to the side, hidden by the darkness. The conversation proved satisfactory, and one of the men re-entered the aircraft. Shortly afterwards, the MiGs began a landing approach. The eyes of the men on the ground were focused on the lights of the approaching jets, just as the eyes of the men in the transport (the many men that Stone was convinced were aboard) were focused on bin Wazari's minions. Stone slunk from the darkness near the tail of the aircraft and was soon under the belly of the old Shaanxi Y-8 transport. One charge of C-4 was attached within each of the main landing gear compartments and Stone quietly withdrew. It was nearly 1:00 a.m.

Once again, Stone watched from the distance. The Chinese airmen were ill at ease, standing near the base of the transport with no other function to perform. The other man on the tarmac was periodically communicating to the man who had returned to the aircraft. Stone had no doubt that the man in the aircraft was in radio contact with Wan Chu. The funds transfer would take place very soon and then, if all went well, the two Chinese pilots and the lead man on the ground would board the aircraft.

***

In Riyadh, bin Wazari's accountant carefully entered the destination code and password for Wan Chu's receiving account. He checked, double checked, triple checked, had his assistant check, and then timidly hit "enter" on his keyboard. Luana's computer in Los Angeles, with access to both the sending and receiving sites and the encryption, was instantaneously aware of the intended transfer, and a preprogrammed subroutine went into effect. Her intent was to bounce the money to a third location, known only to her, using her father's account as the intermediate "bounce point." Timing such an exchange was spectacularly difficult, particularly as she needed to hold the funds at the bounce point for as long as possible in order for that site to send a confirmation of receipt to the sender. Holding too long could be fatal, as she knew that her father would not allow that amount of money to reside in a single account, particularly one that could be associated with him, for any length of time. In fact, she was certain that an automatic protocol on his computer would engage within seconds to execute the requisite series of transfers to Wan Chu's sterile locations. She knew this because she, herself, had implemented this algorithm for him. Luana's computer received the confirmation code that had been sent back to Riyadh. The timing could not be precisely known, as many factors, including loading of her father's computer, available bandwidth for his wireless link, and other random processes would influence the transfer protocol. But there was no doubt that it amounted to no more than a handful of seconds. Luana had settled upon "two" for the point of the transfer, and her computer, precisely counting down the milliseconds, executed the bounce. A brief summary lit up her screen. Funds transferred at time hack 0.000, confirmation of receipt sent at 0.682 seconds, bounce executed at 2.000 seconds, complete at 2.027 seconds.

***

A voice called from the aircraft, and the leader re-entered to be informed that the transfer of funds was successful. A few moments later, he returned to the runway, motioned in an affirmative to the two Chinese pilots, nodded curtly to bin Wazari's men, and re-boarded the aircraft, the two pilots in his wake.

Stone watched intently. The next events would depend on the reaction time of Wan Chu's financial operative. With good luck, the transport would be airborne before that fallible human could discern what had happened, convey the full meaning to Wan Chu, and Wan Chu re-establish contact with the flight crew. Generally, Stone felt it best to never rely on luck, and in this instance, his belief was dead-on. Wan Chu's man must have seen the irregularity immediately and instantly informed Wan Chu that the money had vanished. Stone could almost imagine the scene: the man calling out in a panicked voice, Wan Chu demanding an instant explanation; asking sharp, intelligent questions as to what might have caused this problem, but the old man instinctively and quickly realizing that, whatever the reason, the money simply had vanished. His next action would be instantaneous.

The door on the transport was nearly closed, and the Saudi pilots were making their way to the MiGs, when it suddenly re-opened. Angry shouting was heard: confusion … hostile posturing … imminent violence. Stone melted into the shadows behind a deteriorating mud and plaster wall. *Damn*, he thought, *Wan Chu is one formidable SOB!* Stone pulled his sniper rifle out of its leather case and steadied it at the edge of the crumbling wall. He still controlled the choke point—the door to the aircraft. And unless the men onboard were fanatics and totally committed, they would need to exit from that door.

The first man, the leader and liaison, filled the doorway, raised an automatic rifle, and Stone squeezed off his first shot. He smiled grimly … a clean head-kill. A second man appeared, crouching cautiously, jarred at the last instant by two or three men—the commandos that Stone had surmised—and ruining Stone's ideal shot. That man, instead, was pierced through the neck, a spray of blood jetting from the wound as he tumbled, screaming, down the stairs, tangling with the first dead man, and then … silent … dead before he reached the ground. Stone inwardly smiled. Two bodies at the base of the stairway would seriously inhibit egress from the aircraft.

Stone refocused on the door, preparing for his next target. And then, with no warning, the demons of hell were unleashed. A half-dozen windows on the aircraft exploded outward. *Shit!* thought Stone, as he realized the men onboard were, in fact, totally committed: willing to destroy their own aircraft, their means of escape. They opened a withering fire, focused on the flashes from Stone's first two shots. *Exceptional men*, concluded Stone as he leaped behind the wall, one shot grazing his left shoulder and one passing through his right side, missing his lung by millimeters, but shattering a rib in its violent flight. Stone drove the scything pain from his mind as he landed roughly on the hard-packed sand. Subconsciously, he realized that heat, baked into the clay-like earth during the blistering day, was radiating up into his scraped face, pressed grittily against the ground. A shrieking was heard as Stone saw several of bin Wazari's men go down, dead or wounded. Consciously, he registered that the situation was breaking containment and was slipping out of control. Plan C, the tertiary and final planned option that he had conceived, was all that was left.

Stone drew a deep breath, sucking in dust and sand. He coughed and then bellowed out in Arabic for bin Wazari's men to pull back; to take cover. Stone jammed his hand into his pocket, seized the detonator, and waited for bin Wazari's men to clear. He waited as long as possible … it seemed years … and the Chinese were pouring down the stairs. The pain that Stone had masked returned with a force that he hadn't felt since childhood … since grade school … since the football championships: his West Valley Ravens versus the despised Bulldogs.

***

It was half-time and his arm was swollen badly. Tears ran silently down his trembling cheeks and he longed to remove his helmet, uniform, and pads; to cry and release his pain. His mother had taken his head firmly in her hands.

"James, James, listen to me. Your team needs you. You must, must play in order for you, for them, to win!"

"But mom, it hurts! It hurts!"

She grasped his head more firmly and captured his misted eyes with her own. "NO! You control it. You decide. Play, James, and win! The pain will wait."

And he had played through two agonizing quarters, and the Ravens became state champions. And ... James eventually recovered from a severe fracture with aggravated complications.

***

Stone grimaced, released the safety on the detonator, and flipped the switch. The transport was engulfed in flames, lifting lazily some ten feet off the ground, and then collapsing in an inferno, its fuel tanks ruptured.

All firing ceased immediately, and there was only the roar of the flames and the screaming pain in his side.

Confusion amongst bin Wazari's men changed to elation as they realized what had happened. *Simple fools*, thought Stone, dragging himself to his feet. He called to Ahmed, the leader of bin Wazari's men, "Have your pilots man their planes and get airborne, then round up your men and get the hell out of here!"

"Yes, sir," Ahmed replied crisply, scarcely hiding a grin. "You killed the dogs!" he added. "Allah be praised …" He faltered. "But you, you are wounded. Sir, you are bleeding!"

Stone grasped the man's collar with his left hand, his right refusing to obey him, a hideous stab of pain intervening as he had tried to raise it. "Don't be a fool!" he growled. "Get the jets out of here now! Tell bin Wazari we were betrayed. Tell him what happened. I suspect Vachenko," Stone concluded, planting the seed that would ultimately bear a poisoned fruit.

"But you, sir," Ahmed persisted, staring at the blood welling from Stone's wounds, "You need assistance, a doctor!"

Stone carefully opened his shirt, revealing the nasty entry and nastier exit wound the bullet had made. At first, Ahmed only stared in shock, then called to another man who hurried up to the pair with a small first-aid pack. Stone gingerly mopped the blood from the wound and then shook a powdered antibiotic into the wound. Ahmed handed Stone a syringe, one of three in the makeshift pack. "Poppy," the man said to Stone's unasked question. Stone took the syringe and plunged it into his side near the wound and nodded to Ahmed, who then helped him dress the area as well as possible. He then helped place a bandage on Stone's shoulder wound, bloody, but of no real consequence.

The effects of the drug were already beginning to make Stone feel oddly removed from the world. Surely this wasn't a civilized, stateside morphine dose. Stone blinked hard, summoned all his self-control and stoicism and produced a steely expression. "Now go!" he said.

***

Miles away, in Hasim bin Wazari's palatial home, chaos was taking hold. Ivor was frantically engaged in a desperate conversation with Wan Chu, trying to understand what the old man was telling him. He had the money, but now he had it not. This made no sense to Ivor, whose own laptop had received the confirmation of the funds transfer, but no evidence of any other activity. Ivor kept repeating that he was convinced that the transfer had gone as planned. The angry, accusatory voice of Wan Chu radiated loudly from Ivor's phone, adding to a bizarre sense of the surreal that filled the room.

Bin Wazari was on another phone, hearing an astonishing tale of betrayal: the Chinese suddenly turning on his men; the overwhelming firing from the Chinese transport aircraft; Stone hit and badly injured supporting bin Wazari's men; the spectacular explosion of the aircraft, no survivors possible; Stone's accusation of Vachenko. It was confusing, maddening, and it was well beyond bin Wazari's ability to immediately comprehend. Only two thoughts planted themselves in his overwhelmed mind. The first was that the jets were his. The second, though a logical, calmly analytical mind would have challenged this conclusion, was that Vachenko had betrayed both him and Wan Chu. "Proceed with the plan!" he yelled into the phone before slamming it onto the table. He then motioned to two of his house guards, just a quick nod to each, and then indicated Vachenko. Without the tiniest hesitation, the two sprang to Vachenko and pinned his arms, while a third, at a motion from bin Wazari, relieved Vachenko of his concealed pistol, a 9 mm Glock, and snatched the phone from Ivor's hand, bringing both to Hasim.

The yelling on the other side ceased abruptly as bin Wazari spoke quickly and earnestly into the phone.

"We have both been betrayed," bin Wazari spoke forcefully. "I will honor our agreement, Wan Chu. You will be compensated." There was a pause, with the angry voice somewhat more muted, though still full of venom and death.

"Yes, yes!" bin Wazari insisted, "For the aircraft upon which we had agreed as well as the transport!" Another pause. "Men have died on both sides! I had no part in that! But we have the traitor, and he will pay!"

"I wish him dead, now!" Wan Chu growled into the phone.

"But surely," Hasim argued, "I must have time with him, to learn what he has done, to recover the money!"

"I care nothing for your concerns of recovering money! The fool has betrayed you under your very nose! He will die now, or your life will not be worth a handful of dust!"

"You wish me to pay you twice?" yelled Hasim in turn.

"I wish you to pay me once! Deal with Vachenko now or deal with the consequence, I will not negotiate with you!" Wan Chu screamed.

"Very well," Hasim said, at last. "You will see it done."

Bin Wazari slid the phone into his pocket and motioned to his men to take Vachenko, protesting loudly, out into the dark courtyard.

"Hasim … excellency," Vachenko pleaded, "we have been betrayed! I will find the dogs who have done this, I will search them out, please!" His voice was attenuated as he was harshly dragged from the room. To the third guard, Hasim motioned to a huge, ceremonial scimitar, one of a pair that decorated the wall at the head of the room. The man took the evil-looking weapon, a hideously pleased light burning in his eyes.

Outside, Vachenko was forced to his knees, his arms twisted behind his back so as to force his body into a hunch, his head protruding outward.

"Please, excellency, I beg you! I have done nothing! I only wish to serve you! This is all a misunderstanding!"

"Yes!" bellowed bin Wazari, "A misunderstanding that will cost me $55 million, and you, your life!"

Vachenko continued to struggle and plead as the third man took position at his side, the huge blade raised high. At the last moment, bin Wazari held up a hand, and the man with the sword halted, giving Ivor a momentary, frantic hope for survival. But bin Wazari simply took the phone from his pocket, took a photograph, and sent it to the waiting Wan Chu. The manic grin left Ivor's face and he screamed, "No, no, Excellency, please!"

At that moment, Elaya and four men entered the courtyard. Elaya immediately understood the situation. There was barely an instant of time for her to act. She ran forward, yelling for her husband to stop, but her words were drowned by Ivor's cries.

Bin Wazari nodded, and the blade swept down in a whistling blur accompanied an instant later by a dull, crunching sound; the cessation of noise from Vachenko replaced by a brief jetting of blood from his severed arteries and a muffled thud like a cloth-wrapped brick hitting the ground. Bin Wazari took another photo, hit Send, and replaced the phone in his pocket.

Another woman might have cried out in rage and terror. Another woman might have run to her lover's side. Another woman might have run shrieking at the man who had slain her love. Elaya was not another woman. She boiled with frustration that she had arrived a moment too late to save Ivor. She was overwhelmed with fury towards the disgusting man before her, the man who had taken her like a possession, the great fool who could not see beyond his own nose, and now the brute who had murdered the one man she loved. But she was Elaya Andoori, destined to rule a resurgent Iran long after this fool was rotting in his grave. She flashed a quick look to her men—*her* men—sworn to live and die at her command, despising the temporary necessity of bowing to these Saudi scum. They understood. And she ran to her husband and wrapped him in her arms.

"Hasim, Hasim, blessed of Allah, are you all right? Are you unhurt?"

The "great fool" drew her close, his disgusting smell filling her nostrils. "I am well, my love, but the traitor Vachenko is in hell, where he will forever burn."

She saw the gun, held loosely in bin Wazari's left hand, Ivor's gun, and Elaya struck like a cobra. She pulled back and smiled dangerously at the man who she called husband, his shocked face centered nicely above the sights of the Glock.

"Elaya … wife … what foolishness is this?" Hasim asked, completely puzzled. "Put down the gun, immediately."

Elaya's men had drawn their weapons with swift efficiency, and were covering bin Wazari's men. The man with the scimitar, feeling his own foolishness, lowered the archaic weapon to the ground, and stared with a dumfounded expression at the woman who now controlled this situation.

Elaya spat symbolically into the darkness. "I take no orders now from you, pig! And he will not burn in hell! He will be at the right hand of Allah, and you his concubine for all eternity. Pig!" she yelled again.

"I was forced to endure your groping hands, your foul breath, and the stench of your unwashed body, but no more! All is now well in hand. He and I," she said, motioning to the lifeless, headless body, "would have ruled, as he ruled my heart." She paused, and a tiny tear rolled down her cheek. It was the only sign of weakness that she would show this night. "Goodbye, my love," she directed towards the body. "By your sacrifice, our people will become mighty. We will wipe the stench of the Saud from the air of the Middle East. Rest, now."

"Elaya," began bin Wazari, "I command you to place down your weapon, to bow before your lord!"

It was a foolish, foolish remark, and before the final word had entirely escaped his lips, Elaya had backhanded the gun across his face, breaking his teeth and tearing his lips. Blood and tooth fragments sprayed into the blackness of the night, and bin Wazari fell to his knees. Bin Wazari's men tensed as if to spring, but quickly drew back to a non-threatening posture as Elaya's men prepared to fire.

Bin Wazari began to rise, but Elaya's gun swung again, tearing the flesh of his forehead so that he was blinded by his own blood.

"Stay on the ground, pig!" she commanded. "And tell me what has occurred." Hasim hesitated and brought a hand to his bleeding mouth, a flame of hatred burning in his eyes. The gun arced through the air, tearing a handful of hair and scalp from his head. He cried out and fell to his face on the dusty tiles of the courtyard, only inches away from the body of Vachenko. "Speak!" Elaya commanded. Cowed and terrified, Hasim told Elaya all he knew of the chaos and confusion of the transfer of the MiGs and their payment.

When he had finished, she considered the situation, and made an instant decision. "Forgive me, my Ivor," she whispered, looking at the still pleading face of her former lover. She turned away for the last time, and focused all of her anger and hatred on bin Wazari. "Know this, fool," she purred, threateningly, "The Kingdom of Saud is at an end, and your name will be forever linked to its great fall. Persia shall rule! First in the Middle East, then in the world! And it will not be commanded by the bearded ancients that speak platitudes and live in the seventh century. They shall be swept aside, banished to the dirt and rock of the desert. And as for your kind," she spat again, "the men of the Saudi royal house shall clean our latrines, the women serve as whores, and they shall be thankful! Your own family: wives, sons, daughters, will be killed, and your house shall be at an end!"

She paused and looked back towards her men. They were alert and eager. Then, turning back to Hasim, she spoke calmly, "You argued with Vachenko over the failure of the transfer of the money. He grew enraged and killed your guards." Elaya turned a stony face to the dumfounded men, staring stupidly as their deaths approached. And with a calmness that Jason Stone would have admired, she shot the first guard in the head, and calmly moved her aim to the second. Another shot rang out, and the second guard dropped to the ground. The third man, the unfortunate man who had used the scimitar, dropped to his knees and begged for mercy, but Elaya looked at the bloody sword lying at his feet, and with a dark and hard countenance, killed him as well.

She then turned back calmly to Hasim, who was stunned into silence, his eyes only speaking … fear, fear, fear. "After killing your worthless guards, Ivor beat you for the pig you are, and then sent you to hell to find your ancestors. Words began to form on Hasim's lips, but he never uttered them. A final sharp "crack" rang out in the night, and bin Wazari lay there dead, his blood soaking the ground.

Elaya turned to her own men. "And when you came upon the scene, it was too late. But it was you who fulfilled the wishes of Wan Chu and who served out justice to Vachenko. Well done," she said, flatly. She drew a breath and her body seemed to relax as her mind whirled into action. At last, she spoke again. "We have much to do."

***

Elaya spoke with a clarity and firmness that reassured Colonel Zareb, who had been deeply disturbed by the events that she had relayed to him. Nevertheless, despite the alleged treachery of Ivor Vachenko, the MiGs had arrived at the Saudi air base, the F-14 had been prepared and its deadly cargo loaded, Elaya had transferred *$60* million to a much pacified Wan Chu, who had acknowledged that, despite the unfortunate altercation in Turkmenistan, he was satisfied with the arrangement and would not take additional punitive action. Things now seemed well in hand.

"You are sure, then, that in forty hours you will be ready to execute the mission?" Elaya asked, finally.

"Excellency," Zareb responded, affording Hasim's widow the deference he would have afforded her husband, not for his sake, but in compliment to her leadership, "we will be ready. We only await the word of command."

"The word is given, Colonel. Proceed as planned."

The colonel swallowed roughly with a throat suddenly constricted. Until now, all had been hypothetical; and suddenly, like a thunderclap, the realization of the imminent horror soon to be unleashed, the overwhelming responsibility now given to him, crushed him like a physical weight. He coughed once, and replied with as much firmness as he could muster, "It will be so, Excellency."

Chapter Thirty-One

Calming Down

Becky Amhurst had been asked to join Chuck and Logan in a small, dingy room with both a spin-dial and a cypher lock on the door. Becky looked at Logan questioningly as Chuck introduced himself, but Logan's face had remained blank and passive. Chuck quickly dispensed with the required paperwork, and immediately came to the point.

"Ms. Amhurst …"

"Please call me Becky. I'm nervous enough already."

Chuck smiled a somewhat distracted smile and nodded. "Becky, you and your team were asked several days ago to review your computer reload operation, software logs, backups, et cetera, and to perform a thorough scan through all the material on the new servers using the software provided to you by CyberSecure."

"Yes," she replied. "It was an enormous pain in the … it was quite tedious. It also destroyed our schedule, and the program offices are livid. I assume there was a point."

"I am sorry for the inconvenience, Becky," said Chuck, wearily. It seemed he had worn out many sets of knee pads this week, providing Alpha executives with different variations of this apology. Apologizing without providing an actual explanation was a recipe for receiving abuse, and Chuck had absorbed a considerable amount. His only relief, in this case, was that he could provide at least a partial explanation.

"But first," he continued, "I have to ask whether anything unusual, suspicious, or even unexpected … anything at all … came up."

Becky's anxiety had spiked again at the seriousness of this CIA agent's tone, but she shook her head firmly and replied, "No, absolutely nothing. I reviewed every one of my people's reports personally, and I've got the red, baggy eyes to prove it," she added, with a quick smile towards Logan.

Chuck looked pointedly at Logan, who shrugged, and said, "Apparently, the fish never took the bait. We knew that this was far from a certainty."

Chuck kept his weary, but steely, eyes locked on Logan's for a long moment, and then his features visibly relaxed. He nodded and drew a deep breath, looking suddenly worn, and much, much older.

"Excuse me," Becky asked, "But I am pretty confused here. What, exactly, were you two expecting? And who didn't rise to the bait?"

"Logan, do you mind?" asked Chuck, whose mind had already dropped all consideration of this operation, and had settled back to pondering the last message he had received from Shirley.

Becky turned an inquiring and unmistakably accusatory look upon Logan. Logan attempted a light, friendly smile, which withered under her air of moral superiority, as one who had been deceived.

"Right," said Logan, "I don't suppose buying a round of drinks is going to compensate for this?"

"Oh no," Becky began, "I'll need something a lot more substantial than that … if you get my drift," she added playfully.

Logan laughed aloud, and the tension in the room dissolved like a mist. "Right," he repeated. "Well here it is, from the beginning."

And Logan proceeded to tell Becky of all that had occurred: the suspicion that terrorist activities from Cathie's novels were being put into practice, the growing mistrust of one of Cathie's biggest fans (no name was given), the budding notion that Cathie's fourth book might be used to trap the perpetrators, the suspicion regarding the fire that had destroyed Alpha's servers, the long, slow, painful development of the sting centering around the reload of the new servers.

Logan continued describing the events of the final night: no apparent attempt at stealing the code ever having been made. The subsequent lengthy internal checking to verify the integrity of the files was the process that had so damaged Becky's schedule and irritated the Alpha execs. Chuck remained silent throughout, deeply submerged in his own thoughts, though not entirely disconnected from the conversation.

When Logan had completed his monologue, Becky asked the question that had been troubling her during the latter part of his description. "You must have suspected someone on my team or on the ISG team. Who?" she asked bluntly.

At that question, Chuck resurfaced quickly. "I'm sorry, Becky, we can't address that right now."

"You can't ... what ... you've got to be kidding! So I'm supposed to keep working with an individual that you think may potentially be a spy? Oh, hell, if you don't tell me, I'll reassign my entire team, and I'll fire ISG. They're under contract to me, Logan," she added, turning a stern, professional face in his direction. "And I can terminate that contract at any time!"

Logan looked over at Chuck with raised eyebrows that said, quite eloquently, "What did I tell you?" It was clear that this had been a point of contention between them, prior to sitting down with Becky.

"Ms. ... dammit ... Becky," Chuck began. "It should be pretty obvious that Logan and I disagreed on this point. I have to insist, however." Becky drew a deep breath to begin her protest, but Chuck cut her off, gently. "Please, Becky, all I ask is that you bear with us for, no more than a week. You have to understand that our primary objective has pretty well failed. Give us a week, or even a couple of days, and if you could help out by monitoring activities ..." Chuck faded to silence, under Becky's incredulous gaze.

Logan jumped in, wearily. "Just a couple of days, Becky. It would really help."

Becky finally relaxed her aggressive posture and sat back in her chair. "Boy, do you ever owe me now, Fletcher! One week. And at the end ..."

"We will share our information, I give you my word," said Chuck, quickly.

"Hmmm, the word of a career CIA agent and a beat-up, old, former program manager. I might as well plan on buying my own drinks in the future," she said, with a smile.

***

Logan dropped two dollars into the tip jar and thanked the bartender as he carefully juggled the two brimming glasses of "Old Monkeyshine." As he set Chuck's down in front of him, he counted the empties. This couldn't really be their fourth round? Three Monkeyshines were dangerous. Four were deadly.

But it had been a four Monkeyshine kind of day, the perfect capper to the last couple of weeks: tedious, meticulous preparation for the software sting; poisoning the book and ensuring it got into the hands of the most likely suspect; dealing with Cathie's initial resistance; the insertion of the love story, with the key to the real terrorist plot (if only they'd known!); Logan, Gail, and Randy caught by terrorists; critical F-14 and missile parts stolen; Gail nearly murdered. And now, after all of that, apparently no one had taken the bait on the software. If Becky was right, and Logan was sure she was, there had been no breach during the software reload. All for nothing. All wasted energy. Logan took a sip of number four. Oddly, Logan looked back upon this series of events and considered that there was one other occurrence that had been more destructive than all of the above: Randy's loss of faith in Chuck, and the bitter, resentful hatred that had taken its place.

Logan took what he thought was his next sip of beer and noticed that the glass was half empty. Clearly some time had passed. He shrugged inwardly, took his sip, and began to fashion the words for his next sentence. Chuck's eyes, sharp and alert, looked out from a very weary face, and Chuck spoke first. "Don't bother, Logan. I know what you'd say. Do you think I wouldn't do anything to get him back? I know I lied to him, to both of you, and it nearly cost you all your lives. When I think of that young woman with the knife to her throat … well, let's just say I'm not too damn proud." He paused for a moment as an employee cleared the empty glasses from the table. "But the real problem is, Logan, that considering the stakes … it was what I had to do! I'd be lying again to say I'd do it differently, and he wouldn't believe it anyway. So that's it," he said glumly, pushing his chair back with a grating squeal. "Next round's on me."

Logan stared at his glass blearily. Empty again! Imagine that. It would be an iffy proposition getting home tonight. Logan took the offered beer with a nod, but then placed it on the table. The inspiration he had been waiting for, hoping for, had finally arrived in his weary brain. "You know, Chuck," he began, "You've already made the most convincing apology. Hah!" he said, with a sudden laugh. "Oh my God, why didn't we see it?" His smile broadened. "Yeah, maybe you should have let us in the loop; maybe we could have avoided that situation at Rickman altogether. I would call that a mistake, and a whopper too. But don't you see? When you made that call to … to him, you were admitting your mistake and trying to make amends, and in a big fucking way! It's kind of humbling; hell, crushingly humbling, and I raise my glass to you!" And Logan did, slopping a considerable amount on their table as he brought the glass to his lips.

"Man, if you weren't so drunk, I would not be amused. Still, I'm curious enough to ask, what the hell are you talking about?"

"Don't you get it? You risked everything, and not just an abstract mission and hypothetical lives … but potentially a lot of *real* lives, for me and Gail and Randy. Brudda, if that isn't love, I don't know what is. And you were ready to risk more if your guy hadn't handled it. Man, that's some apology."

A tiny flicker of hope, of possible redemption, lit Chuck's eyes, and a corner of his mouth lifted in what might have been the precursor to a smile. "Well, I couldn't let them kill Randy and Gail, could I?" he said, deliberately leaving Logan out of consideration.

Logan answered with a huge grin. "That's the spirit, brudda. Now, would you like me to have a small chat with the male Grasshopper?" Chuck nodded, just as a huge man, the bar's bouncer, came up to their table.

"I think you gentlemen are just about done. Would you like me to call you a cab?"

"No argument here!" Logan replied.

***

"Randy, you knew that when you went into the agency there'd be risks," Gail began.

"Please, Gail, I appreciate what you're trying to do, but it's no good. Risks for me are one thing. I chose that job. But not for you!"

"I insisted on going with you and Logan, remember?"

"And I was an idiot to let you. What the hell was I thinking?"

"C'mon, Grasshopper, none of us were expecting armed terrorists on the Air Force base. No one could have anticipated what happened."

"He knew! He could have stopped it! And it almost got you killed! I hate the lying SOB and I'm done with the agency!"

"Randy, you're yelling at me," Gail said in a quiet, somewhat hurt voice.

"No … I'm … it's just … oh Gail, I can't stand the thought of losing you, of living without you. I was so, so frightened and angry that night," he said, pulling her close.

"This is better," Gail said, settling into Randy's arms, "much, much better. You know, Randy," she continued after a long silence, when she could feel his breathing and heartbeat approaching something near normal, "I was just as frightened for you, and the thought of you continuing in … the same line of work … terrifies me."

"But then …" he began, but she brought a cool finger to his lips, stopping him instantly.

"But I've known you long enough now to know that, well, you're really good at it and … you love it. Someday, you may decide it isn't for you. Oh, maybe a better situation will come along or you'll get tired of it all, and you'll decide in cold blood to quit. But that's the point. It will be with a clear mind and no regrets, and you won't need to use me as an excuse. And by the way," she added with a laugh, "I'm never going to work with you again, ever! And that's a solemn promise."

Randy considered this for a long time and inwardly acknowledged the truth in everything Gail had said. He finally turned to her with a troubled look. "I wouldn't know how to begin to … talk with him, to try to maybe patch things up."

"Well, if I were you, I think I'd trust my friend Logan. I'm pretty sure he'd be more than willing to help smooth the way. He's a good friend to Chuck, and to you, Randy."

"Chuck and I would need to settle a few things, for the future, or I would still say no."

"But you'd do it, well, a bit more calmly, and I'd support you in any decision you made … because I love you," she added quietly.

Randy hesitated, felt himself flushing hotly, and then spoke in a suddenly awkward way, his throat constricting uncontrollably. "I made another decision, a while ago. And I … well, the truth is I've been a bit of a coward on that one as well." Gail adjusted her position in Randy's arms to look directly into his eyes, and waited for him to go on.

"Gail, I just don't know how to, I mean, that is, what I mean is …" Gail waited quietly, her soft eyes showing no sign of impatience. Randy drew a deep breath and proceeded with as much steadiness as possible, "Gail, I really love you. Will you marry me?"

Her eyes sparkled and a smile lit her face. "Of course I will, Grasshopper," she answered.

***

Randy wasn't really much of a golfer, but it hardly mattered. By the end of eighteen holes, he and Logan had each smoked two cigars and made their way through a pint of single malt scotch. Nor did that matter particularly either, other than to smooth the hard edges of their conversation. What did matter was that Randy had agreed to a brokered meeting between himself and Chuck, after Logan completed the necessary prep work.

Logan had no doubt that the first encounter between these two since the night at Rickman would be tense and awkward, but he had good reason to believe that their relationship could be salvaged, knowing, as he did, the fundamentally solid and honorable character of each.

Logan also had another small triumph to be proud of. He had beaten Randy by eleven strokes! *Not bad for an old, retired guy*, he thought. But a final thought brought an uncontrollable sense of anxiety. Chuck had asked for a forty-eight hour delay before any meeting took place. And though Logan didn't press him, he knew that matters with Stone/Kulwicki were about to come to a close, for better or worse. Better was fine, in fact, more than fine, but worse didn't bear much thought. Based on the little Logan knew, worse could be extraordinarily bad.

Chapter Thirty-Two

That Day is Here

At nearly the same time as Logan's round of golf with Randy, it was coal-bin dark, with a chilly wind blowing, in the barren no-man's-land of eastern Jordan. Stone pulled his jacket tighter around him, and though he was shivering uncontrollably, his brow was beaded with sweat. He reached for his canteen, pulled a Keflex from a pouch with shivering fingers, reconsidered, and pulled two, popping them quickly in his mouth and chasing them down his throat with a quick drink of water. So far, they had done little to subdue the infection that had taken hold from the bullet wound in his side. In addition, he had used the last of the "poppy" filled syringes, questionable stuff in any case, and the dull throb in his side had become a growing agony of malevolent urgency.

He had been in his primary location for thirty-six hours now. No mission had occurred on the previous night, and so here he remained. A hideous fear haunted him that the incompetent fools working with bin Wazari and Elaya would cause a delay, or worse yet, an indefinite postponement. Under good conditions, that is, conditions where he was not suffering from an infection caused by an untreated bullet wound (one that no doubt still contained piercing bone fragments from his shattered rib), Stone felt he could easily have stretched his supplies for ten days, maybe more. As he was, he prayed that he would hear the beep of the F-14's transponder from his receiver tonight, as he had extreme doubts that he could even remain conscious, let alone coherent, for another twenty-four hours.

To distract his mind, Stone checked his gear once again. The receiver for the Tomcat's transponder would be critical. Stone was aware that the

Saudis would be constantly interrogating the aircraft, and it was critical that the jet keep booming out a clearly Iranian F-14 code. The MiGs would be doing the same, of course, but Stone could only be sure of the mission if he received the F-14's signature.

Another critical bit of electronics was the transmitter provided by Luana, the transmitter that would be his final means of directly triggering the destruction of the bomb. It would be a near-desperate act to use this device, as it would mean that the other triggers programmed into the missile's signal processor had somehow failed, and Stone had small confidence in the operating range of this device, particularly as the signal would be attenuated rapidly as the missile sped away from the launch aircraft at many times the speed of sound. How long would he have once the weapon was launched? He would have to react quickly, that was it, just as his father had said, a quick reaction, quick … reaction …

***

They were only fishing for bluegills, but young James couldn't have been more excited or nervous if it had been marlin.

"OK, son, now just keep your eyes on the bobber. It'll take a little hop, and then you have to react fast. Remember what I told you. Don't pull the rod up. Just give it a little tug to the side. And don't overdo it, or you'll pull the hook right out of his mouth. Once he's on, you'll feel a wobbly, bumpy kind of tug. Just keep easy tension on the line, and reel him in gently. Get him right under the tip of the rod and I'll net him. But the most important thing is to watch that bobber and react fast."

It seemed so much to remember, so much to do, so many ways to foul it up, but James nodded tensely to his amused father, and focused on the bobber until his eyes were watering. Suddenly the bobber did a little double-hop ...

***

Stone snapped upright, a move that caused a nearly unbearable pain to jet through his side. His eyes blurred for a moment, and then refocused. Overhead, a beautiful swath of stars arced across the sky, a gorgeous sight, and he thought briefly of Luana. Where was she, again? His mind was groggy and he couldn't quite remember. Was it LA? Perhaps. There would be no visible Milky Way there, the stars drowned by the manmade light of ten million concentrated humans, spoiling the sky as they had spoiled the land, spoiled the lake where he had caught his first fish. And he had been so disappointed … was still so disappointed. His father had just mumbled something about a subdivision, whatever that was, but his mother would explain, he would go and ask her right now …

***

"Mom, Dad says we can't fish in Cedar Lake anymore, but we fished there last year. Remember the bluegills I caught all by myself?"

"Yes I do, darling, and we fried them up and ate them. They were delicious."

"So why can't I go back and get some more? I can fish even better now."

"Because, James, people bought the land around the lake, and dug it all up to build houses, and the dirt and mud ran from those people's yards into that little lake, and now the fish can't live there."

"But that's stupid," James said, bitterly. "Didn't they realize what they were doing?"

"People almost never do ... until it's too late. Never be one of those people, James. Think before you act. Don't be swayed or distracted ..."

***

Distracted! *Damn it*, thought Stone, who at least had not jerked his body this time as his conscious mind had re-awoken. Stone reached carefully in his pack and pulled out another packet of pills: stimulants, damned powerful ones. Stone considered and settled on one, for now. He eased himself to a more comfortable position, and continued to survey his gear. Food and water certainly wouldn't be an issue. He doubted now whether he could last through tomorrow without some help. And there was no help coming. If only he could shake off this feeling of fatigue.

He pulled out his night vision goggles, and scanned the barren waste around him: rock, bare earth, a few hummocky hills like the one where he was now situated. No signs of life as far as he could see. He put the goggles aside and found that as his eyes adjusted to the faint starlight, he could see almost as well as with his night vision gear. Besides, he thought, allowing himself the luxury of being somewhat sulky, there was nothing here worth seeing beyond the stars themselves. Stone looked upward once again and thought of Luana, and how wonderful a night on the beach in Maui would be once this was all over. But he needed it to be over, soon. He felt so, so tired, and the smell of brewing coffee was like a tease …

***

"Isn't it done yet, Mom?" a fourteen-year-old James had asked his mother in the cramped kitchen area of their camper. Today, they would be bow hunting, something that his mother enjoyed even more, it seemed, than his father, and they had settled on a very early start from the campsite.

"Not yet, son, but it soon will be. And since when have you been a coffee drinker?"

"Since I have to get up at three o'clock to go hunting," he said with a yawn. "It smells good."

"Give it a little more time. I'm going to wash up, but I've got some eggs boiling. Here," she said, grabbing a small electric timer, "You just watch the eggs, and when this beeps, turn them off. By then the coffee will be done and you can have some. You might want to put in some cream and sugar, or it might not taste as good as it smells, OK?"

"OK," James said, resting a heavy head in his hand and staring ahead, blearily.

"Now don't fall back to sleep, young man!" she said, as she headed towards the back of the camper. "And be sure to turn off the water when the timer beeps, OK? That's important ... when the timer beeps ... when it beeps ..."

***

A faint but persistent beeping sounded at last, but James was so, so tired. The smell of coffee faded from his nostrils as his eyes fluttered open. A small red light on the transponder receiver flashed intermittently, and a low beeping sound came from the device. The Tomcat was airborne!

No coffee, but Jason grabbed two more of the stimulant pills. He'd suffer later, with every nerve ending in his body, including the ones around his shattered rib, extremely alert and lively.

The minutes passed, and the transponder signal grew stronger. *Good,* he thought, *still approaching.* He pulled his night vision goggles out once again, and slowly scanned the skies to the northeast. Nothing. He repeated the process again, again, again. At last, a tiny blur of light, slightly more to the south than he had expected, appeared and persisted within the field of view, moving faster and faster across the sky against the backdrop of frozen stars. The transponder receiver was now steadily emitting firm beeps at regular intervals. The jets drew nearer.

Stone frowned slightly. He had positioned himself well to the south and east of the proper launch point. The only problem was that on this track, the Tomcat would launch well south of the proper launch point. Had he had the time or the inclination to perform the calculation, he would have realized that he had lost thirty percent of his space buffer. There was still margin, but considerably less than he had counted on, and this only if the fools didn't get trigger-happy and launch early, before they had penetrated well into Jordan. He knew military pilots could panic and launch ordnance well out of range if things got a little too hot. Hopefully, there was some sense of discipline in the F-14 driver and his RIO.

The planes passed immediately to the north of Stone's position, and continued westward into Jordan. They were minutes away from launch.

Stone repositioned himself behind a large cluster of rock that would shelter him from the north and west, pulled his fail-safe device into his hand, and unlocked the trigger. He then put on heavy goggles. He had no desire to melt his retinas out of carelessness. And he waited.

To the north and west of his location, cruising subsonic at thirty thousand feet, the pilot of the F-14 prepared to launch. The escort MiGs were equally aware of the designated launch point, and their orders were to hang back from and below the Tomcat, and to wait until the missile was away, when they were to send a confirmation signal back to their launch base, and break off to head home, followed by the F-14. There had been no radio communication since takeoff, either between the pilots or back to the base. There was no need, and no desire, the steady repeating of the jet's transponders being the only message they desired to send: the wicked Iranians on a sneak-attack mission against Israel.

They neared the launch point, and the RIO informed the pilot he was cleared to shoot. With no hesitation, no extraneous thought, the pilot pulled the trigger, and the heavy Phoenix missile ejected from the forward portside station, and a micro-world of controlled but staggeringly fast activity initiated within the missile's processor.

Among the many, many processes that began with button-push, the missile's computer checked for sufficient g's for a safe launch. Confirmed. Time ticked down and an electronic pulse squibbed the rocket motor. A massive eruption of flame shot from the rear of the missile, and its accelerometer registered the forward thrust anticipated for motor ignition. This thrust would persist as the missile flew downrange and climbed to a surprising altitude where, the motor finally spent, the Phoenix would begin a slow, controlled, coasting dive towards its target.

Missile forward motion was registered within the processor as the motor's thrust first equaled and then greatly exceeded aerodynamic drag. At a safe separation, the missile flippers were unlocked, and began accepting steering commands from the missile's guidance algorithms. At this time, the missile's safe/arm device was locked in safe, as it would be with even a conventional high-explosive warhead, to prevent detonation too close to the launch aircraft. An algorithm patiently counted down the milliseconds and calculated the fly-out until the missile reached the prescribed "safe" distance from the shooter. Though primarily a long range weapon, the Phoenix could be used for shorter range attacks, and so it was crucial to enable warhead arming as soon as possible, consistent with the safety of the launch aircraft. But the warhead had never been a nuclear device. At a "safe" distance for conventional ordnance, the computer dispassionately armed the warhead.

***

On the ground, Stone's gear registered first one and then a second burst of RF energy from the now distant jets. The missile was away! Stone placed a finger on the trigger and began a silent countdown. He and Luana had allotted six seconds.

***

Onboard the missile, the inertial measurement unit calculated position relative to the launch point, showing a growing separation from the shooter, perhaps a half-mile, and a relative missile body pitch of nineteen degrees as it climbed steeply towards its apogee. What followed took only milliseconds.

The newly installed GPS began to communicate with the missile's processor. North, east, and down coordinates were converted to standard GPS location. The designated burst point would be computed based on those coordinates. An airburst had been desired, and the warhead would detonate at or below five thousand feet above ground level when latitude and longitude were within certain limits. If altitude went below one thousand feet AGL, the warhead would detonate regardless, provided that downrange travel exceeded twenty-five miles from the launch point.

But now, an odd bit of new code, undiscovered in testing, began to execute within the missile's processor, insisting that range was growing at an extraordinary rate, while altitude was steadily dropping. Calculations within the GPS software exceeded computational range, overflowing and providing nonsense values, but the GPS computer, designed for such problems, simply re-initialized with new values taken from the processor. Once again, random, nonsense numbers, and once again a reset, and on the third attempt, a protocol, also newly imbedded within the missile's processor, decreed GPS failure, and reverted all arm and fire control to the missile computer, which now showed a fictitious fly-out of nearly eighty-five miles (its true fly-out, less than a mile), and a rapidly dropping altitude. Ten thousand feet (in fact, the missile was higher than its launch altitude of thirty thousand), nine thousand, eight thousand … The downrange coordinates already registered within the specific target coordinate uncertainty boundaries. Seven thousand, six thousand …

***

Stone stared out ahead at the rocky outcropping facing his shelter. The word "five" hadn't yet formed in his mind.

***

… and then: 4,998.72. A simple mathematical calculation showed that all coordinates had now met optimal values, and a flag was set, to be read microseconds later by a parallel processor. With cold, inhuman logic, a fire pulse was sent to the warhead, and the high explosives in the ancient device detonated, sending two semi-critical masses of plutonium into profound, intimate contact. Critical mass.

A dazzling, sun-white blaze ignited in the desert sky, sweeping the nearby area clean of the tiny, man-made flying machines, nearly vaporized by the massive thermal concussion, and then flung to dust by the shockwave that followed.

As Stone stared, his rocky outcropping was suddenly backlit by an unfathomable brilliance, casting a hard-shadowed silhouette onto the facing rock, visible even with his protective glasses. It lasted for less than an instant, and Stone immediately pulled the goggles from his head, the silhouette now glowing a hellish orange. As it dimmed, Stone peered out from behind his rocky cover, and saw, at a great distance, the huge rising-sun fireball lifting lazily up into the dark sky, burning fiercely, but briefly, until swallowed once again by the infinite night. Several minutes passed, and a low, extensive rumble met his ears, as though a huge night-freight was passing on the tracks near his childhood home. Then silence.

Stone quickly grabbed his sparse gear, and forced himself up. The pain sent a lightning bolt, no less brilliant than the nuclear event, shooting through his head, and for a moment, all was black. But gradually, the stars reappeared, and Stone began the long, painful trudge back to where he had left the Land Rover.

***

Somewhere in a seedy cellar of London's east side, Richard Crandall was enjoying a night of wild hallucinations and carnal delights. He would have smiled, knowing that he had earned his money.

***

Stone was never able to completely recall how he had reached the Land Rover, driven to Al Qurayyat in western Saudi Arabia, or bribed a private pilot to fly him to Kuwait where a certain friend of long standing managed to get him medical help, not long before such help would have proved pointless. As it was, Stone disappeared for over a week and neither Luana nor Chuck received any communication from Shirley during that time.

***

Within hours of the "unprecedented nuclear event" as the press was calling it, Chuck Johnson was called into his Oakland office where he heard a weary, anxious Secretary of Defense offer qualified congratulations. "My God, Johnson, the entire Middle East is teetering, but if we make it for the next twelve hours, there's a good chance, an excellent chance, that we can get some unbelievable leverage. First of all, the Jordanians are mightily pissed. Too bad for them that the world doesn't give a shit! After all, as extraordinary as it seems, there appear to be NO casualties on the ground. The IAEA is monitoring the radiation cloud, which seems to be heading towards Saudi Arabia and Iran—a little poetic justice there! But the altitude of the burst minimized the amount of radioactive dust and sand. Still, there are concerns, and a few towns and villages downwind are being evacuated. All in all, though, it might have been the least lethal location on the planet to detonate a device. My hat's off to your man!"

My man, thought Chuck, grimly. *And where is he now? I should have heard. I hope to God the Sec Def is right about there being no casualties on the ground!* But Chuck remained silent, and the Secretary continued.

"We know it was the Saudis, of course, some renegade group, even if we can't prove it, and we've let them know that we know. They're being pretty damned cooperative right now, I can tell you. Israel wants to wipe out Tehran, but State has them convinced they can get a better deal and lose no lives if they just hang tough. We've also committed to back them to the hilt if things go bad. Tehran denies all involvement, of course. But the transponder signals and the tracking data provided by the helpful Saudis, and corroborated by the Israelis themselves, point a pretty heavy finger in their direction. I hear there is already rioting taking place all over Iran, and the people are calling for the heads of the ayatollahs and mullahs. And this time the U.S. isn't going to squander the opportunity like we did in '09. Do you know there is already a powerful group in London that has created a secular 'government in exile'? It seems legit, and has a pretty solid ground game in Iran. Kind of odd, though, it's being led by an amazingly charismatic woman named Elaya … something or other. Of course, she's promised democracy and a pro-Western government if we'll provide a little support. I may need you to work up a profile on her, fast, if things continue to go well."

Chuck shuddered at the name, but remained silent. In fact, the Secretary had now expended more words on Chuck in this conversation than in all previous discussions, and Chuck assumed it was the characteristic need for a person in high authority under great stress to simply share his thoughts. A subordinate, far below his rank, was a perfect target audience, as there was little likelihood of interruption. Chuck was content to be the silent listener for the "great man." Truthfully, much more than half of his mind was given to wondering about Stone. Where was he? Was he even alive? Why had there been no contact? This last bothered Chuck immensely. Stone had proven to be as reliable as the sunrise, and a stickler for affirmative communication. Chuck's logical conclusion: Stone was unable to contact him. It was the "why" that bothered him.

Chuck's reverie was interrupted by a sudden silence on the phone. Had the Secretary asked him a question? Chuck only hesitated for a moment, and then answered with a reply that had gotten him out of many a tight spot: "Well, Mr. Secretary, I think you've exactly captured the essence of the situation, and I agree with your assessment. Please let me know how I and my team can be of help."

"Thanks, Johnson. You've done a hell of a job, and I really value your input." Voices in the background. "Listen, I've got to go; meeting with the Joint Chiefs. Keep me posted on Shirley's status, would you?" The phone went dead before Chuck could provide a response.

Chapter Thirty-Three

A Night for Jazz

Gail was sleeping quietly, and Randy gently closed the door before turning on the television. He froze instantly as he heard the tense, grim-faced reporter describing the powder-keg tensions in the Middle East resulting from the apparent explosion of a small nuclear device in the night sky over western Jordan.

"At this time, the U.S. and Russian presidents, the English Prime Minister, and the president of the People's Republic of China, as well as French, German, and Italian leaders, are calling for calm and restraint as this unprecedented detonation of a nuclear device is thoroughly investigated. Nevertheless, the governments of nearly all the Middle Eastern powers including Israel, Iraq, Iran, Jordan, Syria, Egypt, and Saudi Arabia have put their militaries on full alert. The United States has dispatched its Secretary of State to the region, as have the other world powers, and it would appear at this time that the situation, while extremely tense, is stable. Initial accusations directed by the Saudis and Israelis towards Iran have been vehemently denied, though it appears that the Iranian regime, under tremendous international and domestic pressure may be crumbling. A semi-official government in exile has been declared in England, and is said to be negotiating with world powers for leniency towards the Iranian people and international support to depose the current theocracy. Israel has stated support for this new government, and has agreed to refrain from a counterattack if the current regime can be removed ..."

The news continued, and Randy whistled within himself. And he couldn't help admire the skill with which his one-time antagonist had handled the situation. The missing device was destroyed over a true desert wasteland, no ground casualties were, as yet, reported, and the Middle East hadn't gone to war, nor drawn the super powers into any conflict ... yet. It had been like performing brain surgery with a chainsaw, and yet this man, this agent of Chuck's, had pulled it off. Randy was feeling rather small by comparison; his own deeds, his own work to date, seemed puny. And then he was struck with wondering if even *this man* had survived his own success. A nuclear blast! How close had Stone been? Was he alive, dead, or dying, blood oozing from skin where the DNA had been shattered, his organs turning into soup within his own failing shell? The thought, disgusting and horribly depressing, had just invaded his mind, when the bedroom door opened slowly, and a warm, pink, and bleary-eyed Gail emerged, stifling a yawn.

"Hey," said Randy, quickly turning off the news. "I tried not to wake you."

"Oh, it's time for me to get moving, Grasshopper."

Randy wrapped his arms around her, absorbing some of the lingering bed-warmth, and smelling the fragrance of her hair. Thoughts of Stone were banished for the time, and he just held Gail tightly, thinking over and over *She's safe, she's safe, she's safe*. A few minutes later, when she slipped away to take a shower, Randy resumed watching the news. As long as things remained stable, and he silently prayed they would, it would have been worth it.

***

Logan and Cathie also watched the news with tremendous anxiety and interest, and Logan realized, as Randy had, that the point of maximum danger had passed. With diplomats applying pressure from all sides, war might now be prevented. The collapse of the theocratic regime in Iran was an extraordinary added benefit. But it was when a BBC reporter was allowed an interview with the head of the government in exile, a snippet being broadcast by CNN, that both Cathie and Logan stared at the television screen with dumbstruck disbelief. Elaya Andoori!

She spoke eloquently for several minutes, praising the youth in her country who were coming out in strong support of regime change, and she pledged to the world that a democratically elected government would take the place of the mullahs and ayatollahs, "too long in power, and too wedded to the theocracy of the past." She promised to hold elections within a month of being instated as interim president, and vowed that she would be a sincere and lasting friend to the world, and would work tirelessly to bring about a lasting peace to the Middle East. Logan's shock evaporated with the deluge of standard "boiler-plate" promises and commitments, and he was about to comment on the fact, when he felt Cathie's penetrating gaze upon him.

Logan turned his head cautiously, and met the accusatory look of Cathie, followed by her statement, "How much of this did you know, you and Chuck and Randy? And don't try to BS me, you have that guilty look plastered on your face!"

Logan adopted his most innocent, winning smile, and shrugged his shoulders slightly, which confirmed Cathie's suspicions. But before he could speak, concoct some absurd and childish tale that wouldn't fool a half-wit, Cathie just shook her head, and grudgingly growled, "No 'need-to-know.'"

Logan just smiled more broadly. "I love you, dear," he said, with sincerity.

"Just answer me this," Cathie added a moment later, "Is it over?"

Logan nodded. "It's over."

***

There was considerably more tension in the Chu household as Wan Chu sat glaring at the television, a silent and, for the moment, obedient daughter sharing the room. Though deferential and polite to her father from the moment she had arrived at his Maui estate, there was an undeniable coldness between them. For Wan Chu, the bitter feelings of disappointment in his daughter were new and extremely unpleasant to him. The mishandling of the transfer of the $50 million dollars was in no way her fault, it seemed to him, and yet it had happened, and the arrangements she had made had been breached by the fool Vachenko. No conception of the actual truth had yet cast a shadow in Wan Chu's mind. But the arrangements, which should have been foolproof, had been broken by the simplest of fools. Yes, his daughter bore some responsibility.

His true source of irritation, bordering on naked anger, was her admission that she, upon her own judgment and authority, had stopped the attempted theft of the datalink encryption algorithms. Her repeated insistence that their plans had been discovered and that a trap had been set, and her proofs of such a trap, produced in great detail, did little to diffuse Wan Chu's frustration. Perhaps it was a belief that such an extraordinary opportunity had been wasted due to timidity. Perhaps it was his deep-seated confidence that they might still have succeeded, even if one of their agents had been exposed, even if Luana's involvement had been exposed. But Luana suspected it was really none of the above. In fact, she was convinced that it was simple parental anger that her father felt: she had disobeyed him, had gone against his wishes, and had not first consulted him. It represented a broken trust, a broken filial commitment, and one that could never be repaired. And as the news repeated its droning coverage of a near war, more than half of Wan Chu's mind was occupied with how he would deal with his daughter from this point forward.

For Luana's part, she and Stone had made a pact, one in which her father would play no part. In her mind, her father's reaction had been foolish and petty. Their plan had been discovered; she was still uncertain as to how. But she knew that it would have failed catastrophically. If he refused to see it, then he was becoming blind as well as stubborn. But she had set that aside. It would be as it would be. Even the news was of only minor interest to her, and that only as it related to Jason Stone.

Stone had warned her that direct contact after the event might be difficult for some period of time, considering his location and the heightened state of security that was sure to follow the event. Luana had accepted this, knowing, as he did, that another reason for his failing to contact her quickly might prove to be permanent. They hadn't spoken of his death any more than they had spoken of the possible failure of his mission. Neither event led them down a path they cared to travel.

Luana looked back to their planning in Breckenridge and in London, and was amazed at their own self-assurance in such a risky venture. And while it was true that, unknown to Wan Chu, Hasim, Ivor, or Elaya, the original $50 million destined for Wan Chu was now in an account to which only Luana had access, the thought was like a thin broth, weak and unsatisfying. Without Jason, Luana thought, what would have been the purpose? She banished the notion from her mind. It was fruitless. She would cling to another of the many reasons Stone had predicted might cause his inability to contact her immediately. The news repeated itself endlessly, and she grew bored, walking out onto the huge patio under the cold glare of her father, to warm herself in the sun, and breathe the fragrant trade winds that endlessly rustled the palms.

After what seemed like hours, her father emerged onto the patio, discreetly shadowed by his huge Hawaiian bodyguard.

"Daughter," he began, roughly, "I must make arrangements to travel to Hong Kong. There will be many questions, and my colleagues will wish to know how it was that we failed so completely. This turn of events in the Middle East will also require much discussion, and there will undoubtedly be much desired of you as a consequence. You will leave, now," Wan Chu added callously, "but will return here in three weeks to be told your obligation."

When it was clear that Wan Chu was finished, and that there would be no fatherly acknowledgement of farewell, let alone of love, Luana nodded curtly and left the patio, vowing to herself to never return; not, at least, until she had found a means to wrestle control from this man's weakening grasp.

The large Hawaiian watched her leave, then turned his massive body to the west, staring phlegmatically out to the coastline, and standing as silently as the mountaintop.

***

Stone was beginning to feel his strength returning. Since his arrival in Kuwait over a week ago, he had been feverish, often delirious. After ten days of antibiotics following a successful surgery that finally removed all of the bone fragments from his shattered rib, the infection suddenly collapsed, seemingly out of his body and into the sweat-drenched sheets of his bed. Time had been a blur, though. In lucid moments, his friend had kept him posted on the incredible tensions in the region, the endless pleading for calm and order by world leaders, the teetering and collapse of the Iranian regime, and the sense of the exhausted, though still nervous, peace that had finally settled upon the Middle East. The world exhaled gratefully, and the promised support flowed into the region: radiation testing, investigative teams, negotiators, even UN observers and peacekeepers.

"Best of luck to you," said Stone's friend, with a pronounced Indian accent.

"And my thanks to you, Ganesh. Be safe, my friend."

"As always," he answered, with a bow.

Stone left the house in the seedy neighborhood of Kuwait City that was a bit too near the busy port and warehouses. But before long, Stone had flagged down a taxi, and was heading south, towards the international airport. Flights in and out of Kuwait had resumed near-normal schedules after the initial panic, suspicion, and incredibly tight security following the detonation of the device. But before Stone boarded his flight to London, he went to the airport executive lounge, and logged on to one of the available computers.

His first act was to update Shirley's Facebook page, expressing regrets for not staying in touch with her friends, but relating that she had been overcome, apparently from eating bad shellfish, and had hardly left the lavatory for days. Feeling better now, she would soon give her friends a full update on her traveling adventures.

Chuck Johnson felt an enormous sense of relief as he finally read the words he had been praying for from the computer monitor at the Oakland Library. He read and re-read every word until he was sure he had gleaned every last drop of information. Then, in a spirit of fun he hadn't felt for months, he surfed the web for porn for the next twenty minutes, fitting in perfectly with his nearby neighbors. Afterwards, he made his way over to Murphy's and treated himself to several "Town Drunks," his inner spirits in a state of confusion, a battle between euphoria and extreme depression raging, with no clear winner in sight.

After updating his Facebook page, Stone strolled over to a deserted corner of the lounge near a set of huge windows overlooking the runway. He pulled his recently purchased cell phone from his pocket and called a familiar international number. He was composing the message he would leave when an even more familiar voice suddenly spoke.

"Hello."

"Luana, this is James, your cousin James. We met in Colorado a few months ago."

Total stunned silence for a moment was followed by a cautious, "James, is it really you? I was expecting to hear from you much earlier. I hope you are well."

"Oh," said Stone, casually, "I've been a little under the weather, but I'm on the mend now."

"Oh thank …" Luana halted, struggling to control her emotions. "Well," she continued, "that's really good. You shouldn't worry your cousin like that, but I'll forgive you."

"Good," said Stone. "Say," he said, almost casually, "do you remember that park where we met a while ago? I don't suppose you could get a little time off. We could go back there, maybe catch a play."

"When?" was all Luana said.

"How does Thursday sound, say around four?"

"I'll be there. And James, why don't you see if Shirley would like to join us," she teased.

"I can guarantee Shirley will be there. Well, listen, I've got to go now. But I'll see you soon."

"Soon!" Luana replied.

Stone went casually into a stall in the men's room, removed the cell phone battery, and twisted the unit until a sharp "crack" was heard. As he left, he tossed the phone into a wastebasket. Stone emerged from the lounge just as his flight began boarding first class. He went onboard, settled himself comfortably in his seat and shut his eyes. A few more hours of sleep would do no harm.

***

It was a surprisingly mild spring day in London, but nevertheless, the extremely well-dressed woman standing near St. James's Park Lake had a light jacket and a fashionable silk scarf over her head. The sun, barely veiled in a thin mist, shone out across the lake, and the gabbling geese at its edge, eagerly seeking a handout from the park's visitors, prevented the woman from hearing the near silent approach of the large man. She jumped slightly as he slipped beside her.

"Hello, Luana," he said.

"Oh my God, Jason," she spoke quickly, and wrapped her arms around him crushingly. He let out a wince of pain and she pulled back.

"Oh my darling, are you OK?"

"Still a little bit sore, here," he said, pointing to his lower ribcage. "Had an unfortunate encounter with bullet. The bullet won," he laughed. "It put me out of action for over a week, but now, it's just a little sore."

Luana switched her grip, grabbing his other shoulder in a passionate squeeze. Stone winced again. "Oh my God, Jason, another one?"

"Yeah, just a scratch, but that was it. I must be slowing down in my old age, but at least I managed to dodge the others.

Luana dropped both arms to her sides, but leaned forward and kissed him deeply, Stone's hands grasping her shoulders firmly.

"Ah, better," she said, when they both stepped back.

"Much better," he agreed.

"And you succeeded. I also. And here you are, alive! Jason, the world is ours! What shall we do first?"

Jason frowned slightly. "I owe a very old acquaintance an e-mail. Let me get that out of the way, and then … we're free!"

***

A pleasant rumbling of many voices talking at once filled the air as the seats of the Hollywood Bowl continued to fill. The air smelled pleasantly of pine sap from the nearby trees, candle smoke, and an overall "California" smell that defied description: a blend of dry grasses, oleander, orange blossoms, and jasmine, all releasing their fragrance into the cooling evening air.

Cathie and Joy were emptying the contents of their wicker basket: a white tablecloth, spread quickly across the tiny table around which they sat, two brass candle holders with a long, white taper in each, cloth napkins, and four wine glasses. The preliminaries accomplished, they began unloading the seemingly endless supply of cheese, fruit, crackers, and of course, wine.

"Do you ever expect to hear from him again?" asked Logan, meaning Stone/Kulwicki/Shirley.

"Doubtful," replied Chuck, as he pulled a pair of cigars, his precious Cubans, from a leather pouch, clipped off their ends and handed one to Logan.

"And Mr. Grasshopper?"

"Back at work in a few days. Man, Logan, I can't thank you enough."

"My pleasure, brudda. But it isn't clear where they'll settle down just yet."

"Well, wherever it is, as long as there's a local office, he'll have a job. Hell, he can have mine!"

"The kid's too smart for that. Now, if you would ..." Logan added, extending the cigar.

Logan took a delicate pull as Chuck applied his windproof lighter, a device that reminded Logan of a miniature jet engine, and uttered a deep sigh of satisfaction.

Chuck was lighting his own cigar when Joy turned to him, holding out the two candles, "Now, no shop talk, remember babe? Just be a dear and light these."

"And you, sir," Cathie added, holding out a bottle of Cabernet Sauvignon, "do your duty. And don't forget, we're sharing that cigar."

"I don't recall making that kind of commitment. Married for life, certainly, but do I really have to share this cigar?"

"If you wish to live to hear the first set, I'd recommend it," she said, laughing.

Logan pulled the cork and filled the four glasses carefully.

"I'd like to propose a toast," Logan began.

"Oh, God," Cathie moaned playfully, "this could take all night."

"Please," said Logan, with mock seriousness, "I will be brief."

They raised their glasses, and Logan's look became suddenly quite serious. He looked at each of them in turn, and then said simply, "To friends!"

"Friends," they echoed, sincerely, clicking their glasses and sipping delicately.

"Oh gawd!" said Cathie. "Ambrosia!"

"Yeah, not quite the character of Ripple, but it'll do," Chuck said, earning a punch in the arm from Joy.

"Speaking of friends," Chuck continued, "How's it feel to have a friend who's running a country now? Wonder what she's drinking these days?"

"The sweet, heady nectar of power," Cathie replied. "And … and I don't think I really want to call her friend."

"Never liked her much, myself," said Joy. "But maybe you can work her into your next novel, Cathie."

"As the evil, power-crazy bitch, most likely," Cathie added, grimly.

"So you've got another one going already?" Chuck asked.

"Just started … pretty rough … you know."

"What's it called?"

"It's just a working title, of course, but I was kind of thinking *A Tale of Two Grasshoppers*."

"Sounds like a cross between a camp TV series and Dickens," Logan said, with a smirk.

"Take it back. Or pass that cigar and refill my glass."

"I really have a choice?"

"No."

Logan refilled the glasses all around just as the path lights dimmed and the stage lights came up. An enthusiastic round of applause as Diana Krall crossed the stage and, after bowing all around in acknowledgement of the crowd, seated herself at the huge Steinway grand. Anticipation filled the audience as she played a familiar series of opening chords, and then began to sing "Peel Me a Grape" in a mellow, throaty voice.

Logan's mind flew effortlessly back to the summer evening in El Segundo and his dinner at La Florentine. This song had been playing as he had approached the bar after dinner, and a few moments later he had encountered Ms. Blue Hawaii, a near collision that had foreshadowed the events of the past year. Logan sipped his wine and listened with appreciation until the close of the song, and the resounding applause, cheers, and whistling, but couldn't help wondering whether this was an end or a beginning.

Made in the USA
Columbia, SC
21 May 2018